About the Author

My name is Hernani Medeiros. I am forty years old and live in Canada, although originally from Azores, Portugal. I arrived in Canada with my parents and brother when I was only eight years old, back in 1990. I graduated from elementary and secondary schools, then college with honors, which has been my greatest achievement. Discovering my passion for writing when I was in grade five, it was something I always wanted to do. I hope everyone will enjoy reading Nanook, just as I have enjoyed writing it. Thank you for your support.

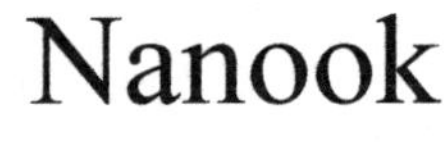

Nanook

Hernani Medeiros

Nanook

Vanguard Press

I would like to dedicate this book to my grandmother,
Maria Jandira Couto Oliveira.

I would like to acknowledge my brother, parents and my close friends for always having my back and believing in me from when I started writing this book to when I finished it. I would also like to acknowledge everyone at Pegasus for making this opportunity come true.

PROLOGUE

People have been calling dogs 'man's best friend' for many generations. They guarded, protected, and have given their lives to save those of people for as long as time can tell, but it was not always like this. Long before dogs became man's best friend, they were his most feared enemy. The story of their origin dates back to twenty-five thousand years ago, to an ice-age world known as Nuna. It was a land full of beauty and danger, where magnificent beasts like mammoths still traveled in massive herds across the plains. Tall conifers and winding rivers preceded roads and buildings, while majestic mountains rose over the land, casting a shadow over the landscape like prehistoric skyscrapers. The landscape of Nuna was quite a sight to behold, but the climate was a little different. It was not the one with which you are familiar.

The summers there were unpredictable. There would be days where it would be cool and other days would be hot, but the winters were another story. They were long, cold, and dark, and hard on life. The herbivores struggled to survive, eating anything green they could find, while others moved into warmer areas, where they would have plenty to eat only to return when the weather warms up again, but winter was a terrible time for the predators. That is because they found it harder to catch the herbivores as they did not adapt well to moving in deep snow, which just slowed them down, unlike the sleek-footed herbivores they hunted.

However, one predator adapted perfectly to these harsh times; they were the true masters of survival. Their ears could locate any sound coming from deep within the snow and their noses could pick up any scent coming from as far as the other side of the meadow, while their paws acted like snowshoes, preventing them from sinking in the deep snow. Winter did not phase them. They could run through the darkness with ease, using their nose and ears as their guide. Those predators were wolves, and they had lived here on Nuna for decades with little to worry about. They were the top predators: even the toughest of mammoths would cower in fear.

Those were the good old days, but as always, all good things must end. Years later, the world they once knew changed. Wolves no longer have control of the land because that role is now being taken over by other predators: people. Wolves had to put up with other predators, like lions and hyenas, before, but they posed no problem because they had their part of Nuna for themselves and there was no competition amongst one another. However, since the people arrived here, the other predators have moved into wolf territory, as well, and made their survival much harder. People are more advanced than any other predator and far more dangerous. They have the ability to use weapons, which can be anything they find lying around, but what makes them deadly are the spears they always carry with them. The wolves' only weapons are their teeth, but they are no match against such a lethal weapon. Spears may look harmless from a distance but are deadly when up close. When any wolf gets struck by one, it is lights-out for them. The people have also, with no remorse, chased wolves away from their kill and since they were too tired to defend it, the wolves have had no choice but to give it up and watch as the people carried away the very food that they worked so hard to bring down.

Long before humans arrived here, there were packs at every corner of the land. Since their arrival, they have long been gone; people have walked into their home and driven them away, mercilessly. All have left except for one pack that remains here, representing the sole and last hope of reclaiming what once their domain. For many years, the wolves and people struggled regarding who would claim the land, but as wolf legend goes, one day a wolf will be born that will stop this decades-long hatred between wolves and humans by forming an unlikely alliance and bring peace to Nuna once again.

CHAPTER 1

Many years have passed since the humans invaded the land.

It is now early morning. Heavy rain throughout the night is still pouring down over the land. The vista appears lifeless and quiet except for the braying of fighting stallions echoing in the distance. Hidden deep within the forest is where the people live, hidden away from the prying eyes of predators. The rain is flooding the immediate vicinity; near the entrance to the cave is a large stump with antelope pelts piled on top of it. They look fresh, as though they were just skinned a short while ago. A young woman steps out of the cave and stands by the entrance as she stretches after a long night. She stares down at the large expanse of water in front of her. It amazes her how wide it has become, just overnight. Three children run out from behind her as she walks out, and begin splashing around in the water, wandering far from the cave.

She calls out to them when she notices they have wandered close to the forest.

"Children! Do not wander far! Stay close to where I can see you…" she warns them, loud enough for them to hear, but the children simply ignore her warning and continue playing. She then looks over to the stump and lets out a scream when she notices the rising water is reaching the pelts. She rushes over to the stump to seize them before the water rises any more. After she has gathered the skins, she walks back into the cave so she can place them over the fire, where they will dry, and calls out to the children as she walks in. The children run past her, laughing. By accident, one of them bumps into her, causing her to drop the pelts.

"Darn you, kids!" she yells. She mumbles to herself as she goes down on her knees to gather the skins. Instead of helping her, the children continue running inside. She gets angrier when she realizes they have left her to pick up the pelts on her own.

"Thank you for your help, I am very grateful!" she yells out.

"You're welcome!" cries out one of the older children as they continue running inside and laughing. She gets up after gathering the pelt and swings them onto her shoulders. Just as she turns around to walk back inside the cave, she hears the snapping of twigs behind her. She looks toward the forest and spots something moving in front of some trees near the camp. She places the pelts back down to look at the trees but stops when someone calls her to get back inside.

The woman turns around and as she is about to pick up the pelts again, she hears the snapping of twigs once more, but this time it seems closer. She turns around to look once again, but spots nothing, so shrugs her shoulders and walks back inside.

In the forest, five wolves are hiding behind the trees, watching her every move. They notice a rack of meat left unattended, leaning against the wall inside the cave. They turn around and walk away in silence.

As the sun sets over the land, a powerful gust of wind blows across the canopy, causing the trees to sway, looking as though they are dancing with one another. The branches from the trees bordering the people's camp are violently blowing around as the winds continue to get stronger, a sure sign that the storm is far from over. One drop of rain comes down, followed by many more, while thunder roars across the night sky, followed by a flash of lightning.

Outside the camp, wolves are sneaking around by the entrance, so the people who are inside will not detect them. Two of them are standing by the entrance, staring deep into the cave. These two wolves are the decoys, and their purpose is to trick the people into thinking they are the only ones who have come, while the other wolves are hiding, waiting to leap out to catch the people by surprise and trapping them inside the cave.

Meanwhile, inside the cave, unaware that there are wolves outside, the family is busy doing chores. Two men are painting along the back of the cave, while two hunters are nearby, carving new spears. Young children run around playing, while an elderly woman nearby prepares to clean the pelts. One child knocks down a bowl of paint that was placed on a rock and causes it to spill onto the antelope pelt. The elderly woman notices the mess that they have made and chases after them while waving her fist.

"Look what you have done!" she yells as she runs after them, but they continue running off and laughing, as one of them sticks out his tongue at her. She mutters to herself as she goes down on her knees and begins wiping the pelt to remove the stain. One man, who is standing behind her, looks over to her and smirks. The other man grins while he shakes his head.

"Come now, Mother… Boys will be boys," he says, while holding back his laughter. She turns to him, giving him a mean look.

"That is easy for you to say. I have to deal with them while you just stand there and paint. They are your kids, not mine. Learn to control them."

As the man is about to comment on his mother's remark, he is interrupted by a scream coming from a young woman who had been standing by the entrance, pointing towards it, believing that she saw something prowling outside. The other man stops what he is doing and runs over to her, sensing that something could be wrong.

"What is wrong, my wife?" he asks, concerned.

"I think I saw something moving across the entrance. It looked like it might be wolves." She says as she points her quivering hand at the entrance.

He looks toward the entrance, expecting to spot wolves but feels relief when he notices that it is just shadows of branches being blown by the wind outside. He looks directly at her big, worried, brown eyes and smiles.

"What you just saw were the shadows of the branches being blown by the wind," he says to calm her down.

"There is nothing out there for you to worry about: it is just your mind playing tricks on you because you are tired. You have never stopped with chores since daybreak — you need to get some rest."

She gives out a yawn and smiles as she starts to calm down. "Yes, you are probably right; I do feel pretty tired."

Her husband looks down at her, annoyed. "Then you should go and lie down for the night. You look exhausted," he says softly to her. He gently pats her on the forearm before he walks over to rejoin the others to continue painting. As the young woman turns around to get ready for the night, she is surprised when she notices that the others are still looking at her. All she does is giggle nervously, while waving at them.

"Sorry, everyone. I didn't mean to get you all scared."

Moments later, she is humming calmly as she prepares to lie down, until once again she catches some movement coming from the entrance. This time she feels certain there is something outside and quickly gets up and runs over to her husband. She frantically taps his shoulder to get him to turn around. He sighs in frustration as he turns to face her, while she stares, expressionless, at him, as if she saw death.

"There is something out there; I am sure of it this time" she says nervously.

He sighs heavily and rolls his eyes. "I already told you, there is nothing out there. Come and I will show you."

He grabs her by the arm and walks with her over to the entrance so she can see for herself that there is nothing there for her to worry about. He looks once more at the entrance and that is when he spots two figures standing there. He rubs both his eyes while crouching down and creeps in closer to get a better look, while his wife anxiously follows him closely behind.

"You do see something, don't you?" she says, in a trembling voice. Without saying a word, he nervously looks over to her, and then looks over at the others impassively before staring back at the entrance once more.

"Maybe it's just—" and before he can say anything else, he gets interrupted by a crash of thunder and that is when he notices that the two mysterious figures have now wandered inside the cave. A flash of lightning exposes that they are wolves. They just stand there and begin growling as they stare at the people ahead. The man grabs his wife's hand without hesitation and they both run to warn the others.

"It turns out she was right — there is something there and its wolves. Grab your spears and let's go and get them!" he shouts out to the other men, as he races past them.

While the men run for the spears, the wolves grab the meat rack and begin to drag it outside. The men shout as they run towards the wolves, but as they are about to go outside, the other three wolves, who were hiding outside, jump in front of them and stop them in their tracks. The men start shouting and thrust their spears to keep the wolves from coming in, but they continue to walk inside, unphased by the threats. In a desperate attempt, the men keep thrusting their spears to keep the wolves from coming in, but their defence does not seem to be working: the wolves have seen this too many times.

The wolves have them backed up into the wall, where they want them. They have them cornered in the same way as many times before. The men, who feel there is no way of escaping them, stick their arms out to protect their family and the leader begins shouting at the wolves, hoping to scare them off.

"Come and get me, you monsters!" he shouts out furiously, but it only makes the wolves angrier.

A black wolf is the first to lunge at him, followed by the other wolves. Moments later, the wolves are walking out. The same black wolf is dragging the leader out by the ankle. Once it gets outside, it stops and releases the man before running off into the darkness. The man then scrambles to get back up so he can run back inside the cave, but the wolves surround him, forming a circle to prevent his escape. He feels powerless as he sits back down, while nervously staring at the wolves.

He hears growls coming from behind, sending chills down his spine and making the hair on the back of his neck stand up. He sees nothing at first, but then the same black wolf, the alpha of the pack, walks out of the darkness like a ghost. The other wolves move aside to let him in. He walks towards the man; he stands over him and leans in closer, until their noses touch, while growling louder and exposing his teeth. The man's terrified face is seen clearly as a reflection in the wolf's yellow eyes. A flash of lightning reveals the wolf's angry face as it leans in closer to attack the man. He begins to scream as the other wolves join in the frenzy.

Deep in the forest, a short way from the people's camp, a flash of lightning reveals an uprooted tree lying across the forest floor. A dark hole is dug up underneath its roots. Inside, a female wolf is lying down on her side, looking as if she is having trouble breathing, but then she stops and raises her head to look behind her. A tiny, helpless pup, crawls out from underneath, followed by three more pups. She lowers her head to lick them dry. The last pup looks up at her just as she bends to clean him up, and it rolls backward to evade her. He crawls away, using all the strength in his tiny legs to escape her. She gasps and reaches out to pick him up in her jaws before he falls outside the den.

"Oh, no you don't — get over here." She picks him up and places him down next to his brothers and sister and begins licking him. At first, he is not enjoying his bath, but he soon calms down as he is enjoying the attention. He looks up at the wolf and smiles. She smiles back as she nudges him to settle him for the night. "Now go on and rest up like your brothers and sister are doing, my little one," she says. The errant pup gives out a little yawn as he snuggles next to his brothers and sister, while the mother lies down again, feeling relieved.

As the storm rages on outside, a group of five wolves approaches the den. A flash of lightning reveals that they are the same pack that attacked the people earlier. They all stand around and stare down the hole while the female wolf and the pups are sleeping, unaware of their presence. The black wolf crawls inside and sniffs the female wolf while the others are waiting around outside, guarding their alpha.

CHAPTER 2

Eight weeks have gone by, and it is a beautiful morning. The sun is shining, adding light to the land once again. The people's camp is now empty. They all left after the night of the attack. The wolves destroyed everything that night so the people will not return. Meanwhile, over by the wolves' lair, everything is now visible. The den is dug up underneath an uprooted log lying flat across a grassy clearing. The log itself provides shelter for its residents because it blocks them from severe weather. There are flowers spread throughout the lair; some blue, some red, yellow, and also orange, adding color to the den. Large conifers reach up into the sky, forming a roof over it, sheltering the pack from rain, snow, and wind.

The female wolf, Sakkara, emerges from the hide. The light of the sun shows she is a light gray in colour, with amber eyes. Four little pups are right behind her as she steps out. Among them is Nanook: he is the same colour but a darker gray. The pups are about to run out, but Sakkara turns to them and snarls.

"Wait there," she demands in a serious tone. She searches the area for any signs of danger. Realizing there is nothing prowling around in the forest, she faces the pups once again, but this time with a big smile.

"Little ones, it is safe to come out now."

Nanook does not hesitate and runs underneath his mother, causing her to lose her balance. The other pups, his sister Aurora and his two brothers, Seka and Denali, run out after him.

"Nanook, wait for us!" Aurora cries out as they try to catch up with him. They race with one another around the lair while Sakkara sighs and gives out a little chuckle as she watches her pups continue playing from the log. Nanook stops running when he notices two legs standing in his way, which causes his brothers and sister to bump into him. They look up but are having a hard time telling who it is because of the sun's glare. The other three run away scared and hide behind Sakkara, but only Nanook remains, looking up at the figure as it lowers down to sniff him.

It turns out the strange figure is Amak, the alpha of the pack, and Nanook's father. He is black all over but his eyes are yellow, just like the sun. Nanook wags his tail and licks him on the side of his face. Amak gives him a smile before walking over to Sakkara, who wags her tail, glad to see that he is back safely. Another wolf walks into the lair: it is Tiyani, second in command and Nanook's uncle. He is a light gray in colour, with a black saddle going over his back and just like Sakkara, his eyes are also amber. He winks at Nanook and nods his head as he walks by him before joining Amak and Sakkara.

Three other wolves jump out from behind the trees roughhousing with each other. One is brown, the other is white and the last is a solid gray. They stop when they notice Nanook staring at them. One of them looks over to the others and sneers as he lowers down, looking like he is about to greet him but instead, he sarcastically snorts at him while Nanook leans back in disgust. They run toward the others, laughing with one another, feeling proud of what they have done as Nanook looks on annoyed. They are Nanook's older brothers, Ila, Miki and Alornek. Although it seems unlikely, one day one of them could be the alpha for the lair. They could have left the pack and started their own but have decided to stay instead and help Amak with hunting and Sakkara with babysitting. With four adventurous pups she needs all the help she can get. Nanook also has sisters but unlike his brothers, they decided to move on. He never met them, and he guesses that he never will, but he is beginning to wish that it were his sisters who had stayed instead. Nanook sits back and watches with joy as his family gather around, greeting each other. It appears that Nanook's family is the same pack that attacked the people, many nights ago, in an attempt to get them off the land so that the pups and Sakkara, at their most vulnerable, would not be harmed by any of them.

Sakkara is giving Miki a bath since he has come back all dirty, while he gives the impression that he is not liking it one bit.

"Mother, not now — you're embarrassing me," he whines, but Sakkara ignores him and continues, anyway. She is about to give Ila a wash, too, but stops when the pups rush in front of her and begin jumping around their brother.

"Let's play, let's play, let's play!" they all shout, while Sakkara looks on with a smirk.

"They are all yours — good luck," she says. Ila sighs with relief, looking down at the pups.

"Thanks, you guys. You just save me from a world of embarrassment. I owe it to you" he whispers, thinking Sakkara will not hear him. What he does not know is that she is still standing behind him.

"I can still hear you!" she cries out. Ila cringes when he hears her and looks back at her with a nervous grin.

"I love you, mother," he says, while the pups giggle. She gives him a mean look before she walks over to Alornek, to clean him up, but as she approaches him, he darts out of the way so he can avoid her.

"I got to go, mom — I think I hear dad calling," he says. He looks over to Amak and calls out to him as he walks by.

"Hey, Dad — did you call me?" he asks but Amak just glances over to Sakkara. He then looks over to Alornek while smiling sarcastically.

"No I didn't," he says, staring at Sakkara once more as he walks past her. She walks over to Alornek with a sly grin on her face and all he can do is stand and gaze at her, stunned as she stares at him, smirking.

"It's bath time," she says, which causes him to scream and run to his den before she can get any closer. She laughs, along with the pups and the others. Amak approaches them, while laughing, and lies down. He rolls on his back and closes his eyes, still chuckling as he dozes off. Aurora sneaks up on him to scare him but just as she gets close enough, he opens his eyes and gives out a loud "Boo!" She jumps back, alarmed, and runs back inside the den to hide from him.

Amak sighs a little, sitting near the entrance, only to see Aurora lying down with her back towards him. He moves in and gently lays his head down, next to hers.

"Come on, now. I did not mean to scare you — come on out," he says quietly, so he can encourage her to come out again. She raises her head up slowly and begins to get up. He sits up outside to wait for her to come out but when she is taking too long, he gets concerned. He lowers himself down to look inside once more, to check up on her, when she suddenly jumps out of the log and catches him by surprise.

"Get over here!" she shouts. Amak rolls over onto his back as Aurora jumps on him.

"Oh no! You're too strong for me! Pick on someone your own size!"

he begs desperately, before turning over on his side with mouth open and tongue hanging out, pretending to be dead. She gets off him and walks in front of him, wagging her little tail.

"Dad! You're not really dead," she says. He suddenly opens his eyes.

"No, I'm not!" he cries out, while she jumps back in surprise. She runs away and begins laughing, running in circles around him.

"I got you again!" he says, laughing. She stops and looks up at him while wagging her tail with excitement.

"You sure did!" she says, full of enthusiasm, "but you have to admit mine was better. I surprised you and you didn't even expect it," she said mockingly. Amak lowers down and whispers to her.

"You sure did. You are turning out to be a better trickster than I am," he says, chuckling. Then he moves in closer and looks at her, while attempting to keep a straight face. "I am going to need to be extra careful so you won't take my other job as trickster of the pack," he whispers to her. Aurora just giggles a little before giving him a lick on the cheek. He reacts by sticking out his tongue jokingly, while blowing a raspberry.

Sakkara is sitting on top of the log, looking down at them, smiling proudly. She clears her throat to get Amak's attention. He looks up at her and she motions for him to come join her. He jumps up on the log and sits at her side.

"So what do you think of them all?" she asks. He looks at her in disgust.

"Nasty little vermin," he says.

"Ha, ha, very funny," she responds sarcastically. He looks at her with a gentle smile.

"I love them. They are perfect additions to our pack," he says, looking down at them proudly. The three pups, along with their older brothers, start racing each other around the den and that is when Nanook excitedly runs over to join his siblings, young and older, in their game. They begin laughing as they race each other around in the lair with their parents looking on, happy that they are all getting along so well.

Night has fallen over the land once again, only this time it is not as stormy. It is, instead, a much quieter night. The moon is full, and the sky strewn with stars. Sakkara is lying down outside the den to block the entrance, so she can prevent the pups from coming out. Two heads peek from behind her. It is Nanook and Denali. Nanook gives out a grin, but Denali does not look so pleased.

"She looks like she is sleeping," whispers Denali, feeling unsure of what they are about to do, while Nanook looks over at him with determination.

"Then what are we waiting for? Let's go outside," he demands. He sneaks toward the entrance while Denali tries to catch up to him.

"Wait, Nanook," he cries out to him. Nanook gets excited as they are reaching the exit.

"Hurry, we are almost there," he calls out to Denali, with exhilaration.

"You know, we could get into big trouble for this," Denali says.

"If you don't want to get in trouble, then you should stay inside."

"I am just saying that we can't be outside on our own yet, especially at night."

"Where is your sense of adventure? Besides, they'll never know. We will get out and sneak back in and mother won't know we have ever left the den at all, so don't waste any more time…"

He looks up when he hears Sakkara rolling over in her sleep and then glances over to Denali, annoyed.

"Let's hurry and get a move on before she wakes up!" scolds Nanook, as he sneaks passed Sakkara with his brother following behind him. They each poke their heads out to see if anyone is awake. Nanook looks at Denali, his tail wagging with great anticipation.

"Coast is clear. They're all asleep. Let's go but remember we just jump out and rush back in," he says. They are about to sneak out but stop when they hear Aurora calling out to them.

"You guys can't go outside by yourselves yet."

Nanook rolls his eyes. "They are all asleep and we won't be long" he says, sounding annoyed.

"We just want to see what outside looks like at night," Denali whispers out to her, but as they are about to step out, they stop. Sakkara is already awake and staring at them, not looking happy.

"You're not going anywhere. Get back inside."

"Awe Mom… We just wanted to see outside at night, that's all," whined Nanook.

"You must never go outside at night on your own. It is too dangerous.

Now get back inside," she said, displeased.

The two pups whimper as they crawl back inside, as Sakkara looks on. Aurora is lying down when the two pups approach her. She watches, grinning slyly as they are about to settle down.

"So what was it like outside?" says Aurora sarcastically.

"We didn't get to go," says Denali, feeling disappointed.

"Mother was already awake," says Nanook, frustrated.

"I told you were going to get into trouble."

"But how did she know?" he asks, sounding surprised.

"She is a mother: she knows everything" says Aurora, as she lies back down and closes her eyes.

Nanook looks up at Sakkara, amazed, as he settles down next to Aurora. Sakkara continues to stare at the pups to make sure they are going to sleep before she lies back down. Alornek and Ila are sleeping next to her to give her some company, even though they have their own dens. Tonight they just wanted to be with her.

As for Amak, he is lying on Alpha Rock, a giant boulder pushing up from the ground. It is an important place where meetings are held. He is on top while his brother, Tiyani, sleeps in a den he dug underneath it. Amak is looking down at his sleeping family and smiles as he watches them. He lifts his head up to the clusters of stars in the sky above and smiles a little when he sees two stars shining brightly.

"Goodnight, Mother and Father," he whispers softly. To his amazement, at that very moment, two shooting stars streak across the night sky.

Meanwhile, in the forest, dead leaves are being blown across the forest floor. A shadowy figure walks through the woods, followed by many more. The figure stops when he notices Amak resting on top of Alpha Rock. The shapes are revealed to be humans, when one of them steps into the moonlight. They have moved back into the land once again and there are more of them this time. They settle down near the lair while the wolves are peacefully sleeping, unaware of their arrival.

The following morning, the people have settled in their new home. The hunters arrive with a kill, a young antelope, which they drop near the firepit, then lean their spears against a large boulder, close by. While one hunter wipes his forehead, his wife, happy he returned safe, rushes over to him and hugs him.

"I am glad to see you back safe. It worries me every time you go out there." He looks down at her big, worried, brown eyes and wraps his arms around her waist, smiling.

"My family is my number-one priority. I will do whatever it takes just so they can eat, even if it means risking my own life," he says. He places his hand over her stomach, revealing that she is pregnant, and she places her hand over his and they rub it together. They both begin laughing when they feel a kick.

"Judging from that kick, my child will be a strong hunter someday and a great leader of his own tribe," says the leader with joy, as his wife looks at him, smiling.

"Or a wonderful wife and mother, just like I am to you — and soon to my child."

Her husband smiles as he gazes at her, before hugging her once more.

Meanwhile, inside the forest, the wolves, are hiding away from view, spying on their new neighbors while they are each doing a chore. The women strip the hide and hang it on the branches to dry and then they each cut at the meat and place it on top of the boulder.

Alornek, the oldest of the brothers, begins licking his lips at the sight of the meat and steps forward.

"Don't even think about it. You don't want to stir up any trouble," Amak whispers out a warning while Alornek whimpers as he backs up next to him.

"But I'm so hungry," he says, whining as he looks up at Amak.

"I understand you are — just like all of us — but we have to wait until it's safe," scolds Amak.

He looks toward the camp, and he notices the women have left to go sit by the fire circle and watch as the men are teaching the children how to start a fire. One child gets frustrated after he fails in every attempt, while his father rubs him on the head for his effort as his mother looks on. The other wolves look over to Amak, waiting for him to give the signal. He checks one more time to make sure that none of them are around. He looks over to the others and nods while grinning.

"They have left the meat unattended; let's go get it," he whispers, smirking as he creeps over to the boulder. The others follow closely behind but Tiyani has accidentally stepped on a twig and the crackling echoes through the forest alerting the human leader, a young man in his thirties, goatee and hair tied in a ponytail. He gets up slowly and motions for everyone to stop what they are doing. He looks toward the forest to find any signs of movement. Convinced that he might have seen something prowling behind some trees near the camp, he gestures to the man sitting next to him to toss him his spear. He runs to the boulder and hands him a white spear with three black feathers tied around it. He grabs his own and stands next to the leader, staring at him, feeling uneasy.

"What do you think it is?" asks the hunter.

"I am not sure," the leader answers, while still focusing on the trees ahead.

"Do you think it could be wolves?" the hunter asks again, feeling anxious.

"Most likely. I heard of a pack living around these parts, led by a large black wolf that is as dark as night and has eyes that are as yellow as the sun. I hear they are the last pack living here," he says with a grin and steps toward the forest, followed closely by the other man. They sneak slowly among the trees, trying not to make a sound, with their spears in hand just in case any wolf jumps out at them. The other man feels nervous and has a tight grip on his spear. He has sweat glistening on his face, but he keeps calm and continues following his leader.

It is all quiet throughout the forest; not a creature is stirring until they hear rustling coming from shrubs next to them. Anticipating it might be a wolf, they immediately turn and face the shrubs with their spears raised. They nervously wait for the source of the noise to jump out at them when, to their surprise, a rabbit pops out of the shrubs and begins bounding around their feet. They both begin laughing nervously at one another. The hunter jokingly thrusts his spear to scare the rabbit away so they can continue with the search. After a while, they stop by a tree to take a break, unaware that they are standing inches away from Amak.

He is by himself on one side, while the others wait across from him. He stands as still as he can and tries not to make a sound. When the men walk away, Amak heaves a big sigh of relief.

After a long time searching, the men spot a clearing close to where they are. The leader looks over at the other man.

"Do you see that clearing over there?"

"Yes, I see it. What about it?" the hunter replies, baffled.

"When we arrived here last night, I saw some wolves sleeping in that exact clearing, so I assume it must be where they live."

"You don't know that for sure. For all we know, they stayed there for the night and left first thing in the morning."

"There is only one way to find out, and that is to go there and see for ourselves," the leader states, and the hunter agrees. Both men move forward to investigate.

Amak glances up and worries when he notices the two men walking toward the lair. He prepares to jump out of the ferns to lead them away, despite the desperate pleas of the others, but stops when he hears a woman calling out from the camp. The men stop their search when they hear her calling and start walking back. The wolves wait for a few moments to make sure the humans have left. Amak raises his head over the ferns and sees no one. He takes a deep breath of relief.

"Okay, they've gone. Let's leave before any more of them come, and make sure that we are not being followed by any of them," Amak demands as he heads back to the lair with the others following him close behind.

Back in the lair, Sakkara and Ila are watching over the pups while they play. They get up when they see Amak and the others burst out from behind the trees. They keep looking over into the forest to be sure that they are not being followed by any humans. Sakkara rushes over to Amak to rub noses with him to settle him down, but he looks down at her, worried.

"You do not know how close you were to being detected by the people."

"They are back? But how can that be?" she asks, alarmed.

"They must have arrived here last night while we were asleep."

"How many of them are there?" she asks, concerned, while looking over at the pups.

"I could not tell, but from what I know it is a lot more than the ones we faced before."

"Did they locate you?"

"No, they didn't because I was lying down amongst the ferns, but they were close," Amak says, while Sakkara stares at him, worried. "They were standing inches from us. We were lucky that they never looked down, but what got me worried was that they may have discovered our lair and I cannot imagine what could have happened if they hadn't been called back and were forced to call off the search."

"What are you going to do?"

"I am not sure yet, but right now I need to warn everyone about them. They need to know about this. Have them gathered by Alpha Rock," he orders.

Amak stands on Alpha Rock, while Sakkara gathers everyone for the meeting. The pups are running over to join them, but she stops them.

"You don't have to come: this is only for adults. Go back in the den and wait until I come back."

The pups look up at her as they head back toward the lair, but they all turn around and raise their heads up with excitement when they hear Amak calling out to her from Alpha Rock.

"They should come, Sakkara — they need to hear this. This meeting also applies to them. It is time that they find out about how dangerous the people are, as well," he says.

She calls out to the pups to come join them at Alpha Rock and they run without hesitation toward her and sit in front of it, looking up at Amak while wagging their tails. Amak looks down at them with a serious stare. They stop wagging their tails, sit up straight and do their best to be serious while he looks away, smirking.

Amak, the pack leader, looks down at the others from Alpha Rock while they all look up at him, waiting for what he has to say. He clears his throat and begins his speech.

"I have discovered, last night, that the people have moved back to the land as we slept and this time there are more of them. Before they were just a family, our numbers were greater than theirs, so we could defeat them, but now they are a clan, which means there are more of them. I have also noticed that they are more advanced than any other humans we have faced before. Besides those large sticks they carry with them, I have discovered that these people carry smaller ones and they shoot them out of weird-shaped branches. We can avoid the larger ones because they cannot go as far, but these smaller ones look much lighter, faster and travel farther, and so are just as deadly.

"I have not thought of a way to get rid of them yet, but until I do, we need to make ourselves as unnoticeable as we can by not making too much noise. We have newcomers to our lair, and they know nothing about how dangerous the people are. We need to make sure that they understand, so they see them as a threat instead of a game. It's for our own safety and their safety," he says, looking at the pups. Then he calls out to Sakkara and Ila. "I will leave the responsibility for them to the both of you. You will watch over them and make sure they don't wander off anywhere beyond the boundary of this lair," he states, while they both nod at him. "And there is one more important thing that I would like to mention before I forget. From now on, our foraging will have to be done at night since it is the only time of the day they are not as active. Let us be safe and most important, let us do our part!" he shouts out, before he steps off Alpha Rock. The pups run over to him and gather around him while Sakkara approaches, and they rub noses.

CHAPTER 3

A month has passed and Nanook and the other pups are now more adventuresome than ever. Nanook bolts out of the den, ready to play, while Sakkara runs out after him in a hurry. She grabs him by the tail and pulls him closer to clean him up before he gets away.

"Okay, okay — I am clean. Can I go play now?"

"Yes, you may, but remember what your father said."

"Yes, Mother. I must stay in the lair's boundary. I've heard it a hundred times."

"And I will say it a hundred times more, just so it gets through to that head of yours." She gives him a mean look as she walks over to take care of the others. Nanook searches around the lair, wondering where Amak and the others have gone.

"Mom, where did Dad and the others go?"

"Oh, they are out in the forest spying on the people. They have always been going there since the day they have arrived," she adds.

He looks at the forest, grinning. "I want to find them myself, so I can show them how brave I am," he whispers to himself.

"You said something, Nanook?" Sakkara calls out to him.

"I said I am going to sit by Alpha Rock and wait for them to come back."

"Good. You stay there and keep watch and when I am done here, the five of us will wait for them together," she calls, as she continues to mind the others, not paying Nanook any further attention. Nanook seizes the opportunity and sneaks into the forest to find the others, so they can see for themselves how brave he is, while Sakkara, with her back still turned, continues cleaning his littermates, unaware that he has wandered off into the forest on his own.

Meanwhile, in the forest, the other wolves are hiding behind some trees near the camp. They have been there since daybreak, waiting for the men to leave. Their target is the fresh meat lying on top of the boulder. The men grab their spears and head out to the meadow to hunt, leaving only the two women and their children behind. Both women are distracted as one is giving a child a bath and the other is busy playing with the other child. The wolves creep gingerly into their camp, so they will not be detected, and they each grab pieces of the meat while Amak keeps watch. When the other wolves have gone, he too grabs a mouthful of the meat. One child sees him and begins laughing. Her mother sees the child pointing at something and walks over to her. She looks where the child is facing but sees nothing there. Amak has left. The woman shrugs her shoulders and picks up her child.

"Come on, now; it's time for sleep," she says, walking back to the cave, as the child continues laughing when she spots Amak and the others running through the forest with their meat.

Once they arrive back at the lair, Sakkara rushes over to Amak, worried.

"What's the matter?" he asks, concerned,

"Nanook isn't here, and I can't find him anywhere. Before I turned around to look after the others, I saw him sitting right here by Alpha Rock. When I finished with them, I looked over again to check if he was still here and he wasn't. I've looked all over the lair, and I can't find him anywhere. I remembered him asking me where you went, and I said you were by the people's lair…" She pauses with a panicked gasp. "What if he snuck into the forest to look for you and got himself lost, or worse — what if the people got him or what if…" She paces back and forth in a panic.

Amak, smiling, looks down at her. "That is quite enough. There is no need to worry like this. I will go look for him. If I know our son, he will not have gone far," he assures her as she stares at him with alarm. "Do not worry — he is fine."

He turns around and runs back into the forest to look for Nanook as Sakkara waits anxiously.

Nanook is wandering through the forest searching for the others but cannot find them anywhere. He walks into the people's camp and bumps into a child playing in the mud nearby.

Nanook freezes, just like Sakkara taught him to do when spotting danger. The child notices Nanook and laughs and smudges him with his muddied hands. Nanook calms a little when he realizes the child will not harm him and licks his hands clean and then his face, as the child giggles. His mother, who is looking for the child, spots Nanook and panics as she grabs her son away from him, yelling at the pup, "Go away, get out of here!" She claps her hands loud enough to get him to leave, but Nanook does not budge. Instead, he just looks up at her, feeling traumatized.

In the forest, Amak hears the noise and believing that Nanook could be in trouble, he does not hesitate and rushes toward it. He is near the people's camp when he notices a woman gesturing and shouting at something, but he cannot see what it is because some shrubs are in his way. He gets in a little closer to get a better look and panics when he notices Nanook simply sitting there, not moving. Without hesitation, he runs to reach Nanook in time. The woman picks up a rock and just as she is about to hit Nanook with it, Amak jumps in between them both, snarling, causing her to jump back in surprise and trip over a root behind her. Amak nudges Nanook's head to get him to snap out of it and as he is about to run into the forest, he sees Nanook has still not budged and he rushes back over to him.

"Come on, we need to get out of here now!" he cries out as he picks up his son before running back into the forest. The woman, who is still in shock, gets up, picks up the child and runs back to the camp while the child is crying, reaching out for the wolves.

Amak rushes through the forest to get away as far as he can from the people's camp. Once he finds they are far enough, he places Nanook down and looks down at him, sternly. Nanook looks away in shame.

"What were you thinking, wandering off like that? You had your mother and me worried. We told you never to wander off beyond the lair."

Nanook looks up at him. "I know, but I just wanted to see you doing what you do; I did not mean to worry you, but I just wanted to show you I was brave, just like you. You are never afraid of anything."

Amak calms down and sighs. "I was today, just at the thought of losing you."

Nanook looks up at him. "I guess even the bravest wolves get scared sometimes…"

Amak nods and smiles a little. "Yes, that's right. I am only brave when I have to be, especially when I have to protect my family." He then looks over his shoulder when he hears children screaming, and shouting coming from the men and women at the camp. "Let's get out of here before they spot us," he urges. He bends down and picks up Nanook in his jaws, and hurries back to the lair.

Before they walk into the lair, Nanook, who is still dangling from Amak's mouth, looks up at him.

"Dad, am I in trouble?"

"You better believe it, but don't you worry — I got you covered," his father says to reassure him before giving him a wink.

They walk into the lair and just as Amak places Nanook down, Sakkara rushes over to him the moment she sees him and hurriedly licks her son.

"I'm okay, Mom."

"I do not care if you are. Even if I have to lick you bald, so be it." Nanook just giggles a little but his smile flips upside down when she stops with the licking, sits up and looks down at him, upset. He flattens his ears and looks down, feeling ashamed.

"Don't you ever do that again — you hear me? You had me worried sick."

"I know and I'm sorry," he whimpers, looking up at her.

"There will be no more playing for you for the rest of the day. Go to the den and don't come out until I say so."

"Come now, Sakkara — there is no need to be tough like that toward him," Amak coaxes, as he stands over Nanook.

"And give me a good reason not to?"

"Because he is still young, and he still has a lot to learn. You were young, just like him, once, and I bet you were the same way as he is now. You always wanted to explore the big world yourself. He is the same way and there is no reason for you to act that way toward him."

"I understand he is still young, but that is not why I am upset with him. It is the fact that he wandered off on his own after I told him not to."

"But he has learned his lesson and he does not need any more. One is good enough for him," he said.

She looks away from Amak and lowers herself down, staring directly into Nanook's eyes. "I do not mean to overreact like I did. I was only afraid.

It is dangerous out there for a pup your age to be on his own. I understand you want to explore, but the forest is not a safe place to go wandering off on your own or anywhere else beyond the lair. Now I am going to need you to promise me that there will be no more sneaking off like that again," she says, not sounding happy, while Nanook looks up at her apologetically.

"I am sorry, Mother. I promise not to sneak away like that again and besides, it is pretty scary out there," he says, while Sakkara laughs a little.

"I bet it is and I hope that experience has taught you a lesson. Besides there is plenty to explore around the lair and…" She pauses, followed by a sigh. "When I say for you to stay put, please stay put."

"I will, Mother, I promise," says Nanook, sounding remorseful.

"I sure hope so, and from now on I will keep both my eyes on you, since I realize one is not enough," she says, while Amak chuckles a bit behind her but stops when Sakkara gives him a mean look. She looks over to Nanook once more. "Now, it is time for you to join your siblings and eat: you must be starving after your adventure this morning," she says, sounding a little calmer.

Nanook smiles as he looks at her and runs off to join the others, wagging his tail as his parents look on, smiling. He arrives by the den and frowns when he sees there is hardly any meat left for him.

"Hey, save some for me!"

"Then you'd better hurry before Seka eats everything," says Aurora.

Nanook dives headfirst into the meat, biting off a huge chunk and swallowing it whole, while Amak and Sakkara have a chuckle at the sight of their children eating. Amak smiles as he watches them eat.

"Remember when that used to be us?" he says, grinning. Then he notices Sakkara staring at him, not looking happy, when he looks over to her.

"Now, I need you to tell me something and I need you to be honest," she says, staring him down and backing him up against Alpha Rock. "Where did you get all that meat?"

Amak looks at her uneasily. "We stole it from the people," he says, grinning nervously.

"And risked being spotted by them. I remember clearly when you said that there would be no more foraging and hunting during the day. It is your own rule, and you broke it."

"But… It applies only to the young ones. The rest of us know what we are doing: we have dealt with the people ourselves, many times," he says nervously.

"It applies to all of us. What if they spotted you? Not only would they kill you, but they could have found our lair and killed us all, as well. Promise you will do the foraging at night from now on and no more during the day," she says in a stern voice.

Amak sighs and places his forehead firmly against hers, whispering, "Fine. I promise that from now on, I will go hunting at night and it starts now."

They both sit on top of the den and begin to nudge their heads and rub their noses together.

"You are still the pup you were many years ago. He has never left," Sakkara says, laughing a little.

"And that is something I am proud of," he says, sounding sarcastic, and they both begin laughing, as the pups look on.

Amak jumps off the den and is about to walk up Alpha Rock, when Sakkara approaches him and places down a piece of meat.

"Here — take my last piece of meat. You did not eat anything since this morning: you must be starving," she says.

She turns around and walks back to the den. Amak jumps off, but before he picks up the meat, he softly calls out to her.

"Hey, Sakkara," she stops and turns to him.

"What is it?"

"Thanks for always being there for me and always having my back."

"Just doing my job and besides, you are always there for us every day. It's the least I can do."

She smiles and walks over to the pups, waiting by the den, while Amak looks on smiling. He grabs the meat, walks up Alpha Rock, then lies down and begins to eat.

As Sakkara sits down behind Nanook, he turns around and looks up at her. She laughs a little at the sight of his face smudged in meat, but she can still see those apologetic eyes within all that mess after she cleans him up.

"Mom, I am sorry again for sneaking off like that. I didn't mean to."

"I am also sorry for being tough on you like that. I was just worried that something might have happened to you," Sakkara responds, looking over to Amak with a grin. "You remind me a lot of your father when he was young. He was exactly like you, very adventurous, and got himself into a lot of trouble, too. I bet he drove your grandmother crazy," she says, chuckling at the thought of it. "Yet he grew up to be a great leader and father."

Nanook looks over to Amak, proudly. "You are right, Mom. He is the best dad and one day I hope to grow up to be just like him."

It is late into the night. Sakkara is once again lying by the den, but this time she has herself stretched across the entrance to keep the pups from coming out. Amak is lying on Alpha Rock, looking up at the stars until he sees a weird black cloud rising into the sky. Realizing that it is coming from the people's camp, he jumps off and disappears into the forest to see what they are up to. Tiyani hears him leave and follows him. After moments of looking for him, he finds Amak sitting by the people's camp, looking toward it as if in a trance, so he does not notice that Tiyani is standing right behind him.

"So, what do you see?" Tiyani asks. Amak is startled.

"Oh, it's you. I didn't know you were there."

"What are you looking at over there?"

"Come here and see for yourself."

Tiyani walks up to where Amak is, and looks in horror as a glowing, flickering light appears before his eyes.

"I don't believe it…" he says, staring and feeling frightened by the glowing light.

"It's amazing, isn't it?" says Amak, as he turns to look at his brother. But Tiyani has already left, terrified by the strange light.

Sitting amid the camp is a massive bonfire, its orange-red flames light up the area and the crackling of the flames echoes through the night. Amak moves in closer, though maintaining distance from the glow of the flames, and looks on astounded when he finds out that humans can handle fire, the deadliest force of nature, whereby many wolves and other animals have perished in its fatal grasp.

The men show up and meet around the fire. Amak snarls at the sight of them and retires into the darkness of the night. The chief catches movement from the corner of his eyes. He gets up and gestures for everybody to be quiet. They all stop making noise and look on. He sees Amak walking back to the lair, and he smirks. Another hunter standing behind him gets his bow ready, but the chief grips his arm and holds it down, just as he is about to shoot.

"But sir, you are just going to let him go? Just think: we take him down and that is one less of them to worry about."

The chief looks at him and grins. "You don't see it, do you? Come here and stand next to me."

The hunter stands next to him, shoulder to shoulder, and the chief points toward the thicket where they see Amak walk behind some trees and the other wolves running over to him.

"You see, my friend, we now know where they all are, so now are you guessing what I am guessing?"

The hunter looks at him with a shrewd smirk. "Why kill one when we—"

The leader interrupts him. "…can slay the entire pack and that means this land will be ours once we take them down." He gives the hunter a pat on the shoulder and heads back to the cavern. "Let's go inside, and at dawn, I am going to reveal to you how we are going to do it."

Meanwhile, Amak and Tiyani have arrived back at the lair. Amak calls Tiyani over.

"We will say nothing to them now. We'll mention it to them first thing in the morning — is that clear?" he says, as he hops back on Alpha Rock and Tiyani lies down underneath it. Amak looks up at the unusual cloud, worried as he settles down for the night.

It is now early in the morning, and heavy mist blankets the land. Over at the lair, Amak is standing on Alpha Rock as he cries out for everybody to meet around him, while Tiyani is making certain that everybody is getting up. He notices Ila is still asleep. He crouches down and yells into his ear.

"Get up!" causing Ila to wake up alarmed.

"What! What happened? Are we being attacked?" he cries out, while Tiyani looks at him with a sarcastic smirk.

"No, we are not under attack. It is time to get up for the meeting," he says, walking away while Ila looks peeved. The pups are already awake and are leaping through the mist. Nanook pokes his head out of the fog and ducks back down to hide when he spots Seka and starts crying out to him.

"Try to find to me!" Seka looks for Nanook once he hears him, but cannot seem to find him anywhere, but he grins when he catches his tail sticking out of the mist and creeps up on him.

"Where might Nanook be hiding? He is too smart for me," he says, while Nanook is lying on the ground trying hard not to giggle. He does not realize that Seka has already found him and is standing above him.

"I found you!" Seka yells so loud that it startles Nanook and makes him jump out of the fog, while the other pups and the older brothers laugh.

"How did you find me?" he sobs as he gets up.

"Your big butt was sticking out; everybody out in the meadow knew where you were hiding," Seka says, trying to hold back his laughter.

"That's not fair. That was cheating and stop calling me fat!" Nanook cries out, while Seka walks over to Alpha Rock smirking. Nanook gets up and prepares himself to charge at Seka, but Amak jumps off and stops him, looking down at them both, not happy.

"Cut it out, you two: this is no time for games." They stop clowning around and rush over to Sakkara and the others, who are already waiting for them by Alpha Rock, while Amak climbs back on top, staring down at all of them to confirm they are all there. Tiyani sits back down in front of Alpha Rock and faces Amak.

"They are all here, Amak. You can start whenever you are ready," he says.

Amak looks down at his brother and nods to him. "Good and thank you, my brother," he says. He looks down at everybody waiting for what he has to tell. He draws a deep breath and begins. "I have gathered you here this misty morning for an urgent meeting to advise you that last night, my brother and I learned that we shouldn't underestimate this human tribe. We have found out they are more advanced and dangerous than we thought. What I am about to tell you may shock all of you, as it did me and Tiyani." He pauses for a moment while he looks, concerned, at his whole family.

"Last night, we discovered that these people have managed to tame fire," he says, sounding worried.

Suddenly, everyone begins talking in an overwhelming panic while

Tiyani tries desperately to stop them.

"Enough, enough! Everyone… please calm down!"

But Amak has had enough and shouts out angrily. "Quiet! All of you!" Everyone stops and stares directly at him. "I am also worried, just like all of you, but like I said before, as long as we follow the rules, they will never know we are here. I know it can be scary, just the thought of them being able to control that wild, deadly force of nature that has swallowed anything in its path. That is why we need to be extra careful."

Alornek, the oldest of the brothers, calls out, sounding a bit uneasy. "How sure are you about this?"

"I am very sure: we have seen it with our very eyes. It was beautiful, mesmerizing and terrifying all at the same time," he said.

Ila speaks up. "Do you have any idea how we can beat them?"

"Right now, no — I do not. All we have to do is be calm until something is figured out to get rid of that menace. We did it once and we will not let it happen again as long as we stick together, but that is up to you."

Amak steps off Alpha Rock as soon as he has finished; everyone moves aside to let him through. Sakkara walks over and looks at him, worried.

"Why are you staring at me like that?" he asks, sounding baffled.

"Every day I worry for you always going out there and risking yourself getting caught by them and now I hear this news that they can control fire… I do not know how much more of this I can take," she says, trying not to get choked up. Amak smiles confidently.

"There is nothing for you to worry about. My father taught me everything I need to know about the ways of humans, and this is not the first time I have dealt with them."

"You say that now, but one day you will not come back. You are a father now and your kids need you around. I won't be able to live with myself if anything happens to you," Sakkara says, sounding emotional.

He stares directly into her eyes. "Don't you worry. Nothing will ever happen to me, and I make sure that I always come back. Besides, I am too smart for them," he says with confidence.

Tiyani, who is nearby, has heard the whole conversation and decides to step in.

"Amak, she has every right to be worried and so am I, after seeing that fire last night. It worries me too and that is why I have decided that it is best that I go foraging tonight, in your place, so you can stay here with your family."

Amak walks over to his brother and looks at him, concerned. "Are you sure you're up to this? You are not as young as you used to be and if they discover you, you will not be quick enough to evade them."

Tiyani takes a deep sigh and looks down at the floor, so Amak does not see him tearing up. "That is a risk I am willing to take. Better me than you. You have four reasons to live but on the other hand, I have nothing to live for," he says, choking up. "And you know what I am talking about."

He looks up at Amak with teary eyes. Amak nods at Tiyani, while smiling. "All right, if that is what you want, then I will stay here tonight and you go in my place, but as long as you promise you will come back," Amak says, concerned.

"Thank you for understanding and I will come back, I promise. And you know I always keep my promises," Tiyani says with certainty as he walks to his den.

Meanwhile, over at the camp, the women and children are still sleeping in the cavern while the men are already awake and sitting by the fire. The three hunters are sitting across from the chief, while he, along with the lead hunter, is sitting facing them.

"I have gathered you here to say that we may have discovered where the wolves live. The night we first arrived here, I spotted some wolves sleeping in that clearing you see behind me. At first, I assumed they were just passing through and would move on the next day and we would not see them again, but I guessed wrong. Last night, as we rested by the fire, we observed their alpha walking past those pines, and the other wolves running over to him to greet him. We have noticed they have little pups with them and so we both came to an understanding that it must be where they are living while raising their young.

That is the only time they settle in one spot longer than expected. Most of the time they are nomads, like us, and they follow the herds wherever they go, just like we do. Their lair is hidden well in the forest's depths. If it were not for their alpha showing us the way, we would never have known we were so close to where they live," he says, grinning while the other men continue to stare at him, confused.

"So, you say that we just walk in there and expect them to surrender their land to us?" one man said.

Thethree men begin to talk amongst themselves. The leader gestures for them to be quiet, but to no avail. He gets frustrated and shouts.

"Calm down all of you and listen to what I have to say!" They all stop and turn to face him. He subjects the first man to an icy stare. "No, I never said that's what we are going to do. I have a better idea. We will burn their entire lair and let the flames swallow them alive."

The other men look on, feeling uneasy. "So how will we do it?" one man asks.

"We will strike while they are sleeping and they won't know what hit them. They won't stand a chance," the leader says, continuing to stare at the flames dancing before his eyes. "We will let the fire do what it does well: surprise them when they least expect it," he adds, entranced by the flickering light.

Inside the cave, the women are waking up, along with the children, who begin crying, causing the leader to snap out of his reverie. He looks up at the sky and sees the sun rising. He gets up to grab his spear.

"Okay, men. Grab your spears and let's go hunting."

They each get up and grab their spears and follow their leader into the woods and out into the tundra.

Night has come once again and Tiyani is foraging for something to bring back to the pack, like he said he would, so Amak could stay back with his family. He looks in every shrub and down every hole that he comes across. He finds an interesting, rotted log that is lying down across the ground, and it entices him to look inside, believing that it might have something to bring back to the pack. But once he sticks his head inside, he pulls it back out and runs away from there as fast as he can. Just as he leaves, an angry badger steps out of the log and chases after him.

Moments later, he is sniffing near a shrub when he spots a family of rabbits close by. He lowers down and begins creeping up on them, so he does not get detected, but he steps on a twig again, which alerts them. One rabbit rises on its rear legs and looks toward the large shrub but goes back down to eating when it spots nothing there. Tiyani has gotten out of sight just at the right time before the rabbit notices him. He is now hiding behind a tree near them. He readies himself and charges, catching the rabbits by surprise and causing them to split up. Two run straight and one runs left. He goes after the single rabbit without knowing it was heading toward the people's camp.

Nearby, a woman is carrying wood back to the camp for the fire. She does not see Tiyani and because he is focusing on the rabbit, he also does not see her but when he does, it is too late: he tries to stop but the moist soil causes him to slip, and he collides into the woman. He gets away in time and jumps into some hedges nearby to hide. The woman takes it as an attack and panics. She gets up and runs, screaming, over to a nearby sentry. He hears her screaming, and he hurries over to her.

"What's wrong?" He asks, concerned

"I got attacked by a wolf!"

"Take me to where you were attacked," he says, worried.

Without hesitation, she leads him over to the spot where she collided with Tiyani.

"It attacked me right over here, next to these hedges. I was just carrying wood to bring back to the camp and then without warning, it attacked me."

"Can you show me where it went?"

"I'm not sure. It happened so fast I didn't have time to check. It just disappeared," she says in a shaky voice.

The sentry looks down on the ground and finds some tracks, which lead him to hedges nearby. He pokes around the hedges with the blunt end of his spear, guessing if there is any wolf hiding there it will jump out, but since no wolf jumps out, he believes it has left. So he turns around to head over to the woman so he can comfort her, when Tiyani runs out of those same hedges and jumps over him, which causes the sentry to fall back in surprise. The wolf canters straight ahead to hide behind some trees and remains there, waiting for the pair to leave.

The sentry and the woman run back to the camp as quickly as their feet can carry them and begin shouting at the top of their lungs, while frantically waving their arms once they get near the camp.

"Wolf! Wolf! We've seen a wolf!" they both scream at once. The leader is the first to hear them and does not hesitate to grab his spear. The other men quickly rise to get theirs and rush over to them. The man and woman lead them to where the woman was attacked and once there, they all gather and listen as the sentry explains how it happened.

"She says she got attacked by that wolf just here. Then I began following these tracks and they led me straight to those hedges behind you and that's when I began looking for any signs that it was still there. Believing there was nothing, I turned around and that was when this huge wolf jumped out, ran past me and vanished behind those two trees, straight ahead."

The leader looks over to the two trees ahead, and slowly walks toward them. The sentry, feeling concerned for his leader's safety, tries to warn him, but he just gestures for him not to worry as he continues on. He stands by one of the trees and looks around it to find any clues. He heads over to the other tree and when he looks down, he notices a clump of hair caught in its bark. He goes down and sniffs at the hair and grins as he begins looking around the area.

"You are around here somewhere, and I will find you," he whispers to himself. He walks over to the others and shows them the clump of hair he has found. He hands it over to one of the men and turns to looks at the sentry and the woman.

"That will do. Go sit by the fire along with the others. You both look like you need a break. We will take it from here." As they both walk away, he grabs the sentry by the arm. "I would like to thank you for a job well done tonight. I know I can always count on you."

The sentry gives him a gentle nod to show that he is grateful and walks back to the camp, together with the woman, while the leader and his group stay back. He looks over to them, grinning.

"Let's go find that demon," he says, raising his spear into the air, and the other men cheer as they march into the forest closely behind him. They gather around the area where the wolf was last seen.

"We will look around these trees, while you two look around those hedges, in case there were others with him. Wolves never wander on their own."

They split up and begin their search with their spears in a tight grip. They look behind every tree and in every bush. They shift through the long grass but there is no sign of him. The leader stops to take a break. One of the hunters stand by him, feeling exhausted.

"We have been looking for a long time and there is no sign of that wolf. It's as though it just vanished into thin air. We will be searching all night and we still will not find him."

The leader wipes his forehead, picks up his spear and looks directly at the man. "They can't vanish into thin air, just like that. He is not far. We have to keep looking harder. If it means we search until daybreak, so be it."

"But he can be anywhere, it moves through this forest like a spirit…"

"They are not spirits, they are demons and it's our job to get rid of them," the leader scolds, but the man, instead of responding, just stands there, staring past him with a terrified look in his face. "Are you all right? Snap out of it," the leader says, feeling concerned for the man.

"Look behind you," the man replies in a shaky voice. The leader turns around and is astounded when he sees Tiyani standing there, simply looking at them before he turns and runs off. They frantically wave their arms to the other men to get their attention and the men quickly rush over to where they are.

"There it is — we found him and look at the size of him!" the leader says.

One of the hunters is about to throw a spear but the leader stops him.

"It is too far; a spear won't reach him, but I have a better idea, and it will for sure reach him," he says confidently, reaching behind him to pull out a bow. He then reaches behind his shoulder, and produces an arrow, looks at the other men and grins as he flicks the arrow in his hand. "This is how we are going to get him."

He sets up the arrow, and the moment he has Tiyani in his sights, he releases it. The arrow zips through the trees in deadly silence, striking Tiyani on the left side as he jumps over a log lying in his way. He yelps in pain as he falls to the ground. The leader grins in satisfaction when he hears the wolf crying out in the distance. Tiyani struggles as he gets up. He looks at the men and sees the leader is getting another arrow ready to finish him off. The wolf runs out of the way, just as the arrow strikes a tree. The leader grins and looks at the other men.

"Let's go: our work here is done. He is dead, anyway — if not by us, by something else," he says as he heads back to the camp.

CHAPTER 4

Early the next morning in the lair, Amak is pacing nervously back and forth, wondering why Tiyani is not back yet. He keeps peeking out to check if his brother is returning from foraging whenever he hears noise coming from the forest. Sakkara, who is sitting by the den, notices Amak's restless pacing and sensing that something is wrong, walks over to reassure him.

"You look nervous."

"I am fine — don't you worry."

"You don't look like you're fine. Your restless pacing is a dead giveaway and don't deny it," she replies, sounding concerned. Amak takes one last look into the forest before looking at her with the most worried look on his face.

"It is already morning and Tiyani is not back yet."

"Calm down — he'll be fine. He has a lot of experience, he has encountered the people countless times. He'll know what to do," Sakkara says.

Amak sighs. "But that's not what worries me. I heard the people shouting last night. What if they got him?" He looks over his shoulder once again, hearing more shouting coming from the people's camp, and worries more. "He could be in trouble. I can't wait any longer. I have to go look for him."

Amak is about to leave, but Sakkara calls out to him "No, stop!"

He hesitantly stops and turns to face her. "But I have to. What if he needs me?"

She smiles as she walks over to him, then sits by him and leans her head on his shoulder. "It's nothing. The people shout all the time — that is their only language; they do not know any other besides that one. I thought you knew that. Come to the den with me. Your kids want to be with their father."

She turns around and heads over to the den. He sighs and calms down a little, but as he is about to follow her, he quickly turns again when he hears movement coming from behind him. Believing that there might be something lurking out in the forest, he stares straight ahead and growls.

Sakkara stops when she hears Amak growling and pads over to his side. The four brothers get up and stand their ground. They all focus their attention beyond the trees when they spot a shadowy figure run across. They stand their ground, suspecting it could be the people, and ready themselves to attack in case any of them jumps from behind the trees. But it is not any of the people who show up: it is Tiyani, who jumps out and stands there, gasping for breath. There is blood dripping from his mouth and nose. It is quiet in the lair as the other wolves stand there, stunned, when they see Tiyani's condition.

Amak approaches him, shocked. "Tiyani, what happened?"

"I… am sorry… my brother. I have… failed you. I did not… keep my promise." Tiyani struggles to breathe, before collapsing to the ground. The other wolves rush over to him. The pups are about to follow, but Sakkara stops them.

"No little ones, stay there. You don't have to see this." They stand around Tiyani, looking down on him as he lies there, gasping for air and drowning in his own blood. Amak lies down next to him, presses his ear against his body while listening to his heart, which once beat with so much life, fade away. They are all quiet while Amak lies next to the body.

"Goodbye, my brother and friend…" he whispers into Tiyani's ears before he looks up at everyone with the saddest look in his eyes. "He is dead."

Sakkara lowers down and nudges him. Amak gets up and walks over to Alpha Rock as the others look on. He walks up on top and lies down with his back facing them. Sakkara, who understands the pain he is feeling, walks over to him and sits down near Alpha Rock, looking up at him.

"I am sorry for your loss, but you should not blame yourself for this."

"Give me one good reason I should not, because I can tell you plenty of reasons to blame myself," he replies, while a tear rolls down his snout. "And one of those reasons is that I should not have allowed him to go on his own: he was too old and could not run fast enough. It should have been me going, not him," he continues as Sakkara sits by him, listening, trying not to cry. "After I had lost my parents and my best friend to those monsters, he was the only family I had left. Since then, we promised ourselves that we would always have each other's backs and protect one another. He said that he had failed me, but he was wrong. I am the one who has failed him."

"You have not failed him," Sakkara says, earnestly.

"Yes, I have. I should not have let him go on his own."

"It was not your fault. He had offered to go on his own."

Amak is about to reply but doesn't when he hears shouting coming from the people's camp. He gets up and faces the forest, snarling.

"You will pay for this, you demons!" he yells out so loud that it echoes through the forest.

Meanwhile, in the people's camp, the leader is standing by the entrance to the cave and hears the barking coming from the wolves. He looks toward the other men and nods.

"You hear that?" he says, grinning. "That is the sound that we have won, and that they are ready to surrender." The other men look at one another slyly and sneer.

In the lair, Sakkara feels the wind starting to pick up. She softly calls out to Amak, who is now lying by his brother's body.

"Are you coming? It looks like it's about to rain."

She looks up at the sky and notices the clouds beginning to obstruct the sun. Heavy raindrops start to come down. Realizing that Amak is not going to join her, Sakkara runs over to the den to shelter from the rain, leaving him alone to grieve his brother's death. The pups look up at her as she arrives.

"What's the matter with Dad?" Aurora asks sadly.

"It is nothing. Your father just wants to be alone, so we shall let him do that. Let's get inside, my children."

Sakkara is lying inside the den, whimpering, while looking at Amak lying next to his brother and not moving a muscle.

It is now night and there is movement coming from deep in the forest, just behind Alpha Rock. It is the leader, standing and sneering while staring at Amak as he rests. Along with the other wolves, the alpha of the pack is oblivious to the human's presence because the rain is preventing them from catching his scent and the wind is blowing from the other direction.

Grinning, the man pulls out his bow and arrow, the same weapon that he used to kill Tiyani, and aims at Amak as he sleeps. Realizing he is too far from the lair, he moves in closer to get a better shot but steps on a cone, which cracks and causes an echo.

Amak is immediately alert. He gets up swiftly, noticing the man standing there. He stands over his brother's body and begins growling, believing the human is there to take the body away. The leader lowers his weapon and walks away while still staring at Amak. The wolf goes over to his brother's side and pulls the arrow off him to throw it back at the man.

"I will not let you take my brother, but you can take this with you, instead," he calls out, throwing the arrow to him. The arrow drops at the man's feet, and he picks it up, nods his head while grinning, and places the arrow back in his quiver as he disappears into the darkness. Not able to pick up his scent any more, Amak assumes he has left, walks back to his brother and lies down next to him, once more.

The next morning, the sun is shining, and the birds are singing. It is a beautiful sunny day, but not for all. Amak is still grieving the loss of his brother; still lying next to the body and not moving from there. The four brothers get up and stretch to start their new day, feeling grateful for the loveliness that befalls the land. Sakkara is next to wake up. She also stretches and gives out an enormous yawn that an entire colony of birds could fit inside. The little pups run around her as they take turns to greet her, before running off to play their games with each other.

She looks over at Alpha Rock and worries when she does not see Amak there. She looks over to Tiyani's body and sighs when she sees him still lying next to it, and begins to walk over to him. She is standing over him and nudges him.

"Come on — it's time to get up. It is a beautiful day. Come join me by the den and watch over the pups as they play," she says, trying to cheer him, but he looks up at her and gives out a sad sigh as he lies back down without saying a word. Sakkara sighs, too, as she lies down next to him.

"I have an idea. Why don't we bury him by Alpha Rock? It is the only way he could be free from this world and be at peace, instead of lying out here like this."

Amak raises his head and without saying a word, he gets up and walks over to Alpha Rock. He begins to dig underneath it, and Sakkara gets up to help him with the task. The older brothers notice them digging and go to help, as well. Nanook and his littermates join in by kicking the loose dirt out of the way.

When the grave is deep enough, Amak and the three brothers walk over to Tiyani's body and together, they lift him over their backs and walk to the grave. They lower their back sides, and the body rolls off, falling into the grave, while Amak and Sakkara look on. When they have filled the burial place back up, they all sit around it and begin howling.

As legend goes, when a wolf dies, their spirit leaves the body and goes through the gateway to the spirit world, but in order for those gates to open for the soul to enter, wolves must howl all together. The wind picks up and swirls around them as soon as the wolves howl, yet stops as soon as the howling stops. Then, they lower their heads and close their eyes, feeling Tiyani's soul leave their realm and enter the spirit world. Amak becomes emotional as he has flashbacks of the great times they had together since they were pups to when they first found this lair and their last day together. A tear begins to roll down his snout and falls onto the grave and that is when he begins to hear his brother's voice coming from all around him.

"It is all right, my brother: don't hate yourself for this. It was not your fault. You did not fail me; you always had my back since the beginning. You are not only my brother but also my friend and I thank you for that. I am fine now and safe: there is no need for sadness but happiness. I am now in a better place and together with my family again. Thank you and until we meet again..."

Amak opens his eyes, astounded, while Sakkara looks over to him, baffled.

"What was that all about?"

Amak looks at her, as confused as she is. "You will not believe this, but I just heard my brother talking to me through the other side," he said, smiling a little.

Sakkara nudges her head against his. "It is your emotions playing mind tricks with you. You miss him so much, they are making you think you are hearing him. It is a phase. It happened to me, too, when I young. You will get over it."

"No, you don't get it: I really did hear him, and he was telling me that he has made it through, and that he is finally together with his family. It was too real to be a fantasy," he said, with so much joy that Sakkara smiles, happy to see the life back in his face. When he remembers what he said while mourning the death of his brother the previous night, Amak looks down at his family and lets out a remorseful sigh. He walks onto Alpha Rock and stands there, looking down at them all with regret.

"Last night, I mentioned to all of you that Tiyani was my only family. It was wrong of me to say that but I only said it in grief. You guys are all my family and it's my priority to keep you all safe. As long as I live, I will make sure that none of us will die by the hands of those monsters. If they want to get to you, they will have to get through me first," he said with confidence. He jumps off Alpha Rock and walks over to his family, hearing Nanook's and the other pups' stomachs rumbling. "And I will start by keeping all of you from going hungry!" he said, as they all laugh together.

Later at night, the wolves are lying near the grave. Sakkara and the three older brothers are down on the ground, facing the grave, while Nanook and the other pups are lying on top of the grave. As for Amak, he is lying on Alpha Rock but tonight he is not looking up at the stars, like he does every night, but looking down at his brother's burial site, instead. This is a sad night for the wolves, but not for the people. They are all sitting around the fire, having a feast for their victory. Amak gets up when he hears them shouting and runs out into the forest.

Meanwhile, over at the camp, the leader gets up and raises his fists in the air.

"Here's for one less wolf for us to worry about, and once we wipe out the rest of the pack, this land will be ours!" he shouts out, as the rest of them cheer him on. The leader takes a bite out of the meat, then he calls out to the other men and they gather by the fire as the women and children walk inside the cave. They sit around the fire, waiting to listen to what he has to say.

"I realized something that made me rethink my original plan. Using fire would be too obvious. They will know we are coming when they see the flickering light of the flames."

"Then what do you propose we do?" asked the eldest hunter.

"We will wait until they go to sleep, and once they do, we will ambush them and trap them in their own lair and destroy them one by one, young and old. We will spare none of them," the leader said.

They all walk back to the cave. As they reach the entrance, he turns to the sentry and places his hand on his shoulder.

"Since you did a good job that night, I think it would be better if you stay on guard tonight in case any wolf comes. And if one does come," he says, handing him his spear, "kill it." He gives the frightened man a pat on the back and walks to the cave, while the sentry goes and sits by the forest to keep watch as he was told.

In the forest, Amak is hiding behind some trees, eavesdropping on them, and the whole discussion has made him angry. He runs back to the lair to warn the others.

Once he arrives, he jumps on Alpha Rock and calls out to the other wolves. He bares his teeth so they will see that he is being serious. They all get up and gather around Alpha Rock while he stares down at them with an angry look in his eyes.

"I was in the forest, by the people's camp, just a while ago, and I heard that they're planning to attack us and rid us from this land so they can claim it for themselves. But we will not allow that, will we? They can drive us away from our food, but they cannot drive us away from our home. Our ancestors — my father and his father before him — fought for this land and we will not give it up this easily. They plan to ambush us when we least expect it, but not if we beat them to it. We will attack them when they least expect it and use their very strength against them, and we will weaken them by turning their very own ally against them. We will fight for our home and our land. Who is with me?" he shouts out, before jumping off Alpha Rock and running into the forest, followed by the three brothers as Sakkara and the pups look on.

Once they arrive at the people's camp, they notice that spears have been placed by the wall near the entrance. Amak grins, knowing that his plan is working out better than expected.

"They left their sticks outside. They are making this much easier for us," he whispers to Alornek.

They are about to sneak into the camp when Amak spots the sentry sitting by the forest. He stops the others from continuing, while Alornek looks at him, puzzled.

"Why have you stopped us?"

Amak motions for him to look into their camp. "Look there: that must be the guard responsible for my brother's death. If it were not for him, he would still be alive." He speaks in a low tone, baring his teeth. "I will take him down. The rest of you stay here and wait for my signal."

He sneaks up behind the sentry. The sentry spots him and is about to yell out a warning, but Amak rushes in and grabs him by the throat, killing him with one twist of his neck. He drags the body into the forest and nods to the others before he walks into their camp. The other wolves follow him in. They each take a spear and run back into the forest. Amak stays behind, with Alornek, grabs a piece of wood and lights it on the fire. He sits in front of the cave entrance, holding the torch in his jaws. Alornek also grabs a piece of wood, lights it up and joins him. Inside the cave, the leader suddenly wakes up to the flickering light and is shocked to see the two wolves sitting in the camp staring directly at them. He swiftly gets up and shouts out to the other men.

"There are wolves outside! Quick! Let's get them, men!"

The other men quickly get up and rush out to the entrance to get their spears, but when they get there, they instantly realize that their spears, their only line of defense, are not there. They look toward the forest and see the other wolves getting away with the spears in their jaws. They stare, terrified, at Amak and Alornek. Amak hurls the flaming torch to their entrance and Alornek throws his. The instant fire spreads rapidly across the entrance, blocking the people in.

The women begin screaming from inside once they wake up to the fire, followed by hysterical crying from the horrified children. The leader shouts to the other men, who are standing there, frozen in fear.

"What are you fools doing, just standing there? Put out this fire before it spreads inside the cave!"

They all desperately gather dirt and throw it at the fire. The leader looks outside and sees that Amak is still standing there, looking at them and snarling.

"This is for my brother. What you made into your ally has turned against you. Let's see you try taming it now."

Amak continues to stand by the entrance for a few moments, watching as the people struggle to put out the fire, before running back into the forest to catch up with the others.

The men have managed to put out the fire and quickly run outside. The leader begins looking for the sentry, when he realizes that he is not nearby.

"Why did that fool not warn us that they were here?" he cries out, angrily.

The lead hunter suddenly notices the dead body, lying in some shrubs near the spot he was guarding, and calls out to the leader.

"Sir, you might want to come and see this…" he cries. The leader goes over to him and is stunned when he sees the body. "This is the reason why the sentry didn't call out a warning: they managed to get to him first," the hunter says, while the leader shakes his head, feeling some remorse for his death. He looks over to the forest angrily and notices Amak just standing there, glaring at all of them. All the leader can do is laugh in disbelief that he was outsmarted by the wolves, an inferior species, as the other men look on shocked.

One of the men places his hand on his back. "We should go and attack now, instead of waiting for tomorrow, and have them pay for what they have done tonight," he insists. The infuriated leader grabs his hand and twists his wrist, as he looks at him with a face that a demon itself would cower from, in fear.

"You want to us to attack them now? How stupid could you be?" he shouts out maniacally. He grabs the man by his arm and walks him to the spot where they had last leaned their spears.

"You want us to attack them back with what? We are defenseless — we have no spears! We can't defend ourselves against their power. We are beat."

He walks back inside the cave without saying a word to any of them, while the lead hunter calls out to him.

"But sir, listen…" but he is instantly interrupted by his frustrated leader.

"I do not want to hear any more foolishness out of you. I am going to lie down." He walks into the cave and lies down for the night, while the other men wonder what to do.

Once the wolves arrive in the lair, they all form a circle and celebrate by howling together, loud enough so the people can hear. Amak looks over at Sakkara with delight, but she does not look happy. She stares at him, unimpressed, before she turns around and walks over to join Nanook and the pups. He rushes over to her and stands in her way.

"What is the matter?" he asks in a concerned tone. She looks at him with an angry look in her eyes and moves out of his way, but he stops her again. "You look troubled. Tell me what's wrong."

"You want me to tell you what's bothering me. Fine, I will tell you. What you did tonight was not right. It was wrong. There — are you happy now?"

He just looks at her baffled. "But I didn't do anything wrong except for making the people suffer," he says while baring his teeth, but she stares straight at his yellow eyes.

"That's exactly my point. You didn't have to destroy their home."

"But let them destroy ours!" Amak shouts at her while everyone stops what they are doing and stares. Amak clears his throat. "I am sorry… but it was the only way to send a message to them that we will not give up to them easily and have them take what is ours. Besides, they deserved it after what they did to my brother. Don't you get it? We are at war."

Sakkara is still not happy with his answer. "That is not the wolf way: we don't do things like that for revenge. Maybe that is what humans do, but never us," she mutters, displeased, as she walks away from him.

Amak looks over to the others who look away, acting like they haven't heard a thing. He walks over to Sakkara, wagging his tail, and whispers into her ear so only she can hear.

"But at least we have won and now my brother can rest in peace," he says to reassure her, but she ignores him instead and sits with her head lowered and whimpers. He sighs and sits next to her, looking at her sad eyes. "I only do this just so we can be safe. I don't know what else I could do."

"It just worries me that one day you won't come back," she says, choked up, as she rubs noses with him and leans her head on his shoulder. Amak licks her cheek.

"Ew, Mom and Dad are kissing!" cries out Denali, while Ila leans over to Alornek and whispers, "Get a room!" and the three of them laugh softly amongst themselves. Amak turns around and gives them a mean look. The three of them stop laughing and hurry over to their dens.

Nanook asks them both, puzzled. "Mom… Dad, what did they mean—"

Sakkara places her paw over his mouth. "It is important that you do not finish that question or even think about asking it ever again in the future," she orders, looking at Amak with an unimpressed stare, while he grins nervously at her. "Let's go inside the den: it's time for sleep. We have had a crazy, long night," she adds, annoyed, giving Amak a mean look once more, before lying down next to the pups. Amak continues looking at her, laughing nervously, then walks up Alpha Rock for the night.

The sun rises, and the birds come out and sing the dawning of a new day. Sakkara walks out of the den and gives a big stretch, while Nanook and the pups run outside and begin bounding around in excitement, ready to play. Sakkara calls out to them as they run off to play.

"Don't wonder off too far, and that includes you, Nanook." He stops and turns around to face her, while she looks at him, crossly. "Come here."

Nanook walks over to her and sits by her feet. "Where dad and the others go? I never see them around in the morning," he asks her, as he looks over at the forest.

"They went out hunting in the meadow. They left early this morning," she says, cleaning Denali. Nanook looks at her with bright eyes and expresses a smile that is brighter than the day itself.

"Wow! The meadow. What is the meadow? Will I ever get to see it?"

"Yes, when you are old enough. Although it is a beautiful place, it is also dangerous because there are animals out there that are ten times your size, and they do not tolerate little energetic pups. And it's where the people go hunting, themselves. We also think that you are not ready to go out there yet."

"But why can I not go now?"

"It is all up to your father. He decides when it is time for you to step out into the meadow and right now, none of us think that you or your siblings are ready."

"I wish I was old enough to go out there now."

"Do not worry," Sakkara smiles, lowering down and nudging him.

"You will get your chance to go. Only in time, but you will. You just need to be patient," she reassures him. "Now go on and play with your brothers and sister."

Nanook looks up at her, wagging his tail, and then turns around and runs toward the others to join them.

Moments later, Amak and the three brothers walk in, each carrying chunks of meat in their mouths, which they drop in the middle of the lair. Nanook and the other pups see the meat arrive and begin racing each other and tugging at one another to see who will get to it first. Amak looks down at them with a harsh look in his eyes that stops them in their tracks. They look up at Sakkara, clueless at what is going on, while she looks at them with a smirk as she passes by.

"Go on to the den. I will join you soon."

The pups, confused, turn and walk back to the den, whimpering. They glance back as they slink away to see Amak still staring at them, harshly. Sakkara fixes her eyes on him, not feeling pleased at all.

"You didn't have to be hard on them like that. They are just kids."

"It's the only way they will learn that the adults eat first, and they will have to wait until it is their turn. Those are the rules," he responds firmly, before taking a mouthful of meat while Sakkara sits by, unhappy about his behavior. The pups sit by the den, waiting for their turn to eat.

Nanook looks down when he hears his stomach rumbling. He gives out a sigh as he lies down.

"What is taking them so long?" he complains.

"I am so hungry," whines Seka.

"That's what happens when you come last. You always end up with the leftovers," complains Denali, watching the adults eating.

"They had better save some for us and not eat everything," protests Aurora, sitting up. After a long time waiting, they all rise when they notice Sakkara backing away from the group and walking toward them, carrying some meat in her mouth. They exchange looks while wagging their little tails in excitement. They run toward her and begin jumping up as she arrives. She drops the meat on the ground and Nanook does not hesitate and dives in. He tries to shake a sizeable chunk out of the meat, but bits of it splatter onto everyone. They all stare at him, irritated, while he just grins.

Sakkara licks the meat off herself and then cleans up Nanook and the rest of the pups. As soon as she finishes washing them, the four hungry pups go right down to eat. She walks up and sits on top of the log. Nanook looks up at her with chunks of meat in his face and she just laughs a little, letting out a sigh, while Nanook shrugs his shoulders and goes back down to eat.

Amak walks over and lies next to her, and they rub noses before he lies down. The three older brothers go to lie down by their dens, feeling full after gorging themselves, and one of them lets out a burp, making the others laugh. Amak suddenly jumps off the log believing he sees movement in the forest. The others stop laughing and watch as Amak stares ahead. They quickly look toward the forest and see what looks like humans approaching their lair. The adult wolves do not hesitate to jump in front of the pups to form a barricade to keep them safe. They begin snarling and ready themselves to attack if the people get anywhere near them.

The leader stops and looks toward Amak. He smirks and nods at him, before giving him a farewell gesture. Amak nods back as a sign of respect. The leader walks away and the others follow him. They all take turns glancing at the wolves as they walk by. The wolves continue to stare until the humans have disappeared into the forest and then they begin jumping for joy, knowing that they have won, and that they are free once again, even though they have been outnumbered. They all gather round and begin to howl in victory. The people stop when they hear their howling echoing through the forest. The leader, who is walking alone, up ahead, smiles and shakes his head without raising it as he continues walking, knowing they are being mocked by the wolves, just like they have been scorned many times before.

Deep in the forest, the people all walk along, following their leader. The women are sobbing while trying to calm their terrified children. The leader feels more sorrow than happiness, knowing that he has failed them when he hears them all suffering. The eldest of the hunters, his best friend, who feels concerned for him, walks over to check up on him.

"Are you feeling, okay?"

The leader looks at him with a smile, not to show that he feels troubled. "Yes, I am okay. Why do you ask?"

"You have been quiet since we have left our camp this morning."

"I have just been thinking: what if I was wrong about those wolves?

What if I had underestimated them this entire time."

"Whatever do you mean?"

"Don't you have this feeling that they might have planned all of that?"

The man does his best to keep a straight face, but he cannot hold it any more and bursts out laughing.

"That's ridiculous! You can't think they are more intelligent than us!"

"Sure — have a laugh, but from the looks of it they have the last laugh because we are the ones walking off this land and they are still here and mocking us, form the sounds of it!" he yells at the man, before turning and walking off on his own again. The hunter and the others watch him walk away. He looks over to the lair once more and lets out a disappointed sigh, as he follows the leader's steps, with the others close behind him.

CHAPTER 5

It has been three months since the humans left and there have been no signs of them since. It is a quiet morning, and it looks like it has just stopped raining. The sun's strong rays emerge through the clouds to warm up the land. The light of the sun breaks through the canopy, lighting up the forest. It is quiet throughout — not even a creature stirs — and then a howl echoes through the forest. Everything comes to life as all the animals scurry around on the forest floor and the birds chirp brightly with song. In the lair the howling is coming from Amak, standing on Alpha Rock, waking everyone up to start their day.

"Come on, everyone — it is time to wake up. It's a beautiful fall morning."

The three brothers are the first to come out of their dens and each takes deep breaths of fresh air. Ila and Miki right away roughhouse with one another, while Alornek just looks on. Sakkara is next to come out of her den and she enjoys a big stretch before walking over to Amak. He jumps off Alpha Rock as she approaches him, and they greet each other by rubbing noses together. They both look over to the den and call out to the pups.

"Come on out, pups!"

The youngsters rush out all at once and get themselves stuck, not realizing they are now too big for the den. "Hey! Look what you've done — you got us all stuck!" cries out Nanook.

"What do you mean, I got you stuck? Said the one with the big butt," says Denali. He tries to squeeze himself out, but doesn't realize his left paw is pressed against Aurora's face.

"Get your paw off my face!" she cries out, pushing him away from her, while he grins, feeling embarrassed. The three older brothers cannot help but laugh when they notice the four of them stuck in the den.

"If only you four could see for yourselves how ridiculous you all look like right now!" Miki cries out before he bursts out laughing. The pups look over to the older brothers, not impressed when they hear them laughing.

"Instead of standing there and laughing, why don't you come here and help us get unstuck?" Seka cries out, feeling annoyed. Sakkara, doing her best to keep a straight face, walks over to them to help get them free.

"Calm down you four, I will get you out of there," but Amak stops her and looks up at her while shaking his head.

"No — don't. I think it's time they learn for themselves."

"But… but… what if they can't?"

"They will just watch," he says with confidence, sitting back to watch.

After moments of pushing and shoving, Aurora suddenly raises her head and looks at them with her ears perked up.

"Hey guys — I just thought of a way that could get us unstuck," she says.

"Oh, yeah and how's that, smartie?" Seka says.

She looks at him irritated. "If you stop moving and listen to me, I'll show you."

They listen to her and stop moving, watching as she wriggles back into the den, loosening the bundle. One by one, they all jump out, cheering. The three of them chant her name with joy as she walks away proudly, with her head raised high.

Sakkara and Amak look at their pups, smiling. "Our little geniuses," they both say, feeling proud that their children are learning to work together. They all look up when they notice the branches of the trees near the lair swaying: a strong gust of wind passes by and loosens all their leaves. The pups begin jumping up and snapping at the leaves as they drift down to the ground. The older brothers join their young siblings as they play, while Amak and Sakkara sit with cheerful smiles on their faces.

"Just look at them play. That reminds me of myself long ago, when I was a pup just like them and when I used to play the very same games that they play with my own brothers and sisters," Amak says with glee. But soon all that joy turns to sorrow when he brings up the past again. "But then it all happened, and I lost everything I ever loved," he adds with regret, while Sakkara looks over to him, concerned.

"Try not to think about it too much."

"I try but it always seems to come back and remind me about it, one way or another. Even watching my own pups playing reminds me of that terrible day. It does not seem to want to go away," he says sadly.

"I have an idea. Why don't we go and join our sons and daughter in their game? It should help you forget all about it."

Amak looks at Sakkara with a soothing smile. "That sounds like a great idea."

They both see a pile of leaves and run straight through it, causing all the leaves to rise up into the sky, colouring it with red, yellow, and orange. The pups jump up and try to get some of the leaves as they float back down. Amak catches one of them in his mouth and taunts them to run after him.

"Let's get him!" the pups shout out all at once, picking up their pace to catch up with him. Amak runs around the lair, laughing as he goes, while the pups giggle, trying to catch him. They are all happily playing as a family, feeling glad that they are safe once again.

By the time evening comes around, the wolves are feeling sluggish after being active all morning, but not Nanook. He is still running around feeling as restless as ever. He picks up a leaf, runs over to Sakkara and begins jumping around her, begging her to play with him.

"Come on, Mom — play with me some more. Please, please, please!" he cries with joyful enthusiasm. She turns to Amak with her eyes still closed and sounding groggy.

"What was in that meat we had earlier?" she says.

"Why are you asking me that?" he responds, annoyed, with his eyes closed.

"Because you were the one who brought it over."

"Why don't you go ask the people? They might know. It was their meat," he murmurs, before rolling over once again.

Realizing that neither Sakkara nor Amak will get up and play with him, Nanook trots over to his siblings to find out if they want to join him, but frowns at them when he sees them all just lazing around.

"I cannot believe that you three would rather lie there, while I am over here having the best time of my life" says Nanook with excitement.

"I am too tired, Nanook," complains Aurora.

"Not me! I feel like I could go on like this forever!" shouts out Nanook, full of enthusiasm.

"Okay, that's nice — enjoy, and I will stay right here," she says, while she rolls over onto her back.

"Okay, have it your way. You still don't know what you're missing," he says, dissatisfied, as he walks away. He is about to grab a leaf but loses interest when he notices a feather twirling toward him, and he jumps up to snap at it. A gust of wind causes the feather to twirl some more, which tempts Nanook to twist and turn along with it. He spins until he gets dizzy, which makes him feel sick and causes him to vomit.

Aurora wakes up when she hears him and looks over to him with a sly grin.

"You still having fun, Nanook?"

"I am having a blast" he yells with joy, as he leaps up into the air to get at more leaves, while she just rolls her eyes.

"Yeah, it sure sounds like it."

He looks at her, annoyed, and as he is about to comment on her remark, he gets distracted by the flutter of wings near him. He notices a bird, blue on top and red underneath, has landed near him and is pecking on the ground, looking for some food to bring over to its nest. Nanook loses interest in the leaves and focuses his attention on the bird, which has its back turned. He crouches down and sneaks up on the bird, readying to pounce once he is close enough, but the bird already knows he is behind and quickly flies away before Nanook can get any closer and lands on a tree near the den. Nanook runs over to the tree and begins running up the trunk and begins barking in excitement as he tries to get at the bird. But each time it looks like he is getting closer, he just slides back down, getting further away from his prize. The bird looks at Nanook, taunts out a chirp, turns around and poops on his face, making Nanook jump back, disgusted. He desperately begins wiping it off with his paw. Alornek is lying by his den, watching the whole thing, and gives out a snort.

"What an amateur..." he says, as he rolls over onto his back.

Nanook looks up, feeling annoyed at the bird as it flutters up three branches. Wedged in a fork is a nest. As the bird approaches it, three heads pop out, wanting to be fed. Nanook starts to walk closer to watch what they are doing, until he feels something beneath him. He jumps out of the way just as a gopher pops its head out from under the ground.

It wipes its eyes before examining its horizon. It sees Nanook and begins chattering at him, making him tumble over on his back. The gopher grabs the feather and drags it underground.

Nanook sits there, clueless. He gets up and walks over to Sakkara and lies down next to her. He feels it is safer by her side, but at 5 months he feels more adventurous than ever before and wants to find out what is out there, beyond the lair. What he does not know is that he will get that chance a lot sooner than he thinks.

Late into the night, Nanook is sleeping alongside his siblings when he wakes up to a rustling sound coming from the woods. He nudges Aurora.

"Aurora, wake up. There is something out there," but all she does is roll over and turn her back to him.

"Go to sleep, Nanook," she complains sounding groggy.

As Nanook looks at the trees across from him, he spots a shadowy figure moving around near the lair. He digs his head underneath Sakkara, waking her up. Sakkara smiles when she looks down and sees Nanook with his head buried underneath her.

"What are you doing under there?"

"There is something scary moving around in the forest," he says in a muffled voice. She looks for herself but spots nothing and begins giggling.

"Nanook, it is okay. There is nothing to be afraid of," she whispers, so she won't wake the other pups.

Nanook pulls his head out from underneath her and looks up. "Are you sure?"

"Yes, I am sure. There is no need to be afraid. Now try to go to sleep, my son," she yawns as she lies back down to sleep, while he shuffles in closer to her and settles down for the night.

Moments later the noise has come back, and it sounds closer, Nanook covers his face with his paws to hide himself from the intruder, when out of the forest the scary creature jumps out with its long furry ears, fluffy cotton tail, big brown eyes and twitching nose — a rabbit.

Nanook raises his head and tilts it to the side, watching the strange creature hop around the lair. He gets up because he has never seen one before, thinking it funny-looking with those long ears and stubby tail. He sneaks up on it to inspect it, but the instant the rabbit spots him, it bounds into the forest.

Nanook takes it as a game and without hesitating, runs after the rabbit.

Nanook is running as fast as he can through the forest to catch up with the rabbit. He does not realize he has wandered away from the lair once again, having promised he would never do so. He continues chasing the rabbit deeper into the forest, getting himself further from home. The rabbit disappears down into a burrow. Nanook pokes his head in and begins barking to get it to come out. The rabbit comes out but from a different burrow, far from where Nanook is. It bounds away, and he spots it and chases it again, calling out to it.

"Hey, wait up — I just want to play!" but the rabbit ignores him and continues bounding away in zigzags, attempting to confuse Nanook. After many attempts at trying to shake him off, the rabbit disappears into some bushes. Nanook jumps in and comes out with nothing but a mouthful of leaves. He continues searching for his new friend but cannot find the rabbit anywhere. After searching for quite some time, Nanook gives up the search.

He looks around to find which way to go back to the lair, but he cannot remember the way. It is a lot different at night than it is during the day. He runs one way and then another. He runs east, west, then north, then south, but he ends up back in the same spot. After realizing he has been running only in circles, he stops trying, convinced that he is lost and that he has gotten himself further away from home than ever. Since it is going to get dark soon, he thinks of the only way that could and will get his family's attention. He raises his head and tries to howl, but a powerful gust of wind blocks out his howling. He stops howling and waits, hoping his family has heard him and that they are already searching for him.

The wind picks up just as night arrives. The clouds are covering up the moon, making the forest darker. Meanwhile, Nanook is still waiting for his family to come and get him. He tries to howl once more but with false hope this time, wondering if they have even noticed he is missing. He hears many scary noises all around him. A winged figure screeches loud as it flies over him, and the wind does not seem to slow down. Nanook senses a storm might come. He hesitates about leaving that spot in case his family comes looking for him but leaves, anyway, to go and look for shelter in case it rains. He walks with caution, looking all around him in case something jumps out from behind the shrubs. Night is a dangerous time for a pup to be all alone. Who knows what could be out lurking in the darkness?

He hears something big moving all around him. He walks a little faster, hoping he might lose it, but trips over a tree root in his way. As he tips over on his back, he sees the figure has caught up with him and is now standing right over him. He closes his eyes, accepting his fate… but nothing happens. He opens his eyes and feels relieved when he notices it is the same rabbit he lost earlier. It just stares at him and begins wiping his face with its front foot, as though mocking him before bounding past. Nanook glares at it, annoyed.

"Thanks for getting me lost!" he shouts out as he gets up. The rabbit stops near a large cave and turns to look at him before bounding away into the night. Flashes of lightning indicate that Nanook has come across the peoples' lair. He explores it with caution and walks toward the cave. He smells it and backs away in disgust. The people may have left, but they did not take everything with them. It still smells of their odour: it is so strong it would make a skunk faint.

To his left, by a large boulder, he notices a branch stuck to the ground; he believes the people placed it there before they left. He walks up to it, and he sees something placed on top. He walks around it, trying to make out what it is, but it is too dark to tell, as the clouds have obstructed the moon. A flash of lightning reveals the object to be a skull of a wolf placed on top of a spear they have left behind. Nanook panics and runs inside the cave. Once inside, he stands by the entrance marvelling at it in awe. He cannot believe this is where the people once lived: it still looks like they have not left at all. He walks by piles of dead leaves on the floor where the people once slept. All around the walls there were many paintings. There is not a spot left bare. He hurries over to one that has taken his interest; it looks like it was just painted. It is of a pack of wolves running from the people as they are throwing those sticks at them.

In his mind, he hears the shouts of the people and the crying of wolves as the spears strike them. He remembers hearing stories about wolves, long ago, who used to roam every corner of this land. Now there are none left, except for his family. Humans have driven away the other packs from this land, with no remorse. He remembers his father was from far beyond the forest on the other side of the tundra, but he ran away here to escape the people who invaded his homeland. He thought he had found peace, but he was wrong. The people also invaded this section of the land and had already killed so many wolves with no mercy. His father has so much hatred toward the people and never trusts them, ever since what they had done to him many years ago. If the people wanted to take this land from him, they would have to get through him first. He has sworn that he will fight to protect this land and all life in it for the future of his bloodline, even if it means sacrificing his own life.

Outside the cave, the rain is pouring down. A flash of lightning reveals a shadowy figure walking into the cave. It notices Nanook looking at the paintings and creeps up on him. He turns around when he hears heavy breathing behind him and sees the creature standing there, staring at him. The wolf pup faces the creature, stands his ground, and gives out a little bark, hoping to scare it away, but the creature responds with a blood-curdling growl followed by a terrifying laughter. Lightning flashes coming from outside reveal the creature to be a cave hyena, and it has made this cave its shelter.

Nanook has heard stories of them. He has heard that wolves and the hyenas have a decade-long hatred for each other and were at war long before the people even arrived here. The hyena has Nanook backed up against a wall. He tries barking once again, hoping to scare it away, but all it does is laugh. She walks up to him, picks him up by the tail and walks toward the entrance, while Nanook struggles to break free.

"Let me go, I have done nothing to you. Help! Help! Can anybody hear me?" he cries out in despair.

The hyena comes to a complete stop as she gets near the entrance and places Nanook down. At first, Nanook thinks there are more hyenas inside when he hears more growling coming from the entrance. He is terrified, but when he looks at the entrance, and realizes the growls are coming from his father and brothers. More relief than fear washes over him. They are staring down the hyena, but they do not faze her one bit, even though they have her outnumbered. She stands over Nanook, holding him hostage.

Amak looks at Nanook and motions for him to look down. Nanook looks down and sees her right front leg is within biting distance. He does not hesitate and bites her on the ankle, causing the hyena to screech in pain, distracting her and giving him the chance to escape from underneath her. He races over to Amak. The hyena, who is now powerless, looks at the wolves as they stare at her, snarling ever louder. Amak lunges forward and drives the hyena out of the cave and the three brothers chase her out into the tundra, while Amak stays back with Nanook. They can both hear the growls from the hyena and the wolves as the chase takes place.

After a few moments, it becomes quiet. Amak is wondering what is taking the brothers so long and begins to worry. Then they both focus in on rustling coming from shrubs in front of them,

"Nanook, quick — get behind me," Amak demands. Nanook does not hesitate and hides behind his father. Amak stands his ground and begins growling, expecting it to be the hyena coming back, but the three brothers run out of the shrubs, instead.

Amak calms down, glad that it is his family and not the hyena returning and he walks over to them.

"Is she gone?" he asks.

"Yes father," Alornek says. "We have made sure she has gone far from here and the lair, but feel that this will not be the last time we'll see her."

"That is fine. I will wait for her in case she comes back," he says, but then he looks down and stares at Nanook. "But now it appears we have another problem," he says, while Nanook looks up at him, knowing he is in trouble and with the feeling that he would have been better off with the hyena.

Amak stares at him. "You have disobeyed us again, after what we talked about before."

"I am sorry but—"

"Let us go home. Your mother and I will have a big talk with you once we get back," Amak states, while Nanook looks up at him, ashamed.

The three brothers and a remorseful Nanook walk into the forest, but Amak stays behind when he notices the branch with the skull. He presses his body against it so that it falls. He picks up the skull in his jaws and runs into the woods to catch up with the others and they all canter together back to the lair.

They have finally arrived at the lair and Amak calls out to Sakkara.

"We have arrived, and we have somebody here who wants to apologize for breaking the rules — again," he says, sounding upset as he looks down at Nanook, who looks away in shame. Sakkara walks out from behind the den and rushes over to Nanook. This time she does not have a cheerful look on her face. She stands inches from him while looking down at him.

"Do you have anything to say?" she asks, sounding disappointed at him, but Nanook does not reply. Instead, he looks down in shame. "Well — are you going to say anything?"

"I am sorry, Mom, for breaking the rules," he murmurs. She is still staring at him with an angry look in her eyes.

"And what else?"

"And for running to the woods on my own again, after I promised that I was never going to it again."

"And what were you thinking, sneaking off like that again, especially this late at night?" she says. Nanook looks away, but she looks directly at him, shouting. "Don't look away from me, and don't you dare look at me like that, either. It worked on me when you were younger, but that trick will not fool me this time. Do you have any idea what danger you put yourself in? The forest at night is no place for a pup to wander off on his own and explore. There are things lurking out there that are worse than the people; things that would find a helpless pup an easy meal. You are lucky that your father and brothers found you before anything else did," she says, sounding disappointed.

Nanook then remembers the hyena and looks up at Amak, who smirks and shakes his head to let him know he will not mention anything about the hyena, this time. Sakkara notices he is ignoring her and calls out to him to get him to pay attention.

"Are you even listening to me?" He quickly looks up at her, feeling apologetic. "I want to hear an explanation from you for sneaking off tonight and it had better be a good one," she said.

"I know what I did was wrong, and I am sorry, but I did not mean to run off like that. If only that rabbit would stay and listen… I mean, I just wanted to play and when he jumped into the forest, I thought he was playing, so I ran after him. I never meant to go that far from home," he says timidly while Sakkara sighs.

"There are so many things you still have to learn. Not everyone is your friend, even though they may seem harmless — but they are not. There are things out there that could really hurt you, and that is something you need to know before you go out there into the meadow or when you decide to leave and start your own pack someday."

"I know, and I promise you both that from now on I will think twice before I sneak off on my own again and stay closer to where you can see me," Nanook said, sounding remorseful, while Sakkara looks down at him with a forgiving stare.

"I sure hope so. Now go join your brothers and sister. It's late." He wags his tail and licks his mother and father before running over to the den.

"We will see you in the morning" says Amak, winking at him.

"And promise me no more of this sneaking off," Sakkara calls out to him.

"Yes, Mother. I promise — starting now," Nanook says eagerly, and goes to lie down next to his sister and brothers.

Sakkara is about to join the pups by the den when Amak calls out to her.

"There is something I need to show you." He walks over to a shrub, and pulls out the wolf's skull. He drops it at her feet, and she stares at him, shocked.

"Where did you find that?"

"I got it from where I found Nanook. The people must have left it there as a sign to let us know we have not seen the last of them. I feel they might be back."

"What should we do?" she asks, glancing over at the pups.

"Don't worry. When they come, I will wait for them. I will not let them harm the pups for as long as I am around. But until then, we just have to keep an eye out for any signs of them."

Amak picks up the skull and buries it underneath Alpha Rock, next to his brother's grave, as Sakkara walks over to the den to lie down next to the pups. He then walks up to Alpha Rock and lies down to keep watch over his family as they sleep.

In the middle of the night, a nut falls on the floor behind the den, making Nanook wake with a start. He looks toward Alpha Rock and notices Amak is still awake. He gets up and sneaks over to Alpha Rock to be next to him, but stops in his tracks when he hears Sakkara calling out to him from behind, sounding upset.

"Where do you think you are going this late at night?"

"I am just going over to Father."

"Your father doesn't want to be bothered. Come — sleep here, next to me," she says. Amak, while lying on Alpha Rock, hears them and calls out to her.

"It's fine, Sakkara. He can come."

Sakkara sighs and gestures for her pup to go, as she lies back down. Nanook runs up Alpha Rock and jumps on Amak's back.

"Hey, Dad — thanks for not telling Mom about the hyena."

Amak looks at Nanook and chuckles. "Your secret is safe with me."

"Why did it look so angry?"

"That is because, long ago, before the people came to this land, wolves and hyenas were at a war with each other."

"But that hyena was looking at you like she knew you."

"That's because she does. When I was young, my father — your grandfather — killed her mother and she vowed vengeance that she would kill his entire bloodline, which, back then, was me, but she has never got that chance." He continues with the story as Nanook listens with enthusiasm.

"Since my father has been dead for a long time and I am no match for her, she thought it would be best to go after my bloodline instead, which is you and your brothers, and by doing that, our blood line would no longer exist and her mother's death would be avenged. And that is why we worry when you wander off like that without telling us."

Nanook looks up at Amak, whimpering sadly. "I know what I did was wrong, and I am sorry that I got you worried."

"That's all right. I accept your apology, but I am not sure about your mother. She was panicking when she woke up and found out you were not there. You do not know how lucky you are that your brothers and I found you. Who knows what that hyena could have done to you if we hadn't got there in time." He quickly looks over to Sakkara when he hears her rolling over in her sleep. He lowers down to Nanook and whispers, "Let's talk low or we will wake her."

"Okay," his pup whispers. "Dad, there is something else I want to tell you."

Amak looks at him. "Oh — and what's that?" He leans in closer so Nanook can whisper in his ear.

"The hyena was more afraid than I was after you showed up."

Amak gives a big grin and puts Nanook in a headlock. "That's because nobody messes with your father."

"Hey, cut it out! Pick on someone your own size!" he cries out. They hear Sakkara shushing them and they both begin laughing softly.

"It's getting late. You'd better go lie down next to your mother," the wolf says, chuckling a little as he lies down himself.

"I am going to be here next to you tonight and help you watch over the lair, if it is okay with you?"

Amak looks down at his son and smiles. "If your grandma and grandpa were here, I know exactly what they would say the moment that they saw you."

"What would they say?" asks Nanook, curiously.

"I know your grandmother would say that you have the same spunk as me," Amak replies, chuckling, as Nanook looks on, trying not to laugh. "And your grandfather would, for sure, say that you will make a greater leader than the both of us put together," he says and smiles a little. Nanook cannot hold it in any more and begins laughing aloud.

"Shh… Not so loud. You don't want to wake your mother," he says, laughing softly. They both look up at the sky as the clouds begins to separate, making way for the moon. Then, to Nanook's amazement, a cluster of stars light up the sky.

"Whatever happened to Grandma and Grandpa?" Nanook than asks Amak. Amak looks down and gives out a sad sigh before answering.

"They died a very tragic death, long ago."

"Do you ever think about them?"

"Always. There is never a day when I don't think about them."

"But how did they die? Do you remember anything about that day?"

"Yes, I do, but I think it is best not to talk about it. Some things are worth remembering and then there are others that we should not: it's those that keep holding us back from moving on. But they are still here with us. They never left us and the same goes for your uncle, since he is now up there with them." Amak looks at the sky and is surprised when he sees three stars are shining brighter than the rest. "Look up at those three stars there, Nanook."

"You mean those three bright ones up there?"

"Yes, your grandfather told me long ago that when we die, our souls enter the spirit world and become stars, once they get through. And from what he told me, that cluster you see up there is how the spirit world is seen by us here on earth," Amak says. Nanook looks up at them. "Every star up there is from every living creature that has passed on in time and those three stars you see shining the brightest are your grandparents and uncle looking down on us. And they are twinkling like that because it's how they communicate with us from the spirit world; and from how brightly they are shining this night, it means they are proud of how big you have grown and that we are not giving up on what they have started."

Nanook stands up with his tail wagging and howls at the stars to greet them, then he lies back down as Amak looks at him, baffled.

"What was that for?"

"I was just thanking them for watching over us, and saying good night," Nanook responds earnestly. While lying down, Amak begins to howl, followed by Nanook, and they both howl into the night.

CHAPTER 6

Months have passed. It is now winter. The entire land is covered in snow. Nanook and his siblings are now eight months old. Since they no longer fit inside the log, they live in their own dens that they dug up themselves during the fall. They come out and it surprises them when they notice the lair covered in white. They walk awkwardly as they lift each paw off the ground so as not to touch the snow.

"Mom, what is this stuff?" asks Nanook, ambling over to her. Sakkara gives a little giggle when she notices how he is walking.

"This 'stuff' is what we call snow," she says, trying to hide her laughter. Nanook jumps on top of the log to avoid the snow.

"Why is snow so cold?"

"That is because it's winter, genius: everything is cold," replies Ila, as he walks by. Nanook sticks out his tongue at him as he walks past, while Sakkara stares at him, unimpressed, before she sits next to Nanook.

"Snow is like water, but only frozen. It comes down as water but freezes halfway and turns to snowflakes coming down to the ground. Since the water is frozen over, and we cannot drink from the pond, we eat the snow to quench our thirst."

Nanook looks at her, shocked. "We can eat this stuff? Can I try some?"

He jumps off the log, not caring about the cold any more and begins eating the snow, then raises his head up and looks over to Sakkara.

"You're right — this stuff is like water!" he cries out with joy, while Sakkara gives a little grin, seeing his face all covered in snow. He runs over to his siblings, full of excitement, to tell them what he has just found out. Seka looks behind him and it surprises him when he sees footprints appear on the snow in his wake.

"Hey, Nanook — there's something invisible following you!"

Nanook looks behind him and freaks out when he sees the tracks. He walks around the lair, looking behind him each time to see if the unseen stalker is still following him, and then runs around the lair, hoping to lose it. He then gets an idea, and he scampers up Alpha Rock, looks down, and notices that the tracks have stopped. He looks at the others and calls out in excitement, wagging his tail.

"It looks like you have some following you, too. Go to high ground and it will not follow you: I think it's afraid of heights!" he cries in excitement. They all join him on top of Alpha Rock to get away from the footsteps while Sakkara, who is witnessing the entire scenario from on top of the log, rolls her eyes and sighs.

"There is nothing invisible following you, silly. Those are your own tracks: you made them yourselves as you were walking," she says, with a chuckle. She jumps off the log and begins walking around the lair herself so they can see for themselves. "I got them, too. And notice how they only appear after each step I take," she says, while Nanook watches, feeling like a fool.

He looks at Seka, growling. "You have made me look like an idiot!" he shouts. Nanook jumps off Alpha Rock and starts chasing him around the lair.

"Stop! Leave me alone! I didn't know! Mom, tell Nanook to stop!" cries out Seka. She grins and is about to stop them, but then hears Amak calling out from other side of the lair.

"That's enough, you two."

Everyone stops what they are doing and looks toward Alpha Rock where they see Amak looking down at them, displeased. They all walk over and gather at the site. They all know that when Amak stands there, he has something important to say.

He looks around to check if everyone has gathered, then clears his throat and begins to speak. "I have gathered you all today to announce that I have decided it is time that we take our newest and youngest members of the pack to the meadow, to show them what it is like to be out in the open." Amak jumps off Alpha Rock and stands in front of it, staring straight at the four confused pups. "Aurora, Seka, Denali and Nanook, come forward," he calls out.

The other wolves form a line as the pups walk toward Amak with no idea of what is happening. They look at Sakkara, confused, as they walk by her while she gazes at them with the biggest smile on her face. They sit in front of Amak as he looks at them with a smile.

"There is one thing in my life, besides being Alpha, that I am proud of and that is to call you all my sons and daughter. Long ago, I founded this lair when I was just a young pup, around your age. I was afraid, alone and with no experience of how to live on my own, but as the years have passed and through helpful guidance, I grew up to be the wolf I am today. I have watched you four grow from helpless pups to fine, young wolves I see before me, and that is why I have decided that it is time to take you to the meadow for the first time tomorrow, away from the isolation of the forest and out into the open." He says.

"At first, it will be scary, but I guarantee the moment you step out there, that will change. I believe you're all ready and the rest of the pack does, too." He pauses and leans in closer to look the pups in the eye. "But are you ready?" Amak asks.

The pups stare at Amak, who is sitting, waiting for their response. "Yes, father, we are ready," the four of them respond at once.

Amak smiles and nods. "Then it's settled. Tomorrow we will go to the meadow before the sun rises."

He walks past them, smiling. The pups look at Sakkara as she walks by them. She knows they are not ready by the look on their faces. She falls into step alongside Amak and looks at him, concerned.

"I don't think they're ready yet," she says.

"They are ready. They are much older than I was when I went out there on my own. If I can do it, so can they," Amak says, without even looking at Sakkara as he continues walking. She steps in front of him, making him pause as she faces him, not looking too happy.

"It is too soon for them," she says,

"They are ready. They told me themselves," he says stubbornly, continuing to do his best not to look at her eyes.

"They only said that so they would make you proud. I clearly saw it in their eyes, as I walked by them, that they were nervous about going there," she says, but Amak ignores her pleas.

"I have made my decision. They are going out into the meadow and that is final," he says, staring her down, but she does not agree.

"Who says?"

"I do, I am alpha and anything I say goes."

"And I am their mother, and it is up to me to decide if they go out there or not," she says, this time sounding angry. "and I say they are not ready."

She walks away without looking at him, as Amak and the others stand around.

"They are ready — I know it. Just you wait and see!" he calls, as she continues walking away from him.

The following morning it is quiet throughout the forest. Light snow is falling to the ground. The laughing of young wolves breaks the silence as they frolic in the white powder. They are rolling on it, sliding along it on their bellies and jumping up and snapping at the falling flakes while the other wolves are walking along, watching as they play. Nanook looks at them with a frown on his face.

"You guys are missing all the fun!" he cries out, while he jumps up to snap at some falling snowflakes. One lands on his nose and Nanook stares it down: it amazes him as it melts away. He loses interest when he hears Denali calling to him.

"Nanook — quick! Come here and look at this."

"What do you see?" he asks, joyfully.

"Look up there, along the tree branch. It looks like it grew fingers."

Nanook looks for a way to reach the icicles, but they are too high up. He spots a shrub behind him with icicles hanging from it and walks over to it. He sniffs them and gets his nose wet.

"Wow! It's water that's stuck in place. That's amazing." He licks another one but only gets his tongue stuck. He tugs at it to free himself, but he cannot. After many attempts, he gets himself free by breaking it off. He walks past the others with the icicle still in his mouth as they just look on, astounded.

"Coming through everyone, nothing to see here and no, I don't have my tongue stuck to this ice crystal," he says in a muffled voice.

Alornek leans to Miki and whispers, "Translation: I have an icicle stuck to my mouth," and they both begin laughing.

Amak and Sakkara exchange glances and smile when they see the way Nanook is walking along with an icicle stuck to his mouth, while his littermates stare at him.

"You look like a boar," Aurora says, while Denali and Seka laugh a little. Nanook breaks the icicle against a trunk of a tree, hides behind it and waits for his brothers, Alornek and Miki to walk by. He jumps out and screams the moment they walk by. They leap up so high that it looks as though they are flying, then both come crashing to the ground, falling on top of one another.

Nanook laughs as he runs off and smacks against a sapling that is in his way. He yelps in pain as he continues running off.

"Hey, Nanook — you know what that is? It is something I like to call karma, and it is a great friend of mine," Alornek cries out.

"I'm glad that you both are getting along," Miki says, grinning, before they laugh as they watch him running off.

The four of them have reached the edge of the forest. They now realize that it has come down to this. They are ending an era of hiding in the forest and starting a new one, out in the meadow.

Nanook peeks over a shrub and ducks back down when he sees large creatures walk by.

"What did you see Nanook?" the other three pups ask when they notice the terrified look on his face.

"I have seen a moving tree, you guys, and this time I am not making anything up," he says.

The three of them look at him as though he's crazy. Seka peeks over the shrubs to check for himself if there are walking trees out in the meadow and ducks back down. He looks at the others with eyes wide open as if he has just seen a ghost.

"He's not lying, you guys. There are walking trees out there and they have these branches growing from both sides of their heads and they are using their roots as legs," he says.

After hearing the calls of the strange creatures, the pups feel nervous about stepping into the meadow. Their three older brothers jump over the shrubs without hesitation.

"Out of the way, rookies — the pros are coming through."

The worried pups look over the shrub and see their brothers frolic in the open, while they are cowering in fear.

"They are out there, and we are hiding here," Nanook says. "Dad went out into the open when he was much younger than we are. If he can do it, so can we."

Seka, who agrees with Nanook, is the first to speak as he sits up. "Nanook is right, there is nothing to fear. Just look at our brothers out there. They don't look like they are nervous, so why should we? Let's get out there and show them we can do it, as well," he says with confidence.

The four of them stand side by side, staring at the bushes that lead out to the meadow. They take deep breaths, while Amak sits back and watches.

"Ready, set and go!" they all shout out at once, as they step out into the meadow together. As soon as they are in the open, the four excited pups jump for joy while cheering. Amak walks by them.

"Now, was that so hard?" he asks, sitting down in front of them, smiling. "I was watching you the whole time and I am proud that you four made it out here all on your own and with none of our help," says Amak to the four of them. He notices Sakkara standing behind them and gives her a mean look. All she does is look away. "I may have been younger than you when I came out here long ago, but I could never step out here on my own. My own parents were the ones who led me out here. You four have shown me that you were ready and capable of coming out here and now it's your turn to enjoy its wonders like I did, many years ago. Welcome to paradise," he says, stepping to one side so his pups can see the meadow and its wonders for themselves. Nanook and the others take a step forward as they look in awe.

"Wow! You weren't lying when you said that the meadow is beautiful, Mom," says Nanook, as he looks on, mesmerized.

"I have never seen anything like it before" murmurs Aurora, while Sakkara looks at her with a troubled smile.

"It is a wonderful place with so much for you and your siblings to explore," she says feeling uneasily.

"Yeah! It is just like you said. It does feel like we entered another world," says Nanook, cheerfully. He hears a sudden honking coming from above, and looks up as goose-like birds fly over them. Out in the distance, they spot a herd of horses. The stallions are fighting to win over a female, but the others just carry on grazing, uninterested. Then a herd of antelope bounds by and Nanook and the pups bound along with them, laughing as they go. They stop when they hear the echoes of loud clashing; they look behind them and see two Irish elk with antlers locked in a shoving and pushing contest, while the females look on, unimpressed, while chewing their cud. They look at one another and roll their eyes as they move away.

The pups nervously run and hide behind their parents.

"What are you so afraid of?" they both ask, confused.

"It's those walking trees we saw earlier."

Sakkara just laughs. "Those creatures are not trees, silly. They are called 'deer'."

They slowly walk out from behind them and Nanook looks up at them, scared.

"If they are not trees, then what are those branches they have growing out of their heads?"

"They are called antlers. They are not branches. They use them for fighting competitions and soon they will fall off, only to grow again, next spring."

"They fall off? That's pretty weird. Good thing that doesn't happen to us. I can't see myself without a tail," he says, looking back at his tail as Sakkara laughs.

"They only need those antlers during the mating season, but they regrow again next season."

Nanook and the other pups look at her confused.

"'Mating season?' What is that?" wonders Aurora.

Sakkara looks at the four confused pups and grins the slyest of grins. "It's… a time for a lot of smooching," she says, making smooching sounds at them. The pups laugh as they run away from her, and she runs after them as Amak stays back, watching them play. Sakkara walks up to him.

"You were right all along; they are ready, and I am sorry for doubting you. They love it out here and I could not be any prouder."

Amak stares down at her. "I knew they were ready; you just needed to trust me," he says, smiling. She leans in closer and rubs noses with him. They both continue to watch proudly as the pups play.

Moments later, the pups stop playing when they hear the grunting alarm calls of the antelope as they bound away. They look over to their right when they hear loud trumpeting, and it surprises them when they see a herd of mammoth approach them. The matriarch trumpets a warning as she passes, while the wolves move aside to give the mammoth their space. The pups are on one side while the others are on the opposite side of the herd.

They all look on in awe as they watch the mighty creatures pass by. A baby mammoth stops and stares at Nanook. They stare at each other, eye-to- eye, before the little mammoth trumpets at Nanook and runs off to join the rest of the herd. Nanook is about to run after it and play with it, just as the herd has passed, but Sakkara hurries over to him.

"I wouldn't do that if I were you!" she calls out a warning to him. Nanook sits by her side, looking at her with so much excitement in his eyes.

"Why can't I go play with it? It looks friendly."

"Remember what I told you before about who is friendly or not? Or did you already forget? Besides, we need to respect the mammoth, since they are the true kings of the land. We do not want to get them on their bad side. What they lack in brains, they have plenty in strength," she said. Nanook looks at the herd as they stop near them to take a break. They use their tusks to sweep away the snow to graze on the grass underneath it. Nanook frowns as he looks at them, not pleased that he cannot play with the baby mammoth.

It is now evening; the sun is setting, and some animals are leaving the meadow. Nanook and the pups are stretching after a long day out in the meadow. They are about to join the others, but Nanook and Denali stop when they hear another strange sound. They spot a ground sloth feeding off a tree near them and sneak up on it to get a better look. The size of the creature amazes Denali as they get close.

"What do you think it might be?"

"I am not sure, but it doesn't look dangerous. Let's find out if it wants to play," Nanook says.

When they get near the sloth, it stops eating, turns around, and spots the wolves. It lets out a growl and stretches out its arms to reveal its razor-sharp claws, sharp enough to chop a tree in half. The young wolves treat it as a game instead of a threat. They get down on their knees and begin barking, thinking the sloth wants to play with them. The sloth, not understanding their behaviour, takes it as a threat. It gives out a roar and approaches them rapidly, swinging its claws in a rage.

Amak and Sakkara hear the roar. They panic when they see their pups are in danger and rush over to them to save them. Just as the sloth is getting closer and ready to strike, the wolf-parents jump in between them in time.

They stand their ground and growl. The sloth stops and turns around. It moves away, while giving out a loud grunt, to another shrub, where it can eat in peace. The pups run over to their parents, jumping with joy, but all Amak and Sakkara do is glare at them, upset.

"Let's go home," says Sakkara in a stern voice. Amak looks down at them, disappointed.

"It's getting dark, anyway. We have had enough adventures for today," he says, as he walks by them without looking at them. The pups know they have done something wrong. They look at the ground sloth as it continues eating, not giving a care. As they are walking back into the lair, Amak looks toward the meadow when he hears the calls of hyenas.

"It looks like we have left in time, before our friends came out," says Amak, walking by Sakkara, who continues to stare out into the meadow. She knows what the hyenas are after and it worries her, but what they do not know is that there is something far worse than the hyenas. From outside the meadow, a shadow appears, followed by a low growl. A shadowy figure stares at the wolves walking away into their lair. It disappears into the forest, sneaking like a ghost to keep up with them.

Amak calls out to Sakkara as they are about to walk into the lair. "I need you to take Aurora and Seka back to the lair with you, I am going to stay here so I can have a talk with these two" he says, glancing back at Nanook and Denali, while they crouch down into the long grass.

Without looking at either of them, Sakkara leads Aurora and Seka back to the lair. The boy pups look up at her, but she ignores them as she walks away, while their siblings look over at them, feeling sorry for them. Amak walks over to the both of them and stares at them without even blinking an eye. They look up at him, feeling apologetic, as he sits in front of them, looking down at them. Then, without saying a word, he gets up and walks toward the forest.

"I need you both to come with me," he cries out to them, sounding disappointed. As he leads them into the forest, they wonder what they are doing out there so late into the night.

"I thought it was dangerous to be in the forest at night," Denali asked him. Amak just sits and stares at the trail that leads to the meadow, ignoring his question.

"Come here and sit next to me."

Nanook and Denali walk over to him and sit by his side while Amak continues to stare ahead.

"I just want to talk to you two in private. This morning, I was proud when I saw you guys stepping into the meadow on your own with none of our help. At that moment, I knew you were ready to go out there, but that incident with the ground sloth made me realize you are not ready yet. You think everything is a game, but it is not. You do not know how lucky you were when your mother and I arrived in time to stop that sloth," scolded Amak.

"But all we wanted to do was play and it looked friendly," Nanook pipes up, while Amak just sighs.

"That's what I mean. You cannot just assume that everything wants to be friends with you. Not everyone wants to be your friend. That ground sloth has claws sharp enough to cut you both in half with one swipe. Even the people are smart enough not to deal with them. That's how dangerous they are."

He is about to continue, but he stops and begins looking around when he hears the snapping of twigs close to them. "I think it's time we head back; we have been out here too long," he whispers to the pups, as he leads them back into the lair. Before going in, he stops and looks at them both.

"I will give you both one more chance to show me you are ready to be out there."

"Does that mean we will still get to go to the meadow?" they cry out with joy.

"Yes, but you must remember what we talked about tonight. You only have this last chance: do not let your rowdy behavior ruin it for you," he says firmly. They both nod their heads excitedly before they run into the lair. Amak is about to follow them in but stays back, when he hears the snapping of more twigs. He walks into the lair and Sakkara greets him.

"You look like there is something bothering you."

"I sensed that we were being watched while I was having a word with Nanook and Denali in the forest."

She looks toward the forest so she can see for herself, but sees nothing. "You are just hearing things. You must be tired after a long day and your mind is playing games with you," she says to reassure him,

"Yeah, maybe you're right," he responds, yawning.

In the middle of the night, Amak is lying on Alpha Rock, unable to sleep, staring toward the forest, wondering what it was he had heard earlier. Meanwhile, a shadowy figure is lurking around the lair and blending in with the trees, so that Amak will not detect it. It gets behind Alpha Rock and moves in closer. As it is ready to jump out from the trees, it steps on a twig which immediately gets Amak's attention.

He turns around and looks at the forest to see what made the noise. He jumps off Alpha Rock and walks in closer to the forest, so he can get a better look, but sees nothing there. The figure has left.

As Amak is about to go back onto Alpha Rock, he picks up some movement coming from the forest to his left and that is when he sees the glare of green eyes looking straight at him, before they disappear into the shadows once again. Amak goes after the movement but cannot find anything. As he walks into the lair, he notices something standing on top of Alpha Rock. Thinking that it might be the hyena again, he growls and raises his mantle to make himself look more intimidating, but to Amak's horror, when the creature steps into the moonlight, it turns out to be a cave lion. Amak has heard stories of them, but he thought he would never get to see one, especially this far up north. They dislike the cold, or so the myth goes.

The lion jumps off Alpha Rock, lands in front of Amak and circles him. Amak does what he can to make sure the lion does not see his family, following its every move and doing whatever he can to keep the lion's attention focused on him, but despite all his efforts, the lion catches some movement behind Amak when Denali rolls over in his sleep. The lion lets out a tremendous roar, making everyone wake up. When they see the lion, the three brothers do not hesitate to stand by Amak, while Sakkara immediately leads the pups into the forest.

"Quick — follow me this way."

The lion sees them running into the forest and begins to chase after them. Amak leaves the lair and races after the lion before it catches up with the pups.

In the forest, Sakkara and the pups are still running. She glances quickly behind her to see the lion is gaining on them.

"Keep running and don't look back!" she shouts out to the pups, picking up her pace while they do what they can to keep up with her. She leads them swiftly underneath the roots of a large tree. The lion catches up just behind them and tries to squeeze through but can't, so it jumps up on top of its roots and begins swiping its paws at the wolves from above. Sakkara instantly bites it on the left paw in defense. The lion lets out a roar of pain before it jumps away. The little family stays inside the roots for a while to make sure it has left. Sakkara sticks her head out of the roots to check if it is safe, before she can the lead the pups out.

Instantly, the lion appears again and tries to squeeze itself through the roots once more. It swipes its paws at the pups, trying to get at least one of them and suddenly gets hold of Seka's tail and drags him out.

"Mom! Help me!" he cries out in terror, as Sakkara looks helpless. Once the lion has dragged Seka outside, it stands over him and just as it is about to finish off the pup, it gets distracted when Amak suddenly arrives.

Seka grabs his chance and gets away from under the lion and runs behind some shrubs. The lion focuses his attention on Amak as the alpha wolf stands his ground, growling as loud as he can. The lion lunges to attack him but stops as Sakkara immediately stands next to Amak and begins ferociously growling with him, but the lion does not feel threatened and lets out a roar. Just as it is about to attack them, the three brothers turn up next to them, as well. The lion knows it is outnumbered and gives up: it will not stand a chance against the adult family, so it turns around and runs back into the forest and out into the tundra, realizing it is no match for a pack of wolves.

The wolves are still waiting around to make sure the lion has left for good. After waiting for a while, they sense the lion will not be coming back any more. Sakkara walks over to the tree roots and pokes her head inside, calling out to the pups.

"You can come out now."

The pups walk out and nervously look around.

"Are you sure the monster has gone?" asks Nanook.

"Yes, it is my son. Now all of you, come out so we can all go home."

They all come out, feeling traumatized by the experience, while she looks down at them, smiling. She then begins to panic when she does not find Seka anywhere.

"Seka — where did you go?" she calls out to him, hoping he will answer. She calls out to the others, panicking. "Seka is not here. Did any of you see where he went?"

The others run off right away to search the area while Amak goes to look behind some bushes.

Meanwhile, Seka is looking for a spot to hide but stops when he spots two figures staring right back at him, over by some trees. Instead of hiding, he just freezes. The two figures are about to approach him but instantly hide behind the trees when they spot Amak. He breathes a sigh of relief that he has found Seka safe and calls out to the others to let them know he has discovered his son.

"I found him! He is right here. He is safe and sound." He is about to head back to the others with his pup when he notices Seka just staring straight ahead. He looks for himself, but he spots nothing. He lets out a smile as he lowers down and nudges his head.

"Hey, calm down, buddy. You look like you've just seen a ghost. I know what you experienced was pretty scary, but it's safe now. The danger has gone. Let's go home," he says softly, while trying to reassure him. Seka speaks, though still feeling traumatized.

"That is not why I am afraid. I saw two other scary monsters right past those trees, but instead of doing the smart thing and hiding, I just froze as they stood there, staring at me, and then you showed up just as they were about to walk over to me. And when I looked over there again, they've completely vanished," Seka says.

Amak looks down at him, concerned. "Do not worry about it: you were just seeing things. There is nothing there. We should go back; your mother is worried sick."

Seka follows Amak, while still looking over to the trees, and together they walk out of the shrubs to join the others, who are waiting anxiously for him.

Sakkara, relieved that Seka is safe, rushes over to them just as they step out of the shrubs. "I am so glad you're okay! I thought I'd lost you," she says in such a worried voice, and then she looks up at Amak.

"Thank you so much for finding him, Amak," she murmurs, while the alpha wolf looks at her teary eyes and smiles.

"I am just doing my job. Now that we are all here, how about we go home?" he says confidently, but at the same time trying to hide that he feels troubled. Sakkara knows him too well and senses that something is wrong:

she can see it in his eyes and beyond that grin. As they are walking away, the same two figures that Seka encountered have come out of hiding. They stand behind some bushes staring at the wolves as they leave. The light of the moon reveals them to be the people, back once again.

The pack has arrived back safely, and everyone feels glad that the danger is over, except for Amak. He still thinks there is something worse than the lion out there. Everyone enters the lair except for him. Sakkara turns to him when she notices he is staying back.

"Are you coming?" she said, but he just shook his head at her as she looks on confused.

"I need to go back to where I found Seka."

"What for?"

"When I found him, he told me he had seen some shadowy figures looking back at him over by some trees, close to where he was. I feel it may be worse than the lion and I have to find out what it is," he says. He is about to run to the forest, but stops when he hears a concerned Sakkara calling out to him.

"Be careful!"

"I will. I promise," he calls back, and runs out into the forest.

He arrives at the spot where he found Seka and saunters toward the two dead trees, where his son said he spotted the two figures. He sniffs around the area to find any signs of anything nearby. After moments of searching the area, he looks down, and is shocked when he sees a print that looks like a human footstep. He looks up when he sees two shadowy figures, close to where he is, creeping toward the lair. Believing it might be humans, he crouches down behind the shrubs and runs swiftly back to the lair so he can warn Sakkara.

Sakkara, who is still waiting for Amak at the same spot since he had left, rushes to him to moment she hears him arrive. She knows something is wrong when he looks at her with worry in his eyes.

"Did you find anything?"

"I am afraid I did, and you will not like it."

"Well, what is it?"

"I was by the trees where Seka had seen the figures and when I was searching, I noticed what looked like the peoples' footprints, so I think it may have been the people Seka had spotted."

"Are you sure it was the people?" she says, sounding more concerned.

"I am very sure it is the people. No other creature I know makes tracks like that. He says, worried.

"But how can that be? We saw them leave last summer."

"I am afraid they may have returned, and I think I saw two of them heading toward the lair and for all I know they could be anywhereright now," he says, sounding concerned and making Sakkara feel more uncomfortable.

"What do you think we should do in case they do arrive?"

"I will stay up and keep watch."

"I will also stay up with you. We will both stay up the entire night and take turns guarding the lair."

"No, you don't have to. Go lie down with the pups and rest. I will be fine" he says, but she disagrees.

"No, I will not leave you. I cannot rest at all knowing that the people could still be lurking out there," she insists, worried for the safety of the pups.

Amak looks down at her worried eyes. "I am not willing to put you in danger and the rest of our family. Go, and I will stay and guard the lair," he says. She does as he asks and goes to join the pups. She lies down and looks at Amak as he walks up to Alpha Rock.

Late in the night, it is quiet throughout the lair. Amak is not lying on Alpha Rock as he does every night. Suddenly, two men poke their heads from behind some shrubs and begin looking around the lair to see if any of the wolves are awake. They have covered themselves with mud to cover their scent so the wolves will not know they are there. One man is about to come out of hiding until another man stops him. He kneels back down, looking at the scout with an unimpressed stare.

"What is it now? You've been acting weird since we got here."

"I still cannot believe that we are back here," the scout replies in a shaky voice. The hunter rolls his eyes and places his finger on his lips to shush him.

"Be quiet. You don't want to wake them up, especially their alpha. He's the one we need to worry about and from the looks of it he is nowhere to be seen. He must have gone foraging… Please try to be quiet so you don't wake the others, or they will do us both," he says, as he is about to step out into the lair.

"So, what's the purpose of coming back here and dragging me along with you?"

"We're going to find the spears they took from us and bring them back to the…" He slowly looks over his shoulder when he hears growling coming from close by. Amak is standing behind them, baring his teeth. The two men nervously turn around and gesture for Amak to stay back.

"You stay right there and do not come any closer," they both call out nervously, but suddenly, without hesitation, Amak lunges toward the two terrified men. They turn tail and rush away into the night, screaming, with Amak cantering closely behind them.

In the lair, Sakkara suddenly wakes up when she hears a loud noise coming from the forest. She looks over to Alpha Rock and worries when she does not see Amak lying on it. She quickly turns around when she hears rustling coming from behind the den. She slowly gets up and starts sneaking toward some bushes, staring at one of them nervously as the rustling gets closer. Amak jumps out from behind another shrub near her, panting heavily. She is relieved that it is him and walks over to him.

"What was all that noise I heard coming from the forest?"

"Remember when I told you earlier that the humans might have returned?"

"Yes…"

"Well…It turned I was right, and I believe they were the same ones I saw heading toward the lair" Amak says, grinning while Sakkara looks at him concerned. "There is no need to look at me like that. I made sure that after tonight, they will never be bothering us again," he says, walking up Alpha Rock to lie down for the night. Sakkara looks at him with suspicion as he sits on the rock.

"What did you do?"

"I gave them the fright of their lives," he says, trying to hold back his laughter.

"You should have been there to see it all for yourself."

"You're sure that they will not be coming back?"

"Yes, I am positive. I made the message clear to them," he replies, giggling a little.

Sakkara slowly turns around and goes back to her den to lie down for the night, feeling relieved that they are no longer in danger, thanks to Amak.

Meanwhile, walking out in the meadow, the two men are heading back to their camp, empty-handed. The smaller man has one of his hands clamped over his rear because a piece of clothing is missing from his pants, bitten off by Amak as he chased them off. He continues walking awkwardly as the other man laughs hysterically.

CHAPTER 7

Two months have passed, and the seasons are changing. After a long winter, the snow is melting; a sign that spring has come. Green grass is growing while flowers are blooming, adding color to the meadow once again, while the buds in the forest trees are sprouting leaves. The meadow has come to life as the animals have arrived to enjoy the spring weather, gorging themselves after a long, cold winter. A herd of antelope grazes the fresh green grass. Meanwhile, out in the distance, horses are gathering around the waterhole, drinking the fresh water after it was frozen over in the winter. The forest is full of life and birds flutter along, singing cheerful tunes; a true sign that spring has arrived.

Meanwhile, in the lair, the growing pups come out of their dens. They run toward the other wolves who have gathered by Alpha Rock, ready for another day out in the meadow, while Amak stands on top.

"So is everyone here?" he says, looking down at everyone to check if they are all present. "Then what are we waiting for? Let's go to the meadow."

As the wolves prepare to head out to the meadow, two men are hiding near the lair, waiting for them to leave. They are the same two men that Amak chased away back in the winter. As they head out, Amak catches them out of the corner of his eye. The men hide behind the trees just as Amak looks back. He looks away when he sees nothing, but he knows too well that they are there. He is only pretending that he did not see them. He sits back as he waits for the other wolves to get far enough and without them knowing, he runs back, in the opposite direction, to sneak up on the men.

After a long time waiting, the two exhausted men have come out of hiding. They sneak around the lair, looking for their lost spears. The scout looks around, feeling uncomfortable, freaking out at every sound he hears, thinking it might be the wolves returning.

The hunter sighs with frustration. "Stop it, already. There are no wolves here — they have left. You saw it yourself."

"Easy for you to say. I still cannot believe how you dragged me back here. You remember the hole their alpha ripped out of my pants the last time we were here, or did you forget? Who knows what he'll do when he sees us back here again," he says, fidgeting with his fingers. The other man remembers that night and tries to keep a straight face before he turns to look at him.

"You need to stop worrying. We won't be here for long. As soon as we find our spears we'll leave, and they will never even know we were here," he says, continuing to look around the lair. "Now, if we were wolves, where would we hide those spears?"

He spots the log and walks up to it, noticing there is a hole underneath it. He kneels down and looks inside while the scout looks in from the other side. The hunter sees the spears and signals to the other man to come over to where he is. He kneels down next to him and pulls out a spear. They both smile and celebrate, but they cut their celebration short when they hear deep growling coming from the top of the log.

They look up and panic when they see Amak standing on top, staring at them and snarling. Both men look at Amak as they get up slowly.

"Whatever you do, do not panic. I will count to three, and that's when we run out into the forest. Ready? One, two, and—" And without saying three, the two men turn around and run into the forest, screaming.

"What about the spears?" The scout cries out.

"They can keep them!" the other man cries out.

A sly grin crosses Amak's face and he races out into the forest in pursuit.

Meanwhile, the rest of the pack is out in the tundra, waiting for Amak's return. Sakkara wonders what is taking him so long, when she notices the pups are getting bored from all the waiting. Nanook is doing his best to keep entertained by blowing at a blade of grass. He sits up and lets out a yawn.

"I am so bored, Mother. Why do we have to wait for Dad to come? Can't we just go, anyway?"

"We have to wait for your father. We cannot go into the meadow unless he gives the word, and because he has not arrived, we cannot go. Those are his rules," she replies, losing her patience.

"Where could he be?" Seka whines.

"I don't know. He was right behind me when we left the lair. I only realized he wasn't there when we got here."

"What could he be doing that is more important than being out here, teaching us how to hunt?" asks Aurora.

Sakkara sighs. "I don't know, maybe he is—"

She is interrupted by screams approaching them. They all look toward the forest to check where the noise is coming from, when the two men run out from the bushes. They rush past the wolves as they scream, paying no attention to them, as the wolves watch, surprised. Amak races out after them. Sakkara gives him a mean look before leaning over to Aurora .

"Does that answer your question?" she asks sarcastically, while Aurora looks up, just as surprised.

"Yup, it sure does," she nods.

Amak stops running when he notices Sakkara and the others all looking at him. Sakkara gives him a mean look when he sits by her, panting with excitement. She grins a little when she sees him acting this way. It reminds her of the same pup she met years ago, so instead of getting mad she just sighs and giggles, gesturing for him to continue chasing after the retreating men.

"Go finish what you started."

"Did I ever tell how much I love you?" he says gleefully, before running off after the men again. Sakkara rolls her eyes. The men in the distance look back and panic when they notice Amak is gaining on them.

"We must run faster! He's gaining on us!" yells one of them as they pick up their pace in the hope that Amak will not catch up with them. They look back once more, and realize he has stopped. They glance at one another, grinning, then turn around and start mocking Amak.

"What's the matter? Are we too fast for you?" says one man, pulling funny faces, but he stops when he feels the other man cautiously tapping him on the shoulder.

"I wouldn't look if I were you. I just found out why he's stopped running after us."

"I would have loved it if you'd never said that."

The hunter turns around and freezes when he notices that there is an angry ground sloth standing inches from them. It gives out a loud roar and the men shriek in fright. They duck down just as the sloth swings its massive arm over them and then start to run away again.

Meanwhile, Amak is sitting down and watching with a sly grin on his face, as the men run screaming in terror with the angry ground sloth chasing them. The others walk over and sit next to him to watch, as well.

"I'm so glad you have joined me," he pants.

"Was it fun?" Sakkara asks, unimpressed.

"Yeah, it was. You don't know how much I miss this!"

"You have missed it so much that it made you forget the real reason we came out here," said Sakkara, while Amak looks at her, baffled.

"What are you talking about?"

"You promised to show your sons and daughter how to hunt. You kept them waiting this whole time," she scolds him. He looks back at the pups, lowers his head, and takes in a deep sigh of regret.

"I forgot, and I am sorry, but I had to make sure the people left," he says, sounding apologetic.

"The people have left. Now apologize to your sons and daughter for keeping them waiting all morning for you," she says in a stern voice. He sighs, then gets up and walks over to the pups. They sit up when they see Amak approaching them.

"I am sorry for making you wait so long after I promised you that I would show you how to hunt. I was so caught up in something else that I forgot about you guys."

The pups begin wagging their tails as they stand up.

"It's okay, Dad. We were enjoying watching the people run away from you!" says Nanook, while Amak just chuckles.

"That was pretty funny, wasn't it?" he whispers to them, with a chuckle.

Sakkara clears her throat. "Are you going to teach them, or do you want me to do it?" she says, annoyed.

Amak turns to her with a humiliated grin before he turns around and faces the pups, who are patiently sitting and waiting for their father to begin.

He has the pups sit in single file as he walks along while staring at them. The pups are all sitting up and do not move a muscle except for an occasional wag of a tail or twitch of an ear. Amak smiles when he sits in front of them before he begins his lecture.

"All right, guys. Time to listen up. The real reason we are out here today is so I can teach you four how to hunt. You are going to need this skill if you are to survive on your own one day. I will show you how my father taught me, long ago, when I was young myself and just like him, I will start by showing you how to hunt a small target. Then, when I see you are ready, we will move onto hunting bigger prey. It's not that hard; it is a lot easier than it looks, but I am going to need you four to pay close attention if you are going to perfect it."

The pups focus their attention on Amak, except for Nanook. He is too busy looking at a butterfly fluttering over him. Unimpressed that Nanook is not paying any attention, Amak clears his throat loudly. Nanook looks and grins while the others glare at him, annoyed, and Amak rolls his eyes and sighs. He walks over to a patch of flowers near to where they are.

"Now that I have attention from all of you," he says, sounding annoyed and giving Nanook a firm look, "I am going to start you off with something much simpler, like how to locate and take a gopher right from under the ground. I will show you the same way your grandfather showed me, but you have to pay close attention because you will have to do it on your own once I am done. So — get ready," he demands, feeling self-assured.

The pups watch as Amak lowers down and presses his ear to the ground, then starts walking around the patch of flowers. Then he stops, jumps up, lands and begins digging. He stands back up and walks toward them with a gopher in his mouth, while the pups watch, amazed. Then he walks and sits behind them, licking his lips.

"And there you have it. Doesn't look so hard, does it? Now it's your turn to try." He speaks in a muffled voice, his mouth full of gopher, as the pups stare in awe, not realizing it's their turn. "What are you all waiting for? Don't just stand there — go try it out!" he cries aloud, dropping the dead gopher and startling the pups, making them snap out of it.

The pups trot over to the flower patch to try out their luck. The other three seem nervous, while Nanook is the most confident of the bunch.

"You look pretty confident for someone who's doing this for the first time!" shouts Seka.

"That's because I have already hunted before."

"Since when?" his three astounded siblings shout at once, as Nanook stops and looks at them with a big sly grin in his face.

"That rabbit I chased out of the lair so long ago."

"Ooh! You mean the one that outsmarted you and got you lost 'so long ago'?" Aurora shouts out.

Nanook ignores her comment and continues walking along ahead of them, with his head held high. He then pauses while the other pups slow down behind him.

"Why have you stopped?" asks Aurora, while Nanook looks over at them, astounded.

"Why don't you guys come here and see for yourselves."

They walk over to his side and look in awe at a gopher, sitting just inches from them with its back turned, seemingly oblivious to them standing right behind it.

"Why are we just standing around here for?" whispers Aurora. "Let's go try to get it. Don't you want father to be proud of us?"

The four of them lower themselves down and sneak up on the gopher, while Amak and the others watch. Once they get close enough, they all pounce, but the gopher knew they were sneaking up and dives back underground, causing all four to collide with each other, forming a cloud of dust. As the dust clears up, they hear Denali call out with joy.

"I got it! Look everyone — I got it!" but when he opens his eyes, he sees Aurora staring at him, not looking happy.

"Yeah, good job, genius. You got my tail," she grimaces, tugging her tail from out of his mouth while everyone else tries hard not to laugh. Amak, almost managing to keep a straight face, walks over to them and looks down at the four disappointed pups.

"You guys did your best and I couldn't be any prouder. As for you, Denali — good job catching something but if only it was that gopher," he jokes, while the three older brothers begin laughing between themselves as they run back into the forest. Amak and Sakkara both notice that it will be dark soon and they lead the pups out of the meadow and into the forest back to the safety of the lair before the bigger predators come out.

When they arrive in the lair, Amak gathers the four pups near Alpha Rock, feeling remorseful.

"Hey, sorry I didn't pay much attention today. I was busy focusing on something else instead of you guys. Today we may not have had enough time to learn how to hunt, but next time I will make sure to spend more time teaching you," he says, while the pups look at him with smiles on their faces.

"That's all right, Dad. We understand," they all cry out.

Nanook goes to lie down next to Sakkara. "Someday, mother, I will get that gopher and I won't give up until I do," he says with determination, as she looks down at him, smiling.

"Now that's the spirit, and with that attitude I am sure you will," she whispers, lowering her head to sleep, but Nanook cannot sleep because he is still feeling excited from the day's events. Instead, he looks up the stars. His littermates notice that he is still awake and walk over to him.

"You can't sleep, either?" whispers Aurora, trying not to interrupt Sakkara as she sleeps. Nanook sits up and looks over to her.

"I feel this rush coming over me after what happened in the meadow today. Can you imagine, someday, we will be the ones joining Father when he goes hunting out in the meadow," he says, while his siblings also quietly look up to the sky. "I know today we didn't do well, but tomorrow will be a new day and if we keep trying, we will get that gopher because we have the best teachers to show us, both here on earth and in the sky above." He lies down for the night and tries to fall asleep. Up in the sky, three stars begin to twinkle as the wolves are peacefully sleeping below.

CHAPTER 8

Six months have passed; it is fall once again. Early in the morning, thick fog has blanketed the meadow. There is no life at all in the meadow except for three Irish elk who are browsing by the pond; a large male with a doe and a young buck. They are eating by the pond's edge when the buck looks up and begins prancing and grunting a warning to alert the others. He is nervous as he looks around, but since he senses nothing nearby, he calms down and goes back to eating.

Near to where the deer are feeding, four wolves are creeping toward the herd, using the fog to blend in. Their fur is also wet, which is the reason the deer have not caught their scent. As they continue to walk out of the fog, it turns out the wolves are Nanook, Denali and Seka, now a year old, with their older brother, Alornek, walking behind them. The pups have moved up from hunting small game and are now experienced enough to join the others to go hunting bigger game. They slow down their pace as they are getting closer to the herd, who are oblivious to their presence. Each time the deer look up, they freeze and only move forward when the deer go back to eating.

"Listen up, guys. Let's move in a little closer and on 'three' we run ahead and separate the herd. Don't forget what Father has taught you," whispers Alornek, while Nanook looks over to him with a self-assured grin.

"You need to stop worrying. We got this. Father has taught us everything we need to know," he says with confidence. They move a few inches closer and once they get near enough, Alornek whispers out to them.

"Let's stop right here. This is as close as we will go."

They stop and crouch down on the ground, waiting for Alornek's signal. Up ahead, they notice the deer have turned their backs to them, so that they can sneak up on them.

"Okay — listen," Alornek mutters. "I will count to three and we charge. Ready? One, two, three... Go!"

Nanook, Seka and Denali run full-tilt toward the elk as fast as they can. The deer suddenly notice the wolves and take off in leaps. The two adults swerve to their left and the young buck, confused, bounds to the right, getting himself separated from the safety of the adult deer. The wolves have caught up with the young buck. They run on opposite sides; Seka to the buck's left and Nanook to its right, while Alornek and Denali run behind it.

"Now that we have it boxed in, you guys need to prevent it from getting past you," Alornek shouts out, "so every time it moves over to either the left or right, you guys flank it to keep it from escaping."

The deer tries swerving to the right but Nanook shoves against it, preventing it from getting past him.

"Way to go, Nanook! That's how it's done," Alornek yells proudly from the rear, when he sees that Nanook has stopped the deer from getting past him. They continue chasing the buck toward a large shrub where Amak is waiting. He is watching proudly as his sons are doing exactly what he has taught them. When the deer gets close enough, Amak readies himself and leaps out just as it races by. The deer tries to outmaneuver him but instead, it slips on the muddy ground. Amak quickly rushes in for the kill before it gets up again. He grabs the struggling deer by the throat and kills it by breaking its neck. The deer lies motionless; the hunt was a success. The others reach him, panting, and look down at the deer.

"Good job ! I am proud to see how you've gone from young pups who couldn't even catch a grasshopper to successfully bringing down this large elk," Amak says proudly to Nanook and his siblings. "And thanks to your success today, we all get to eat," he adds, with pride. He points his muzzle to the sky and howls to the rest of the pack, who were waiting patiently in the forest, to come out of hiding and rush over and join them in their feast.

Later in the evening, as the wolves are lying around the lair, feeling full after their meal, a herd of mammoth approach and begin feeding off the trees near the lair. The wolves stand their ground the moment that they arrive. One of the mammoths pushes down a tree and begins eating the leaves, while another nearby, a young female, begins to relieve an itch by rubbing against another tree. Nanook walks over to inspect the herd and begins wagging his tail in excitement, when he recognizes that the young mammoth was the same one he encountered when he first stepped out into the meadow, back when he was still a young pup.

"Hey, I recognize that mammoth and just look how she has grown! Do you think she still remembers me?" he says, joyfully.

Sakkara, who is standing behind him, thinks otherwise. "Nanook, don't get too close. Remember what I told you about the mammoth."

Nanook ignores her warning as he continues to stare, amazed at the sheer size of the mammoths. He barks aloud to get the young mammoth's attention. She stops what she is doing when she hears the barking. She turns around and rumbles when she spots the wolves staring at her. The matriarch stands in front of her to prevent the wolves from coming any closer, while she too rumbles a warning, so that they will not go near them. The other wolves stand by Nanook and stand their ground as the mammoth sways her trunk side to side in a threatening posture and to show off her mighty tusks. The wolves ready themselves to run in case they charge, but lucky for them, the mammoths calm down and continue eating as Nanook watches. Sakkara calls out to him, and he walks over to her,

"Why don't you stay with us and give them their space? We were lucky this time but if we continue to stare at them like that, they will get irritated and they will charge, and believe me, you do not want to be standing in their way when that happens," says Sakkara as she lies down by the den. Nanook goes to lie down by his den and watches in amazement as the mammoths continue eating in peace.

It is now night, and it is quiet in the land, but the trumpeting of frightened mammoths breaks the silence as they echo through the night. Over at the lair, Amak and the rest of the wolves are sleeping, unaware of the noise. The loud screeching of frightened birds causes Amak to wake up as they fly over the lair. He looks beyond the trees, hearing loud crashing coming from the forest.

He jumps off Alpha Rock and moves in to get a better look. Sakkara, who was already awake, spots Amak standing by the forest. She pads over to him.

"What is wrong?"

"Something must have spooked those birds that just flew over us."

They look toward the forest once more, hearing what sounds like branches falling. Amak sees a large, shadowy shape heading towards them and without hesitation, he turns around and runs out of there.

"I think what scared the birds is heading our way! We need to move out of here fast!" he yells as he runs past Sakkara. She also sees the shapes running toward the lair and panics when she notices they are getting closer and runs to catch up to Amak. They both run past the others.

"Quick — get up!" yells Amak, running past the three brothers while Sakkara races over to Nanook, Aurora, Seka and Denali. "Quick! Follow me to the forest!" The siblings get up rapidly and follow Amak and Sakkara into the forest, just as a mammoth crashes through the lair, followed by the rest of the herd. Something must have spooked them. They all get away except for Seka, who is in a deep sleep.

He wakes up blearily and panics when he sees the stampeding mammoths heading his way. He gets up and tries to get out of their way, but he is not fast enough. Sakkara is about to run over, but Amak stops her.

"No — stop! If you go, you'll get trampled yourself!" he cries out to persuade her. The young female swings her trunk and sends Seka flying across the lair. His back hits hard against a tree, leaving Sakkara helpless as her son lies there. The pack stays hidden in the forest until the herd passes. They immediately come out of hiding and rush over to Seka when the danger has passed. Amak nudges his head against his son's to get him to wake up, but he does not. Instead, he lies there, motionless. Sakkara approaches and Amak looks at her, full of sorrow.

"Our son is dead."

She does not want to believe it and rushes to Seka, nudging her head against his, whimpering so loud that it echoes throughout the night. The others watch while she attempts, with false hope, to wake him. Finally, she stops and just sits there, looking down at the body, Amak slowly walks over to her.

"There is nothing you could have done," he says to her softly, but Sakkara looks at him and snarls.

"Why did you have to stop me? If I had come earlier, he could have been saved. It's because of you he is dead," she cries. She runs away and goes behind the log. Amak walks over to her and sees her lying there.

"I had to stop you or you would have been trampled by the mammoths. What else was I supposed to do?"

Sakkara raises her head and looks at him with a sad look in her eyes.

"You should have let me go. Right now, the way I feel, I wish that it were me in front of that mammoth, instead of my son," she says. Then she lies down again as Amak stares at her. He whimpers sadly as he leaves her to be on her own, and walks over to the others.

The pack gathers around the body, each placing a fern leaf over it for burial. Sakkara feels hesitant about burying her own son as she places the fern over him, and sits, unable to hold back tears. Amak sighs and sits by her side, trying to reassure her.

"You have to stop hating yourself like this: there was nothing you could have done," he says, but all she does is stare back at him, angrily.

"There was something I could have done but you just chose to stop me," she says, as she runs back to the log. Amak follows her and stands behind her as she stares straight ahead, giving him the cold shoulder.

"So then explain to me what I should have done instead of stopping you!" he yells.

Sakkara, snarling, gets up and stares Amak dead in the eyes. "You could have let me rescue our son."

"And watch you get trampled?"

"Yes! Better me than him!" Sakkara shouts. Amak stares at her, astounded, while the others look alarmed. They have never seen their mother act this way before.

"It sounds like you're blaming me for this, like I had something to do with it—" Amak begins.

"Yes! I am! Because you stopped me from saving him!" Sakkara shouts again, choking up. There is a quietness throughout the lair. Sakkara, trying to catch her breath, stares coldly at Amak. "If you had only let me go in the first place, our son would still be alive, but because you didn't, he is dead!" she yells at him, before lying back down and turning her back toward him.

He whimpers sadly as he walks over to join the others. They form a circle around Seka's body and begin howling to mourn his death, while Sakkara lies very still, in grief.

The following morning, Amak and the others walk around the lair, shocked by the damage caused by the stampede. Amak stands on Alpha Rock and barks out to the others to gather round, but he does not see Sakkara. He looks over to the log and sees her still lying there. She has been there the whole night and has not moved since. He lets out a sigh as he jumps off Alpha Rock and approaches her. He crouches down, and nuzzles her to encourage her to get up, but she ignores him and keeps staring straight ahead. He gets up, stands in front of her and lowers himself down, smiling gently at her.

"What are you doing over here by yourself? Come and join us," he urges, but instead of getting up, all she does is lie there and continue to stare straight ahead.

Amak sighs a little as he turns around and walks over to Alpha Rock. Then he stops and smiles gently when he hears Sakkara getting up. He glances over to her and smiles more when he sees her walking over to him. They exchange caring looks and both walk together to Alpha Rock to join the others for the meeting.

The pack gathers around the rock and waits for Amak to begin as he looks down at all of them.

"Something spooked those mammoths last night, and it must have been something big because mammoths don't get spooked that easy."

"What do you think it might have been?" asks Alornek, but as Amak is about to answer he is interrupted by a guilty-looking Nanook, who thinks he could be the one responsible for the stampede.

"I think I had something to do with it," he mutters. "I mean, they were feeling uncomfortable by my presence earlier in the evening, so I feel like I was the one who caused it. If only I had listened to Mother and stayed put, they would not have felt threatened. I was the one who caused this and I do not blame you all for holding me responsible for my brother's death." He lowers his head and looks at the ground, while Amak listens.

"No. We're not blaming you for any of this. It wasn't you or any of us. We may be predators, but we are no threat that is big enough to cause a stampede like that." He raises his head up when he hears Sakkara shouting out from the pack.

"Whatever it was will die for this!"

"We will kill no one. Remember you told me yourself: it is not the wolf way," Amak protests, but Sakkara stares back at him with fire in her eyes. He jumps off Alpha Rock and stares at her. "This is not like you," he says to her, as she calms down and looks over at the others.

"I am sorry. I am just so angry at the loss of your brother," she says, sadly and apologetically, while Amak reaches over and rubs noses with her.

Amak hears the mammoths have not left. He strolls over to them so he can get a closer look, hiding behind a tree and trying to stay downwind so they will not catch his scent. They still look restless from last night. If they detect him, they could start another stampede. He looks over at the large matriarch and it astounds him when he notices a spearhead still attached to her shoulder hump. He snarls as he walks back to the lair, where the others are still waiting for his return.

"Did you find anything?" asks Sakkara, quietly.

"You should see this for yourself. Come with me."

He leads her back to the mammoth herd, and it shocks her when she sees the spearhead on the mammoth's shoulder hump. Sakkara walks stiffly back to the lair, with Amak following her, trying to calm her down.

"Don't be like that," he says. She stops and stares at him with an angry look.

"Think of one good reason I should not feel like this, and it had better be a good one," she snaps. "The people caused the stampede last night that killed our son. They will pay for this, whether you like it or not," she declares, running back to the lair, while Amak tries to keep up with her.

Sakkara arrives back at the lair and walks past the others, who look confused. Amak walks over to them so he can leave Sakkara be.

"What's the matter?" asks Alornek.

"It was the humans who caused that stampede, and that has upset your mother."

"How do you know it was the people who caused this tragedy?" said Alornek, angrily.

"Because I saw the tip of their sticks still attached to the large mammoth's shoulder," Amak says, lowering his head, feeling shamed. "And I believe it must have been my fault. I have a bad feeling that the two I chased away in the spring , as we were out in the meadow, might have come back and this time brought more people with them, and they caused that stampede as an act of vengeance after what I did to them."

He looks over to Sakkara, sitting by herself, and lets out a heavy sigh. He leaves the brothers, walks over to her, and sits by her side, taking a deep breath.

"You are right about everything you said last night. You have every right to blame me for this. I should have listened to you and left the people alone and not chased them off like I did. If I had listened to you in the first place, none of this would have happened. I am blaming myself for all of this and because of my selfish actions we have lost our son — and our home," he says, wholly remorseful as he nudges his head against hers. "I am truly, deeply sorry and from now on I will think twice about what I do, so I will not regret it later, and from now on I am going to learn to start listening to you more, I promise" he said.

Sakkara looks up and begins speaking to him, struggling with her emotions. "I am not blaming you for this. I am just angry for the loss of our son. How could anyone do something like this and take the life of another, especially when they have done nothing to them?" she says with a fiery stare. "If you do not think attacking them is a good idea, then what do you think we should do?" she asks, sounding upset.

Amak replies, though feels unsure of what he is about to say. "I am not sure if you are going to like this, but judging from the damage caused by the stampede, I have decided that we cannot be here any more. I think it will be better if we move elsewhere."

"And where would that be?" Sakkara asked

"This is the part you are not going to like. I have chosen to move back to my father's old lair," he says, as Sakkara looks surprised.

"You are planning to go back."

"Yes, I am, unless you have another idea."

"You remember the reason you left there or did you already forget?"

"Yes, I do," he says, sighing a little as she continues.

"I am not sure that going back is the right choice. You came here to escape the past and now you are running back to it."

"We have no choice. As long as we stay here, the people will keep coming. This time it was the mammoth stampede; who knows what they could be planning next at this very moment."

Sakkara looks around before she stares back at Amak and sighs. "I think you are crazy, but as much as I hate to admit it, you are also right. So, when are you thinking of leaving?"

"First thing tomorrow, before the sun rises, so we get to the other side before dark."

"It will be a long and crazy trek across the open, but I am with you every step of the way."

"Thank you for understanding, Sakkara. I will tell the others near dusk. I don't think now is the right moment to mention anything about this," Amak says, while Sakkara stares at him, unsure of his idea, as he walks away.

Later that evening, Amak is standing in front of Alpha Rock for a meeting of the pack, instead of standing on top. The other wolves find it unusual to see him standing at the same level as they are. Sakkara sits next to him and they exchange looks, as they still feel uncertain about their decision and how they are going to word it, while the others look on, feeling uneasy.

Amak stares at all of them with a sad look in his eyes before he begins. "Today I gather you all here to announce to you that your mother and I have made a hard decision. It has been the hardest one we have ever had to make in our entire lives, but it is for the best if we are to survive." He stops speaking and looks at Sakkara, full of regret, before he walks away, while the others watch as he walks past. Sakkara looks at all of them and continues for him.

"What your father is trying to say is that he and I have decided that we are going to leave here and move somewhere else, where the people will not find us. I am sorry that we did not tell you sooner, but we thought it was not the right time to mention anything about it."

Alornek is outraged about the news and steps in. "How dare you make that decision without telling us first? This is our home. We grew up here and we have our fondest memories here and you are making us leave just like that. Fine! I understand it was hard all these years, struggling with the people, but we have fought so hard protecting the place and now we are just leaving… Can you please explain why?"

Sakkara looks at him, full of regret. "I know how you feel. It pains me as much as it does you, but we have to leave. As long as we remain here the people will keep coming back. We have lost your uncle to those demons. Then we lost your brother just recently. They are picking us off, one by one, and they are doing it when we least expect it. That mammoth stampede was just a warning: who knows what else they have in store for us next? And I, for one, don't want to stick around to find out," she says, staring at Alornek, who sits back down, still uncertain about the idea of moving away.

"Where are you planning to go?" Nanook asks, sounding disappointed, while Amak speaks from the log.

"We are going to the forest on the other side of the meadow, which is where I came from."

Miki speaks up, feeling stunned at the news. "We are going beyond the watering hole and that means we will have to cross the barren lands and last time I checked, that's hyena territory. They will kill us all if they catch us trespassing on their land."

"I am aware of that," Amak responds, "and that is why we are leaving before the sun rises, so we can make it to the other side before it gets dark. So, let's all get a good rest tonight, because we have a long journey ahead of us."

He steps off the log and lies down by the den.

Sakkara lies down next to him. "I hope we made the right choice…" she murmurs.

"So do I," Amak replies, feeling unsure of his idea before he lies down to sleep, as does Sakkara.

The following morning, the family pack gathers around Seka's grave. They all howl together to say their last goodbye. They leave the grave and walk into the forest for the last time, knowing that they will not be returning. Amak waits for Sakkara, as she is still standing by the body. He walks over to her and stands by her side.

"Come, Sakkara — we need to go."

She nudges her head against her son's, one last time, then stares at Amak. "This is the hardest thing I have ever done," she whispers as she turns around and walks over into the forest, while Amak stays back for a last look around.

He has flashbacks to when they first discovered this lair, many years ago, back to when they were young themselves. He lowers his head, not quite believing he is leaving it forever. As he is about to turn and follow the others, he catches some movement near Alpha Rock. He looks back, and is wholly surprised when he sees Tiyani lying underneath it. He blinks his eyes, believing he is seeing things, but he is not. He sees his brother sitting there like he had never left. Amak walks toward him, looking astounded.

"Is that you, my brother, or am I going crazy?"

Tiyani just stares at him while giving a little sarcastic smile. "Hello Amak. Yes, it is me, my brother, and no, this is no dream."

"What are you doing here?"

Tiyani gets up and walks over to him. "I just came down to have a talk with my dear and loving brother. I also heard you are leaving our home, after all the hard work we went through to protect it and that I died for" he says, while Amak looks away in shame.

"I know what I am doing is wrong, but if we stay here the people will keep coming back. It is for the good for my family. I need to leave," Amak says, while Tiyani walks around him.

"Where are you planning to go?"

"Back to our old lair; the one where we grew up."

Tiyani stops and looks at him, stunned. "You mean back to the one you ran away from to escape your past, and now you are running back to it again?"

"Yes, I have no choice. I cannot think of anywhere else. The people have taken every other spot," he says.

Tiyani looks at him with a smirk as he faces him. "You are still the naïve Amak I knew many years ago," he says, laughing a little. "There are people there as well. I have seen them for myself," he says, but Amak looks at him, not believing it.

"You are just saying that to convince me not to go. But no matter what you do or say, I am still going, and you will not stop me. I have made my decision and I am not turning back on it."

"I am telling you the truth and they are much stronger. You are not protecting the pack by taking them there. Instead, you are just going to get them all killed!" shouts Tiyani, trying to convince Amak.

"I am still going and that is final," Amak says stubbornly.

"Why are you so stubborn?" his brother yells once more. Amak rushes over to him and stares directly at him, snarling.

"It was my stubbornness that got us this far!" he shouts out. "Besides, I have dealt with humans my whole life. These will be no different if they are there!" he yells. He turns around and prepares to run into the forest while Tiyani looks on grinning.

"I sure hope so," he says. Then, before he vanishes, he looks to Amak once more. "There is one more thing I came to warn you about..." He pauses for a moment, then grins. "Never mind. You'll find out when you get there — and for that, you will not be ready," he says sarcastically, before he vanishes.

CHAPTER 9

Meanwhile, out in the meadow, the others are still waiting for Amak. Sakkara does not look happy when she sees him walk out of the forest.

"What took you so long? The sun is almost up. Wasn't your plan to leave before sunrise?" she says, but he does not reply. Instead, he smiles at her.

"I was just saying my final goodbye to our old home, that's all," he says, while at the same trying hard not to mention that he had encountered Tiyani or anything that he had warned about: it could just make her want to change her mind about leaving. He looks over at everyone else, while smiling. "You should all do the same and have one last look before we head over to our new home," he says as he walks by them.

They all stand around by the edge of the forest to have one last look at their old home before they begin their trek, as the sun rises high above the sky. They have wasted too much time and now make their way across the meadow. They will have to pass the pond and through the barren lands, which is hyena territory and the last place any wolf would want to venture into. Nanook looks behind him and sees that they are getting farther from their old home. It hurts him, knowing that he is leaving it forever and will never be returning. Sakkara is feeling the same way, but she continues anyway. He can see in his mother's eyes that she's heartbroken about leaving their home as well, but she has no choice and nowhere else to go but follow Amak.

The sun is already high in the sky by the time they reach the pond. Amak looks toward the barren lands: there is nothing but a blur. There is no trace of life or another drop of water anywhere. He looks down at the others as they drink.

"We will need to drink as much as we can because when we cross the barren lands there will be no water until we reach the other side."

Once they have quenched their thirst, Sakkara walks over to him. "It is too hot for us to make this journey across the barren lands. I think it would be better if we wait it out."

"We cannot stop. We need to keep going if we are going to make it to the other side before dark," Amak insists, but Sakkara disagrees and walks underneath a willow tree near the watering hole. Its long branches dangle down until they touch the ground, making it a perfect shady shelter. She stands underneath the branches, while staring at Amak.

"At least until it cools down a bit," she says. Amak smiles as he walks over to her. "Fine. Only until it cools down, but then from here on, there will be no more stopping." He looks over to the others as he stands underneath the tree. "Your mother has a valid point: it is hot for us to make this crossing, so I believe it would be a better if we go underneath this willow tree for some shade while we wait until the sun moves south, when it will not be as hot." They all walk underneath the tree. They lie down in the shade to wait until the sun shifts away from them.

Later in the day, heavy rain begins pouring down. The wolves are still sleeping underneath the willow tree. Amak wakes up to the new sound, gives a yawn and watches the falling rain. He then gets up and stretches, then when he realizes it will be dark soon, he rushes out from under the willow tree, startling the others awake. Sakkara walks over to him to calm him down.

"What's gotten into you? You need to calm down. You are scaring all of us," she whispers to him.

He has a worried look in his eyes. "We have wasted too much time. It's almost dark. We have to move now," he says and without saying a word, he runs ahead while the others do their best to keep up with him. Sakkara catches up with him and looks up at him, irritated.

"This is madness. You need to slow down right now."

"We can't slow down. We have already wasted too much precious time. We need to get to the other side before dark." Amak looks up at the sky and sees the first signs that it will be dusk soon, as bats are flitting above them. He looks at the forest ahead and sees that it is still too far and has doubts that they will make it across the barren lands in time.

The rain is coming down much harder now and turning the soil into mud. The others are having a tough time keeping up with Amak because the slippery ground is making it impossible for them to get a good grip. Amak notices them lagging and calls out to them.

"Don't stop — keep running!"

Moments later, the mud becomes deeper, making running impossible. Amak realizes the depth is slowing him down and stops running, which gets Sakkara concerned.

"Why did you stop?" she pants. He looks down at her while trying to catch his breath.

"The rain is flooding the entire area, and it's just slowing us down. We won't make it across in time," he says, breathing fast. He looks down and notices his paws are buried deep in the mud to the point where he cannot see his toes.

Sakkara looks at him, displeased "What do you want us to do?" she asks again, but Amak looks at her without saying a word and just lies down. "Don't tell me you are giving up. I will not let you do this. I was against your idea of coming back here at first, but you convinced me to come. We have come this far and now you are giving up just because a little mud is slowing you down," she scolds, while Amak looks up at her, exhausted. "Shame on you! You drag us all this way and now you decide not to continue? I will not allow it and do you know why? Because, for one, I am not willing to die out here. Now get up!" she demands, hoping to knock some sense back into Amak. It seems to work when he gets up and stares back at her.

"Now that's the Sakkara I came to know and love." He turns and continues running, shouting, "Let's go, guys! Let's not waste any more time!" Sakkara smiles when she sees Amak running ahead, full of hope once again.

The rain has stopped. He looks up at the sky and notes that it will be dark soon, but instead of being worried, he looks back at the others with confidence and gestures with his head for them to keep going as he begins running again. Nanook, puzzled by his father's sudden change of behavior, runs over to Sakkara's side.

"What did you say to him?"

"Sometimes, when you feel down, all you need is a little motivation to put you back up on your feet," she smiles proudly, watching Amak running ahead. "And that is what I did."

The sun is setting, and it is coloring the sky with shades of red and orange; a sign that night is on its way. Amak sees they are getting close to the forest and smiles, believing that they are going to make it on time.

"Keep on running, guys — we are almost there. If we hurry, we will make it across and reach the other side before dark, like we planned," but his hopes are short-lived. Aurora, who is lagging, is doing her best to keep up with them. She does not see a rock in her way and trips over it, letting out a cry as she falls to the ground. Sakkara hears her cries, turns around and runs over to her. She stands by her side and sees that Aurora is in a lot of pain.

"What happened, Aurora?" she pants.

"My ankle hurts real bad after I tripped over that rock," the young wolf winces, holding back the pain. Sakkara looks at her left leg and notices it swelling up. She licks it, hoping it will ease the pain, and encourages her to get up.

"Try to see if you can stand…"

Aurora does her best to get back up on her feet, but she cannot and just lies back down.

"I can't, Mother — it hurts so much," she groans. Sakkara looks at the others, worried as they are gaining ground ahead, and she howls to get their attention. Amak hears the howling and notices Sakkara and Aurora have stopped. Suspecting something could be wrong, he turns around and runs back to them.

Amak arrives and feels concerned when he sees his daughter lying on the ground, unable to get up.

"What's happened?" he pants, heavily.

"She sprained her ankle when she tripped over a rock, trying to keep up with us, and now she can't get up because of the pain. We need to stop somewhere so she can heal," Sakkara says.

Amak looks down at her ankle. "You're right: it looks bad." He glances over at the forest up ahead; they still have a long way to go before they reach safety. "We will be vulnerable if we stay out here. We're not that far from the forest. I will carry her the rest of the way and once we reach the other side, that is when we will stop so she can rest and have some time to heal," he says while Sakkara nods.

Amak calls out to the others, who have stopped to take their breath, and they run back to him. "I need you guys to help me carry your sister the rest of the way. You three will line up next to me and we will carry her together."

They agree and walk over to Aurora. They lift her up on Amak's back and then each line up next to him, so she can lie comfortably over their backs. But as they are about to walk, Amak looks over to his right, believing that he might have caught some movement out in the distance.

"On second thoughts, I will try to carry her myself, while you guys run ahead. Once you arrive, do not come back for me," he says, sounding a little desperate.

They leave him be and continue ahead while Amak tries carrying Aurora on his own, but her weight is slowing him down and he cannot go far. The others stop and begin walking back to him and stand by him. He looks up at them.

"I thought I told you guys not to come back for me."

"We are a family, and we will always have each other's backs until the end," says Sakkara. Amak gets up and smiles at all of them. He is about to lift Aurora over his back again but stops when he notices Nanook and the three brothers lining up next to him.

"You don't have to carry her on your own. We will carry her together," says Alornek, while Amak smiles. They all lift Aurora over their backs, and they walk together the rest of the way.

Amak stops when he hears the one sound he had hoped never to hear while still out in the open: it is the terrifying whooping calls of hungry hyenas in the distance. He tries to see if he can locate where they are coming from, but it is too dark to tell. They place Aurora back down and form a circle around her when, to their horror, they see the hyenas approaching from afar. The hyenas know they are there, and they pick up their pace.

Amak looks over to Sakkara. "You must take Aurora to the forest. The rest of us will stay here and hold them off."

She agrees and rushes over to Aurora, who looks up at her scared while Sakkara offers a gentle smile to reassure her. "There is no need to be afraid. Everything will be fine. I am going to need you to forget about everything that is happening around you and focus on me right now. I need you to get up once more but do it slowly and don't rush." Aurora nods and tries to get up, only to collapse back down because of the pain in her injured ankle.

"What is taking you so long? They are getting closer," Amak cries out in desperation.

"She can't get up. She can't put any weight on her injured foot," Sakkara says and suddenly notices Denali lift his back paw off the ground. That gives her an idea. "I know you are afraid, Aurora, but I need you to get up again and this time try standing on your other three legs and keep the affected one off the ground. That way, you won't put too much pressure on it."

Aurora tries it out and lifts her injured foot off the ground, getting herself balanced on the other three legs while Sakkara smiles.

"That's great and now, on the count of three, walk by my side and we will walk together. Try to keep up with me, okay? Ready — one, two, three and let's go."

They sneak away from the pack and start heading toward the forest before the hyenas arrive. Sakkara does her best not to go too fast so Aurora can keep up.

The hyenas slope closer and surround the wolves while staring them down, but the wolf pack continues to stand their ground and growl to show them they don't feel threatened by them. Nanook recognizes one hyena when he notices the scar on her front right paw and he smirks. The hyena, the leader of her pack, also recognizes Nanook and just grins.

"You remember me, don't you? So much has changed since the last time we met," Nanook says.

The wolves continue to stand their ground and do their best to trick the hyenas into believing that Aurora is still behind them, but their effort is short-lived when one hyena notices Sakkara running off with Aurora in the distance and lets their leader know. She notices them running away and laughs as she sends two hyenas to go after them. Amak sends Nanook to stop the hyenas and without hesitation, he runs after them, while Amak and the others stay back to keep the rest of the hyenas, including their leader, from going after him.

Sakkara is running alongside Aurora, doing her best not to go fast so she can keep pace and stay by her side. She looks back to see how the others are holding up and notices that two hyenas have gone past the group and are gaining on them fast. She looks down at Aurora and gives her a smile.

"We have to keep going and whatever you do, do not look back — promise me," she whispers to her daughter, trying to hide her unease. Meanwhile, Nanook is not far behind them. He picks up his pace when he notices the hyenas are gaining on his mother and sister. He runs alongside one and gives a few snaps at her flank, causing her to jump up to avoid him, but she loses her balance and tumbles over when she lands back down. The other hyena looks back and notices that Nanook has brought her partner down and that he is right on her tail. She picks up her pace so he will not catch up with her while he just grimaces and runs just as fast. Once he is close, he snaps at her hindquarters. The hyena runs in zigzags, hoping he will lose his balance, but he is nimble.

Then Nanook has an idea. He slows down to trick the hyena into thinking he has given up and disappears into the fog. The hyena looks back and begins laughing when she does not see Nanook behind her any more. Believing that he has surrendered, she focuses on her quarry up ahead and picks up her pace, but what she does not know is that Nanook has been running next to her the entire time. He comes out of the fog and clears his throat to get her attention. It shocks her when she sees him running by her side, emerging from the mist like a ghost. He glares at her with a sarcastic grin on his face, running alongside.

"What's the matter? You look like you have just seen a ghost."

The hyena picks up pace to get away, but Nanook pushes against her, making her fall. Sakkara looks back and sees he has stopped the hyenas and smiles as she keeps on running.

"That's my boy!" she pants with glee.

Amak and the others are doing what they can to hold back the hyenas' leader, so that they can give Nanook and Sakkara time to bring Aurora to safety, but despite all their efforts, the matriarch has seen that Nanook has brought down the other hyenas. She gives Amak and the other wolves a cold, dark stare and an evil grin before she goes after them herself.

Amak yells out to let his running family know their leader has gotten past them. "Keep running! Their leader has passed us and she's coming after you!"

Nanook hears the warning and looks back, seeing the hyena leader gaining on them. He is about to run toward her and try to divert her from getting near them, but Sakkara stops him.

"I will hold her back; stay with your sister."

"Are you sure you're up to it? She is three times stronger than you."

"I can, and I will. I still have some fight in these old bones of mine," his mother says.

She turns around and runs straight toward the hyena while Nanook stays back with Aurora. She stops the hyena in her tracks and begins growling and raising the mantle on her back to make herself appear more intimidating, but her threat does not phase the hyena. All the hyena does is stare her down while grimacing before knocking her down to the ground. She is about to continue running after Nanook and Aurora but stops halfway when she hears Sakkara's faint voice coming from behind.

"Is that all you got? My grandmother can do better, and she's already dead!" she cries out as she gets back up. The hyena walks over to her and stares her down again before head-butting her and knocking the wolf down once more. Nanook hears Sakkara's cries. He looks back to see the hyena has brought her down. Aurora looks up at him, like she is about to give up.

"Just leave me and go help Mother," she says, regretfully, while Nanook looks down at her like she is crazy.

"What are you talking about?"

"It's me they're after. Just leave me here and I will slow them down. It will give you guys a chance to escape," she says, full of sorrow, which just makes Nanook angry

"No! I will never allow you to do that. Do you even know what you're saying?" he yells, but she looks up at him with regret in her eyes.

"I am just slowing you down: just do what I say."

"No — never. You will not die like this. I will not let you. I just lost a brother, and I am not willing to lose my sister, as well. You are a fighter, not a quitter. Don't quit on me now!" he cries out.

She listens to Nanook and picks up her pace to keep up with him. Nanook smiles when his sister runs on.

"That's it! That's the spirit! Now stay by me. Just a few more steps before we reach the forest," he says.

They finally reach the forest and Nanook hides Aurora behind some shrubs.

"Stay here, sister. I am going to go and help Mother. I'll be back!"

He runs out of the shrubs then stops when he hears Aurora calling out to him.

"Promise me you will come back and bring them all back, as well," she says, as Nanook looks at her.

"I will, and I promise," he nods, before running off to help Sakkara.

Nanook runs as fast as he can to get back to his mother. She is lying on the ground with the hyena standing over her. He gets himself ready to tackle her from the side as he gets close, but something runs across him and stops him in his tracks. He rushes over to Sakkara to check up on her, but is shocked when he does not see the hyena anywhere in sight.

"Where did the hyena go? It's like she just vanished…"

Sakkara looks at Nanook, smiling as she gets back up. "Why don't look and find out for yourself."

He looks to his right and grins when he sees Amak and the hyena fighting with one another. They are growling and snapping at each other while Nanook watches, amazed that even a creature as powerful as the hyena is no match for his father. Moments later, as the fight continues, the hyena is getting the upper hand and Amak is showing signs of struggling. Nanook spots the reason when he looks down at the ground: it is still muddy from the earlier rain, making him slip. He remembers when Amak was teaching him and his siblings how to hunt gophers, back when he was younger, and this gives him an idea.

As Nanook is about to bound over to the fight, Sakkara calls out to him, sounding concerned.

"Where are you going, Nanook?"

Her son looks at her with a big grin on his face. "I have to help Father. I have an idea that could help him win this fight."

Once he gets near the fight, he jumps up in the air and when he lands back down, mud spatters everywhere and some splashes onto the hyena. The hyena gets distracted, looking over at Nanook, growling. Amak spots her inattention, gets up and pushes against her real hard, knocking her down to the ground. He bounds up to her and stands over her, staring straight at her and snarling.

"It looks like the hunter has now become the hunted," he hisses.

The hyena pushes Amak off. Grimacing, she gets up, shakes the mud off her and stands her ground, ready for another fight. Amak stands his ground and growls while the hyena emits a terrifying laugh that would send chills down the backs of anything living. She stares at Amak, not concerned one bit by the threat. She is about to charge but stops when Sakkara suddenly shows up next to him, also growling. Nanook comes next, followed by Denali and the three older brothers.

The hyena continues to laugh, not feeling at all bothered until she realizes her pack is not around. She looks back and sees them fleeing, instead. She stares at the wolves, stunned, realizing she is now outnumbered.

Amak glares at her, smirking. "I believe it will be for the sake of your own life that you turn around and do the same," he snarls, while his family stands firmly by his side. "I am never alone and never will be, but as for you — you will always be alone and when you need your pack the most, they are never around. My pack always supports me, as you can see for yourself."

The hyena backs away each time the pack takes a step forward. Without hesitation, she turns tail and flees to catch up to her pack, while Amak and the other wolves watch proudly as she disappears into the darkness. They continue waiting, just to be sure the hyenas are gone, in case it's another one of their tricks to make them believe that they have left, only to catch them again, off-guard.

Sakkara notices that Aurora is nowhere near them and begins to panic. "Nanook, where is Aurora?"

"She is safe. I hid her in the forest so the hyenas wouldn't detect her," soothes Nanook. Sakkara sighs with relief while Amak walks ahead of them.

"I think it's best that we do the same — who knows what else is lurking out there? Can you show us where you hid Aurora?"

Nanook agrees and leads them to some shrubs covered in yellow flowers, where Aurora comes out of hiding the moment she hears them. She limps over to them to greet them, wagging her tail excitedly while Sakkara begins to lick her, feeling glad her daughter is safe. Amak is still out in the meadow. He recognizes the yellow flowers and collects some before joining the others. He walks over to Aurora and lays some of the petals on the affected leg.

"That should do it," he says, as the others stand around, looking down at him as he continues to apply more pedals on the injured ankle. When he has finished, he looks up at them to see them all staring at him, puzzled. He smiles.

"These flowers grow only on this side of the meadow, and they bloom only at night when the moon faces north. My mother told me many years ago that the petals of these flowers have a healing effect, and so they should ease the swelling. In three days, Aurora will be a lot better and be walking again. We will stay here to give her time to heal, but as soon as she is recovered, we won't waste any more time. We will continue searching for my parents' old lair, or whatever's left of it."

As he lies down, he starts to feel unsure if coming back was a good idea. It has been years since he has been here, and he is worried that what Tiyani's spirit has warned him about might be true. He looks up at the sky and sees only one star shining brightly. Believing that it might be his brother's star, he gives out a sigh as he lies down to sleep, while Sakkara looks on, feeling concerned, while the star continues to twinkle up above.

Three days have passed, and the pack is still waiting for Aurora to recover. Amak arrives with breakfast, and everyone gathers. Aurora gets up, too, and limps over to the others so she can join them as they eat. Sakkara notices her condition and walks over to Amak while he stares, feeling concerned for her.

"She looks like she's getting better," she observes.

"Yes, she is, but she is still limping, and I don't know how much longer we should be here," Amak murmurs, looking at her. "We just need to collect more of those flowers. They seem to be working." Sakkara says.

Amak is distraught when he hears her mention the flowers. "I hate to break it to you, but there are no more flowers left. I picked the last ones the other night but I still don't get it — her ankle should have healed by now."

"So what do you want us to do?"

"We still need to move on. We will each take turns carrying her on our backs and hope that we find more of those flowers along the way. We don't know what might lurk out there. Those hyenas might come back. They know Aurora is weak, and they will stop at nothing until they get her. That's why I believe it is time we move deeper into the forest, far from the meadow and its prying eyes," he says.

He walks to the center of the clearing and calls for everyone to gather around him. "I know it was crazy to drag you all on this journey and the trouble it has put you through. But I would like to thank you all for coming along and believing in me every step of the way," he says with pride, while Sakkara stares at him with a sarcastic smirk.

"We are family: we will always support your ideas, no matter how they crazy they are," she jokes, while Amak exchanges a grin right back at her before he looks at all of them, proudly.

"Then what are we doing standing around here? Let's go home!" he cries. He lifts Aurora onto his back and leads the way through the forest with the others continuing to follow him.

CHAPTER 10

It is late in the afternoon and the pack has now moved deeper into the forest to stay away from the meadow. Nanook and Denali are idly wrestling with one another, when Nanook spots Alornek approaching them and hides behind a tree as he gets close, to scare him, but when Nanook jumps out, Alornek has disappeared. He looks behind a large tree near him and begins searching, believing that he may have hidden himself behind it, but is shocked not to find him there. He notices a large shrub near the tree and smirks as he pokes his head inside, expecting that his brother is hiding there.

"I found you. You thought you could hide from—"

Alornek suddenly jumps out from behind another tree, across from him, yelling "I'm right here!" and startling Nanook. He tumbles backwards and falls on an ants' nest. The ants bite him as they try to defend their home. Nanook runs away, yelping in pain, while Alornek just giggles, watching his brother leaping about. Amak stares at him, unimpressed, as he walks past him.

Meanwhile, as he dances around, yelping and shaking off ants, Nanook trips over something in his way. Amak and Sakkara rush over to him to check if he is okay, but stare past Nanook, astonished. He finally frees himself from the biting ants and looks behind him to see what they are staring at. Shocked, he realizes he tripped over the body of a human. They spot three more bodies lying in some shrubs near them. The others arrive and it stuns them when they see the human bodies lying everywhere.

Amak approaches one body and begins sniffing at it. "They smell fresh. They were just killed overnight."

"What do you think might have killed them?" asks Sakkara.

"I am not sure, but from the looks of these claw marks on this old one's back, it must have been something big to take down a group of them." Amak looks around the area and notices some movement beyond the trees. "Let's keep moving: whatever attacked the people might still be around," he says, concerned, as he walks away followed by the others. Amak takes one more look at the forest where he last saw the figure but it is there no more. Just as they leave, a shadow appears over one body, issuing a low growl before it drags it away.

Later in the day, Amak is tiring of carrying Aurora. He stops and tells the others to do the same.

"We will stop here for now and rest."

They all gather some dead leaves so Aurora can lie down, and then they gather around her, when a herd of ground sloths stop near them and begin rootling through some leaves. They spot the wolves and begin to swing their arms furiously to reveal their claws, and roaring loudly. Amak quickly picks up Aurora once again and without hesitation, they quickly move out of there. The ground sloths begin to calm down as soon as the wolves leave. Nanook looks over and notices why they are acting that way. Coming out of hiding are two baby sloths and they begin to play around their mother as she feeds. Nanook begins to smile as he realizes the sloths are just protecting their babies, in the same way that his pack is protecting his sister.

Late into the night, the pack is asleep until Amak wakes up. He hears the crackling of twigs coming from the forest. The alpha wolf gets up and looks toward the forest, believing that he has seen some movement coming from behind the trees ahead of him. He stands his ground as he looks toward the forest, growling as the figure creeps through the trees. Nanook wakes up when he hears his father's growling. He also spots a shadowy figure creeping through the trees, so he gets up and stands next to him. They both begin growling together, hoping they will scare it away, but it seems ineffectual as the figure is walking toward them. It then stands there for a while, staring at them both with its gleaming green eyes. It is a lion.

Then it bursts out through the trees and lets out a thundering roar, waking the rest of the wolf pack. They all gather in front of Aurora to form a barricade to protect her from the lion. Amak believes that it is the same lion that attacked them, back in the old lair, when he notices the scar on his left paw, where Sakkara bit it to protect the pups. The lion is pacing back and forth, trying to get past the wolves, but after many attempts, it shows signs of giving up and runs back into the woods, disappearing into the night. The wolves calm down when they believe it has left, but all of a sudden, the lion catches them by surprise, bursting out from behind different trees near Aurora, reaching out and grabbing her by the tail.

Aurora cries out for help as the lion drags her into the forest, while the rest of them watch helplessly, when a mysterious wolf runs out from behind the trees across from them. They ready themselves to attack it, just in case the wolf could be in league with the lion, but the wolf runs past them and begins taunting the lion before running back to the forest. The lion loses interest, releasing Aurora, and instead runs into the forest to chase after the wolf as the rest of the pack looks on, astounded.

"Who was that?" asks Nanook, surprised.

"I am not sure, but I am sure grateful that it is on our side," says Amak, feeling relieved that Aurora is no longer in danger. They all lie down around her for the rest of the night, while Amak and the three older brothers stay awake to keep watch as the others sleep, in case the lion returns.

Early the next morning, the stray wolf is trudging through the forest near where the pack is asleep. He stops and moves in a bit to get a better look. Amak is already awake and notices him approaching them. He gets up to go thank him for helping them chase away the lion, but he stops when he hears Sakkara call out to him from behind.

"I would not do that if I were you: you don't know who he is or where he is from."

"But what I know is that he helped us save Aurora from the deadly grasp of that lion last night and if it weren't for him, we would have lost a daughter." He approaches the wolf, surreptitiously, but before he can get close, it turns around and snarls. Amak stands still and stares nervously at him. "Hello there — I am Amak and I am here to—" but before he can say anything else, the wolf turns around and runs away instead. Amak runs after him, but the wolf is too fast, and he disappears out of sight.

Amak stops and begins sniffing around the area to catch his scent, but he has no luck. It is as though the lone wolf had not been there at all. He arrives back and everyone is already awake.

"Did you get to say anything to him?" asks Sakkara.

Amak sighs. "No, I didn't. He ran off before I could say anything and vanished without trace. I do not think we will ever see him again, but I am still grateful for what he has done."

He stares toward the forest and shouts so the wolf can hear him. "You hear that? I said thank you for your help!" They stand around for a while to wait for a response. They hear nothing and continue on their way and then, walking from behind the trees, the wolf appears, and stares at them as they are walking away.

"You're welcome," he whispers, before he backs away and disappears into the forest once again.

It is now late in the afternoon, and it feels hot. The wolves are exhausted from the heat. Nanook, who is thinking that Amak is leading them in circles, walks over to Sakkara's side, and gives her a weary stare.

"I have this feeling that father has been leading us in circles. I think he's got us lost. Does he even know where he is going?" he says, sounding frustrated, while Sakkara looks at him smiling with confidence.

"Although he may not have been back here for a long time, I believe he still knows where it is."

"But how does he know that it's still there?"

"He feels it in his heart, my son. You just need to believe in him, just like I do."

Meanwhile, Amak is walking ahead of them and has overheard their conversation and believes what they are saying about him getting them lost could be true. He stops underneath a willow tree, puts Aurora down, and turns to face the others.

"We will stop here to rest for now."

He walks away feeling regretful and lies down near some reeds. Sakkara, sensing that he feels troubled goes over to him.

"What's the matter, Amak?"

"I heard the conversation you were having with Nanook a while ago, about me knowing the way and feeling it in my heart. But I hate to break it you — I do not know where I am taking you. I think Nanook is right about me getting us all lost. It has been years since I have been here, and I am not even sure where here is, or if it is still there. I have been walking in circles and I am taking you guys along for the ride," he says, sounding upset. Before Sakkara can reply, Amak suddenly raises his head and looks towards some taller reeds behind them, while Sakkara looks puzzled. He looks over at her with a smile on his face. "Did you hear that?"

"I hear nothing."

"I think I just heard what sounds like splashing coming from behind these reeds."

They both turn their ears toward the reeds, and hear more splashing.

"I think I hear it, too," Sakkara says, with enthusiasm. They walk into the reeds, and as they step out to the other side, what they see astounds them.

They have come across a large river. There is a cascading waterfall flowing down a ravine. They look down at the river and see fish swimming in the clear water, some of them jumping up to snap at passing insects and splashing back down into the water.

"That explains the splashing we heard," Sakkara says, while Amak stares at the grove across the river and feels like he is remembering where they are.

"What's the matter?" she asks gently.

"I have this feeling that I know this place. I think I have seen it once before," he says.

They both call out to the others to come and join them. They are all gathered by the riverbank and begin drinking the fresh water. While he is drinking, Amak notices a reflection in the water. He looks up and sees the same wolf sitting on the other side. He crosses the river so he will not scare the wolf away, but it runs away again before he can get any closer. Amak is about to run after him but decides not to, and as he is about to walk back to the others, he notices a paw print near the spot where the wolf was sitting. At first, he looks down at it, wondering who could have made this print, and then, when he notices that there is a claw missing from the middle toe, he remembers it belongs to his father. He jumps for joy and starts calling out to the others as he runs off.

"Quickly! Follow me this way. I remember where we are!" he cries out to them, sounding ecstatic. They all cross the river and try to keep up with him.

When they have finally caught up to him, they see Amak sitting down, looking up at some trees that look like an X. He is looking up at them, mesmerized, as the pack slowly approaches him. He looks over at them, smiling. Sakkara sits next to him while he continues to look up at the trees.

"Are you remembering where we are?"

"Yes, I am, and I have that wolf to thank for this. If it were not for him showing up, I would never have noticed my father's print, which had me remember where the lair would be." He takes a deep breath and walks over to some bushes full of berries. He stands next to one bush, looking at them, wagging his tail in excitement.

"Beyond these shrubs is our new home and the start of our future," he announces as he walks into the shrubs. The family looks astounded as they walk toward the lair where their father was born. In the middle of the lair, they see a huge stump: it is Alpha Stump, and that is where Amak's father held his meetings long ago, just like Amak did on Alpha Rock, back in the old lair. They notice Amak already sitting on top with the biggest smile on his face. He thinks back to when he was a pup, playing with his siblings in this very lair while his parents looked on, smiling. He snaps out of it when he hears Sakkara sit next to him.

"It is beautiful, Amak. It must have been a while since you have been here."

"I just hope that I made the right choice coming back here and that the people are no longer here… I do not want what happened to me before happening to us again," he says, as he remembers what Tiyani warned him about.

"You need to stop thinking about your past. This is now our future and it's up to you to change that," Sakkara says to reassure him, while he looks over to her with a smile. He sits up.

"You are absolutely right. The past is over, and our future begins now. We are home and that is all that matters." He looks over to her and he places his forehead against hers. "You have always believed in me and trusted me ever since the day we met, and you never gave up on me no matter how stubborn I can be, and I thank you for that motivation."

He gets up and begins howling. Sakkara and the others howl along with him. The wolf, who is nearby, howls as well when he hears them. His howl echoes through the forest. Amak stops when he hears him and responds to let him know how grateful he is for his help. The wolf hears him, and he smiles a little as he walks away.

As night falls over the land, the pack is settling in for their first night in their new home. In the forest, behind the lair, the same wolf is hiding behind some trees, blending in with the darkness so he will not be detected by any of them. Amak manages to spot him from the corner of his eye, and he quickly turns to him. As a sign of gratitude he nods his head, while the wolf nods back before he walks away.

Early next morning, the pack finds an elk carcass lying out in the meadow and they rush over to it to eat. Meanwhile, the stray wolf is hiding in the forest, watching them as they eat. They know the wolf is there, but they pay no attention to him. They just continue to eat and once they have their fill, they walk away, back to their lair. The wolf walks out and stands over the carcass and begins eating, while still staring at the pack as they walk away. Amak and the others have not left at all but are, instead, watching him from behind some bushes as he eats while trying to keep out of sight.

"I have had it. We need to see what he wants from us and why he's helping us" says Alornek. "How did he even know you were trying to find the lair?"

"I don't know, but I know how we are going to find out. Come, let's go back and I will tell you what we are going to do," Amak says, walking away while the others look confused. Nanook looks out into the meadow and sees the wolf standing there, looking at him. Nanook nods at the wolf before turning around and walking away to catch up to the others. The wolf stares and grins as he goes back to eating.

Late into the night, the lair is empty. The pack is nowhere to be seen. Amak raises himself and looks over to the forest to check up on the others and make sure they are all in position. He is lying so still on Alpha Stump and his dark fur is blending in with the darkness, so that no one would know there was a wolf there at all. Meanwhile, the others are hiding behind some trees as they wait for the wolf. After a long time of waiting, they hear some movement coming from the forest, and suspecting it to be the wolf, they all crouch down to hide from him.

Over by the forest, the wolf is trudging through the trees as stealthily as he can. He looks over to the lair and it surprises him when he does not see Amak or his family around. He walks toward the lair while Amak smirks from on top of the stump.

"I got you now. Let's see you get away from me this time," he murmurs under his breath. He looks at the others as they are getting themselves ready to jump out as soon as Amak gives the signal. The wolf creeps around the lair. He sniffs around Alpha Stump. He is so focused that he does not realize he is being closely scrutinized from above, until Amak sits up and yells out.

"Now!"

The wolf hears him and is about to run away but the other wolves stop him by jumping out from behind the shrubs and have him surrounded. He tries to do whatever he can to escape, but the others block him in, making his escape impossible. He gives up when he realizes they have him trapped. Amak jumps off the stump and saunters toward the wolf, who stands his ground and growls as he gets close, but all Amak does is smile.

"Calm down. I am not here to harm you; I just want to talk," he says as softly as he can, so he won't scare the wolf again. "I just want to thank you for helping us."

The wolf stops growling and calms down when he sees that Amak and the others are no threat. As Amak approaches him, it shocks him when he notices the wolf looks more dead than alive. His fur is out of place and covered in mats and some claws in his right paw are missing. He is missing a canine tooth while the rest of his teeth are rotten, and part of his left ear is missing, as though it got bitten off during a fight.

"Where are you from?" says Amak, quietly.

The wolf just stares at all of them at first and then mutters, "I… am… from… here. I never left," he mutters as Amak looks puzzled.

"So you are saying you never left this spot. And what made you stay here this all time?" he asks, while the others look on as they patiently wait for the answer.

"No, I haven't ever left, Amak. I have been here waiting for your return."

Amak jumps back, as startled as the others. "How do you know my name? Have we met before?"

"Yes, we have met before — many years before, but it has been so long that you have forgotten who I am, Amak. It is me — Lukka."

The wolf grins as Amak just stares, shocked at first but then turning to joy as they both begin jumping and shouting with happiness before the rest of the pack. Amak walks him over to Sakkara for an introduction.

"This is my best friend, Lukka," he says with great joy as Sakkara smiles.

"Nice to meet you, Lukka, Amak has told me a lot about you," she says happily, while Amak smiles.

"I thought you were dead that night after we got ambushed by the people," he admits. "All these years, I never stopped blaming myself for it and now, after all this time, here you are standing right in front of me alive and well, like you just rose from the dead. No offense," he says, overjoyed to see his friend alive.

"I guess I came back from the dead. Let us just call it a miracle of some sort..."

"Whatever happened to you that day?" Amak asks, but Lukka changes the subject.

"Hey, Amak, how about you introduce me to the rest of your pack?" he says. Nanook watches, feeling suspicious. Amak agrees with him and leads him over to the others for an introduction and straightaway they all welcome him into the pack. When they reach Nanook, however, his reaction is different; he snarls at Lukka as he gets close. Lukka is surprised at Nanook's reaction, as is Amak when he leads him away from him.

"Forgive my son Nanook: he is acting a little weird... Too weird," he says, looking over to Nanook, unimpressed. "Come — I will show you where you will spend the night," he says, as he leads him to Alpha Stump, under Nanook's watchful eye. "You will be staying here, next to me; you could dig a den yourself or sleep out in the open. It is all up to you."

"I prefer to sleep out in the open, under the stars. It's what I've been doing all these years. I would feel uncomfortable living in a tight den," Lukka says, as Amak looks at him, baffled.

"What about when it rains? You will get yourself all wet."

"Same old Amak — you have never changed," Lukka replies, laughing a little. "Don't worry. I will manage. Besides, I cannot dig: I barely have any claws left, as you can see," he says, wriggling his toes. Amak rolls his eyes and grins.

The following morning, Amak and Lukka are out scouting the forest. Lukka stops Amak and gestures for him to look down. It shocks him when he sees a trap, set up by the people, just under his feet.

"Watch your step. You don't want to get caught in one of these," Lukka warned him. It shocks Amak when he looks around and notices there are more scattered everywhere. "The people have set these here. That's what they use to catch their food."

"They are still here. I need to warn the others."

"Before you go, there's something you need to see first," Lukka says, walking away. Amak follows him.

In the lair, Nanook wakes up and does not see Amak or Lukka anywhere. He gets up, wondering where they could be. Denali wakes up and rushes over to Nanook when he sees him behaving strangely.

"What's the matter? I have never seen you acting like this before."

"Father is not here. I think he went on his morning patrol with what's-his-name, and he could be in trouble. I am going to find them," he says, and begins to run towards the forest.

"Hey — wait up! I am coming with you!" cries out Denali, running after him.

In the forest, they begin looking for Amak and Lukka. Denali walks over to his brother.

"You still didn't tell me why you're acting like this. It started just as Lukka showed up."

"You have just answered your own question, my brother. I do not trust Lukka."

"You're overreacting. I see nothing suspicious about him and father trusts him, and he trusts no one besides us."

"I just find it suspicious that he changed the subject, instead of answering father, when he asked him what happened to him long ago. I feel in my gut he is up to something, and we need to find them before he does anything to our father," he replies, concerned.

Meanwhile, Amak and Lukka are sitting by the peoples' camp watching as they go about their morning.

"They have never left," Lukka says.

Amak looks astounded. "How can that be? It has been years since we left here, and their leader still looks the same."

"He is not the original leader. He died long ago. That's his son. He is filling in for him now."

They hear loud banging near them and go to find out what it might be.

They notice two of the people are practicing their fighting skills. Lukka purposely steps on a twig as they get close, and alerts them. They stop what they are doing and close in on the forest to investigate.

"What is it?"

"I heard something — a noise coming from the forest," replies the leader.

"Do you think it could be — you know — wolves?" The other man says, sounding concerned as the leadertries hard not to laugh.

"You are crazy! There have not been wolves in these parts for as long as I can remember. My father got rid of the last pack many years ago. They have been gone since," he says, as he readies his spear to continue sparring. "Forget about it — you're just hearing things. Come on, let's carry on practicing."

"Yeah, you are probably right. I might be losing my mind," the man says, getting ready to spar. "Let's see what you got," he taunts, and they continue with the sparring.

The wolves are lying down in the long grass to hide from the humans. Amak has his back turned toward Lukka, who sees his chance and is about to pounce on him, when Nanook and Denali appear, just in time. Lukka is not happy his plan has failed and growls, as Nanook looks down at him suspiciously before going over to Amak.

"I woke up, and I did not see any of you. I had to see if you guys are all right," he says, as Amak looks back at his son.

"Yes, we are fine. We were just scouting the forest and we came across the people," Amak says, as Nanook looks shocked to see more of them again.

"What do we do?"

"Stay low. They look far more advanced," Amak says, as Nanook stares, worried. "We should go now, before they notice us."

He walks away, followed by Lukka and Denali, but Nanook stays behind. Near to where he is hiding is a young man, in his twenties, sitting on a log and eating some fruit from a pile brought by the men earlier in the morning. Nanook stares at him with interest. It is like he feels something different about this one. He senses he is not like any of the others.

Denali surprises Nanook when he walks up behind him. "What is it?" he whispers.

"It's one of their young ones, but he doesn't look as dangerous as the others we faced, as we were growing up," he says, in a low voice, but Denali disagrees.

"Remember what father says. We can never trust them, contact them, or let them know we are here. Remember what happened at our old lair..." he warns, as he walks away. He notices Nanook is still looking at the boy and calls out him, "Are you coming or what?"

"Yes, I'm coming," Nanook says, walking over to Denali. The boy turns around, looks at them and grins as he sees the wolves walking away.

"Don't worry — your secret is safe with me," he whispers. He gets up and walks away to be with the other humans.

The wolves are hurrying back to the lair to get as far from the people as they can, while Lukka is lagging behind, not pleased at all that his plan failed. He growls low enough so no one can hear him, but Nanook hears it and looks at him suspiciously. Lukka is about to run in the opposite direction to arrive at the lair before any of them do, but he stops when he hears Amak calling out to him.

"Lukka, come walk next to me. What are you doing by yourself back there?"

"Coming right over, Amak," Lukka calls back. He walks past Nanook and stares at him. "You had better stay out of my way," he says, while Nanook watches, feeling uneasy. They arrive back at the lair. Nanook, without saying a word, walks over to his den to lie down. Denali senses that something is troubling him and walks over to his brother and lies next to him, rolls over on his back and grins.

"What is wrong? Come on, you can tell me," he says while Nanook continues to stare at Lukka.

"This time I think he is up to something, and I think it has something to do with Father," he whispers to Denali, looking at him, concerned. "We will need to monitor him."

"Are you sure about all this?"

"I am very sure. Where we just found them, by the people's camp, he looked like he was about to harm Father when he had his backed turned. I want to tell him, but he trusts Lukka too much and he will never believe me. I have to tell everyone about him, and it will reach Father, but for now we will need to watch our backs, especially Father's back, or else what happened to father before might happen to us again," he says, firmly.

Sakkara rushes to greet Amak when she hears him arriving. He looks down at her with a concerned look in his eyes.

"What's the matter?"

"Wait here. There is something I need to show you." He walks back to the forest, picks up pieces of the snare and drops them by her feet as she looks at him, shocked.

"What's this?"

"It's the people's tricks; at least, one of them. There are many more scattered out in the forest. You need to watch your step, so we don't get caught in one of them."

"They are still here, after all these years?"

"Yes, but the leader of the tribe is not the same one that killed my family. It's his son, and from the looks of it they are heavily trained, and they don't look like they will give up without a fight." Then he remembers Tiyani's warning and looks away in regret, so Sakkara won't notice, but she does.

"There's something you're hiding. I can see it in your eyes."

"There is something I have actually been meaning to tell you. Back at our old lair, before we left, Tiyani appeared before me to warn me about the people still being here. But I did not believe him," he says. Sakkara looks shocked.

"First you hear ghosts and now you see them," she says to him, sounding skeptical about the whole thing.

"You don't understand. I saw him and that is the reason I took so long to meet you guys out in the meadow."

"So, you're trying to tell me that Tiyani's spirit came before you to warn you of the people here. Why should I believe you?"

"That's because he did! I did not believe it at first. I thought I was imagining things, but he really was there. He told not me to come, but I ignored his warning. Now I am regretting it."

She looks at him, trying her best to believe him, "So, if what you say is true, why did you not tell me about his warning in the first place?" She says angrily

"Because I knew you would change your mind about coming here.

Besides, I had no other choice. It was the only place I could think of that would be safe for us. All I want is the best for all of you, but this time I have failed you all instead," he says, as Sakkara stares at him with an angry look in her eyes.

"I knew it was a bad idea to come back here in the first place and so did you, but you still pushed us to come here, even when Tiyani came down to warn you about this."

"I am sorry, and I will do whatever it takes to make sure that they don't know we are here," he says, feeling remorseful.

"You had better. Because of you, we are stuck here now," she says, sounding upset. She turns around, leaving Amak behind.

Lukka has been eavesdropping on them by Alpha Stump and has heard the entire conversation. He laughs to himself and lies down next to the stump, pretending to be asleep as Amak walks past him. Meanwhile, Nanook is lying down by his den, not liking the news one bit.

CHAPTER 11

Many months have passed since Lukka's mysterious and unsuspected appearance. It is now winter and night-time, and a powerful snowstorm rages across the land. The trumpeting of terrified mammoths echoes throughout the land. Amak is still awake and listens as the trumpeting continues. The next morning, snow is still coming down and lying by the falls is the carcass of a mammoth that the people brought down during the night. The wolf pack is sitting at the bottom looking up at the carcass but as they are about to climb up, Amak stops them when he spots some movement on top of the carcass.

"Stop — don't move. There are still some people near the carcass."

"Really! There's nothing there," said Lukka.

"He is over at this side, near the back thigh."

Nanook looks and spots another   humankneeling just behind the ear, cutting away pieces of meat.

"I spot another oneover on my side."

"I see one more, over here. He is over by my side, cutting along the front leg," Alornek says.

"If we take that carcass from them, we will have enough food to last us the whole winter," says Lukka as he climbs up the slope, but Amak tries to stop him.

"We will come back later, when they are gone. If we go now, they will know we are here and it's best that they don't," he says, sounding concerned. Lukka ignores him and climbs up the rocky slope while looking back at Amak with a sly smirk on his face.

"Don't worry, I've got an idea," Lukka grins. "Me and you will walk up on the carcass and get them distracted, while Nanook, Alornek, and Denali sneak up behind them and take their sticks. They are powerless without their sticks. It's a sheer win for us and I promise no harm will come to either of us or them."

Amak and the others feel unsure of the idea but climb up after him, anyway. Once they get to the top of the rim, Lukka and Amak walk up to the carcass and begin growling to catch the people by surprise, while Nanook and the others sneak past them and grab their spears without them knowing. The three men reach over to grab their spears but are shocked when they realize Nanook and the others have already thrown them over the falls.

The humans are now defenseless and standing by the edge of the falls. They have nowhere to go but down. They are preparing to jump but decide against it when they look down and realize it's a long way down. Instead, they do the smart thing and go down on their knees and raise their hands to show they have surrendered as the wolves continue to stare at them.

"We give up. You win. You want this carcass — it's yours. Please just let us go," says one hunter in a shaky voice. The wolves stop growling, except for Lukka, who looks shocked that the others are not going to do anything.

"I can't believe you are just going to let them go."

"They have surrendered. They are not going to do anything," says Amak.

Angered by Amak's choice, Lukka rushes at the youngest of the men and pushes him over the falls. The man is falling into the thundering water, screaming as he falls to his death. The other men look helpless and stare nervously at the wolves, awaiting their fate. Amak and the others run to the edge and try to find the man, but he has disappeared.

"He is gone. The falls have swallowed him up," Nanook says.

Amak looks at Lukka angrily. "What is it with you? Have you any idea what you have done?"

"I did the right thing. Do you have any idea what will happen if you let them walk away? They will go back and warn their clan and lead them straight to us and I know you do not want that. I heard the conversation you had with Sakkara. I have saved your entire family, Amak!" Lukka cries out, but Amak does not agree.

"Killing them is not the wolf way. My father — our father — taught us that or did you forget that? And now because of what you have done, they will know we are here and put us all in danger." He looks over to the other men and realizes they are gone. They all look down the ravine and they see them running into the forest. Lukka stands next to Amak, angrily. "And now, because of your stubbornness, we are all dead anyway," he says, as he walks down the slope.

Amak stands on top of the ravine, not looking happy as he watches Lukka walk away. He is about to go after him, but Nanook stops him.

"Father — just let him go and let's all collect some of this meat and bring it back to the lair."

Amak smiles and heads over to them, but he still feels some remorse, believing that Lukka may have been right.

It is now late in the evening. Hidden in the forest and close to the pack's lair is the people's camp. This one differs from the other human camps that Amak and his pack have ever faced. Instead of living in caves, the people live in tents. They use poles and tie them up together with vines and wrap them with deer or mammoth hide because they are best for keeping the cold from going in and the heat from going out. Everyone in the camp is performing their own chores. Standing on top of a boulder in the middle of the camp is a tall man, in his mid-forties, black hair with shades of gray tied in a ponytail, and brown eyes. He is supervising as the rest of the people carry out their tasks. Two men walk by carrying a mid-size log. They both look at the man, who points toward the firepit.

"Place that over by there. We will use it for the fire tonight," he says.

He is about to help a group of men repair some tents that have tears on them, when he hears what sounds like someone clearing their throat. He turns around and sees a woman standing a few feet from him. She is his wife. She looks at him, plainly unhappy, as he looks at her.

"Why are you looking at me like that?" he says, sounding confused.

"What are you doing?" she asks in a stern voice.

"I am observing everyone as they do their chores; that is what I do. That is because I am the leader here," he says, in a patronising tone, but the woman is unamused.

"You are so busy being a leader that you forget about your other job of being a father," she says, angrily. He scratches the back of his head as he remembers what she is talking about. "You never pay attention to your own son" she continues.

The man looks over at his son and he sees him all by himself, doing some target practice. He looks at his wife as she stares back, displeased, crossing her arms to show him she's being serious.

He lets out a sigh. "I'll go talk to him," he says, rubbing the back of his head as he walks away. She continues to stare him down.

"You'd better" she says, sounding serious before she heads back to do her chores.

The man stands by his son, who is scrawny looking, with brown eyes and messy, shoulder-length hair, and watches as he tries to strike the swinging target with his spear. He grins and sighs when he realizes he is holding the spear the wrong way.

"What are you doing, Kho'ta?" asks the leader, scratching the back of his head once more, while Kho'ta continues with target practice

"What does it look like? I am practicing how to wield my spear on my own, since my father never has the time to teach me," he says, as the leader looks at him with regret.

"I know I haven't been paying any attention to you in a while" he says, while Kho'ta lowers the spears and stares at him, balefully.

"In a while! Don't you mean my whole life? You are always too busy caring about everyone else instead of your own son!" he shouts out angrily.

"I know I have not paying too much attention to you, my son, and I do not blame you for acting this way. I am just too busy looking after everyone in the camp and I am sorry about that. But I am here now," he says with open arms. They stand there and look at one another in an awkward silence.

"I know why you came: it was because Mother told you to. If it were not for her forcing you to come, you would have never showed up at all," he says, sounding upset. He raises his spear, turns around and goes back to practicing striking with his spear, which he keeps on failing as his father watches him. "I am never going to get this right," he sighs with frustration, while his father just laughs a little.

"That is because you are doing it all wrong. The way you are holding the spear is wrong: you have been holding it by the rear with both your hands, leaving the front dangling," he says, while reaching out his hand. "Give me the spear and I will show you how," he adds, as Kho'ta looks on, shocked, as he slowly hands the spear over to his father. "You do it like this: your left hand holds the rear to give it leverage while your right hand grips the front just below the spearhead for control — like this," he says, showing it to Kho'ta and then he thrusts the spear at the log and manages to strike it as his son looks on amazed. The man laughs a little and hands the spear back to Kho'ta.

"Now you try it," he says, as he watches Kho'ta hold the spear the way he showed him and with one thrust he attempts to strike at the log, but it bounces off the side of it. He looks at it with a smile on his face. "Let me see you do it again, but this time aim by looking at the tip of the spear. Hold your breath and strike where it's going to be and not where it's at. You got it," the man says, patting his son on the shoulder.

The boy does exactly what his father has said and thrusts the spear and this time he strikes the log. He screams with delight as he pulls the spear out and begins jumping around with joy as his father smiles. He is about to say something to his son when he hears some sound coming from the woods. He readies his spear and looks at Kho'ta, concerned.

"Quick — go back to the camp," he says as Kho'ta walks away. The man focuses his attention on the forest when he starts to see some movement. He looks back and notices that Kho'ta is still standing behind him. He starts to frantically gesture for his son to leave and then looks into the forest once again, but this time he sees nothing. It is quiet. He looks beyond the trees, with his spear ready, and sees some figures quickly coming toward him. The man has his spear in the thrust position and readies himself to attack whatever is approaching him.

As the figures get close, he begins to feel a flow of relief when he notices that it is two of his men, the same men who escaped the wolves, rushing out of the forest. They both go down on one knee and breathing heavily, they look up at him with terrified faces, like they have just seen a ghost. The leader lowers his spear and sighs.

"Am I glad to see that it is you two! I thought you were something else," he says, walking up to them to greet them both on their safe return. But he stops halfway when he realizes that only two of them have come back and not the third. "Where is my nephew? I thought he went with you?" He stares at them with a worried look on his face and all they do is look down in shame. "What happened to him?" he yells. "What have you done to my nephew?"

The other men stare at him without saying a word. One of them gets up and nervously looks his leader in the face.

"We were cutting at the carcass of the mammoth we killed the night before, just minding our own business, and then they came out of nowhere. We didn't stand a chance: there were too many of them. They had us outnumbered," says the man, sounding shaky. Khi'da looks directly at his eyes with anger in his face.

"That still doesn't answer my question. Where is my nephew?" he begins to yell out, as the two men cower in fear.

"We surrendered to them and as we were kneeling on the ground, one of them pushed him off the edge and he fell down the falls to his death," he says, nervously.

The leader looks down at him with disbelief in his eyes. "And you did nothing? You just let him fall?"

"There was nothing we could do. It happened so fast, we had no time to react!" the desperate man shouts out, nervously.

Khi'da looks at them both and without saying a word, walks past them toward the camp, but then he stops and turns. "What was it that had you outnumbered?" he asks.

"Wolves, sir. They are back," he says anxiously, as the leader looks at him, stunned.

"How can that be! I thought my father had them all wiped out from this land. When will these demons ever leave us be?" He starts to run back to the camp to warn the others as the two men watch. Khi'da turns back to the two men and gestures for them to come to him. "I need you to come with me because it's not going to be me that's going to tell them the news. You are." They walk in front of him back to the camp.

Once they arrive at the camp, Khi'da stands on a rock and the two hunters kneel in front of it while looking down at the ground, ashamed and awaiting their fate. The rest of the tribe gathers around to listen to what their leader has to say.

"I heard some terrible news this morning, from two sources. First, as we all know, late last night, I sent a hunting party to find us some food that would last us the winter. Then this morning, I sent these two and my nephew, Attah, to gather some meat for us. I asked them to watch out for him and bring him back alive, and these were the words that came out of their mouths before they left. They said they promised to bring him back in one piece and I had nothing to worry about," he says, looking at both men as they lowered their heads yet further in shame. "But they didn't keep their word, because they didn't return with him."

He jumps off the rock, stands in front of them, and looks them both in the face with an icy stare. "I am going to leave the rest to you. You are going to tell them what you told me." The crowd focuses their attention to them. "Go on: tell them!"

"We got ambushed by wolves, surrendered to them and one of them knocked Attah over the falls," they both say, afraid as the crowd instantly gossip amongst each other in overwhelming panic. The leader gestures for them to calm down and turns to the stricken men. He leans in close.

"And you did nothing to prevent that!" Khi'da shouts, as the two cower in fear.

One of the men stares him in the eyes. "How could we? They threw our spears over the falls: we were defenseless! If we did anything, they would have pushed us over the edge and the falls would swallow us, as well!" he cries out, shaking.

The leader leans in closer. "Better you than my nephew." He then turns to the others. "This is an example of failure. I trusted these two to look out for my nephew and they failed me. They promised to come back with him, but they didn't keep that promise." He turns to stare at them. "Did you?"

"Like I said, we couldn't do anything!" one man shouts.

The leader gets up and looks at both men in anger. "Unlike you two, I will do something about it and you will both lead me to those waterfalls," he says in a barely controlled voice and walks away. Everyone else does the same and walks away as they stare at both men, disappointed.

Hiding behind some bushes, close to the camp, Lukka hears the whole thing. He jumps out of the shrubs and begins barking and making noise to get their attention. The two men, who are still kneeling by the rock, spot him. One man quickly gets up and begins shouting to get their leader's attention.

"He is here! Come here — quick!" The leader turns around and sees the wolf pacing near the men and runs over to them. Lukka then disappears deep into the forest before the leader even has time to see where he went.

"That was the wolf that knocked Attah down the falls!" the man says.

"Are you sure?" he shouts, staring at the forest.

"Yes, it is! I swear!" he replies.

"You two walk with me. We'll find him and hopefully it will lead to the others, and we will get rid of them — or my name isn't Khi'da," he says with confidence, as he walks away with the other men following right behind him.

One of the men walks next to Khi'da with a worried look on his face. "That wolf has followed us here: it knows where we are. What if he has gone to call the others to come get us?"

Khi'da looks down at the man. "I will get them before they have time to react."

"How do you plan to do that?" said the other hunter.

"We will go to the valley tonight."

"Tonight? But it will be dark soon and we won't see anything. They could sneak up on us and we won't even know it."

"Don't worry. I have an idea and I am going to need the dark of night in order for it to work," the leader grins, looking at him as the man looks back puzzled.

"Don't worry. I'll explain everything once we get there," he said.

Khi'da is standing by the forest. Standing by his side, the other hunter feels nervous. He is angry when he does not see the other man and looks for him.

"Where is your partner? I thought he was coming, too." He looks around for him but does not find him. "Does any of you know where he is?"

One man speaks up. "I remember seeing him walk into his tent and he hasn't come out since."

"I will make him come out," Khi'da says angrily, striding toward the tent. He opens it and sees the man cowering in the corner.

"Are you coming or not? We are waiting for you," he shouts. The man turns to face him and it shocks Khi'da when he sees the terrified look on his face and the trembling of his chin as he pleads with him.

"I can't go out there again. Please don't make me go, I beg you. I've got a wife and kid, and they need me. I beg for mercy — don't make me go…" he cries, turning around again and rocking back and forth as he mutters to himself, "Don't make me go. Don't make me go. Don't make me go…"

Khi'da looks at him and feels sorry for him. He leaves the tent and looks at the rest of the tribe. "He is in no condition to go tonight and since he can't go, we won't. We will go in the morning, instead," he says, sounding disappointed as he walks away. He stops when he hears a faint voice calling out to him from the crowd. He turns around and looks for whoever has spoken up. It surprises him when he sees his son emerge from the crowd.

"I will go, Father. I will come and avenge Attah and I am ready," Kho'ta says, tightly gripping his spear. It surprises Khi'da when he hears that his shy, insecure son wants to go with them. "Even though I don't believe wolves are relentless killers, this is for my cousin, and I will do whatever it takes to avenge him."

His father stands before him and gives him a pat on the shoulder. Kho'ta looks up and smiles nervously as his father leans in closer to him and presses his forehead against his.

"I know you will, my son," he says with pride, as his wife Kara stands by their tent and smiles. He gets up and looks at the tribe with a big smile on his face. "We are still going tonight because my son has agreed to join us," he says loudly, as he proudly raises Kho'ta's arm in the air, and they all cheer.

Kho'ta gives a nervous smile, feeling unsure that he has made the right decision. They walk into the forest leading out to the valley as everyone bids their farewells. The rest of the camp all stand and watch as the men disappear into the darkness. Standing by their tent, Kara feels nervous as she watches her young, inexperienced son walk out into the meadow next to his father.

Moments later, the men have reached the grove and are hiding behind some trees near the falls. One of them peers over and notice that the wolves are still by the carcass.

"They are still there. They never left."

Khi'da looks for himself, and grins. The two men and Kho'ta stare at him, wondering what he's planning, and feel nervous. Meanwhile, on top of the ridge, the wolves are eating, unaware of the people hiding in the grove. Lukka stops eating and raises his head, thinking that he caught movement near some trees. He grins when he spots the people hiding by the falls.

He notices Nanook staring at him and goes back to eating. Nanook looks to see for himself what Lukka was looking for and stares at him suspiciously when he sees nothing. He turns to Denali, who is eating next to him.

"We need to watch him. I think he's up to something," he says, but Denali doesn't believe him.

"How can you be so sure?"

"Just now I noticed him looking down the ravine. There is something hiding down there, and he knows about it and he is not warning us."

Denali also looks down the ravine, and he sees nothing. "There is nothing down there," he says. He takes one more look, and suddenly he sees a man peeking out from the trees and swiftly pulling back in. "I take that back. You might be right. I just caught some movement coming from behind those trees by the river," he says.

"Now you believe me? We need to monitor Father. You stay here and I will go beside Father," Nanook says, and walks over to Amak's side.

Over by the river, the hunter and Kho'ta stand around Khi'da to listen to his idea. The leader smirks when he notices the clouds obstructing the moon, making the area darker.

"It just got dark. We will use it to our advantage. I will have you two lay down on the ground and I will walk over to the ravine, call out to their alpha and lure him to you, and that's when you will come out of hiding and ambush him. The rest will see their alpha is in trouble and will come down to help him and then we will trap the entire pack."

"What if they spot us? They will evade us and go around us," the hunter says.

Khi'da looks for a way to help the humans blend in. He looks at the ground, scoops up some mud with both hands, and presents it to them.

"You will blend in by covering yourselves with mud. It's perfect camouflage and they will never realize you are there, and when they do it will be too late."

The hunter and Kho'ta prepare themselves for the ambush. Khi'da walks into the middle of the grove. He looks at the other two as they are preparing their disguises before they hide. The hunter gives a signal to let Khi'da know they are in position. He walks closer to the ravine and shouts as loud as he can.

"Hey down here! Come and get me! I got nothing on me!" he shouts out as he jumps and waves his arms to get the wolves' attention.

Amak is the first to see him. "They've come back," he growls. "We can't let them take the carcass from us."

He is about to run down when Nanook calls out to him.

"Father, don't go! It could be a trap!"

Lukka steps in. "Amak, can't you see he is alone and defenseless? Now is your opportunity to avenge your father and get rid the bloodline of the man who killed him and now threatens to kill your entire family."

Amak, already consumed by revenge, listens to Lukka, ignoring Nanook's warning, and runs down the slope. Lukka stares at Nanook with a sinister grin and then goes back to eating without a care. Nanook is about to confront him, but Denali stops him as he realizes Nanook's instincts are correct.

"No, don't. You don't want to stir things up. Just leave it."

All Nanook can do is watch helplessly as Amak, his own father, runs alone down the slope to face the most dangerous predator in the land, with no idea of what he is up against.

Khi'da sees Amak running down the slope and waits until he gets close. "That's it, you demon, come to me!" He runs toward where the others are hiding and Amak follows. "Now!" he yells, running past the men, and they jump out of hiding just as Amak runs by. They shout and thrust their spears. They have Amak trapped, and he cannot think of a way to escape amidst the noise. He does whatever he can to grab at the spears, but they are too fast for him. After many attempts, he is showing signs of slowing down. Khi'da sees the wolf is becoming weary and smirks. "He is getting tired. Keep it up and soon the rest of them should come to help him and that's when we'll get them."

Near the carcass, Nanook and the others see Amak is in trouble, and they all rush down the slope to help him, except for Lukka. He continues eating, not seeming to care. Nanook sees him and calls out to him.

"Hey, are you coming to help?" he cries out, before heading down the slope. Lukka stops eating and watches the pack running down the slope to help Amak. He begins to run down the slope but instead of following the others, he runs in the opposite direction to avoid the fight and heads back to the lair.

The pack picks up pace so they can reach Amak quickly.

"We're almost there! Let's all scatter and pick them off one by one," Nanook cries out.

They all split up. As soon as they arrive, Nanook leaps forward and bites Khi'da's calf. The man lets out a scream as he falls to the ground. The other wolves run past Kho'ta and the hunter, catching them off guard. They form a circle around Amak and growl while staring at the men. The hunter readies his spear and is about to thrust it toward Denali but Khi'da stops him. He nods his head at the wolves as he lowers his spear.

"Let's go, men. They have won this fight, but next time they won't be so lucky." Khi'da walks away, and the other men follow him. He gives one last look and grins when he sees the wolves still have them in their sights.

After they are sure the people have left, the pack gathers around Amak to check if he is okay. He stands up and looks at them, smiling. He is about to walk back to the lair, but collapses, tired from the struggle. Nanook and Denali lift him over their backs and carry him back, instead.

They are walking back to the lair, looking all around them to make sure that they are not being followed by the hunters. Amak wakes and feels rested.

"Thank you, guys. I will walk the rest of the way." They stop and Amak reaches the ground. Instead of walking ahead of them, as he normally does, he walks behind them, instead. Nanook notices his father lagging and walks over to him.

"Are you all right, Father?"

"I am fine."

But Nanook knows him too well. "No, you're not. You're wondering where Lukka is, aren't you?"

"Yes, I am. How did you know?"

"Because you would have been walking ahead of us right now, instead of being back here."

Amak gives a big sigh. "You're right. I did not see him with you guys when you came to help. I hope he is all right."

"The last time I saw him he was behind me, but he never showed up to help you."

Amak stares at him, not liking the answer. "What do you mean by that?

Are you telling me he turned his back on me."

Nanook faces him. "No…" He pauses for a moment to think about what he is going to say. "And yes. I think he led the people to us. How else could they have known we were there?"

All Amak does is stand up and stare his son down. "You are wrong. He would never do that. He is like a brother to me. How could you say something like that?" he says in a stern tone, before running past the others as Nanook watches him leave. Denali witnesses the whole thing and walks over to Nanook.

"You did what you could," he says, while trying to encourage his brother, but all he does is look at him as though he has failed.

"But it wasn't enough. Father trusts him too much: he will never believe me," he says, and walks away as Denali watches.

They arrive at the lair and see Amak lying on Alpha Stump, sound asleep, still exhausted from the struggle with the hunters. Sakkara, Aurora and Lukka see the returning wolves, and run over to them.

"What happened out there?" asks Sakkara, concerned.

"We got ambushed by the people." Nanook notices Lukka standing behind Sakkara and gives him a mean look. All Lukka does is turn around and walk over to Alpha Stump to hide. Sakkara looks up at Nanook, her face etched with worry.

"Can you tell me everything that happened?"

Nanook nods and leads her away from the stump so they can be alone. "We were on top of the ridge by the grove, collecting some meat from the mammoth so we could bring it back here, and the people showed up by surprise. Father went after their leader, thinking that he was alone, but there were more of them hiding by the trees and they ambushed him. If it weren't for us coming to his rescue, who knows what might have happened?" he says, as she feels some relief come over her.

"Thank you, Nanook." She then looks at the others. "Thank you, all of you, for saving him." Amak wakes and jumps off Alpha Stump. Sakkara runs over to him and gently nudges her head against his. "You had us all worried. How do you feel?"

Amak looks at her, smiling. "I will be fine," he replies, sounding exhausted, then he looks at all the others and gives them a smiling nod as a sign of gratitude.

Lukka hears Amak is awake, walks out from behind Alpha Stump and rushes over to greet him, but Nanook stops him. He stands between them both and stares directly at Lukka, growling, while everyone looks surprised, but not as surprised as Lukka.

"I have come only to greet him," he protests, but Nanook continues to growl and bare his teeth at him as he steps in closer, while Lukka lowers himself down in submission. Sakkara has had enough: she gets between them both and looks straight at Nanook with a stern face.

"What has gotten into you? He has done nothing."

"That's what he wants us to believe," Nanook replies, staring Lukka down. "He led the people to us. How else would they know we were there? And you know what else? Instead of coming to help Father, he ran back here instead, like a coward."

Lukka gets up and stares at him. "I came to warn your mother and sister, in case the people came here."

Nanook looks at him, not believing a word he is saying. He stares directly at Lukka's terrified eyes.

"You are lying, and I can see it in your eyes."

Amak, who has had enough of all this fighting, stands in between them both. "Enough of this, you two." They stop as Amak stares down at them both with a stern look. "Right now you are both starting to sound like the people from the way you are behaving." He looks at Nanook. "What do you have against him? You have been acting this way ever since he arrived. I trust him, your mother trusts him and so does the rest of the family, but why don't you?" he asks, but all Nanook does is continue to stare straight at Lukka with suspicion.

"I have a feeling that he is planning to attack the moment you have your back turned," he says, while Lukka looks mystified.

"What?" he says, chuckling a bit. "Why would I do that to your father? He's like a brother to me," he continues as Amak stares at them both.

"Then why did you not come and help him? Why did you run instead? You are nothing but a coward," he says.

Lukka has had enough. Growling, he rushes over to Nanook and they both stare each other down.

"Like I said, I came to warn your mother and sister," he states.

Nanook still does not believe what he is saying and readies himself to lunge at him, but he is stopped by Amak, who stares him down, baring his teeth.

"If you want to get to him you will have to go through me first," he says, snarling. Nanook takes a deep breath and looks up at Amak, displeased.

"Fine. I will stop, but if he causes any problems, I do not want to hear I didn't warn you," he says, as he turns and runs into the forest.

Amak walks over to Lukka. "Are you all right?"

"Yes, I am fine. Thanks for standing up for me. I am really grateful."

"No need to thank me. We are a family and that is what we do — we stick together," he says, while looking at the forest, wondering where Nanook went. "At least some of us think so."

"He will come round," Lukka says, trying to keep a straight face.

"I sure hope so," Amak says. He turns around and walks up Alpha Stump to lie down. Lukka goes to lie down for the night, as well, and when he looks at Nanook's den, he gives a sly grin, realizing that Nanook won't be back for a while. Now that his threat is finally out of his way, he believes that his plan will go smoothly.

Amak is lying on Alpha Stump, looking down at Lukka, when he hears him laughing and starts to wonder what if Nanook could be right about him all along. He begins to worry when he looks over to the forest. Nanook is not far from the lair at all. Instead, he is hiding behind some trees, staying there and waiting for when they are asleep. He believes that is when Lukka will attempt to harm his father and that is when he will rush out and expose him, and prove to them all that he was right about him being a fake.

It is late into the night; the entire pack is sleeping by their dens, while Amak is sleeping on his own on Alpha Stump. A shadow appears over him as he sleeps. The light of the moon reveals it to be Lukka. He looks down at Amak with his gleaming green eyes. He steps over him and as he is about to attack him, he stops when he hears growling from behind. He turns around and sees a shadowy figure staring at him. It is Nanook, who growls loudly as he runs up Alpha Stump and tackles Lukka to the ground.

The noise makes Amak wake up. He looks down, and it surprises him when he sees them both lying on the ground. "What are you two doing down there, making all this noise so late in the night?”

Lukka, with no hesitation, gets up. Amak becomes concerned when he sees the terrified look on his face. “What has happened here?”

“I was sleeping, and Nanook appears out of nowhere and attacks me.”

Amak looks at Nanook angrily. “Is what he said true?”

Nanook does not believe that his own father is falling for that. “No! He was going to attack you and I stopped him.”

Amak jumps off Alpha Stump and stands between them both. “Is that true, Lukka? Were you going to attack me as I was sleeping?” he asks, while Lukka stares at him.

“No, it is not true. I would never do that,” he stutters.

Amak stares at them both, unimpressed. “This has to end. From now on, I will keep a close eye on you two,” he says, walking away. Lukka, not feeling happy that he almost got caught, goes to lie down by Alpha Stump. He growls a bit when he sees Nanook still staring at him. Amak is sitting on top of the stump and spots a broken claw and fresh blood close to where he was lying down earlier, and looks down at Lukka suspiciously.

Late at night, Nanook wakes up to growling. He is startled when he sees Lukka standing over him with his eyes gleaming green and teeth bared. Nanook gets up and stares him straight in the face, snarling.

“If you are trying to scare me, it is not working.”

“Who says I was trying to scare you? I only came to tell you to watch your back. One of us is going to slip and I’ll make sure that it will be you,” he whispers as he turns around to go back to lying down. Nanook stares at him, unfazed.

“You are the one who needs watch your back. When my father finds out the truth, it will all be over for you. Nothing will save you.”

Lukka stops and grins. “He will never believe you. It will be my word against yours and from what we experienced just now, he will always believe me,” he sneers, before walking away.

CHAPTER 12

It is now morning, and spring has arrived. The sun is shining once again, adding light over the land after a long, dark winter. The meadow is once again full of life; birds are singing as they fly about. In the forest, the sun glints through the canopy, lighting it up after being dank for a long time. The animals are scurrying about looking for food, feeling hungry after a long winter. The meadow is once again littered with life; the herds are back and bring with them their young, who frolic in the long grass.

A loud clattering echoes through the forest, waking Nanook. He panics when he does not see Lukka lying down by the stump, and he notices Amak is also wondering where he is.

"Where is Lukka?"

"I was wondering the same thing."

They look toward the forest when the clatter begins again. Nanook gets an idea where he could be.

"I think I know where he is."

"And where might that be?"

"He's by the people's lair. I know it."

He is about to run out and find him, but Amak stops him.

"I will go get him. Stay here with your mother."

He is about to look for him, but Nanook stops him. "It is better if I go instead, and you stay here. I will prove to you I am right about him, and this is the only way."

He runs toward the forest while a concerned Amak stays back, watching his son disappear into the brush.

Nanook is hiding near the people's camp. He is lying low in the long grass so he will not be spotted. The clatter is coming from Khi'da trying to teach Kho'ta how to fight using spears. The young man struggles to keep a firm grip on the spear as his father keeps knocking it out of his hand. Khi'da sighs in frustration, picks up his spear and tosses it to him. He goes back into position and readies his spear as Kho'ta sighs, unsure that he can do it.

"I can't, Father, and I never will."

Khi'da is not impressed and once again tries to encourage his son.

"Of course you can, but you need to focus. Come on — try one more time but pay attention to every move I make. You understand?" He thrusts his spear at Kho'ta. "Ready? Let's go."

Kho'ta nods and grips his spear. Just as he is about to charge, he stops when his father stares toward the forest.

"Be quiet... I hear noise coming from that direction."

"What could it be?" asked Kho'ta.

"I don't know, but I am going to find out."

He walks in the direction of the sound with his spear in hand. Nanook sees Lukka close to where he is hiding. He is pacing back and forth near the people's camp, trying to make as much noise as he can to get their attention. It looks like it's working because Khi'da is heading straight for him, as he has his back turned. Nanook, who is witnessing the whole thing, wonders whether to call him crazy, suicidal or both. He sneaks in closer to see what Lukka is up to, but Kho'ta spots him moving through the long grass toward his father. He tries to warn him, but all Khi'da does is gesture to be quiet.

Nanook stops once he is close enough and lies down, but he does not realize that he is beside an ants' nest. The angry ants crawl up Nanook's body and begin biting him, making him jump out of the long grass, yelping in pain. He runs past Kho'ta and Khi'da, who just stare in shock as he races by. He collides with Lukka and they both fall on each other, creating a dust cloud. Lukka is the first to run, with Nanook not too far behind. Khi'da picks up a rock near him and throws it at both wolves as they run back into the forest, disappearing out of sight.

"Those demons don't seem to leave us alone," he complains, as both father and son stare, astonished, at the wolves disappearing out of sight.

In the forest, both wolves are running as fast as they can to get away from the people. Nanook looks back to make sure they are not being followed by them. He does not realize there is a trap in his way and suddenly hears a snap. He yelps and chews on the rope to set himself free, but it is hopeless. Lukka stops when he sees Nanook in trouble and walks up to him, standing before him, with a grin.

"It looks like you got yourself all tied up there."

"Yeah — can you set me free?"

"Nope. I will not. You are on your own." Lukka turns around and walks away.

"Where are you going?"

"I am going back to warn the others and tell them of the bad news."

"What bad news?"

"That they have lost a beloved son and dear brother. Bye-bye now."

Lukka walks away, leaving Nanook to fend for himself. He yanks at the snare, hoping to snap the line, but no matter how much he tries, it is too strong. Lukka hears him struggling, and he turns around, grinning, and walks back to him. Nanook smiles once he sees him approach and assumes he has come back to rescue him.

"Great — you are back."

"Yes, I came back but only to warn you of something." He shows Nanook a string of bones that is dangling from the trap. "You see these right here? That is what they use to alert them that they have caught something. From the way you are struggling, you must have alerted the entire camp by now. You have made it worse for yourself."

He laughs as he walks away, while Nanook looks at him, growling. "When I break myself free, you will pay for this."

Lukka stops and faces him with a grin on his face. "You can, if you get out of this alive, but there is no need for me to worry because I doubt that will happen."

Lukka runs off and leaves Nanook behind for good. He continues to try to break free before the people realize he is there. Kho'ta and Khi'da are walking back to their camp when Khi'da comes to a stop, hearing the rattling coming from the trap.

"You hear that?" He looks toward the forest, and smiles when he sees that something has got caught in the trap he had set up earlier. "Sounds like we've caught something." He is about to check what it is, but he hears his wife calling him and turns to Kho'ta. "Go check what got caught in the trap, and whatever it is, kill it. You got me?"

"Okay, Father," says Kho'ta. He turns around and heads to the forest all alone, while Khi'da shakes his head with regret, walking back to the camp.

In the forest, Kho'ta is creeping toward the trap. Once he gets near, he gets low and hides behind a shrub. He peeks over the shrub to see what got caught in the trap and surprises him when he sees Nanook chewing on the cord as he tries to break free. Nanook senses he is being watched, faces the shrub behind him and begins growling when he sees Kho'ta hiding behind it. Realising Nanook knows he is there, Kho'ta gets up, tightly grips his spear and prepares to strike. Nanook closes his eyes, accepting his fate.

Meanwhile, in the lair, Lukka walks in, panting. Amak and the others rush to him to see what the matter is.

"What's wrong? Where is Nanook? He went out to go look for you. Why didn't he come back with you?" Amak asks.

Lukka looks at up, him pretending to be full of regret. "It happened so fast. We got attacked by the people. I ran, and I lost Nanook. I tried to find him, but there were too many of them. I am afraid to say that they may have him. I am sorry, everyone."

Amak is about to run and find Nanook, but an anxious Lukka calls out to him. "No, don't go!"

Amak looks suspicious. "Why shouldn't I go?"

"Because… they still might be there… searching the area," he stutters, which gives more reason for Amak to feel suspicious as he walks over to him. He sits near Lukka, glances back at the forest and sighs.

"You're right. I don't want to stir up any trouble." He stands up again and walks away as Lukka watches, grinning. "For your sake, I also think it is better that you stay here, as well. It will be a tragedy if we lose the Alpha of the pack, and we wouldn't want that," Lukka says, slyly.

"What a tragedy that would be. And with me, gone, who would replace me as the next Alpha? You!" Amak says, laughing as he walks onto Alpha Stump while Lukka sneers.

"That's exactly who it would be." Lukka gets up and walks over to join the others by Alpha Stump.

Meanwhile, Kho'ta is still standing over Nanook, taking a deep breath and wondering whether he should kill him. "You can do this, Kho'ta," he murmurs. He raises his spear, but he resists and then lowers it. "No, I can't."

He kneels down and pounds at the ground with both fists. Nanook opens his eyes and feels relieved when he sees the young man has lowered his spear. He continues to chew frantically on the trap to set himself free, as Kho'ta looks at him, smiling.

"You cannot bite through that. We made that cord from mammoth hide. You'll chew on that for days and it still won't break. Here, let me help you." He reaches his hand out to untie the trap, but Nanook growls at him and attempts to bite him. Kho'ta pulls back his hand in time. "Take it easy. I am only trying to help you." Nanook stares him down and bares his teeth so he will not come near him. Kho'ta notices Nanook staring at the spear next to him, so he picks it up and smiles. "So this is what's bothering you. I don't blame you. They use this on you plenty of times, am I right?" He tosses the spear aside. He raises his hands and waves them in front of Nanook so that he can see he does not have the weapon any more. "See? No more. It disappeared." He moves in a little closer, while whispering to Nanook. "Now let me help set you free." He reaches down to his ankle, pulls out a knife and attempts to cut the snare, but Nanook panics at the sight of the knife and snaps at Kho'ta's hand once more, giving him a hard time. "You need to calm down. I am not like the others. I will not hurt you."

He tries to cut the rope to free Nanook from the trap, but it is useless. He gives up and sighs in frustration. Kho'ta places the knife back and stands up. "I give up with you. You don't want me to help you. Go on and free yourself."

He walks away, but he does not go far when he hears a whimper coming from behind him. He turns around and smiles when he sees Nanook lying down and panting. He rolls his eyes, walks back to Nanook, then kneels in front of him, pulling out the knife again and cutting the rope. "I feel glad that we have come to an understanding." As he continues cutting, he stops and realizes something is not right as he glances down at Nanook's eyes. "How do I know you are not plotting this, and you will maul me instead the moment I set you free?" He feels unsure of what he is doing. Nanook whimpers a little, sits up, and places one of his paws on the young man's knee.

Kho'ta feels more comfortable and smiles when he realizes he will not harm him. "All right, I will set you free, but remember — no funny stuff," he says, pointing his finger firmly at him. He lowers the knife and cuts the rope, releasing Nanook. He quickly stands back and waits for what the young wolf will do. There is a long awkward silence between them as they stare at one another. Kho'ta is breathing heavily as a drop of sweat rolls down his forehead. Nanook is still staring at him but instead of lunging at Kho'ta, he turns around and runs away.

Slowly, the young man gets up, wipes his forehead and sighs in relief as he turns to walk back to his camp. He takes one more look back and spots Nanook staring at him, while hiding behind some trees. He smiles as he continues to walk away, while Nanook does the same.

It is now evening and Amak is pacing back and forth. It worries him that Nanook has not arrived yet. Lukka notices his restless pacing and walks over to him.

"What's the matter, Amak?"

"It is getting late and Nanook is still not back. I hope he is safe."

"He is fine. Trust me, he will be back. Not sure when, but he will." He sees Amak is still worried. "I have an idea. What if I look for him and bring him back when I find him?" Lukka is about to run into the forest, but stops when he hears a very familiar voice behind him. He turns around. It surprises him when he sees Nanook approaching Amak and Sakkara, staring at him with a sly smirk.

"Hello, everyone. I am back, and do I have some news to tell you..."

Lukka looks astounded. He smiles and tries his best not to show that he is nervous as he walks over to him. "You are back, but how did you manage— I mean, where have you been? You had us all worried sick." Lukka pretends to be worried, so the others won't find it suspicious but Nanook knows he is faking it.

"Oh, I was all caught up in something, you know what I mean, right Lukka?"

Amak stares at him, feeling suspicious. "What is he talking about, Lukka?" Lukka looks panicked which gets Amak suspicious.

"Yeah, tell him what happened, Lukka," Nanook says, walking around him waiting to hear how Lukka can get out of this situation.

"I... I... was by the people's lair and they were training with their sticks. It looks like they're planning to attack."

Nanook stares straight at him with a wry smirk on his face. "Now, go on and tell him the second part of that story."

"I don't know what you're talking about," Lukka says, emitting a nervous laugh.

Nanook has had enough of his lies. He leans in close to his ear and whispers to him. "Oh, you don't remember what happened in the forest earlier, so I will make this easier for you. I will tell them and maybe it will help you refresh your memory." He looks away from him and faces the others who are waiting for a response. "What our dear friend Lukka is trying to say is that earlier this morning, he was by the people's camp planning to lead them to us and kill us all, but it has all backfired. isn't that right, Lukka?" He looks at him, smirking, while Lukka looks away trying his best not to blow his cover. "We got away from there and as we were running, I got caught in one of their tricks, the same one that Father brought in to show us. Instead of setting me free, he just left me there and saved himself, just like a coward would." He walks over to Lukka and whispers to his ear again with a sneer. "I told I would get you for this." He walks away and leaves Lukka to fend for himself, just like he had done to him, and lies by his den to watch the whole thing.

Amak walks over to Lukka. "Is this true? Were you planning to lead the people here?"

"Never. He is lying. I would never do that."

Amak looks down at Lukka's terrified eyes and knows he is lying. "You are saying that you would never hurt me or any of us, is that right?"

"Of course not: you are my family."

Nanook has had enough and runs to Amak's side.

"Can't you see he is lying?"

Amak quietly looks over to Nanook, while grinning, and motions to him to look down. Nanook looks down and notices that now Lukka's left paw has a broken claw. Smiling slyly, he backs away. Amak walks over to Lukka and begins circling him.

"I need you to tell me exactly which paw had broken claws again."

"Just on my right paw. Why do you ask?"

"Because now your left paw has a broken claw. Explain to me how you broke that one, since it was only your right paw that had broken claws."

Amak smirks while Lukka looks at him with a terrified look in his eyes.

Nanook just grins from his den.

"I must have broken it while I was getting away from the people."

Amak does not believe a word. "That's strange, because I saw a broken claw on Alpha Stump on that very night you claimed that Nanook tried to attack you as you slept. Tell me the truth. You broke that claw when Nanook tackled you to the ground, when you tried to attack me as I was sleeping. Then you tried to set up Nanook to make it look like he attacked you when he was only protecting me. You blamed him just so you could cover up your traitorous hide and finish me off when I least expected it. I want to hear the truth."

Lukka, now realizing that his cover is blown, walks up to Amak and stares at him, snarling.

"You want to hear the truth? Fine. I will tell you everything you want to know. What Nanook said is true: I was planning to lead the people over here to kill you all — especially you, Amak. You got away from me once, a long time ago, but again, after years and years of waiting, I saw it as a sign from the ancestors to continue with my plan once you arrived. I tried once again to kill your entire bloodline, so I could take over the pack and the land and start my own bloodline." He walks around Amak, who stares at him, shocked.

"So all that was a lie — our friendship, when we found you cold and alone. That was all a set-up just so you could get us to trust you."

"Yes, Amak — that's right, and I almost got what I wanted. I managed to bring the people over that night and got your father killed, along with your brothers, but unfortunately you escaped."

"But Lukka, you had vanished. We thought you were also killed by the people…"

Lukka grins. "It was all a cover-up, to make it look like it was an accident, but the truth is I was hiding in a hole I dug up, before I led the people to you. I was hidden well underneath all the long grass and out of plain sight, so none of you would even notice that I was there, and it worked perfectly. I was watching the whole thing and loving every moment of it. But this time, I thought I got you where I wanted, and I wasn't going to let you escape this time. It looked like I was going to get away with it, too, if it wasn't for somebody getting in the way." He looks over at Nanook while baring his teeth. "My plan would have worked if it weren't for you. I would have gotten you killed and I would have taken over your pack and I would be the hero." He turns around swiftly and runs to the forest.

Nanook sits by Amak's side. "What a coward. Just turns and runs away like that. I cannot believe that you used to call that traitor a brother."

Amak pays no attention to him and stares toward the forest, feeling apprehensive. "I have a bad feeling about this. He is heading over to the people so he can lead them here. I need you to follow him and stop him before he stirs up anything."

"No problem," Nanook replies, and runs into the tundra to spy on Lukka.

It is now night. Lukka is hiding behind some trees near the people's camp. Nanook arrives quietly and hides behind a rock so he will not know he is there. Lukka suspects he is not alone, when he catches some movement from the corner of his eye. He scans, but he sees nothing. Nanook hides behind some shrubs. The rustling caused by the bushes catches Lukka's attention and this time, suspecting that he is being watched, he saunters over to the shrub. Nanook gets ready to lunge at him as Lukka gets close, but Lukka stops when he hears people talking, and loses interest. He sneaks in the camp's direction to spy on them. Nanook peers through the bushes to get a better look at what Lukka is doing. While in the camp, Khi'da and Kho'ta are having a talk while they sit by the fire.

"Kho'ta, how many times do I have to tell you? Wolves are demons that kill for pleasure — they do not do it to survive. They crave blood, our blood, which is what keeps them alive."

"That is not true, Father. You are wrong. Wolves also kill to survive like we do. They are not demons: they are living beings, like us."

Khi'da disagrees with him and places both hands on his son's shoulders, looking directly at him. "You are wrong. If that were true, my grandfather would have lived a long life. Wolves are the reason he died young."

But all Kho'ta does is walk away from his father. Lukka sees him with his back turned and runs out from behind the trees, charging toward him. Khi'da sees the wolf and pushes him out of the way as he jumps past Kho'ta. Lukka quickly turns and runs back to the forest while Khi'da shouts, causing the other men to wake up. They quickly rush out of their tents and grab their spears.

"Let's get that monster!" Khi'da runs out into the forest, followed by the rest of the men, but Kho'ta stops him as he is about to enter the forest to get the wolf. He grabs his son by the arm and pushes him aside. As he walks past him, he looks down at him with an icy stare.

"What do you think of your wolves now?" He walks into the forest as Kho'ta stares after him, then looks down at the ground, feeling distressed about the whole situation. He begins pounding the ground and shouts to let out his anger.

Nanook emerges from hiding and runs off as quickly as he can to warn his family. Kho'ta sees him and stares sharply, believing that Nanook was the wolf that attacked him.

"I saved you and you thank me by trying to attack me…" he says. It startles him when he sees a shadow standing over him. He looks up and stares, wide-eyed, when he sees his mother standing in front of him, holding his spear, and looking at him crossly.

"If you want to make your father proud and prove to him that you can and will be great, lying in the dirt will do you no good." She throws him the spear. He stares at it and grins as he gets up. "I know you can do it; I believe you can," she says, and walks back to the tent. Kho'ta smiles and then charges off to the forest to catch up with the others.

Meanwhile, Nanook is running through the forest, to get back to the lair before Lukka does, and warn his family that the people are heading toward them. Lukka is running out in the tundra, taking his time so he won't lose the people. He gasps when two spears strike the ground just a few inches from him and jumps just in time to avoid them. Lukka looks back and grins when he notices that Khi'da and the men are running closely behind him. He picks up his pace and runs into the forest. Khi'da watches Lukka run into the forest and grins.

"He won't get away from us this time. Let's follow him to his lair and if there are any wolves there, we will chase them out of there, as well!" Khi'da shouts, running into the forest after him.

Nanook arrives at the lair, relieved that he has beaten Lukka. Amak rushes to him the moment he sees him and looks at him, concerned.

"What happened? What's Lukka doing?"

"He's leading the people to us, and this time it's the entire camp,"

Nanook pants heavily.

"Let them come. We will be ready." Amak jumps onto Alpha Stump and calls everyone to gather around him. "Many years ago, my father died in this very lair while trying to protect his family and now I know why: because someone I used to call my brother has set it all up. He is planning to do it again, but this time against us, so he can kill us all and take over the land. But we will not allow him to go through with this and get his way. We will fight and we will succeed and that is because we are ready; because we went through this before. This encounter will not differ from any other we faced in the past. Evil has come to our home in the form of those monsters and tried to take us out, but we will face it and smile upon it when it falls." He lets out a howl and the others howl with him. "Now let's get them!"

He looks toward the forest when he hears the men are getting close. "They are here. Let's hide in the forest so they will think we've left, and that's when we come back and catch them by surprise."

They each run into the forest, with Amak in the lead. The pack hides in the ferns and stays there, waiting for the humans to arrive.

Lukka grins when he arrives at the lair, but is surprised when he finds it empty. He runs and hides behind a tree near Alpha Stump before the men arrive. The men shout and ready their spears as they burst out of the trees. It astounds them when they spot no wolves, but Khi'da grins because he knows they cannot be far.

"It may look like they have left, but I know they are here by their smell."

Dark clouds have formed over the land and very suddenly, heavy rain pours down on them. The wolves come out of hiding and surround the lair. Amak looks at Khi'da and bares his teeth.

"That one is mine. I will do to him what his father did to mine," he snarls, and with one thrust of his paws, he rushes toward Khi'da. The man turns around when he hears Amak running out of the trees and readies his spear to strike at him as he gets close. But Amak is quick, and jumps over to the side, pushing against him, causing Khi'da to fall. Amak picks up the spear and tosses it aside, but Khi'da will not give up that easily. He gets up and pulls out a knife from underneath his sleeve and stares at Amak.

"Come on, show me what you got!" he shouts, running toward Amak, but suddenly gets knocked to the ground just as he was about to stab him. It surprises Amak when he sees Sakkara standing over the man and staring him down, snarling. She looks over at him and smiles.

"Thank you," Amak breathes out.

"No need to thank me. Go find that traitor," Sakkara hisses.

Amak smiles and nods at her before he runs to the forest to find Lukka.

Meanwhile, Nanook and his brothers have the upper hand: some of the people have retreated into the forest. He looks up when he hears a familiar voice and sees Kho'ta charging toward him, shouting and with his spear aloft. Nanook grins and moves aside as Kho'ta trips over a rock, falling flat on his face in the mud. Nanook looks down at him, grinning sarcastically as he walks by him. Denali is surprised, seeing what happened.

"How did you know he was going to fall like this?"

"I saw him fighting and he is terrible," he grins back.

Lukka is still hiding behind the stump, enjoying the carnage he has brought upon the lair. He crawls out of hiding, hoping not to be seen, and runs into the forest to get away, but Amak spots him and chases him. He catches up with him and stops him in his tracks.

"You are leaving so soon, but the party has hardly started," Amak growls at him.

Lukka snarls. "And you're the guest of honor."

He lunges at him. Amak pushes hard against him, knocking him to the ground.

"Why don't you stop this foolishness and join us?" Amak coaxes, but Lukka is not fazed by his words.

"I will never join you. I will not stop until your bloodline is dead," the rogue wolf snaps back at him.

"Why do you hate us so much?" Amak asks.

"Because you are doing everything wrong. This whole thing about not killing. How many of us did the humans kill?"

"Is that what this is all about?"

"Yes — it's not right. You let them go and they just keep coming: you kill them, and they are gone for good."

"You really think so? You killed one of them and look at what you stirred up. Is this right, to put us all in danger?"

"Yes, it is. That is one less of them on this earth for us to worry about."

Lukka is about to lunge at Amak once again but stops when he notices the people running past them, screaming. Amak is distracted and when he looks back to Lukka, he is gone. He has vanished once again. Amak runs back to the lair, believing it is where he may be heading. He charges through the trees, then stops and begins looking for Lukka but cannot spot him. But it shocks him when he sees the aftermath that he has brought to the lair.

Nanook and Denali are picking up the broken spears and dropping them into the forest. Miki, Ila, and Alornek are dragging two bodies into the forest. Aurora comes out of her den, having looked around to make sure all is clear before emerging. Sakkara, while feeling a little shaken up, walks over to Amak.

"Are you okay?"

"I will be, after I do this," he says, looking over at Nanook.

"Do what?"

"There is an apology I need to make," he says, leaving Sakkara smiling as he walks by her.

Nanook has dropped off some broken spears into the forest and it startles him when he looks up to see Amak standing next to him with an apologetic look on his face. Nanook looks away, giving him the cold shoulder as he begins to walk away.

"I deserve that, my son, but you need to listen to me."

"I need to listen to you? But what about when I told you to listen to me? You turned your back on me and only listened to what 'Lukka' said."

"I know the way I was behaving toward you was wrong, and I do not blame you for being angry with me. You've got every right to be. I should have listened to you and because I didn't, I caused this instead. That was wrong of me. Can you ever forgive me?"

Nanook stands in front of his father, staring at him before he grins. "Yes, I forgive you. After all, we're not all perfect and we've all made mistakes."

Amak smiles when he remembers the trouble Nanook caused when he was a pup. He looks his son in the eyes.

"And I promise I will think twice before ever doubting you again."

Alornek sees his father and little brother not doing anything and walks over to them.

"Are you ladies done making up yet? We've still got a lot of work to do."

Nanook and Amak look at one another and laugh.

CHAPTER 13

Months have passed since Lukka vanished. It is now late fall, and the canopy displays brilliant shades of orange, brown, and red. The forest is quiet since the birds left. The days are shorter, and the nights are longer; the larger animals have left to find land full of fresh grass in the south. The land is once again bare and lifeless.

Nanook, Denali, Alornek and Amak are walking across the frost-bitten ground. They are trying to find anything to eat. Out in the distance, they find what looks like a dead horse. They run over to it and scan the horizon in case there are any predators nearby, then howl to call out the others who are waiting in the forest. Sakkara, Aurora and the other two brothers rush out of the forest and run over to them and once they arrive, they all eat.

Over by the forest, the people are hiding behind the trees so the wolves will not know they are there. The leader, Khi'dagets up and walks over to Kho'ta, smiling at him as he places some stones in his hands.

"Are you ready, my son? I know you can do this, so make me proud." Kho'ta nods as he places the stones in his sack. Khi'da looks at the other men and nods.

"It is time."

They all walk out of the forest, shouting loudly and banging their spears together to get the wolves' attention. Khi'da, who is walking in front of the group, stares out at the wolves in the distance. He gestures for the others to stay back as he takes a few steps forward, closes his eyes, and suddenly drops his spear on the floor. It shocks the other men when they witness what he has done. Khi'da takes a deep breath and shouts as he runs toward the wolves, making as much noise as he can. Amak sees him coming, and with no hesitation, he runs toward him. Khi'da grins when he sees his plan is working. He pulls out a rock from underneath his skins, then he stops. Amak notices that the man has stopped and snarls as he picks up his pace while Khi'da waits for him to come closer. Amak is gaining on him, believing that the man is unarmed and readies to pounce at him.

Khi'da pulls out one rock and flings it at Amak when he is close enough. He yelps in pain as he falls to the ground. Khi'da pulls out another rock and taunts Amak with it. He gets up and runs back to the pack. Khi'da throws the rock, but Amak dodges it this time as he continues to run away. The others see it as a signal and throw their rocks at the rest of the wolves. The wolves run for cover, abandoning the carcass to evade the rocks as they rain down on them.

Khi'da shouts in victory with his fists raised up high. The other men jump with joy where they are, before running to join Khi'da by the kill. Once they arrive, they kneel down and start cutting pieces of meat from the carcass.

In time, they walk back to their camp, singing along the way, filled with joy. Kho'ta is the only one who is not singing. Instead, he walks quietly behind them. He looks toward the forest, and sees the wolves staring at them as they are leaving. The young man feels bad for taking the meat from them. He looks ahead at his father, who glances back at him proudly. His father is full of pride, but Kho'ta is not happy that they took what wasn't theirs.

He looks back at the forest once more and notices that the wolves have left. He lowers his head in shame as he walks away, following the rest of the hunters. Nanook is still in the forest watching as the men, along with Kho'ta, leave. He walks away feeling that Kho'ta has betrayed him again.

Late into the night, Nanook wakes when he hears a sound coming from the forest. He gets up to check and sees a shadowy figure moving through the trees. He is about to step into the forest to see who the figure is but stops when he hears Denali calling softly to him from behind.

"Where are you going, so late in the night?"

"I think there's something in the woods. I'm going to find out what's out there."

He hides behind some trees and sees that the figure is Kho'ta and he looks like he is carrying something in his hands. He sees him kneeling down near a tree stump and laying some strips of meat on top. Nanook moves in closer and steps on a twig, alerting Kho'ta. He looks over his shoulder and is startled when he sees Nanook staring directly at him. Kho'ta raises his hands to show the wolf he means no harm.

"I am not here to hurt you, but I have brought you some meat. They took it from you, and I am here to give it back."

He gets up and walks back to the camp. Nanook walks over to the stump and grabs the meat left out for them. Moments later, Kho'ta is walking in the meadow. He suddenly stops when he hears a noise coming from behind him. He smiles, assuming that Nanook has followed him.

"If you want more, you are going to have to wait until tomorrow."

He turns around but realizes it's not Nanook. He feels nervous when he sees a silhouette of another much larger creature walking toward him, growling. Kho'ta stands his ground and claps his hands so the creature might leave.

"Go away, whatever you are."

His defense is not working, as the creature lets out a terrifying laugh that sends a chill crawling down the young man's spine. The figure steps out into the light. It's a cave hyena. Kho'ta realizes he is in trouble and begins to run, but the hyena reaches out its sharp paw and trips him. It slowly walks up to Kho'ta and as it stands over him, he yells out desperately for help, hoping that someone will hear him from the camp.

Nanook is nearby the lair when he hears Kho'ta's anguished screams for help. He turns when he hears the growling that follows and runs to help him. He jumps out into the tundra and picks up his pace when he sees Kho'ta being attacked by a hyena, then leaps forward and tackles the hyena to the ground. The hyena gets up and races off as Nanook watches it retreat. He runs over to Kho'ta and sees him kneeling on the ground, not saying a word. He raises his trembling hand and there's a deep cut to his palm. He then rips his sleeve with his good hand and ties the cloth around the damaged hand to stem the bleeding and not to attract any more predators. Nanook is lying down inches from him, watching him as he tends his hand. Kho'ta looks at him and smiles.

"Thank you for saving me, my friend. I owe you one."

Nanook looks at him, confused, and tilts his head as he gives out a whimper, while Kho'ta giggles a little.

Back at the camp, Khi'da wakes suddenly, hearing sounds coming from the meadow. He rushes out of his tent and heads over to Kho'ta's tent, but worries when he doesn't see him there. He grabs his spear and sets out to the forest to look for him. The lead hunter sees him leave and hurries over to him.

"Where are you going?"

"I heard loud sounds coming from the meadow and Kho'ta isn't in his tent. I believe he might have gone out and may be in trouble." The hunter grabs his spear and follows him into the forest. "What are you doing?" asks Khi'da.

"I am coming, too. I can't let you go out there alone at night. Things worse than those wolves are lurking out there."

Khi'da does not approve. "No, you stay here. This is between me and my son."

He walks into the forest to find Kho'ta as the hunter watches him, worried. He walks by a boulder where they placed the meat and sees that some of it is missing.

Meanwhile, in the meadow, Kho'ta moves in closer to Nanook, who does not snarl like he used to do. Kho'ta reaches out his hand to pet him. Nanook takes a sniff of his hand and licks it, as Kho'ta laughs.

"You don't want to hurt me — you never did!" He reaches out his other hand to scratch behind his ear. Nanook seems to like it, as he wags his tail furiously.

In the forest, Denali and Aurora are watching the whole thing and it shocks them when they see their brother is letting a human get close to him. It gets them worried, wondering what Amak would do to him if he ever found out.

Nanook looks straight past the young man and snarls, then turns and runs swiftly back to the forest, while Kho'ta watches, wondering why he left so suddenly. He gets up and when he turns around, it surprises him to see his father walk out of the mist — and he is not happy. Kho'ta walks up to Khi'da, placing his hand behind his back so he will not notice the wound. He stands in front of his father and stares at him while Khi'da looks down at his son, displeased.

"What are you doing out here in the middle of the night? Don't you know it is not safe to be out here this late?" Kho'ta nods his head shamefully, while Khi'da looks down at him, unimpressed. "Come, let's leave here before a predator shows up." Kho'ta walks by his father, who notices he has his hand placed behind his back. "Why do you have your hand behind your back? Are you hiding something?"

Kho'ta continues to walk. "It's nothing," he mutters, doing his best not to look at Khi'da.

"Show it to me: I want to know what you are hiding behind your back" but Kho'ta just shakes his head refusing to show him the hand.

Khi'da becomes angry. "Stop walking and face me right now!" Kho'ta stops and turns to face his father. "Show me your hand now!" But Kho'ta still refuses to show him. Khi'da has had enough of his son's defiance and pulls his hand from behind his back. He tries to open it up, but Kho'ta has it in a tight squeeze. "Open it up. Open it up now!" he shouts, frustrated while Kho'ta continues to disobey.

They stare at each other without saying a word. Khi'da realizes he is scaring Kho'ta and calms down.

"I am sorry for my behaviour, but I am worried about you, and I want to know what happened to your hand, so please show it to me." Kho'ta agrees and opens up his hand, showing him the wound, while his father looks up at him, worried. "How did this happen to you?"

"Like I said, it was nothing. I fell down because—"

He is interrupted by Khi'da. "Because you were being chased."

"No — nothing was not chasing me, I swear."

Khi'da is not buying it. "You must never come out here," he says, turning and walking away as Kho'ta follows him. "Hurry — let's get to camp so I can treat that hand better," he says, sounding disappointed as he walks away.

Nanook is still hiding in the forest, watching the two humans as they leave. He walks back to the lair, where Denali and Aurora are still awake. They sneer as he walks by them. He notices them acting strange and looks at them, baffled, as he lies down.

"Why are you both looking at me like that?" he whispers.

"We have found out you have been allowing humans go near you," Denali said, "and you allowed one to touch you—"

"Which is against the rules," interrupts Aurora. Nanook gets up and moves in closer to them, checking whether any of the others are awake, and whispers to them.

"Can you say it any louder?"

"How long has this been going on?" Aurora asks.

"Not too long." He stops and looks up when he hears Ila rolling over in his sleep. "Remember that night when Lukka arrived alone without me?" They both nodded. "I got caught in their trap and the human arrived, but he did not kill me. Instead he did the opposite: he set me free," he says, as the others look stunned, but eager to hear more. "At first, it confused me but then I realized: he was not like the others we witnessed while growing up. This one is different. He's not greedy at all, but kind."

He is going to continue with his story, but Aurora interrupts him. She gets up and begins circling around him.

"Oh! You think so. So, then explain this to me. Remember that evening, months ago, when Lukka led the people to us? I remember the human charging toward you, and it looked like he was going to attack you. He did not look kind then, now did he?"

Nanook stares at her, annoyed, before answering. "It was all an act, so his father would not find it suspicious. That trip was all for show. He did not want to hurt me at all; at least, that's what I think," he says, because he knows if Kho'ta wanted to hurt him, he would have done it already, but Aurora does not buy it.

"Are you going to meet up with him soon?"

"Yes, tomorrow night," Nanook says, while Aurora walks over to her den.

"I would be careful if I were you," she warns him, as she lies down for the night.

Meanwhile, Khi'da and Kho'ta arrive back at the camp. Khi'da stares at his son with anger in his eyes and calls him over.

"I need you to come here."

Kho'ta walks over to him, still staring at the ground, trying not to look his father in the eye because he feels in his gut that he is in trouble. Khi'da kneels down so he can look at him and places both hands on Kho'ta's shoulders.

"Tell me the truth, son: were you attacked by a wolf?" he asks, hoping to get something out of Kho'ta but there is no response. "Can you please tell me, and I promise I will not get mad." But all Kho'ta does is shake his head, continuing to look down at the ground. He walks away from Khi'da without saying a word and heads back to his tent, muttering to himself. This catches Khi'da's attention. "You said something and if you did, speak louder so I can hear you."

Kho'ta turns around and stares at his father, but he still says nothing. Khi'da's smile turns to a frown because he has had enough of Kho'ta's disrespectful attitude toward him.

"I need you to come here and tell me the truth right now" he says, sounding frustrated.

"I told you already: nothing happened. I just fell," his son replies, shakily.

Khi'da looks at him and saying nothing, gestures for him to go. As he is about to enter his tent, Khi'da calls out to him, remembering the missing meat.

"When I went looking for you, I noticed some meat missing from the boulder. Do you know what happened to it?" he asks, sounding suspicious, which causes Kho'ta's heart to sink. He pauses for a moment before he can answer his father.

"I don't know what you're talking about," he responds in a hoarse voice, making Khi'da even more suspicious that he is hiding something.

"Okay then. We should monitor that meat and stop whoever is taking it. We need it if we're to survive the winter."

Kho'ta enters his tent while Khi'da stares over to him before he goes inside his own tent.

The following morning, it is quiet throughout the land. A herd of elk is feeding on the willow tree by the watering hole. Khi'da and four other hunters are hiding behind some trees. They have been watching the deer the whole morning. They spot their target and Khi'da signals for the team to move out. They step out on to the tundra. The male deer sees them and grunts to warn the others in the herd. They leap swiftly toward the forest to hide from the people, but three more jump out from the long grass, catching them by surprise and making the deer split up to escape. The buck is running on his own as he heads in the direction where Khi'da is hiding. Then a rapid swishing sound comes out from the forest as an arrow strikes the deer and it collapses to the ground. Khi'da and the other men stand over it.

"Give me your knife," Khi'da orders.

The man next to him pulls out a knife from behind him and hands it over. Khi'da stands over the elk, looking down on it as the animal struggles to breathe. He crouches down and stabs the deer in the heart. The beast grunts before dying. The men tie the deer's legs to one of their spears and they carry the body on their shoulders to their camp.

The wolves are nearby, watching as the people carry away the deer. They walk over to the site of the kill, looking for something to bring back to the lair but find nothing. Amak whimpers as he walks away. They arrive at the lair, where Sakkara is lying inside the den on her side. Amak walks over and rubs noses with her. She raises her head to rub noses with him and four little pups appear from underneath, as Amak looks at her with a sad face.

"I brought nothing back. It's been three days since we had anything. The people have learned to leave nothing behind. I am sorry." Amak looks down at the nursing pups with regret, while Sakkara smiles. "I will do whatever it takes, even if it means sneaking over to their camp and taking some of their meat."

"It's not your fault. Try again some other time," Sakkara replies.

"I am not doing this for me; I am doing it for you. Without getting enough to eat, you cannot produce enough milk and the pups will starve."

Nanook is by his den, hearing the whole thing, and he begins to worry for his new brothers and sisters.

Late into the night, Nanook wakes up when he hears the shuffling of leaves coming from the forest. He spots a shadowy figure creeping through the forest and gets up so he can see what it might be. He looks over at Alpha Stump to make sure that Amak is sleeping before he sneaks off into the forest. He walks behind some trees so he can sneak up on the intruder, but when he realizes the figure is Kho'ta once again, he rolls his eyes and sighs. Kho'ta gasps and turns around when he hears noise coming from behind him, suspecting it might be his father, but when he sees that it's Nanook, he feels glad to see him.

"It's you. I thought you might have been someone else, like my father."

He pulls out his sack and takes out some pieces of meat and lays them across a log. He looks at Nanook, realizing that he is hungry. He places a piece of meat in his hand and throws it a few feet away to get Nanook to get closer to him.

"Don't worry— I will not hurt you. Come and get it," he says, but Nanook stays where he is instead of going over to him. Kho'ta looks frustrated.

"Really! I thought you would have been used to me by now. Well, there you are. If you don't want to take the meat from my hand, I guess you'd feel more comfortable taking it from this log."

As he is about to walk away, he turns around when he hears whimpering and smiles when he sees Nanook still sitting there, licking his lips. Kho'ta sighs as he walks over to him. He kneels down and stares at Nanook.

"I know you do not trust me yet, especially after that night I tried to attack you, but I did not mean to do it. I had no choice. My father was there. I had to do it," he says, with remorse. "I want to make him proud, for him to respect me more. But I am an outcast. I am picked on and laughed at by the others in my tribe because of what I am; because I believe killing for revenge is wrong. They want me to be like them. But I don't want to be like that." He picks up his spear and looks at the feathers hanging from it. "In my tribe, each feather represents our rank. They come in different colours: black for leadership, red for courage, brown for hunter and…" He raises up his spear and looks down at it, ashamed. "And this one — white for cowardice — is mine," he says, sounding choked up.

Nanook looks at him. Smiling, Kho'ta reaches out for another piece of meat, places it in his hand and reaches out to the wolf to get him to eat off it once more. Nanook sees the meat, crawls over to Kho'ta and eats it off of his hand as the young man laughs. After Nanook has eaten enough, Kho'ta gets up and heads back to camp. He turns around and sees Nanook staring straight at him before gathering all the meat, then the wolf turns around and walks slowly back to the lair. Once Nanook arrives, he places the meat in a pile in the center of the lair and goes to lie down to sleep.

Meanwhile, Kho'ta arrives at the camp and sneaks to his tent. He opens the flap, and is surprised to see Khi'da inside, already waiting for him. Khi'da steps out of the tent and looks down at his son, crossly.

"Where did you sneak off to?"

"I went to relieve myself."

Khi'da does not believe him. "In the middle of the night?" he says, while Kho'ta is speechless. "There is no more need for secrets. I know who is responsible for the missing meat," he says, looking Kho'ta dead in the eye. "I bet you know, too," but there is no response from Kho'ta. He grabs him by the arm and walks him to the middle of the camp, calling out, "Come on out, everyone. My son has something he needs to tell all of us!"

Everyone, including Khi'da's wife, comes out of their tents and gathers around them both. Kho'ta looks around nervously at everyone before he looks up at his father, who forces him to go down on his knees. He moves Kho'ta's hair away from his eyes, so they can look directly at each other while everyone else is quiet.

"Go on, tell us. Tell us why the meat has been missing!" Khi'da shouts.

"I already told you, I don't know!" Kho'ta yells back. Khi'da stares directly at his son and sneers. He gets up and climbs up a boulder in the middle of the camp and looks at everyone, while Kho'ta stands on the ground, in front of the boulder, looking nervously at everyone. His mother, behind the crowd, looks concerned. Khi'da looks down at Kho'ta angrily, once again.

"It's okay, son: I know your secret. You do not have to hold it in any more. Go on and say it." Kho'ta still refuses to say anything and looks away. "Fine! If you do not tell them, then I will!" he cries out as everyone stares. "Every night for the last few days, I have noticed meat has been missing from our camp, and do you know why? Because my son here has been giving our meat to the wolves." He steps off the boulder and places both his hands on Kho'ta's shoulders and stares deeply into his eyes. "Is that right, Kho'ta? Go on — tell them that you were taking our meat that we need for our own survival and feeding it to those monsters!" he says, sounding maniacal while Kho'ta looks nervously at him.

He looks beyond the crowd, and he sees his mother in the back, staring at him and nodding. He gains some confidence as he stares directly at his father's eyes, but this time, he is no longer afraid.

"Yes! I did! Are you happy? Is that what you wanted to hear?" There is an awkward silence all around the camp.

"Good, that is exactly the answer I wanted to hear coming from you.

Now you can tell all of us why you were doing that."

Kho'ta gulps as he looks at the others, nervously, once more. "Because I believe that they have rights to this food as well. We are taking it from them; they were here before we arrived, and we have driven them off this land and taken what is theirs, which I think is wrong. Don't you get it? They are living beings just like us!"

Khi'da looks at his son like he has heard enough. He stares down at him angrily. "You are talking like they have a soul, but they don't. They are demons, brought here to destroy our kind. Just think about what they have done to your great-grandfather..." he says, but Kho'ta shakes his head, disagreeing.

"They are not demons. The only demons I see here are us. They kill for survival — we kill for revenge. Maybe your grandfather got what he deserved."

Khi'da raises his hand and smacks Kho'ta. He falls to the ground while everyone, including his mother, looks shocked. There is an awkward silence as Kho'ta gets up and walks back to his tent without looking at his father. He passes the others as they clear the way for him while Khi'da silently watches him leave. The rest of the tribe all stare at him, displeased, as they walk away. His wife stares at him, upset, as she turns around and walks back to their tent, while Khi'da shakes his head, feeling regretful for what he has done.

Early the next morning, everyone in the lair is surprised when they wake up and see a pile of meat next to Alpha Stump. Amak and Sakkara sit by the pile and stare at it, confused.

"Where did all this come from?" asks Sakkara, while Amak shrugs his shoulders.

"I am not sure; I am as surprised as you are."

"Did you sneak off in the night to get all this meat for us?" she asks.

"No. This time I had nothing to do with this, I swear." He realizes it might have been Nanook who brought it over when he sees he is still in his den. "I believe I may have an idea who has been bringing us the meat."

He walks over to Nanook. He stands over him and nudges his head against his son's, to get him to wake up. Nanook opens his eyes and gets up, startled, when he sees Amak and the others all gathered around his den with smiles on each of their faces.

"Why are you guys looking at me like that? Did I do something wrong?" he asks.

Amak looks at him with a smile. "No, you did nothing wrong. We only want to thank you for bringing us this meat." But all Nanook does is look away. "Oh yeah, I forgot about that," he says, while Amak looks at him, surprised.

"You do not have to be ashamed of this. You did nothing wrong; we want you to tell us how you got all this meat."

"From the people," Nanook says, as Amak looks shocked.

"So you're saying you risked yourself by sneaking into the people's lair in the middle of the night, stealing all this meat from them so you could bring it over to us?" he says.

Nanook stares at him and all the others and feels guilty. "That's not how it happened, exactly."

"What do you mean, son?"

"I was not taking the meat from the people…" He pauses as he looks at everyone.

"Go on: we are all listening," Amak urges, sounding suspicious.

"It's the other way… the people have been giving me the meat. One of their young ones has been leaving meat for me to bring it over to us every night."

Amak laughs. "That's a good one. The people have been bringing you meat…" The rest laugh.

"Why are you all laughing?" Nanook asks.

"Because you are still alive. The moment the people see any of us, they try to kill us. We will be lucky to get a few feet close to any of them without them striking at us. That should be no surprise to you: it has been like that before, and it will always be like that"

Nanook looks at his father. "But not this one. He is different. He is nothing like the others."

Amak and the others look shocked. "So, you are not joking. You are being serious about all of this. You actually let the people approach you?"

"Yes, I have. I was going to tell you this when it was time."

Amak stares at him, displeased. "How long has this been going on?"

"Since that day I got caught in their tricks when spying on Lukka. He was the reason I escaped."

Amak turns around, without saying a word and the others do the same. They walk past the meat without even looking at it.

Aroura and Denali walk up to Nanook. "You did the best you could," said Denali.

"Did I? Really? Then why do I feel this bad?" Nanook mutters, slinking back into his den, feeling disappointed.

CHAPTER 14

The sun is rising over the land. Winter has passed, and the meadow is full of life once again. Everyone in the lair is awake and ready to start their day. Amak and the others are still ignoring Nanook after they discovered he was allowing the people to approach him and kept the information from them. Amak walks past Nanook, without even looking at him, and he jumps up on Alpha Stump.

"Can I get everyone's attention?" he calls out to the others. "I am gathering you all around so I can talk to you about honesty. As all of you already know, back in the fall, I discovered that someone in our pack had been keeping a secret from us, but that is not what we do in a pack, is it? No, it's not. In a pack, we keep nothing from each other. We never lie!" He is about to keep going until gets interrupted by a guilty Nanook.

"Father, please listen to me. I was going to tell you about this when I thought I was ready," but Amak stares at him with an angry look on his face.

"When was that going to be? When I was dead?"

"No — never, Father. I was afraid to say anything about it sooner. I am sorry, Father, and I am sorry, everyone."

Amak refuses Nanook's apology. "A wolf is never to approach any of the people, young or old. It's against the rule. You are placing yourself and all of us at risk if you continue to see him."

Nanook rolls his eyes. "He will not harm me. If that was the case, don't you think he would have done so already? But no, he didn't. You need to stop being so stubborn."

Amak does not agree. "It won't be my stubbornness that will get us killed or driven off our land, but your ignorance will!" He jumps off Alpha Stump and stares at his son. "If I ever catch you going near him or any of the people again, I will exile you from this pack."

Aurora and Denali, sensing that Nanook could be in trouble, step in to stand up for their brother. "If he gets kicked out of this pack, we will go, too."

"Step aside. This does not concern you two. It's between me and your brother here."

Nanook looks at them both and nods, but they ignore him and stand between their brother and Amak.

"No, Father. We will not let you do this. We also do not act like this in this pack: we do not turn on each other. We are family," says Denali.

"Besides, he is right about what he is saying. He is not lying. We have seen it for ourselves," insists Aurora.

Amak stares at both of them. "You knew about this as well, and you told me nothing!" he yells at them, snarling.

"We were going to tell you," Aurora urges. "But we were afraid to say anything because we knew you were going to act like this."

Amak begins to calm down "I will keep an eye on this and if I sense anything suspicious, I will step in and stop him. And I will not go easy on him, I promise you that." He turns around and walks away.

"Thank you for forgiving us, Father, and we promise we will tell you everything that happens from now on," Nanook says.

"Just because I said I will keep watch, it does not mean that I have forgiven you," Amak snaps with a stern tone.

Nanook looks at his brother and sister, appreciatively. "You did not have to do this; you were risking getting yourselves exiled, as well."

"We had to," insists Denali. "You are our brother, and we will never let him do that to you. Life here would never be the same without you around."

Nanook looks over to Alpha Stump and sees Amak lying down, with his back toward them. "I have no idea what has gotten into him."

Sakkara hears her son and walks over to him with a smile. "He's just having a bad day; he will get over it."

"I sure hope you're right," Nanook says, and turns to walk back to his den, feeling thankful that the whole confrontation is over.

In the middle of the night, Kho'ta is standing in the meadow by the forest. He whistles, hoping to get Nanook's attention. In the lair, Nanook wakes up when he hears the strange sound coming from the meadow. He gets up and sneaks by Alpha Stump. As he is about to walk into the forest, he stops when he hears Amak calling out to him.

"Where are you going so late in the night?"

"I heard some strange noise coming from the meadow. I thought it would be best if I check it out."

"What kind of noise?" Amak asks.

"Sounded like some kind of strange bird."

Amak lies there and stares at his son suspiciously. "I hope you're not going to meet with 'him'," he says.

"No, I'm not, Father — I promise," Nanook says, before running into the forest to get to the meadow, while Amak watches him.

Nanook arrives at the meadow. He wags his tail with joy when he sees Kho'ta standing there with a smile on his face, but growls the moment he sees the spear behind his back. Kho'ta tries in vain to calm him down.

"No, you don't understand. I only brought it with me so no one from my tribe would know I am coming out here to meet up with you. I made them believe I came here to hunt. I would never harm you."

Kho'ta goes down on his knees and strokes Nanook behind the right ear, calming him down. Kho'ta gets back up and leads him to the watering hole. He sits down by the bank and looks up at the sky. Nanook, hesitant at first, walks over to him and sits by his side. They stare at one another, and they each see their reflection when they stare at the water.

"Do you ever wonder why we fight like this?" Kho'ta asks, rubbing Nanook's lower jaw. He sits back and looks up at the sky. "But don't you ever wonder how great it would be if we worked together instead of fighting one another? What a great team we would make…" he says. Nanook makes happy sounds while Kho'ta scratches behind his ears and laughs a little. "I am sure you do, as well, but if only my father understood the same. He hates your kind. Long ago when he was young, he saw his own grandfather get dragged out of their cave and killed by a pack of angry wolves, in front of his eyes. Since that night, all he wants is to rid this land of every single one of you." Kho'ta looks away in shame. "He expects me to be like him, but because I am not, he looks down on me, like I have no right to be walking on the same ground he does. I need…" he pauses as he looks at Nanook and smiles a little, "…we need to team up and stop this fighting and show both our fathers we can do a lot better working together than fighting each other."

He looks at the sky and is surprised to see streaks of colourful light flashing across it. He points up to show Nanook. "See those lights up there? It is said those lights are paths that lead us to the sky-world when we die." He looks down, upset. "My great-grandfather is among those up there and for sure he is angry at what I have become."

He gets up and throws a branch in frustration and causes an excited Nanook to run after it when he sees it flying through the air. He brings it back and drops it at Kho'ta's feet. The young man picks up the branch and looks at it, confused at first, unsure of what to do with it. He smiles when he sees Nanook sitting there, wagging his tail furiously and it brings a smile to his face.

"You enjoyed that, didn't you?" He throws the branch once again and laughs with joy when he sees Nanook run after it. Kho'ta kneels down when Nanook approaches him and scratches him behind his ears while he laughs.

Further in the forest, hiding behind some trees, Amak is watching the whole thing, but instead of running out to attack Kho'ta, he turns around and walks back to the lair.

Kho'ta, sensing that he has been out too long, begins to worry that his father might be looking for him.

"It's getting late. I need to go before my father comes looking for me. I don't want him to see that you are with me: it will make him mad. We'll meet again tomorrow." Nanook, with the branch still in his mouth, watches him leave.

The following morning, a light rain is coming down. The land is lifeless, except for a herd of horses grazing by the willow tree. The stallion raises his head and calls out a warning before cantering away. The other horses do not hesitate and immediately follow their leader.

A spear strikes the ground near them as they are running away. Kho'ta approaches the spear and picks it up off the ground. It frustrates him when he sees the herd running away. He kneels down on the ground and lets out a scream to release his frustration, then gets up and walks back to the camp, feeling ashamed that he will come back empty-handed again. As he is walking, he hears a low grunt coming from behind him. He turns around, and is taken aback when he sees a young ground sloth feeding off of the willow-tree branches. It has its back turned and does not realize that Kho'ta is a few feet away.

He grins and grips his spear as he sneaks up on the sloth. If he brings it down, the most dangerous animal to walk the land, he will prove his worth to his tribe. He crawls long in the long grass to get closer. Once he finds himself close enough, he gets up, throws his spear and it strikes the sloth in the back. He jumps for joy, thinking he has got it, but soon panics when the sloth turns around and looks straight at him. The beast stands its ground and spreads out its arms to show off its mighty claws.

Kho'ta does not hesitate and runs in the opposite direction as the sloth lets out a roar and charges toward him. Kho'ta glances back and panics, seeing the sloth is gaining on him. He trips up on a rock as he is running and tumbles to the ground, then tries to get up but panics even more when he sees that the sloth is already standing over him. It raises its arms up, and as it is about to strike him down, it stops and stands in place while taking deep, fast breaths.

Kho'ta opens his eyes. He reaches out for his dagger when, suddenly, the sloth collapses next to him with a loud thud. Kho'ta gets up and uses the blunt end of the spear to poke the body to check if it is dead. He is startled when the creature shifts its head to one side and lets out one last roar, before dying. The relieved young man laughs and starts shouting for joy before he kneels down and begins cutting out strips of meat to carry back to his family.

Meanwhile, in the forest, a shadowy figure passes through. It looks toward the meadow and sees Kho'ta kneeling by the carcass. The creature, which turns out to be a lion, steps out of the forest and sneaks toward him. Kho'ta is oblivious to the lion's presence as he cuts away at the carcass. When it's close enough, the lion readies itself to pounce but Kho'ta raises his head and turns around when he hears low growls coming from a short distance behind him. He panics when he sees the lion staring at him with its green, soulless eyes. The lion lets out a roar and rushes at Kho'ta. The young man does not hesitate and reaches out to grab his spear, but he is not fast enough. The lion swipes it out of his hands before he has time to thrust it in defense. A shocked Kho'ta peers up at the lion's face as it lets out a roar, blocking out his screams.

Meanwhile, in the lair, the pack is eating. Nanook looks up when he hears roaring coming from the meadow. He drops everything and races out into the forest, sensing that something might be wrong, as the others look up.

Denali and Aurora worry for their brother's safety and decide to follow him. In the meadow, the lion is standing over Kho'ta, staring down at him and about to deliver the fatal bite. Nanook appears just at the right moment and instantly tackles the lion from the side, winding it and sending it tumbling to the ground. He rushes over to Kho'ta to check up on him, lowering down and licking him when he sees him cowering in fear.

Kho'ta looks up and is relieved when he sees it is Nanook who saved his life and gives him a hug as he tries to hold back tears.

"Thank you… I would have died if it were not for you," he stutters in a shaky voice. They quickly turn around when they hear growling coming from behind them. The lion has recovered and Nanook stares him down as the large beast circles around them, trying to get past him, but the young wolf stands between them both, preventing it from coming closer. The lion charges at Nanook. He jumps over to the side to dodge the lion and bites it hard on its paw. The lion roars in pain and pounds Nanook on the ground to free his paw from his grasp, but the wolf does not let go, despite all its efforts.

Moments later, Nanook releases the paw, beginning to feel exhausted. He sinks down, panting with exhaustion, and the lion glares at him. As it is just about to finish him off, Kho'ta calls out to it.

"Hey! He's not the one you want. I'm the one you want! Get me!" he cries out, before turning around and running. The lion lets out a tremendous roar and sets off after him. Kho'ta tries to reach his spear before the lion approaches, but loses his balance and crashes to the ground. He tries to reach for his spear, but it is out of reach. He is frantic when he sees the lion is closing in on him and closes his eyes, accepting his fate. But nothing happens. He opens his eyes and smiles in utter relief when he sees Nanook is distracting the lion once again. And this time he has it by the hindquarters. He still won't give up, even though he's exhausted.

The lion swings around and exposes its razor-sharp claws as it swipes its paws at Nanook, but he dodges every time, while Kho'ta watches in horror.

Over by the forest, Denali and Aurora watch, wide-eyed, as their brother is trying in vain to hold back the lion on his own. They exchange swift looks and nod before they each take a deep breath and run out to the meadow to help him. Kho'ta lets out a terrified scream as he watches the struggle between Nanook and the lion. Nanook gets distracted when he hears Kho'ta scream and looks toward him to make sure he is all right. The lion sees his chance and swipes his paw at him, sending Nanook tumbling to the ground. Kho'ta realizes he is close to his spear and drags himself to get it. Once he finds he is close enough, he reaches for the spear with his leg and drags it toward him. He grabs the spear once it is within reach and places it behind his back.

Meanwhile, the lion is once again lowering down on Nanook, about to mount the final attack. Denali and Aurora arrive just in time. Using all their might, they tackle the lion together, knocking it down hard onto the ground. They both rush over to Nanook to check if he is all right. He looks up at them, exhausted.

"Thanks, you guys," he pants. "I would have been a goner…" He offers them a relieved smile.

"We are a family: that is what we do," says Denali.

"And besides, we wouldn't sit around and let you have all the fun!" Aurora adds, while Nanook grins.

They hear growling coming from behind. The lion is getting up. They turn around to face its fury and stand their ground, growling to keep the lion away from Nanook. Suddenly, Kho'ta starts yelling out to the lion. The beast turns around and seeing Kho'ta sitting on the ground, it rushes toward him. The young man pulls out his hidden spear and thrusts it as the lion pounces at him. A huge dust cloud forms and everything is quiet, while Nanook and the others stare, waiting for the dust to clear. Moments later, the cloud clears. They see the lion's body lying on the ground, but no sign of Kho'ta. Nanook walks around the body, pawing the lion's head to check if it is dead, while the others stay back and watch. Nanook stares at them and starts whimpering, suspecting that Kho'ta must have died as well, since he cannot find him anywhere.

He sees one of the lion's front paws moving. He stands back, growling, believing that the lion is still alive. Denali and Aurora go to his side and growl along with him. They stop when they hear a faint voice calling from underneath the lion. Nanook looks down and wags his tail with joy when he sees Kho'ta's hand reach out from underneath the body.

"A little help here!" he cries out from underneath.

Nanook, Denali and Aurora grab him by his sleeves and begin to pull him out. The young man takes a deep breath of fresh air when his head finally pokes out from underneath the lion's body. Once he is finally out, he sits down, shocked, when he looks at the huge, dead lion, not believing that he managed to kill it on his own, without the help of anyone from his tribe, while Nanook stares at him and happily licks his hand. Kho'ta snaps out of it, takes a look at Nanook, and gives him a big smile.

"I did it. I cannot believe I killed a lion on my own!" he says, with enthusiasm. He reaches out to Nanook and gently pats him. "And I could not have done it if it weren't for you. Thank you," he says, feeling grateful for Nanook coming to his rescue. He looks up and is shocked when he sees Aurora and Denali standing there, emitting low growls at him. Nanook looks over to them and rolls his eyes, then walks over to them. He looks at them both, while smiling.

"What are you two doing, just standing there? Go and greet him — he's waiting for you," he says, while the sibling wolves look at him, uncertain if they even should go near a human.

"I am not sure if that's a good idea, we are not even supposed to go near his kind. Father will not like it," Denali states. Nanook stares at his brother.

"That is true, but he is not around and what he does not know will not hurt him. So, let me introduce you to him," he says confidently, while the others nervously follow him.

Kho'ta is kneeling on the ground when they approach him. They stand a few feet from him and just stare nervously while Kho'ta smiles. As he reaches behind him, the wolves quickly react by baring their teeth, but Nanook looks at them, smiling.

"There is nothing to worry about. Just watch closely."

Kho'ta looks at them and sticks out a closed fist in their direction, while Denali and Aurora lean in close, with eyes wide open, wondering what he has in his hand. He slowly opens his fingers to reveal pieces of meat, while Nanook smiles. The siblings look at Kho'ta, astounded, when they see the meat in his hand.

"See? I told you. Now go take it from him, one at a time," Nanook says.

Denali steps forward, gingerly, and takes the first bite as Kho'ta laughs a little, but Aurora feels hesitant when it comes to her turn. Nanook walks over to her to offer some encouragement. "It's okay. Trust me: he will do nothing to you."

She slowly walks over to him while Kho'ta speaks softly to her. "It's okay. Don't be scared: you can trust me." She leans in closer and begins to sniff the meat before she takes it from his hand. Nanook smiles proudly that his brother and sister have faced their fear and actually got close to Kho'ta. Then he reaches out his other hand, while they both look confused wondering what he is doing. Nanook goes over to them and explains. "Do you see what he is doing right now? He's reaching out his hand to lay it over you guys so he can scratch you behind the ears."

They look at Nanook confused.

"What is the purpose of that?" asks Denali.

"Go over to him and see for yourself. Believe me, you won't regret it at all," he says confidently, while looking over to Aurora, gesturing for her to approach the human. "Go on — don't be afraid."

Kho'ta is gazing at them, smiling as he waits for them to get closer. They each nervously stand by him as he slowly reaches both his hands and begins scratching behind their ears. They slowly begin wagging their tails as a sign that they are enjoying the experience. Nanook sits back with a smile, feeling glad that now his own siblings seem to be trusting Kho'ta, as well.

Meanwhile in the forest, Amak has been hiding behind some trees, watching the whole thing, feeling some concern for them. He lets out a howl before he turns around to head back to the lair. The three of them hear his howls and head back to the lair. Kho'ta stands there as they leave. He also thinks it is getting late, and he quickly kneels by the carcass and cuts pieces of meat to bring back to the camp. He gets up and looks toward the forest and sees Nanook and the others standing there. He stares back at him before they head back to their lair.

Kho'ta arrives back at the camp and kneels by a creek to wash the blood off his hands so his father will not know that he got attacked. He places the meat down by the boulder and sneaks past his parents' tent so he will not wake them. He opens the flap, when, to his surprise, Khi'da walks out. He stands by his tent with his arms crossed, staring at Kho'ta, not looking happy.

"Where have you been?"

Kho'ta looks up at him. "I have been out hunting to bring some meat back to the camp; to pay back what I took from us," he stutters, but Khi'da does not buy his son's explanation.

"I do not believe you. I want to see that meat for myself," he says, as he walks toward the boulder. He looks down, and it surprises him when he sees a pile of fresh meat lying there. "Where did you get this meat from?" he asks, puzzled.

"I got this meat myself. I brought down a ground sloth," Kho'ta responds.

Khi'da stares at him, astonished, when he hears his son has brought down a sloth. He smiles the biggest smile as he reaches out to hug Kho'ta. He looks down at him with pride, but the smile turns to a frown when he realizes Kho'ta does not feel proud at all.

"What is the matter, my son? You should be proud of yourself for bringing down a sloth, of all the creatures out there! When I younger I never had the courage to face one on my own, but you did and you won!" he says with joy, and grabs him by the hand to tell the others of his son's success. Kho'ta pulls his hand away while Khi'da looks at him, this time feeling more concern than pride. He looks at his son.

"Something else happened," Kho'ta states. He looks down at his hand and opens it to show his father the injury. It shocks Khi'da when he sees the gash in his hand.

"How did this happen? Do not tell me you got attacked?" he says with concern.

"Yes, I did, Father. I was attacked by a lion while I was out there hunting on my own, to prove to you all that I can, and at least try to make you proud of me for once. Because I feel you are never proud, no matter how hard I try!" he cries out, causing everyone to emerge from their tents when they hear the shouting from outside. "And do you know what else, Father! I have also killed a lion. If you don't believe me, go out into the meadow, and see for yourself!" he yells while everyone else, including Khi'da, looks astounded. "And I could not have done it if the ones you call 'monsters' hadn't arrived. But they did! That's why I am still alive! But that would not matter to you, because I matter nothing to this tribe!" He yells loud enough so everyone can hear, then strides away and throws the spear down next to the meat before heading off to his tent.

Khi'da and the others are speechless. He looks to one of the hunters and calls him over. "Stand by his tent and make sure that he does not come out. I cannot have him wandering off and meeting those wolves any more. It is for his own safety and ours, as well. I cannot risk him bringing those demons over to us."

The hunter nods his head without saying a word, and walks over to the tent to keep watch over Kho'ta.

Meanwhile, Nanook and his siblings are strolling through the forest.

"You were not lying about that one. He is nothing like the others," Aurora says with glee.

"I'm glad you like him," Nanook says, smiling a little.

"What was that thing he was doing behind our ears? I enjoyed that. Too bad it had to stop. I wanted to stay there the whole day," Denali says joyfully.

"I am not sure what those are. He also does that to me, plenty of times, and I enjoy it because it is very comforting," he replies.

"Why didn't you tell us about him when you first met up with him?" asks Aurora walking beside her brothers.

"I wanted to, but I wasn't sure how you would react; you could have run off and warned Father about it," he said.

"Like we said before, we would never do that," Denali says. "You can trust us. We are not only your siblings, we are also your littermates. We will always support your ideas, no matter how crazy they may be. And besides, I like him. Next time you meet up with him, I want to come too, so he can do that thing behind my ears again,"

Nanook smiles. "It makes me happy to know you guys like him. I wish Father would think the same way as you do," he says, with resentment.

"He will. You need to give it some time," Aurora urges.

"Right! That will happen after I die," he says ruefully.

They arrive at the lair and are glad to see everyone, but it surprises them when they notice everyone is not happy to see them. Nanook walks forward and smiles as he calls out to get their attention.

"Hey, everyone, we are back!" but nobody answers. Their older brothers do not even look at them as they walk into their dens. Sakkara whimpers as she turns around and walks away from them. The siblings stare, clueless about what is going on.

"Why are they all acting like we are not here?" Denali asks Nanook.

"I'm not sure. But it's not good."

They look over to Alpha Stump and see Amak standing there, looking down at them with a dead stare. He jumps off and walks over, looking down at them as he walks past. Without saying a word, he gestures them to follow him into the forest. They do what he says and follow him. They see him staring straight ahead and they walk up to him. The three of them sit behind him and wait for what he has to say. He turns around and snarls, looking straight at them.

"Whatever you are planning had better stop now," he says, angrily.

"What are you even talking about?" asks Nanook, baffled.

"I saw the three of you out in the meadow with the human before you came back. You thought I didn't know," he yells.

Nanook rolls his eyes. "How many times do I have to tell you that he will not do anything? He could have done so the moment he discovered me at the trap. Instead, he set me free. He is nothing like the others. Give him a chance, just like Aurora and Denali did, and I know you will feel the same way" he says calmly, sounding reassuring and hoping Amak will change his mind, but his father stubbornly looks away without saying a word. Nanook thinks of an idea that will help him change his mind about Kho'ta.

"I tell you what — I will bring him over just so you can see how he is for yourself" but Amak rejects the idea and faces his son.

"You will do no such thing! If you ever bring him over and he endangers our family, I will personally end his life," he declares, angrily.

Nanook looks impatient. "But he won't!"

"Enough! You may have manipulated these two but that will not work with me!" Amak shouts before he walks away, back to the lair. Nanook, not liking how his own father has acted toward him, runs out into the meadow as his siblings stand and watch.

Night has come. Over at the people's camp, everyone is sitting by the fire, feasting on the meat that Kho'ta has brought over, except he is not there with them. He is, instead, inside his tent, frustrated by watching them eat without him. He looks down at his stomach when he hears it grumbling. He feels some pain, and he presses his knees to his stomach so the pain might go away. He looks up when he hears someone approaching and lies down, pretending to be asleep, in case it is his father. The flaps of the tent open up and his mother smiles when she sees him pretending to be asleep.

"You do not have to pretend to be asleep: it is not your doubtful father but me, your loving mother, instead," she says with pride.

Kho'ta gets up and gives her a tight hug as he cries, "He is eating the meat I brought over and that almost took my life. He did not even call me to join in. No matter what I do to make him proud, I only make him more disappointed. Tell me what I am doing wrong?" he says, wiping away his tears while his mother looks at him with a calming smile.

"You are not doing anything wrong. He is more than proud to call you his son and he loves you more than you know it. He worries for you," she says, to reassure him.

He looks away in shame. "He sure has a funny way of showing it."

"That's because he does not like to show the others that he is sensitive. It's how he is, but he is proud of you. Believe me when I tell you this. He acts that way toward me, too, but it doesn't mean he does not care about me," she soothes. She reaches inside her skins and pulls out pieces of cooked meat, handing them over to him. "Eat this and when no one is looking, go search for that wolf. I also believe all this hatred toward the wolves is wrong, but I am his wife. I have no choice but to always agree with him. It is up to you to show him how right you are yourself. You need to believe in yourself and who knows — one day he will realize you are right."

She walks back out of the tent as he looks at her, smiling, before he takes a bite out of the meat.

It is late into the night. Everyone is now sound asleep in the camp after an evening of eating. Kho'ta wakes up and steps out of his tent. He sneaks past his parents' tent, trying not to make any noise to wake up them. He freezes when he hears his father rolling over in his sleep and waits for a while to make sure Khi'da is not awake. Kho'ta reaches the meadow, very glad he did not get caught by his father or anyone in the tribe. He wipes his forehead before running over to the wolves' lair.

Moments later, the flap of his parents' tent opens up. Khi'da pokes his head out and looks around. As he is about to step out, he feels a tug from behind. He turns around and notices that his wife is awake.

"Where are you are going so late in the night?" she asks him, groggily.

"I ask the same question about our son. I think I heard him sneaking off into the meadow," he says. She sits up, rubs her eyes, and looks over at him.

"Leave him be. He knows what he is doing. He went to relieve himself. You need to stop worrying about him and go to sleep," she yawns, as she lies back down and turns onto her side.

"That's not what he's going to do. He's going to meet that wolf. I have had enough of this."

Khi'da walks out while his wife sits up and watches him. He then opens the lead hunter's tent, startling the couple who are sleeping inside. The hunter's wife wakes up, screaming in fright, not knowing what is happening.

"Are you trying to give us both a heart attack?" the lead hunter shouts.

"There is something important we need to do…"

"It had better be important. You scared us half to death," he cries out.

"There is no time for this," states Khi'da. "Get up, get your spear, and meet me in the forest. We are going to pay our friends, the wolves, a visit," he says, replacing the flap, leaving the man wondering what is going on. He looks over at his wife and shrugs as she stares at him, still traumatized. He steps out of the tent, grabs his spear to go and meet with Khi'da.

He finds him in the forest, crouching near some shrubs. He kneels by his side and looks at him.

"You had better have a good reason for waking me in the middle of the night and almost giving my wife a heart attack," he mutters to him, frustrated.

Khi'da stares at him with an angry look in his eyes, making him nervous. "Kho'ta's looking for that wolf and I will put a stop to this. It's time we pay those wolves a visit. Go call out our best hunters and meet me back here so I can tell you my plan," he orders.

The hunter nods and walks back to the camp to get the other hunters and meet Khi'da back at the forest. He is standing behind a tree, looking toward the meadow with a smirk on his face. The hunter walks up to him and looks in the same direction, beginning to feel uneasy.

"So what do you plan on doing if he does locate that wolf?" he asks, nervously.

"I will catch that wolf off-guard and get him cornered. That's bound to attract the Alpha and he will come running to the rescue, but what he won't expect is that he'll be the one who needs to be rescued," he says heatedly, as he gets up.

"But Khi'da — wait and listen to me!" he cries out to him. "What if your plan backfires?"

Khi'da stops and rolls his eyes, annoyed, and responds without even facing him. "You don't have to come if you don't want to. It's your choice. But I will," he states, walking off while the others stand, looking at him.

Meanwhile, over at the lair, a rock drops right beside Nanook's den, waking him instantly. He looks around the lair to see what might have caused it before lying down again. He then hears noise coming from his side of the forest and turns quickly, seeing a figure standing close by. He growls as the figure continues to stare at him but stops when he realizes it is Kho'ta, as he steps into the light. He wags his tail as he about to walk over to him, but quickly looks over at Alpha Stump to make sure Amak is sleeping before he runs out into the forest to join his human friend. He jumps into his arms and licks him with much joy before Kho'ta places him back on the ground.

Amak wakes with a start when he hears a noise coming from the forest. He glances over to Nanook's den but does not see him there. He sits by the forest and feels disappointed when he spots his own son playing with Kho'ta. He continues to stare as they frolic with one another and does not notice Sakkara standing behind him. She walks closer to him and sits.

"What are you staring at?"

"Just look at our son playing with 'him'. That is outright wrong."

Sakkara looks for herself. "I see nothing wrong. He looks happy and 'him' does not appear like he is going to harm our son at all," she says to reassure Amak.

He stubbornly presses on. "You see nothing wrong. But I do."

"What do you find wrong about our son playing with that young one?"

"Everything. They are the enemy, and he is acting like they are not. He is turning his back on his own kind.”

“You might believe they are the enemy, but he doesn’t. This is not the first time you’ve doubted him when he was right about something,” she says as he looks over to her, baffled.

“When did I ever doubt him?”

“You remember when he was trying to tell you that Lukka was lying to you, but you never listened to him?” she suggests, while Amak looks away without saying a word. “Maybe he thought you had betrayed him when you listened to Lukka more than you did to him. You never thought about that?” she continues. “You should give ‘him’ a chance and who knows — you might like the young one, too, like Nanook does,” Sakkara adds before she leaves and walks over to her den to lie down. Amak continues to look toward the forest, thinking that she had been right about everything she had said before. He walks up to Alpha Stump.

Amak is settling down on Alpha Stump, getting ready to sleep, when he catches some more movement coming from the forest. He looks up when he spots three more shadowy figures prowling through the forest, near where Nanook and Kho’ta are playing. He realises it is the rest of the people sneaking up on them from every direction. Amak senses that it might be a trap and begins to run toward the forest to help Nanook.

Meanwhile, Nanook stops playing with Kho’ta, and snarls as he looks past the young man, much to his confusion. Kho’ta turns around to look behind him and panics when he sees his father rapidly approaching them, with his spear aimed at Nanook. Kho’ta is about to run toward Nanook and push him out of harm’s way, when Amak jumps in between them both and snarls, stopping Kho’ta in his tracks. Believing that his son could be in danger, Khi’da does not hesitate and thrusts his spear to attack both wolves but Kho’ta turns around and stands in front of his father, just in time, with his arms outstretched to stop him from getting anywhere near either wolf. Amak sees both people are distracted and spots his chance to attack them from behind.

“Quick, Nanook! I take one and you take the other!” but Nanook steps in front of him and stops him from moving forward, while Amak looks at him with an angry stare.

“I will not, Father. Stop acting this way and listen!” but Amak refuses. “Then, step aside. I will handle this myself if you’re not going to help!”

shouts out Amak. Nanook does not move and stares at him as if he's had enough, much to Amak's surprise.

Kho'ta looks at him and nods to thank his young wolf friend for stopping Amak from attacking him. Khi'da continues to stand in front of him with his spear still held tight.

"What are you doing standing there?" he yells at his son. "Get back to the camp!" he orders, staring at both wolves. "I got you now, demons. You won't get away from me this time," he rages.

Kho'ta continues to stare him down. "I will not go; you cannot make me, Father. In order to kill them, you're going to have to kill me first!" he yells.

It surprises Khi'da when he hears his son talk that way and Amak looks up at him, surprised, when he realizes Kho'ta is standing against to his own people.

Nanook looks hopeful. "Are you now seeing it for yourself, Father?" he urges, joyfully.

Confused, Amak does not respond and turns to walk away, back to the lair. Khi'da sees Amak with his back turned and readies suddenly to throw his spear at him, but Kho'ta immediately stops him by grabbing his arm and pulling the spear away.

"You need to stop this right now, Father. I will not let you harm them, no matter how hard you try," he insists, as he tries to push his father away from the wolves. Khi'da feels rage come over him and will not tolerate his son's defiance.

"Move out of my way!" he yells, as he pushes Kho'ta aside. He picks up his spear and runs toward Amak, about to strike him. Nanook stares helplessly and yells out to warn his father of the incoming threat.

"Father! Watch out!"

Amak turns swiftly and stands his ground as Khi'da approaches him. Just as he about to strike Amak, Kho'ta leaps in his father's way once again, shocking him with his determination.

"Kho'ta, I said move!" Khi'da yells, but Kho'ta does not move a muscle. Instead, he lowers himself down and stands over Amak, much to his surprise.

"No! These wolves have saved me twice; back when I got attacked by a hyena and then by that lion on the night I brought you back that meat, which you have never thanked me for!" he cries out in anger. "When will it ever sink into your head that they don't want to attack us!"

Khi'da rolls his eyes and sighs deeply. "I am deeply concerned for you. I do not want anything bad to happen to you. You are my only son and next in line to being leader of this tribe, like my father once was," he says, with seriousness.

"You do not have to be concerned because nothing bad will ever happen. When will you ever realize that? If they wanted to hurt any of us, they could have done that right now. At this very moment they are just as scared as we are. You believe that they have nothing in common with us, but they do — and that is the will to survive," insists Kho'ta, with hope when he sees his father lowering his spear. Khi'da drops to his knees and looks directly at his son while trying to hold back tears.

"Those are the words of a true leader. I always knew that you would make me proud, my son." He reaches out to Kho'ta and gives him a hug, which to Kho'ta's surprise is something that he has never done before. He hugs him back while Amak and Nanook just stare. Father and son stop hugging and Khi'da presses his forehead against his son's, while choking up. "What will I ever do with you?" he murmurs, while Kho'ta looks at him with a smile.

Khi'da gets up and walks away, with his son following closely behind. They approach the other men, who were hiding away in case they got attacked. Khi'da nods and smiles at them as he walks by. He raises his hand in the air and motions for them to move on. They all walk back to the camp. Kho'ta looks up at his father and smiles, knowing that he has finally earned his parent's respect.

Over at the lair, everything is not fine. Amak, who still feels too proud to admit he was wrong, walks up to Alpha Stump and lies down, while the others look at him. Curious, Denali and Aurora walk over to Nanook.

"So what happened out there?" asks Denali. "We heard so much noise."

"We were ambushed by the people and the young one saved us from them, but from the looks of it Father still doesn't want to accept that he is good and not like the others."

"He will get over it. Just give it some time," soothes Sakkara confidently from behind them. "He lost his family to them, and he has not trusted any of them since. He is just confused and does not know whether to trust them or not. I am on your side. I believe what you say is true and the young one does seem to be kind: I can tell from how you speak of him all the time. Your father still needs some time to think. Eventually he will realize it, as well," she says.

"I sure hope you're right," Nanook replies. He turns around and heads back to his den to lie down for the rest of the night. He looks over to Alpha Stump and notices that Amak is still awake and looking up at the sky, while giving him the cold shoulder.

The following morning, Nanook is startled when he wakes up to find Amak standing by him with a smile on his face. The alpha wolf gestures for him to follow as he heads into the forest. Nanook, though confused, gets up and follows him. Once inside, they sit a few feet from the lair and Amak looks over to him while Nanook tries to explain once again.

"Father — please tell me why you are being—?"

"It is all right, Nanook. You don't need to explain anything to me. I experienced it for myself, and it has all sunk into this thick skull of mine while I was lying on Alpha Stump last night. I now realize you were right about 'him' all along. When he stood over me like he did, to stop his father, I realized he was nothing like any of the people we faced in the past. I was only confused at first. That is why I was acting harshly towards you. I didn't know how to react to this, especially after all that they had put us through before. I am sorry for my behavior."

Nanook looks at him with a smile spreading across his face. He feels glad that Amak is realizing the truth about Kho'ta.

"I forgive you, Father, and thank you for understanding. Besides, there is no need to be sorry. I would feel the same way if anyone harmed any of you, but you need to give them a second chance. It is that one chance we all need so that we can be at peace again."

As Amak is about to respond, they both hear Kho'ta calling out to Nanook.

"Go on, you don't want to keep him waiting," Amak says, looking at his son with pride. Nanook gets up and runs into the tundra. The young man and the wolf frolic with one another as they walk out into the tundra, while Amak looks on from behind the trees and smiles before he heads back to the lair.

CHAPTER 15

A year has passed. Nanook is now two years old. It is summer, and the worst of winter is over, but the summer itself isn't as promising. The meadow, which was once filled with every colour of the rainbow, is now barren. A powerful gust of wind blows an immense cloud of dust that blocks out the sun. There is no life at all on the land. The grazers left since the grass on which they depend has dried up. The skeletons of some that succumbed to the heat and lack of water are all that remain. The watering hole is dry, except for a few isolated pools. Inside each pool are crowded schools of fish trying in vain to keep within the remaining water. Others are struggling in the mud where the water has drained away. Four shadowy shapes are cast over the pools. It is Amak and the three brothers. They lower down to grab some of the fish and head back to the lair.

When they arrive, they walk over to the den and place some of the fish by the entrance. Sakkara, looking like death, pops her head out and smiles when she spots the fish. As she steps out, four little pups come out in a single file. They scamper over to the fish and eat. Sakkara is the last to join, while Amak and the others watch them eat. They feel relieved that she and the pups got something to eat. After Sakkara has had her fill, she lies down next to the log and Amak lies next to her, looking at her, concerned.

"You look like death," he whispers but all she does is smile.

"I will be fine," but Amak continues to stare at her because he knows she is just saying that to calm him down.

"You don't look fine to me. You are nothing but skin and bone and you haven't eaten for days. Those fish I brought over were not enough to feed all of you. I wish that there was more that I could bring that would feed you enough to bring you back to good health."

"Don't worry about me. I've lived my life. The pups need it more than I do."

Amak sits up and looks down at Sakkara's terrible shape and whimpers as he walks over to the others. He looks at all of them, concerned.

"I hope Nanook, Aurora, and Denali bring back something better than these fish," Amak says.

"I am sure that they will, especially when they got 'Him' with them," Alornek responds with confidence.

"I sure hope you are right or else your mother will not make it past the summer." Amak turns around and heads back to Sakkara and lies down next to her while the Alornek and the others continue to stare out into the meadow waiting for the others to return.

Meanwhile, out in the tundra, Nanook, his siblings and Kho'ta are approaching a herd of wild hogs, the only living wild game that has stayed behind. They are digging the ground hoping to root out some water, unaware that Kho'ta and the wolves are sneaking up on them. The wolves stop to study their quarry while Kho'ta crouches down next to them. He sees they are near a large boulder, on the south side, where it is shady, to shelter themselves from the sun's glare. The largest of the boars look up and glances their way. They crouch down to the ground to blend in with the dry soil. Sensing that they are being watched, the boars wander behind the boulder as they continue in their search for water.

Nanook has an idea and walks over to the boulder as the others follow his lead. He sneaks over to one side of the boulder, while Denali and Aurora hide by the other side and lie in wait. Kho'ta climbs up to the top of the boulder and crouches down so that the pigs don't know he is there. They all wait for Nanook to make his move. He takes a deep breath and leaps out. It startles the hogs, and they scamper away from Nanook, but Denali and Aurora jump out and block their escape. The smaller hogs escape, but before the larger one even has a chance, Kho'ta jumps off the boulder and strikes it from above, just at the base of the neck, and instantly kills it. He pulls out the spear and begins shouting out with joy as the wolves jump around him, feeling just as happy as he is. Nanook is equally happy because he knows that this mass of flesh will feed his mother and she will feed his younger siblings.

Kho'ta lowers down and begins cutting away the meat. He takes some time to gather enough to take back to the tribe. "I have what I need. Now you can help yourselves and take as much as you need. We made a great team today and because of that, we have plenty to eat that will last us through this drought," he smiles.

They realize the wind is picking up. A huge dust cloud forms around them. The four of them huddle inwards together so they won't breathe in any of the dust. Once it clears, the wolves look up at the sky and see clouds forming. They hear thunder from out in the distance, while flashes of lightning streak across the sky. Sensing that a storm is coming, they gather as much meat as they can before running off to beat the downpour. Kho'ta runs back to the camp, shouting with joy, believing that rain is approaching much sooner than expected. The wolves feel that something doesn't seem right about this storm: they stare up at the sky before running back to the lair.

Once they arrive back at the lair, Amak is looking up at the sky, as well. Nanook notices the concerned look on his face as he sits by him.

"You also sense that there's something wrong with this storm."

"Yes. I find it odd that there is no rain coming down. It should have come down after the first roar of thunder. Instead, all I see are the flashes of lighting and only the wind but not a single drop."

"It will come soon. We need to wait," Nanook says. Amak looks over at him, worried.

"Rain does not choose when it comes down. Something doesn't seem right. We need to prepare ourselves. I will need to make sure your mother and the pups are safe in the den. I do not want to put them at any risk." He gets up and rushes over to Sakkara. "I am going to need you and the pups to go inside right now."

"What for?" she asks, baffled, just as a streak of lightning strikes at the exact spot where Amak had been sitting.

"Does that answer your question?"

Sakkara doesn't hesitate and leads the pups inside the den. Amak and the others stand around the spot where the lightning struck. They all sense that something is not right about this storm and go to hide in their dens to shelter themselves, as well.

Meanwhile, out in the meadow, the wind is getting stronger. The roaring of thunder echoes through the night, but still no rain. Once again, a streak of lightning strikes the ground and smoke appears. Over at the camp,

Kho'ta arrives, and it surprises him when he sees everyone throwing all the supplies into the forest. Khi'da rushes over to him the moment he sees him. Kho'ta reaches behind his back and shows his father the meat, but Khi'da does not seem to care about it at the moment. He looks down at him with a worried stare.

"I going to need you to put that meat away and come help us. Something does not seem right about this storm."

Kho'ta nods and grabs some coltsfoot leaves to wrap the meat in, then buries it by the forest, so no animal can find it. He runs over to help the others as they put away the supplies and prepare for the storm. Moments later, as he gathers arrows, he hears the frantic calls of the wolves coming from their lair. He is about to walk over to make sure they are okay, but stops when he hears Khi'da calling out to him.

"Where do you think you are going? We need you here with us," but Kho'ta shakes his head.

"I have to go, Father; the wolves might need help!" he cries with concern, but Khi'da does not agree.

"They can take care of themselves. You are needed here, with your own kind, not with them," he shouts. Kho'ta is about to walk over to him but then he hears the howling coming from one wolf, who he believes is Nanook.

"Kho'ta, do not go. I am ordering you to stay here" Khi'da cries angrily.

Kho'ta refuses. "I have to see what's wrong. They could be in trouble. I am going there and do not come after me. I can take care of myself. Besides, I know you would have done the same if it were one of your friends."

He drops the arrows on the floor and runs into the forest. Khi'da looks worried. As he is about to go after him to bring him back, he feels a hand being placed gently on his shoulder. He turns around and sees his wife standing behind him.

"Leave him be, Khi'da. If you want him to be the man you expect him to be, you just have to let him be that man on his own. He knows what he is doing. I trust him and so should you," she says to reassure her husband. He looks over to the forest and sees his own son running off on his own to help his friend and begins to smile when he realizes that his wife is right.

He gives her a hug.

"Where would I be without you?"

"You would have been killed," she says sarcastically, walking away. Khi'da looks at her with a smile on his face before he walks over to help the others. He hears thunder once again and looks up the sky and still sees no rain. He looks out into the forest, worried, and whispers, "Be safe, my son, and come back soon."

When Kho'ta approaches the lair, he feels something is not right when he finds Nanook pacing back and forth up ahead. Nanooks spots him and runs toward the lair. Kho'ta, with no hesitation, follows him. Once he arrives at the lair, it shocks him to find that a trunk of a tree has fallen, caused by the powerful gusts of wind earlier, and has blocked the den. He sees Nanook standing by the den and walks over to it. Alornek sees him and snarls, but Denali stops him. Kho'ta walks by them. He approaches the den and just as he is about to kneel to check inside, it surprises him when he hears Sakkara snarling at him from on top of the log. She believes he is going to harm the pups inside.

Nanook walks over to her. "It is all right, Mother; he will hurt none of them. He is only trying to help. Trust him," he says, as Amak and the others monitor him. She calms down and backs away from the den. Kho'ta stares and nods as Nanook sits by him to guard him from the others, in case they choose to turn on him.

He steps over to one side of the den, picks up a rock, and with three hits, he cracks it open. He looks inside, and he can see the pups. The pups back away, scared, the moment they see him. Kho'ta speaks to them in a soothing voice so he will not scare them.

"Don't be afraid. I am here to help you."

He slips his hand through the crack to let one of the pups lick it. The pup sniffs it and licks his fingers. Kho'ta sees it as a sign that the pups are trusting him, and he gets hold of one of them and pulls it out. The pup looks up at him when he places it down. He lowers his hand, and the pup licks it once more before running over to the others, who are waiting for its safe return.

After he has freed all the pups, Sakkara walks over to him and stares at him. This time she isn't defensive, but thankful. She leaps up on him and licks him while Kho'ta laughs.

"You are welcome!"

Amak and the others wag their tails and trot over to him. Nanook is glad that his family is also trusting Kho'ta, and realizing that he differs from any of the others of his kind. They all stand in front of Kho'ta as he looks at all of them, baffled. He opens up his hand and reaches out to them, and they each take turns licking his hand to let him know he is a part of the pack. They all form a circle around him. They all howl and Kho'ta howls along with them but suddenly stops and gets up quickly when he hears his father calling out to him.

"I have to go," he says swiftly, but before he walks out into the forest he looks and smiles at Nanook and the others, and howls one more time before he runs out into the forest and back to the camp. Amak and the others look up and notice smoke rising into the sky. They begin to feel uncomfortable as the cloud of smoke builds up.

As Kho'ta is running back, antelope bound past him. He looks in the direction they came from, and it shocks him when he sees fire spreading rapidly out in the meadow. He notices it is getting near the lair of the wolves and worries for them. Meanwhile, over at the camp, Khi'da sees the smoke. He panics and calls out to everyone to come out. They freak out the moment they see the fire.

"Everyone, calm down. There is no need to panic. Remember what we have trained for in case of a fire." But everyone else is too busy gathering their equipment to escape from the fire. As he is about to calm them down once more, he turns around when he hears his wife, Kara, calling out to him. He rushes over to her.

"What's the matter, Kara?" he asks, concerned.

"Kho'ta has not come back!" she cries out.

Khi'da widens his eyes in shock. He runs over to the boulder and grabs his spear, and is about to head over to forest when his wife follows him.

"Where are you going?"

"I am going to get Kho'ta: he must still be with the wolves."

"You are walking out into the forest?" she asks, panicking.

"I will be back safe and with Kho'ta by my side. You need to go with the others. I will catch up with you," he assures her, as he runs into the forest. Kara watches him disappear into the smoke. She sees the rest of the tribe are moving deeper into the forest, north of the camp, to get away from the fire and she follows them.

When Kho'ta arrives at the wolves' lair, it scares him when he sees that the fire has reached it before he has. He looks around, hoping to find any signs that they are still there. He is about to run back to the camp, believing that they might have moved somewhere, when he hears faint barking. Kho'ta turns around and notices that the fire has trapped the wolves.

He looks around quickly to find anything that could be useful to get them out of the fire. Close to where he is, he finds a dead tree, which gives him an idea. He hurries over to it, presses his back against it and pushes it with all his might. He feels the tree loosen around the base, then he hears it crackling before it snaps in half and starts falling. He shouts with joy when it falls right by the den. He calls out to the wolves.

"You've all got to hurry and run across this tree before it catches on fire!"

Amak is the first one to cross. He jumps on it, to test its strength, then sees it's secure and runs across, followed by the others. They all look up at Kho'ta with gratitude as they run past him. Sakkara then realizes the pups are still in the den. Amak is about to go in and get them, but Nanook stops him.

"I will get them. You go ahead with the others," but Amak stops him.

"Let me come with you. Two heads are better than one. We will locate them quicker."

Nanook agrees and they both go in as the others watch as they disappear into the thick smoke. They locate three pups hiding inside the log but worry when they do not see the fourth. They look for him but cannot find him. They lower their heads, believing that the fire may have taken him. They rush out of the fire. Sakkara sees them approaching and feels relief, but then panic when she sees only three of the pups have made it back.

"Only three? Where is the fourth one?" she says, worried, while Amak and Nanook lower their heads in remorse.

"We could not find him. We may have lost him in the fire," says Amak, full of sorrow. Sakkara runs by them so she can look for the pup herself, but the others stop her.

"Let me pass! I need to find my son!" she shouts out.

Amak walks up to her. "There is nothing you can do. We lost him," he says, sadly, while Sakkara stares at the raging fire. "We need to get out of here as fast as we can!" Amak cries out.

They all turn to escape the fire except for Nanook, who is still looking at their home as it burns. A tree near him snaps at the base and topples down toward him. Amak notices it just as the tree is about to crash down on his son. Amak leaps, just in time, and pushes Nanook out of the way but gets himself pinned underneath the tree, in the process. Nanook jumps over and sees that Amak is stuck under a branch. He uses all his strength to try and pull himself out, but gives up when he realizes that he is wedged. He looks up at Nanook.

"You must leave me. Go — and lead the others to safety," Amak orders his son, sounding as though he is giving up, but Nanook ignores him and begins to dig to free his father, but he must do it quickly before the fire swallows them both.

Kho'ta picks up a rock and runs over to Nanook and helps him dig. Nanook jumps over to one side while Kho'ta digs on the other. Moments later, after a lot of digging and breathing in smoke, they feel the branch's grip loosening around Amak. Kho'ta tosses the rock behind him and begins pulling Amak out to set him free from underneath the tree, but he loses his balance and slips on the rock behind him, hitting his head against it.

Amak, finding himself free, jumps over the young man and runs back to the others. Nanook does not leave. He stays behind to help Kho'ta as he lies there, unconscious. He grabs him by the back of his shirt and tries to drag him, but he is too heavy.

Amak has arrived to join the other wolves and panics when he does not see Nanook there with him.

"Where is Nanook? Why is he not with you?" Sakkara says, sounding worried.

"I thought he was right behind me. He must have stayed with 'him'. I must go back and see if he is all right."

"Be careful and please come back safe," she says, holding back tears.

"I will come back, I promise. Take the others and wait for me by the river, and I'll meet you there," he says. He then turns around and runs back into the fire to go look for Nanook, while Sakkara watches him leave.

After a long time of searching for Nanook in the fire, Amak finds him. He runs up to him, seeing that his son is trying to drag Kho'ta out of the fire. At first, he feels hesitant about helping him. Just as he is about to run back to join the pack, he remembers that Kho'ta put himself at risk to save his life, and he goes to help. It surprises Nanook when he notices Amak has come back. He looks into his eyes and notices how exhausted he looks.

"He is much too heavy for you to drag on your own. I will grab this sleeve and you grab on to the other and we will pull him out together," Amak suggests.

Nanook smiles and agrees and grabs a hold of one sleeve while Amak grabs on to the other, and they drag the unconscious young man out together. Fire and smoke build up all around them while burning debris falls everywhere, but they press on, switching sides each time.

Meanwhile, by the river, Sakkara is waiting for their safe return. She tries to look beyond the thick smoke, hoping to glimpse them, but loses hope when she cannot see them at all. Just as she is believing that they have not made it, she sees shadows appearing from the smoke and she smiles when she spots Amak and Nanook walk out of the fire, dragging Kho'ta. She, along with the others, runs over to him to greet him as they each take deep breaths of the clean fresh air.

They all stand around the unconscious Kho'ta. Sakkara goes over to the river, gathers water and sprinkles it onto his face, hoping to wake him up. The young man opens his eyes and coughs, after breathing in all the smoke. Nanook licks him when he begins to sit up, while Kho'ta just laughs and reaches out to hug him. He looks toward the tundra and smiles when he hears his father calling him. He gets up and begins calling out to him, "I am over here, Father!"

Out in the tundra, Khi'da hears him and smiles as he runs over to the river. The moment Kho'ta sees his father running out of the smoke, he does not hesitate: he runs up to him and hugs him. Khi'da cries while hugging him.

"Thank the ancestors that you are okay," he says, filled with emotion. Kho'ta looks up at him and cannot believe that his own father, the brave leader of the tribe, is crying.

"Why are you crying?" he asks, while Khi'da looks at him with watery eyes.

"I thought I had lost you." He hugs his son once more. "Let's head back to the others. They are waiting for our return, especially your mother." As they both walk away, Khi'da looks over to the wolves and nods at them to show his gratitude. "Thank you for keeping him safe," he whispers to them and runs back to the camp.

The wolves do the same and run across the river. Kho'ta is looking back as they cross the river and it gives him an idea.

"Father — look. The wolves are crossing the river and it looks like the fire gets put out the moment it touches the water, so it will not reach the other side. Why won't we do the same and cross the river?"

"That's not a bad idea," Khi'da replies. "The other side looks untouched by the fire. If the wolves find it safe to go there, so shall we. But we have a problem we have to explain to the others, and they will not like if we tell them to go where the wolves are going, after what they put us through."

"But we've got to try, Father. I know they will listen to you," Kho'ta said with confidence.

"I sure hope so," Khi'da said, feeling unsure.

Over by the other side of the tundra, Kara and the rest of the tribe are waiting for Khi'da to come back with Kho'ta. She looks toward the trees and worries when she spots shadows heading toward them. The others have their spears ready when they spot the shadows and prepare themselves to attack, in case it is a predator. Kara motions with her hands for them to lower their spears. Once she sees they have downed their weapons, she smiles and runs towards the two figures, while the others look at one another, baffled. She picks up her pace as she gets closer to them. Meanwhile, Khi'da sees his wife running toward them and runs over to her. They give each other a hug while Kho'ta stands behind them with a smile on his face. She cries as she goes over to him, hugging and kissing him multiple times.

"Never, ever scare me like that again — you hear me?" she says, hoarsely.

"I will not, mother — I promise."

They both walk over to Khi'da and hug each other once more, before heading back to the others, who are also glad to see them both back safely.

They all gather around them, cheering, when they arrive. Khi'da sees the lead hunter, walks up to him with a smile, and stands by his side. The lead hunter looks at him doubtfully.

"Tell me what troubles you, my friend," Khi'da says while the lead hunter looks baffled.

"Can you not see for yourself what is wrong? The fire is spreading, and we still haven't moved out of here. We have to leave fast before it reaches here and traps all of us. I say we keep heading north and look for high ground." Khi'da disagrees and the lead hunter looks confused. "Then for your own sake, I hope you have a better idea," the hunter says.

Khi'da stares at him with a curious look on his face. He turns to Kho'ta and gestures for him to walk over. "I don't, but Kho'ta does. Tell him your idea, my son. Why don't you tell everyone your idea?"

Kho'ta looks at all of them as they stare at him, waiting for what he has to say. He clears his throat, and looks once more over to his father and mother, who gaze at him with pride.

"Go on, say what you told me as we were walking back here," Khi'da encourages. Kho'ta stands up straight and stares at them all once more before starting his speech.

"As we were walking here, I noticed that the wolves and all the other creatures were crossing the river to the other side. The fire will not reach there because it cannot cross the river. If we find a way across the river, we will cross it like they all have and escape the fire," he says with confidence.

There is an awkward silence as the entire group stare in disbelief but the silence is broken when the lead hunter laughs. Kho'ta looks over at him unimpressed.

"I find nothing funny about this!" but the hunter looks at him as though he's crazy.

"You think this is a good idea — following the wolves? The ones that have taken our food from us? And killed your great-grandfather?" he cries out.

Khi'da steps in and tries his best to speak up, but the others keep ignoring him. He has had enough of how they are ignoring his son and yells out.

"My son is trying to say something, so all of you shut up and listen to what he has to say!"

Kho'ta climbs up a nearby stump so they can all see him. "The wolves know this land more than we do and that is why I believe we should cross the river like they have. If they think that's a smart idea, then so should we!" he shouts, as they all stare up at him.

One elderly man speaks up. "So what you are saying is that we should trust the wolves? They will kill us, like they always have. This idea is crazy!" he cries out, raising his fist into the air. The others start chanting 'Kill us all!' multiple times.

Kho'ta glances over at his father with a look indicating he is about to give up, but Khi'da nods at him and smiles, giving him confidence once again.

"Just like we have killed them and driven them away from their home? You may not trust them, but I do!" he cries out. The old man looks up at him, astonished.

"Is that so? Then tell me what they have done that makes you trust them?" he sneers, looking over to the others and laughing.

"I am still here and talking you. That's what got me to trust them. If they were the killers that you believe them to be, I would have been dead by now, but they are not. Instead, they saved me; not once, not twice, but three times!" he cries, as the old man glares at him without saying a word.

Then, out of the crowd, a younger man standing next to his family yells out.

"You are as crazy, just like your old man. It must run in the family!" The others scream with rage at the three of them. Khi'da steps in before they all turn on Kho'ta.

"Listen, everyone — you need to calm down! What he says is true. It wasn't me that saved him from the fire; the wolves did. By the time I arrived, they had safely removed him from the fire, and they would not leave until he was rescued," he says softly, to calm them down. The old man walks up to Kho'ta and stares him straight in his eyes.

"You want to follow your wolves? Fine, go ahead, and anyone else foolish enough to follow him can go ahead, too!" he says, angrily. He walks past the others. "If there is anyone who wishes to come with me, then do so. It will be a wise choice, instead of staying to die," he declares as he walks away.

Kho'ta looks at him. "It will not be. You will be sorry!" he cries out,

but the old man ignores him and continues walking in the other direction.
Three of the younger men and their families look away and follow the old
man. The others all watch as they disappear into the darkness of the forest.
Kho'ta jumps off the stump with remorse.

"You are the real fool — not us. May the ancestors go with you and
guide you on your path," he whispers. He looks over to his family. Khi'da
goes down on his knees and the others do the same as Kho'ta looks down
at all of them with confidence.

"We will do whatever you say, my son. I trust you and so do the rest
of us," Khi'da says with pride. He gets up, along with the others and they
pound their chests with their fists and all shout out at once, "Wooo!"

Kho'ta looks east and smiles. "The fire is spreading fast. We must head
east and cross the river," he says. He turns around and leads the way with
his fist raised in the air. "Let's go home!" he cries out. The rest of the tribe
follow him, cheering.

Late into the night, they are moving as fast as they can to get away from the
fire, with Kho'ta in the lead. The smoke gets thicker, a sign that the fire is
gaining on them. Kho'ta looks down in shame, wondering whether the old
man may have been right about coming this way. He feels his parents'
hands on each of his shoulders. He looks at them while they both smile at
him to give him encouragement. He smiles back and leads them north to
get them out of the smoke.

"This way, everyone."

After some moments of walking, he looks up when he hears the rushing
of water and begins to run. His father calls out to him.

"Where are you going in such a hurry?"

"I hear the river! Follow me this way," he shouts with joy. Khi'da and
Kara exchange looks and run behind him, together with the rest of the tribe.
They catch up with Kho'ta and see him standing by the riverbed.

"What's wrong, son?" says Khi'da, concerned. "The river is too rough.
It's not as steady as it was by the wolf's lair. We cannot cross here."

A young man shouts out from the crowd. "You've led us to our doom!
The old man was right!"

But he quietens down when Khi'da gives him a cold stare. He looks
over to his son and sees the disappointment written all over his face. He

places both hands on his shoulders.

"Don't let them get to you. I believe in you, and I know you can do it. That's all that matters."

Kho'ta smiles. He turns around to face the water, and looks downriver to find anything they can use to get across, but he sees nothing. When he looks upriver, he notices a dead tree leaning over the water with only three roots keeping it from crashing down. It gives him an idea.

He runs over to the tree, leans his back against it and pushes it with all his strength until the trunk falls over the river, creating a platform so they can cross. The others all look at one another, smiling, and run over to where Kho'ta is standing, beckoning them.

"We will use this trunk to cross the river."

He allows his parents and the others to cross first, and he will go last. Once they all make it to the other side, Khi'da calls out to his son.

"We've all made it across! Now it is your turn, but be careful — the middle is not so sturdy. It might give way at any time. Trudge across it and you should be fine!"

Kho'ta nods. Before he walks across, he stands by the base and jumps on it to check its strength. Judging that it will be strong, he walks across, but once he gets to the middle, the trunk snaps, tipping him into the rough water. Khi'da is about to jump in to save his son, but two other men hold him back. The strong current pulls Kho'ta downriver as his parents and the others stare as he screams for their help.

Nanook is not far away when he hears Kho'ta's cries for help, and he rushes to help him. Amak and Denali run to his side. In the water, Kho'ta spots an overhanging branch and attempts to reach out for it, but it is too far, and he cannot grab hold of it. Further downriver, he sees a boulder rapidly approaching and somehow, he clings on to it. After several moments of rushing water smacking into his face, he loses his grip, just when Nanook jumps in and grabs him in time, before he gets pulled underneath the raging river.

Nanook swims toward the shore, but Kho'ta is too heavy, and he struggles swimming against the current. Amak once again jumps in to help him and together they pull him to shore. Denali, who is waiting by the bend, helps them lift the young man onto land. He sits there, shaken up, and Nanook licks him. Kho'ta smiles gratefully at him and at the others.

"Thank you… Thank you, again. This is the fourth time you saved me!"

The wolves run off when they hear the other humans approaching. Kara cries and hugs her son and Khi'da places a fur over him to warm him up. The others build a fire so Kho'ta can dry in some warmth. Once the fire has started, they have him sit near it, so he can hold his hands over the flames, and feels relieved when he feels the warmth. He looks toward the trees and smiles, grateful to Nanook: had it not been for the young wolf's intervention, he would have drowned.

In the small hours of the morning, they reach a spot by some shrubs covered in berries and decide this is where they will set up camp, until they decide when to move on from there. Out in the tundra, the fire rages on and the clouds of smoke block out the moon. Kho'ta is standing by the river, wondering if the other men are safe, just like they are. He walks over to the others and sits by the fire.

CHAPTER 16

Three weeks have passed since the fire ravaged the land. It shocks Kho'ta, along with Nanook and Denali, as they walk through the area that was once full of life, witnessing it now filled with nothing but death. They step over the charcoaled carcasses of those not so lucky to escape the flames, and feel glad that it was not them. Nanook and Denali look at one another and whimper when they remember they have lost one of their youngest brothers to the fire. Kho'ta looks at them when he hears them. He goes down on his knees and hugs them both.

"You did the best you could. I was not your fault. The fire was too powerful," he says, holding back tears. He gets up and together they continue to search for anything worth bringing back to their families.

Meanwhile, the pack is getting accustomed to their new lair. They are busy picking up any debris they find lying on the ground and scrape away any dead leaves spread across the lair. Over at the people's camp, they are also cleaning up whatever debris they come across, tossing it over to the wolves' lair on purpose, which Amak does not approve of. He still does not trust the people, and the same goes for Khi'da, but at least they are no longer trying to kill one another. They just stare at one another, while Sakkara readies herself to stop Amak in case he attacks. Instead, they turn their backs and walk away, much to Sakkara's relief, as she goes back to lying down and watching as the pups continue playing.

One of them sees a child. He walks up to him and plays with him as Sakkara keeps a watchful eye on the two youngsters frolicking with one another. Amak watches from Alpha Stump as they play, with a distrust look in his eyes. Sakkara gets up and walks up to the pup.

"Leave it be and come with me," she whispers to the pup. She walks by Amak, unimpressed, but he ignores her and continues to monitor the child. A woman walks out of the bushes to pick up her child and Amak gets up and growls. It startles the woman when she sees him staring at her. She picks up the child while still staring at Amak, gets up and walks backwards toward the bushes and back into the camp. Sakkara, not impressed by the alpha's behavior, walks up to him.

"Stop this right now. You are behaving like a pup," she says while Amak stares at her.

"You may trust them, but I still don't. His father killed mine or did you already forget?" he snaps, before lying back down.

"That was then, but now they seem at peace and let us make sure we keep it that way."

"For now they may be at peace," Amak replies, "but we still need to watch our backs because you never know — one day we will have them turned and they will attack us when we least expect it — and it won't be the first time that will be done to us."

Sakkara looks down at him, displeased, and lets out a whimper before walking back to lie down by the log, looking over toward the people's camp, believing that Amak may have a point.

Two months have passed since the fire and the meadow is gradually recovering. The grass is growing back once more, adding some color to the vista. New seedlings are growing to restore the burned trees the fire took down. They are sprouting leaves once again and some fruit is growing along the branches. Flowers are blossoming and are spreading across the meadow, coloring it like a rainbow that has collapsed to earth. Bees and other insects that rely on them for their own survival have also appeared. Since there had been no flowers in the recent months, some insects had submerged themselves underground to wait for the flowers to sprout once more, and as for the bees and butterflies, they moved to other parts that were not damaged by the fire. They are filling the air with the sound of their buzzing once again. The insects are not the only ones to arrive. Birds are snatching up the insects as they land to forage on the blossoms near the branches where they were roosting. They are filling the skies with their songs, after a long time of nothing but silence.

The large herbivores have also come back and they wander among the remains of their decayed brethren. Horses neigh and buck each other, in the distance, for the rights to the finest patch of grass. Near the pool, the antelope spring into the air as they ready for the mating season. Mammoths are wallowing in the pool while giant sloths browse off the new fruits from trees near the water. Across from where the mammoths are wallowing, the beasts get spooked when they hear screaming accompanied by a big splash. Something is swimming beneath the surface and as it breaks the surface to catch a breath, it is Kho'ta, and he waves with excitement to two wolves in the far distance. They are Nanook and Denali, lying by the bank watching him, as though he is odd.

"What do you think? Should we go in and join him? It doesn't look so bad," says Nanook, joyfully.

Denali feels nervous when he sees the mammoth on the other side of the pool, making him afraid. "I am not sure if we should. I don't trust those mammoths," he responds, but Nanook disagrees and tries to coax him to go in.

"Come on! Why are you so nervous all the time? As long as we stay clear of them, they will do nothing."

"Easy for you to say. Did you forget what happened to Seka when they smashed through our lair?"

"I try not to, but that was then, and they only did that because they got spooked and those don't look anything near that. They look calmer. Besides, we're not much of a threat to them like the lion was."

Denali still refuses, which annoys Nanook, but he grins when he thinks of a way that will get his brother into the water. "I'll tell you what. How about we race each other? I win, you jump in. You win, then you don't go in. Does that sound good?" he says.

Denali nods and they both stand side by side, then run toward the pond.

Nanook is in the lead, but he slows down as he gets close to the water's edge. Passing him, Denali looks back and begins teasing Nanook.

"Am I too fast for you?" he cries out.

Nanook grins. "You sure are!" he shouts out.

As Denali turns back to race his brother to the pond, he suddenly realises he is getting close to the edge, panics and tries to stop, but too late. He falls in, with a loud splash. Nanook laughs while the rest of the other animals watch. Denali comes up to the surface to catch a breath and struggles as he swims back to shore. Once back on dry land, Nanook stands near him with a sarcastic grin.

"Was that so hard?" he says, holding back his laughter.

Denali does not look happy, and he gets up and shakes off some of the access water, spraying some on Nanook. He notices Nanook standing by the water's edge, watching Kho'ta as he swims, and sneaks up on him. Once close enough, he pushes Nanook into the water. He breaks through the surface and notices Denali staring at him.

"How is the water?" he asks with a sneer on his face, when suddenly the loose soil where he is standing collapses, tipping him into the water again with a loud splash. He does what he can to keep afloat and notices Nanook staring at him with a grin on his face.

"I don't know. You tell me!" He swims away laughing leaving Denali treading water. Denali laughs and then swims to catch up to his brother. They both join Kho'ta, frolicking with one another in the water right up to nightfall, while the rest of the animals graze around them with nothing to worry them.

As night falls over the land, Kho'ta is sitting by the pond, along with Nanook and Denali, looking up at the sky. It amazes them when they see a meteor shower streak over them. The other animals have all moved out of the open and into the forest for safety and shelter, except for the mammoths and ground sloths. They do not seem to worry about being out in the open because they have no predators to worry about, so they continue feeding while their young play in the water.

Kho'ta gets up and walks back into the forest, followed by Nanook and Denali. As they walk by the river, they hear a loud splash and look down. It surprises them to see huge fish swimming upriver. One of the fish leaps out of the water to snap at a passing insect before falling back into the river with a loud splash, much to their amazement. Kho'ta looks down at the wolves as they look up at him.

"What a surprise it would be if we showed up with fish this size! They won't be expecting this," he grins. He wades into the knee-deep and chilly water with his spear in hand. Spotting a fish nearby, he sneaks up on it. He strikes at the fish once he is close enough and quickly lifts the spear out of the water, shouting with joy when he reveals the struggling fish at the other end. He throws the fish over to the shore before continuing to search for more fish.

Nanook and Denali walk into the water to get some fish themselves to bring back to the lair. Denali spots one swimming upriver as it passes inches from where he is standing. He lunges at it and pulls it out of the water, much to Kho'ta's surprise.

"You got a big one there!" he says, sounding impressed.

Nanook makes his attempt, spotting a fish swimming by Kho'ta. He prepares to dive in and lunge at the fish, but then stops when he notices something much bigger swim just underneath the young man. Kho'ta stops and turns around when he hears Nanook growl a little.

"What's the matter? Upset you can't catch any fish, but your brother did?" he asks. Nanook looks up and snarls while Kho'ta readies his spear. "It's not that big a deal. You can take some of mine," he says.

He suddenly feels drips of water on his head and looks up, believing it could be rain, but instantly spots a giant snake looking down on him from a tree limb directly above him. The dripping he felt was from it's saliva. Kho'ta panics and as he steps back, he slips in the water. The snake strikes at him. Nanook immediately jumps in between them but gets himself caught in the snake's coils. With every rapid squeeze of the snake's body, the young wolf finds himself losing consciousness and then sees only black as he passes out. The snake is about to strike at Kho'ta. Denali rushes in and plunges his teeth into the midsection of the snake's body, to try and save his brother. The snake writhes to free itself from Denali's grip, and while doing so, it loosens Nanook from its coils.

Kho'ta rushes over to the unconscious wolf, picks him up, and carries him back to shore. He places him down and rubs his side to revive him. Nanook gains consciousness, coughing and taking deep breaths as Kho'ta looks down, smiling. When he knows that his wolf friend is going to recover, he grabs his spear and wades back to the struggle between Denali and the snake. He readies his spear and waits to strike the snake's throat. He focuses, but every time he is about to throw it, the snake lowers its head and hides its vulnerable throat. He wades behind the snake and aims to strike it at the base of the neck. He takes a deep breath and throws the spear, but he misses, much to his frustration.

He knows Denali is getting exhausted and so he thinks of another risky way to stop the snake. He grabs a rock and throws it at the snake's head. It stops and turns around to face Kho'ta, giving Denali the chance to run. Kho'ta pulls out his bow and grabs an arrow from behind him. Taking a deep breath, he aims. The snake lunges at him with its mouth open and as it is about to strike, Kho'ta releases the arrow, which hits directly inside the snake's mouth and comes out from the back of the head.

The giant snake crashes down to the water, inches from Kho'ta's feet. Taking heavy breaths, he looks down at the stricken creature. He approaches it and taps at its body, to make sure it is dead, before jumping for joy. The wolves run over to him, and they celebrate together. He places the bow back over his shoulder and he pulls out a stone from his pouch and starts cutting away at the snake. They each carry pieces of meat back to their families.

Four months have passed, and the sun rises over the land. It is now late fall, and it is a chilly morning. Out in the meadow, it is lifeless. The herds have moved away to areas with fresh new grass, except for a few horses who have stayed behind, and since there is no other herbivore remaining for competition for the greenest patch of grass, they graze as much as they can until the grass gets covered up by snow. The stallion looks up and the others prance as they ready themselves to run at the first sign of danger. The stallion keeps focusing into the distance and then, coming out of the mist, he notices two silhouettes coming toward them. They turn out to be Nanook and Denali and the horses neigh when they see them, but the wolves seem not to be interested in them as they continue to frolic with one another, much to the stallion's confusion. Then a loud swish from an arrow comes from behind them and strikes down a mare near the stallion. The other horses run for their lives the moment they see Kho'ta rushing at them. Kho'ta kneels down and cuts away at the fresh meat. The wolves arrive and bite off some chunks for themselves as the young man looks at them and smiles as they eat.

After the wolves have had their fill, he kneels down and hands them some meat. "Here — you can take some back to your lair and feed your family. They must be hungry, just as you are," he smiles. The wolves take the meat, and they turn around and head back to the lair with their mouths full of big chunks of horse. Kho'ta stays back and ties the horse's two back legs with some rope and drags the corpse over to the forest, but it is too heavy. Nanook and Denali turn and notice him struggling and rush over to help. They grab both ends of the rope, and the three of them drag the carcass back to the people's camp.

Deep in the forest and hiding behind some trees, a shadowy figure watches as they carry away the carcass. Giving out a low growl, it walks away.

Meanwhile, in the forest, close to where they live, Kho'ta places the horse carcass next to some bushes and covers it with fallen branches to hide the meat from other hungry predators. He walks back to the camp and his parents welcome him with open arms. They embrace each other and walk together back to the camp.

Nanook arrives back at the lair and drops the meat in the middle area. The pups race toward the pile of meat, dive in and begin gorging themselves as Nanook looks down at them, smiling. Amak approaches and takes some of the meat. He looks up at Nanook.

"Thanks for the meat," he says, sounding grim. He turns around and lies down near a large boulder while Nanook looks at him, smiling before walking over to Sakkara.

"So how is he handling all this? I mean, being this close to the people this time?" he asks, concerned.

"He still doesn't trust them. He has been standing near that boulder just staring over at their side since daybreak," Sakkara says, while Nanook sighs with disappointment.

"At least they're not trying to kill one another."

"Don't worry — he will get used to them. Just give it some time. He'll get over it one way or another, since he has no choice," Sakkara says, wisely.

"I sure hope so, if we want to be at peace. He'll have to stay put or one wrong move and we will fight one another again and this time we have nowhere to run," Nanook replies.

"Don't worry. I will monitor him, and you know he always listens to me. Now, go on and lie down and rest. You look stressed," Sakkara soothes to reassure Nanook. He looks at her and smiles, then goes over to his den and lies down. Sakkara joins the pups by her den while Amak stands on top of the boulder and continues to face the people's camp, keeping watch on them as the rest of them sleep.

It is late into the night, and everyone on each side is asleep. Amak stirs awake to the sounds of rustling coming from within the forest. He watches, annoyed when he notices it is just a mouse, and goes back down to sleep once again. Moments later, he wakes up to rustling coming from all around the lair. This time, sensing that it cannot be mice, but something big, he jumps off the boulder and stands in the middle of the lair. It surprises Nanook when he wakes and sees Amak standing in the middle of the lair, looking straight at the forest. Sensing that something could be wrong, he goes to stand by his side.

"What do you see?"

"There is something moving around out there… At first I thought it was a mouse. When I heard the noise a second time, I realized it's too big to be a mouse."

Suddenly, a large, bulky figure moves across from them.

"That sure is one big mouse," Nanook says, concerned. They then hear movement coming from all around them and realize that there could be more than just one of the unknown figures and that they are surrounded. One shape stops, stands across from them and then walks toward them.

Amak recognizes the figure as it gets close; it is the same hyena that they encountered when they first crossed over to this side. This time she is back with a vengeance. Nanook growls, too, and the wolves' noise causes everyone else in the lair to wake up. When they see the hyenas, they swiftly get up, stand their ground and begin growling, as well.

Over by the camp, Khi'da wakes up when he hears noise coming from the wolves. Sensing that something might be wrong, he steps out of his tent, grabs his spear and heads over to their lair.

The lead hunter, also awake, feels concerned for him, goes to his side, and looks toward the wolves' lair, hearing their growling.

"Do you think they are planning to attack us?"

"No, they're not. They have not tried to attack us ever since we got here. I have a bad feeling it could be something worse," Khi'da responds quietly. As he gets close to their lair, he panics when he sees hyenas have surrounded the wolves. He stands there with his eyes wide open.

"What's the matter?" asks the hunter, feeling uneasy.

"Come here and see for yourself, but I must warn you: you will not like what you see."

The hunter walks over to him and is shocked when he sees the hyenas. "What should we do?" he asks in a shaky voice.

"Grab your spear and call out the other hunters. We have to be ready in case the hyenas attack us next."

The hunter agrees and walks away to grab his spear, calling out to everyone to wake up. They all stand by Khi'da and prepare themselves in case of an attack. The lead hunter stands next to him, feeling uneasy.

"We are all here."

"Thank you for calling them all out," Khi'da says. "and don't forget to thank the wolves, as well. If it were not for their growling, the hyenas would have ambushed us as we slept."

"Yes, you are right," the hunter says.

"They have warned us of the danger, which made us aware of it before it happened," Khi'da says.

They all stand their ground with spears in hand and ready themselves in case of an ambush. Kho'ta pokes his head out of the tent to find out what is going on, then panics when he realizes Nanook is in trouble. He rushes out and grabs his spear and runs out to the wolves' lair to help him, much to Khi'da's despair.

Over at the wolves' lair, Amak and the others are still facing off the hyenas. The pack is too busy focusing on the matriarch hyena to realize that there is one sneaking up on Nanook. Spotting the hyena, he turns around swiftly, but has no time to react as the creature lunges at him.

A spear suddenly whooshes from out of the forest and strikes the hyena just in time. It collapses to the ground, much to Nanook's surprise, as he looks down at the lifeless body. He turns around and snarls when he sees some movement running toward them, but stops and begins wagging his tail when he sees Kho'ta coming out from behind the trees. The young man looks down at the dead hyena and pulls out his spear. He cringes when he spots the large female, staring at him with a hungry look on her face. He stands his ground and readies his spear to help defend the wolves.

Another hyena appears from behind him. It suddenly jumps on Kho'ta, pinning him to the ground while he struggles to keep it off by swiftly moving his spear between himself and the creature. It keeps on snapping at him so dangerously close that Kho'ta can see inside its mouth. Nanook is about to help his friend but is stopped in his tracks when another spear whooshes out of the forest and strikes the hyena right at the base of the neck. He looks toward the forest and sees Khi'da and the hunter running toward the lair. Khi'da arrives and kneels by his son and helps him up, looking at him as he holds back tears.

"Never do that. You had me scared," he says, sounding choked up as he hugs him. He looks down at Kho'ta with concern and calls the lead hunter over. "Take my son back to the camp," he says.

"What about you? Are you not coming as well?" the hunter says, sounding worried. Khi'da looks up at him, shaking his head.

"No, I will stay here and help the wolves fend off these hyenas. Now look after the others. I will be fine," he orders as the hunter nods, turns around, and walks back to the camp with Kho'ta. The young man looks back to his father, who just smiles and nods. "In case I do not come back, my son — take care of your mother for me," he whispers.

He gestures what could be a last farewell before he turns around and readies his spear, while the wolves look over to him. They all exchange looks and smile at one another, glad Khi'da has joined to help them. They face the hyenas and snarl at them. The threat does not faze the remaining hyenas: they just laugh as they charge at the wolves. The wolves also charge at the hyenas for the fight for their lives, and what might be their last, for some, in the effort to rid the land of this menace for good.

The sun rises over the land, dawning a new day, but this time it is not silent as echoes of growls fill the air. Over at the lair, the battle rages on. It has been going on all night. Nanook and others are doing their best to keep the other hyenas from coming near Amak as he is fighting their matriarch, who has grown stronger since their last encounter. Standing not far behind him is Khi'da, trying in vain to stop another hyena from lunging at him by thrusting his spear, but the hyena laughs and grabs at the spear. Khi'da does what he can to release it from the beast's grasp but despite the effort, she breaks it in two with just one bite. Khi'da stands helpless as the hyena stares at him, preparing to charge. It rushes toward him while he stands his ground and readies himself to grapple with the animal, but it is no use: the hyena overpowers him and pins him to the ground. It snaps at Khi'da while he struggles, using every ounce of his strength, to get the foul creature off him.

Meanwhile, over at the people's camp, they are all cowering in fear inside their tents. The lead hunter hears Khi'da's screams and he worries for him. He brings his family closer when he hears the growls coming from both wolves and hyenas as they battle. He cannot take it any more when he does not hear Khi'da. He gets up, and as he is about to head out, he feels his wife tugging at him. He looks down at her and sees a frightened stare on her face. He smiles and kneels down next to her.

"You look frightened, my dear wife, and why is that?" he asks.

"I do not want you to go out there. I am afraid that you won't come back," she replies.

He places his hand under her chin and raises it up so she can look straight into his eyes.

"But I must go. Our leader is out there fighting alone, and I do not think it is right for me to stay here and cower while he risks his life. Besides, he would have done the same if any of us were at risk of losing our lives," he says.

"He can take care of himself," his wife protests. "You have children and they need their father around. They need a father figure to teach them how to hunt and build the fire and that is something you know. I can't lose you. I just can't!" she calls out, trying not to cry. Despite her pleas, he ignores her and leaves.

She brings her sons closer and begins crying as he closes the flap of their tent. He looks back when he hears his wife crying and feels regret coming over him as he grabs his spear. He calls out to the other men to come out. They poke their heads out of their tents and when they see him standing in the middle of the camp, holding his spear and looking at them all with a serious stare, they step out of their tents and walk over to him. Once they have gathered around him, he looks at all of them.

"Our leader is sacrificing himself over by the wolves' lair to protect us. He is doing that for us, as he always has. All we ever did was cower away while he did all the work. Now that he needs us, we are not there fighting by his side, but that ends tonight. We will go over there and help him and return him back to the safety of the camp. I am telling you this because that is what he would do if it were any of us in that same situation. He would not hesitate. Instead, he would rush in with a spear in his hand to help us. I am not saying that you have to come, but I say that you would be doing the right thing if you did. Now, as I stand here talking to you, our brave leader is fighting a powerful threat, far more powerful than any wolf. So, I ask you one question: are you going to help or are you going to stay here and cower away? The choice is yours."

He looks all around and stares at each one of their terrified faces and gets no response. He feels disappointed as he picks up his spear and walks out to the wolves' lair to help Khi'da. He is about to walk into the forest but stops when he feels a hand grasping his shoulder. He looks behind him and sees all the men staring at him with smiles on each of their faces. He acknowledges them and walks out into the forest as the rest of them follow his lead.

Meanwhile, in the sky overhead, the clouds are covering the moon as they form. The wind picks up, while lightning streaks across the sky above them, followed by heavy rain. Over at the wolves' lair, the battle still continues. The hyenas feel the wolves have them outnumbered, since they brought down many of their pack members. So, they run out into the meadow to escape them. The wolves, along with Khi'da, do not hesitate and chase after them. Once they have caught up with them, they line up and stare at each other. The matriarch steps forward and calls out to Amak for a challenge. He accepts the challenge and steps forward but stops when he hears Sakkara calling out to him from behind.

"Amak, please do not do this!"

"I have to do this. I have to rid the land of this menace once and for all!"

"But she will kill you!" Sakkara cries out with anguish.

"Then I shall die knowing that my bloodline is safe and will continue to live on in peace."

Amak walks toward the hyena while the others watch. The alpha wolf and the matriarch hyena stand, then begin pacing back and forth, not leaving each other's sights. Some hyenas are about to walk closer in case they need to intervene, but the other wolves hold them back and prevent them from getting any closer. Khi'da lowers his spear and kneels down, waiting to watch who will come out of this alive.

The animals stare at one another once more, snarling, and suddenly they lunge at each other. Their growls echo through the night as they fight one another. In the forest, the others hear the growling. They run toward the meadow, and crouch behind some trees to witness the fight for themselves.

Moments later, Amak is showing signs of tiring and begins slipping underfoot. The hyena sees her chance and moves back, causing Amak to fall from exhaustion as the others watch, helpless. The matriarch stands over Amak as he struggles to get up. She lowers her body over him but Khi'da pounds his spear on the ground to distract her. She looks up and growls when she spots him and then suddenly leaves Amak alone and runs toward him. As she gets close enough, she lunges at him. Khi'da closes his eyes to meet his fate but instantly, an arrow whizzes past him and strikes the hyena right in the eye.

All is silent. Khi'da, breathing heavily, opens his eyes and looks down. It shocks him when he sees the hyena's lifeless body lying there with an arrow pierced through her eye. He gets up and looks around to find where the arrow came from. He glances toward the forest and grins when he sees the others running out of the forest, shouting. The hyenas sense they have lost this battle, turn around and run away before the other men arrive. The wolves, along with Khi'da, howl with joy as the hyenas continue to retreat into the distance.

The lead hunter and the other men run to their leader and celebrate with him. Khi'da gives the hunter a pat on the shoulder, happy to see him.

"Am I ever glad to see you, my old friend. If it were not for you, I would have joined our ancestors in the sky-world above," he says, with a smile on his face.

"I am only looking out for my leader, like you have always done for us. It is now our turn to repay you for all your sacrifices," the hunter announces with pride. Khi'da looks at Amak, nods and smiles at him, before he and the others walk back to their camp.

"It looks like Kho'ta was right about them. Those wolves saved us all this night," the leader states with relief, while the hunter nods in agreement with him.

Meanwhile, the remaining people, still hiding in their tents, worry when they hear nothing. Kara brings Kho'ta closer and clings to him, sensing the worst is yet to come when she hears noise coming from outside. She peeps outside to see what is making the noise and shouts with joy when she realises it is Khi'da and the others walking into the camp. The other camp dwellers breathe a sigh of relief from inside their tents. Kara does not hesitate and runs out to give her husband a hug.

"I am so glad to see you back safe! I thought you would never return. I was so scared," she says tearfully, while Khi'da looks down at her.

"I made it back like I promised, and I brought back some good news," he said.

"What?" she asks.

"Go sit by the fire and I will tell you," he says joyfully, as he heads over to the fire. Everyone leaves their tents and they all sit by the fire to hear what Khi'da has to say, while he looks at them with a smile. "The battle tonight was the toughest battle I have ever fought. Our enemy was far stronger, but I am here sitting before all of you to say that the worst is over and the hyenas, the very creatures who brought our nightmares to reality, are no more," he announces. He points toward the wolves. "If it were not for those wolves warning us, the hyenas would have ambushed us, and we would never have known of their presence until it was too late. So, from now on, if any of you even thinks about harming a single hair on those wolves' backs, you will have to answer to me," he says in earnest, while Kho'ta smiles.

Khi'da looks at him and calls him over as he stands up. Kho'ta gets up and walks over to his father. He stands by his side and Khi'da grabs his arm, raising it in the air.

"If it were not for my son here uniting us with those wolves, hatred would have still been eating me from the inside, and we would have been dead. He made me realize we could be allies and fight alongside the wolves, instead of against them, and that is why we came out victorious tonight!" Kho'ta looks up at Khi'da and he can see in his eyes that his father is proud of him, and he tears up. Khi'da once again looks over at everyone. "There is one more thing that I would like to announce tonight. From now on, when I am out hunting, I will leave my son in charge of what goes on in the tribe. Is that understood? If any of you has a problem with that, come tell it to my face."

Kho'ta looks over to his mother, amazed, while she smiles at him. Everyone else in the camp is quiet for a while until the lead hunter gets up and claps, followed by everyone else, as Kho'ta looks amazed. He raises his fist in the air and howls and everyone else does the same.

Over at the lair, the wolves hear them and howl along with them, filling the night sky so the world can know of their victory. Over by some trees, a shadowy figure walks by the lair as the wolves continue to howl in celebration, unaware of its presence.

CHAPTER 17

It has been four months since the bloody battle fought against the hyenas and it has been a while since one has been heard or seen since that night. With the hyenas now gone, the barren lands belong to the wolves and the people. The grass and flowers are growing once again. Instead of this part of Nuna being filled with death, it is now full of life once again. The songs of birds fill this part of Nuna with songs. The herbivores are also back; this time the live ones, instead of dead ones, like before.

Over at the lair, Nanook is sleeping in his den. He wakes up when he hears Amak calling him from outside. He walks out of his den and stretches, before looking over at his father.

"What is it? Why did you wake me so early? The sun itself isn't up yet..." he complains, sounding groggy before he lies back down. Amak does not tolerate his son's laziness and yells in his ear.

"Get up!" he shouts, causing Nanook to get on to his feet.

"Okay, okay — I am up," he says, startled, while Amak gives him a sarcastic grimace.

"Good. Come and follow me out to the meadow," he whispers, so not to wake any of the others.

"Why do I have to be the only one to be up while the others are still sleeping?" Nanook grumbles.

"Because I want only you to come out into the meadow with me. And keep it down or everyone else will wake up," Amak hisses. He walks out into the meadow while Nanook follows him, feeling a little sleepy.

"This had better be good," he mutters to himself before letting out a yawn. They cross the stream, which is now flowing calmly, unlike the last time they needed to cross it. They walk by their side of the meadow as Nanook looks on, wondering where Amak is taking him. They walk past the watering hole and a herd of horses, who become wary of them the moment they pass.

Amak then stops in the middle of a field of flowers and stares ahead as the breeze blows through his hair. Nanook stands by him and looks over to his father, baffled.

"Why did you bring me all the way out here and— where is here?" he asks, puzzled.

"You don't recognize where we are, Nanook?" Amak asks, while Nanook shakes his head, confused. "This is that same land we had to cross to get here, and where we had that encounter with the hyenas that almost destroyed our chance with our new life," he says, while Nanook stares at the horizon, amazed.

"This is the barren lands!" he says, sounding surprised. Amak looks at him with a smile on his face.

"Yes, it is, my son. And look how much it has changed in just four months. With the hyenas now gone, it is recovering back to its old self, as it once was," the alpha wolf states.

"It can't be. I thought the barren lands were supposed to be… well, barren. Isn't that why we called it that?"

"Yes. that's right. But it hasn't always looked that way. Yet this is not the reason we are here."

"Then why are we here?"

"We are out here so I can tell you the real reason I hated the people, originally" Amak says, while Nanook looks shocked

"I already know why, Father. The people caught you by surprise and got your entire family killed and that's why you ran away to the other side — to hide from them," Nanook responds, sounding surprised.

"Yes, that is correct, but there is more to that story than simply my family being killed. That's half of the story. There is more to it than you know," Amak says.

He then gets up and walks toward the pond and sits by the shore. Nanook sits next to him.

"So are you going to tell me what happened that made you hate the people so much? If you're still willing to talk about it?"

Amak replies, "I want to talk about it. Are you ready to hear the truth?" Nanook nods his head. "I thought you'd want to and so here I go." He takes a deep breath followed by a depressed sigh. "Long before the people arrived here, there were wolves at every corner of the land. We had everything we needed: water, food, and shelter. The hyenas had their own side, but it was not like ours, and so jealously, they tried to get rid of us and take it for themselves. Hyenas are just too lazy to get their own things and instead, they take from others." He is about to continue but Nanook interrupts.

"So, how did the hyenas end up on this part of the land and why weren't they stopped since there were wolves living at every corner?"

"We did whatever we could to stop them. Every time they trespassed on our land, we had always outnumbered them, but then the people arrived and drove the packs away, so the hyenas took that to their advantage and moved right in. First it was the mountains, then the wetlands, then the meadow, and all they needed to claim Nuna for themselves was the forest, but they still had one obstacle between them and their prize. My father — your grandfather — was not going down without a fight. Every time the hyenas attempted to take away his territory, he fought with all his might. He risked his life fighting off the hyenas and he led the remaining packs that were left to fight them off, but the hyenas just got stronger, and it looked like they would not go down easy. To show that they would not give up, they destroyed everything. They drove and killed anything that moved — herbivore or carnivore — to convince my father to leave. They even drove away the herds, our very food, but despite all that, it still did not faze him and that made the hyenas want it more.

My father knew he would not win in the face of such a threat, so he produced the only solution and that would be to challenge their leader, thinking that it would cause them to leave our land. He knew it was risky and it could cost him his life, but he proceeded anyway. He headed toward their territory, alone at night, to confront them. He stood there and called out their leader to challenge him and she accepted, feeling confident that she would win, but she thought wrong. My father killed her, but instead of bringing peace to the land, it got worse. Her daughter avenged her death and continued on with her legacy. Her quest for revenge brought them to us. They thought they had overpowered us when they confronted us, out in the meadow, but they thought wrong," he says, while looking straight ahead, as a mammoth passes by.

Nanook looks astounded by the story. "Now it all makes sense why you hated the people so much. Not just because they ambushed and got your family killed, but if they hadn't driven away the wolves from the land in the first place, the hyenas would never have attempted to take over the land and they would have left you all alone."

"Yes. That is correct, Nanook. Although the people ambushing us had something to do with why I hated them, that is not the actual reason I acted that way toward you when you tried to unite us. It was because I was being consumed so much by my hatred toward them for weakening us and making our enemy far stronger. If it were not for them driving away all wolves, we would have won much sooner. But I also made a mistake of my own and that was by running away. And because of that cowardly act, the hyenas thought they had won, since the last of my father's bloodline had run off."

"But you had no choice but to run away!" says Nanook.

"Yes, that is true. But if I remained here, instead of running away, the hyenas wouldn't have taken over; but because I did, they claimed this part of Nuna for themselves since no wolf was around to fight them off." He pauses for a moment. "I remained hidden all these years in the forest, far from the meadow, so they would continue to think I was dead so that I could keep all of you safe from them. But since that encounter in the cave, I had to expose myself to save you. That night, they discovered I was not dead at all. So, their quest for vengeance pushed on, and from the looks of it, they would not have stopped until they had us all killed," Amak says, with a sigh.

"That explains why they wanted to kill every single one of us out in the meadow that night. It was all an attempt to get rid of grandfather's bloodline, because the matriarch hyena knew we could be the only ones to bring her to her knees. And if she got rid of us, there would be no other wolf strong enough to stop her, and this whole land would have belonged to hyenas." Nanook was working all this out in his head as he spoke.

"Yes, but that night, four months ago, proved otherwise and they did not stand a chance because we have gotten much stronger over the years. And we have another powerful ally and that was their downfall. That's why I am certain they will not bother us again," Amak says with confidence.

"How sure are you about that?" Nanook asks, feeling uneasy.

"I am very sure. Since their leader is dead, they have no other leader to motivate them and because they are the ones who are now powerless, they will think twice about setting foot here again." He stares at Nanook with a smirk.

Nanook looks at his father as though he is understanding him better, now that he knows what he has gone through before.

Amak then gets up and walks past Nanook. "We had better hurry and get back before the others wake up. Your mother will worry when she does not find us there." They walk back and before they enter the forest that leads back to the lair, Amak stops and faces Nanook. "Do me this favor: let us not talk about this to anyone. It stays between me and you — you promise. Your mother does not want to hear about it any more. The experience was bad enough for her and it traumatized her."

Nanook's face is serious. He nods to agree with his father.

Meanwhile, over at the people's camp, Kho'ta is asleep. He wakes up when he hears walking near his tent. He turns around, and it startles him when he sees the shape of a figure standing outside. He pulls out his dagger and points it toward the entrance, as the flap opens. It is Khi'da, his father who shows up, and he is is shocked to see a dagger just inches from his face.

"Kho'ta — what are doing pointing that knife in my face?" he utters, sounding terrified. He moves it away from his face as a frightened Kho'ta stares at him.

"It is all right, son. It's only me," Khi'da says, to calm him down. Kho'ta feels relief as he puts the dagger away.

"It is not every day I have someone walking outside my tent this early in the morning," the young man breathes out.

Khi'da grins as he rubs the back of his head. "Sorry about that. I did not mean to scare you."

"Next time, if you want to see me, just call out my name. It's not that hard," Kho'ta complains.

"I just came to tell you to come with me. Take your bow and your spear and walk with me to the meadow," Khi'da says.

Confused, Kho'ta quickly gets dressed, places the bow and arrows over his shoulders, and steps out of his tent. He takes hold of his spear, which he had leaned beside his tent, and walks over to Khi'da, who is waiting for him by the forest. They step out into the meadow, spotting an antelope grazing nearby.

Kho'ta pulls out his bow and aims an arrow at the antelope, but is confused when Khi'da reaches out and lowers the bow, shaking his head as he looks at his son.

"I did not bring you out here to hunt," he says.

"Then what did you bring me out here for?"

"There is something I need to talk to you about."

"If we are here so you can talk to me, why did you tell me to bring my spear and bow?" Kho'ta says, sounding annoyed.

"Just in case your mother woke up. She would not let me take you out into the meadow if we were just going to talk," he says, while Kho'ta continues to look at him, annoyed.

"Whatever it is you want to tell me better be important," he mutters.

"What I want to say is important. I feel you are ready to know why I hated the wolves so much for all these years," Khi'da says. They walk toward a boulder, and they sit on it.

"So, what made you hate them so much in the first place?" asks Kho'ta.

"A long time ago, when my father was a teenager, his tribe settled on this land and called it their forever home. They had everything they ever needed. A pond where they could fish and have fresh water, when needed, and plenty of game to hunt. His father thought this land was perfect, but they thought wrong. The wolves had already claimed the land, and they wanted us out. One night, as we were bedding down, they ambushed us and dragged my grandfather outside and had him surrounded. He tried to escape, but they stopped him. As he just sat there, helpless, their alpha walked up to him and delivered the first bite and that is when the others joined in. My father just watched from inside the cave as they mauled his father.

"When your grandfather was about my age, a wolf appeared before him. My father and the rest of the men did not hesitate and chased it into the forest. The wolf led them straight to its lair and they killed off every single one of them, except for three. They had escaped. So, believing that they had left for good, we went back to our lives again.

"Many years passed, and we had seen no trace of them. I took over my father's place as the new leader of the tribe and I promised that I would continue what he started. I became the father of a beautiful baby boy who I thought would lead this tribe to greatness, and I was right. It was not the way I expected, but you have still brought greatness to our tribe by uniting us with the wolves. I could not have been any prouder, and that is why I am also here to apologize for being so harsh to you, at first, when you were trying to bring us together. Can you ever forgive me, my son?"

Kho'ta nods, smiling. "I forgive you, Father, and now, after hearing the entire story, I understand why you hated them so much. I also felt hate toward them when they killed Attah, and I know how that feels," he says.

Khi'da smiles as he rubs the back of his head before he continues. "My hatred consumed me from the inside and I found it hard to see for myself that you were right all along. Our kind walked into the wolves' home and drove them away and took their food from them, feeling no remorse. When they did the same to us, we thought of them as murderous demons. They could have thought the same way about us when we stole the land from them," he says, now feeling remorseful.

"What made you see they are not evil, like you always thought?" Kho'ta asks.

"That very night, when they got you out of the fire. Instead of leaving you there, they stayed by your side until I arrived and that was I when I realized that they were not the demons I once thought they were. And then there was that battle with the hyenas. We fought them together like a team. If we'd had to fight them off ourselves, we would have been no match for them, and they would have killed us. But together we won and got rid of that menace forever," Khi'da says with pride.

He stands up when he hears his wife calling and looks across at Kho'ta. "Seems like they are awake. I just heard your mother calling. How about we go back home?" he smiles.

They walk together back into their village. As they walk by the wolf lair, Khi'da notices Amak staring at him and gives him a nod before walking over to his wife, who welcomes them with open arms.

It is now night. Over at the lair, Amak is sound asleep, along with the others. He wakes up when hears something walk by. He gets up, noticing movement behind some trees.

He walks behind Sakkara's den and snarls when he notices a figure standing there. It looks at him before it runs off, waking Nanook up. The young wolf feels concerned when he notices his father standing by the forest, staring straight ahead as though he is in some kind of trance. He gets up and walks over to him. He then stands by him and stares ahead, as well, but feels uneasy when he sees nothing.

"What do you see, Father?" he asks.

"I woke up to the sound of something walking by and when I looked, I swear I saw this figure staring straight at me near those trees, in that direction, but when I came to see what it was, it just vanished," he says, sounding concerned.

"Maybe it could be the people out on patrol or going for a drink over by the river," Nanook says, sounding assured.

Amak does not agree. "No, it's not the people; I am sure of it. They are all sleeping. Not one is out except for their guard, and why would they come out into the forest in the middle of the night just for a drink? Besides, it looked like it was walking on all fours, not on two legs like they do," Amak whispers, while Nanook stares skeptically.

"I have an idea that I know will make you see for yourself that you are only imagining things. In the morning we will both scout the forest and look for any signs of that 'mysterious figure' that you say you saw walking around tonight, but I assure you it is only your mind fooling you and tomorrow I will prove that to you" he says.

Amak agrees with him and goes back to lying down next to Sakkara and the pups, while Nanook walks over to his den. Before he goes in, he looks toward the forest when he, too, hears rustling among the leaf litter. He shrugs it off when he thinks it could just be the wind. "Now I am the one going crazy," he mutters to himself, before he goes back inside his den for the night.

Meanwhile, over at the people's camp, the sentry is guarding the area as the others sleep. He is busy carving a new spear out of a branch. He turns around when he hears movement from behind him. He picks up his spear, gets up, and stares beyond the trees to try and work out where the noise is coming from. He then readies his spear when he hears something running toward him, but he brings it down when he realizes it is just a rabbit bounding across. He nervously laughs as he sits back down and continues to carve at the branch. He does not see a large shadow standing over him, and before he can scream, he gets dragged into the forest by a mysterious figure.

Khi'da emerges from his tent when he hears a noise from outside. The lead hunter also rushes out of his tent. He goes over to Khi'da feeling concerned for him when he sees his friend just staring out into the forest in the middle of the night.

"What's wrong?"

"I thought I heard something, and I came out to see what it was."

The lead hunter stands by him and looks toward the forest. "I see nothing. Are you sure that you aren't just hearing things? Go back to sleep. It is late," the lead hunter whispers, patting him on the shoulder. Khi'da is about to go back into his tent when he notices that the guard is not at his post.

"Do you know where the guard went?" he asks but the lead hunter just shrugs his shoulders and lets out a sarcastic chuckle.

"He went to relieve himself. He will be back soon enough. Don't worry," he says to reassure the leader before he crawls into his tent. Khi'da is also just about to re-enter his tent, when he hears growling coming from the forest and worries that there is something out there.

Early the next morning, Amak and Nanook are scouting the forest. They are looking for any signs left by the mysterious figure Amak claims has been prowling around the lair for the past night. Amak runs over to two trees, convinced they are the ones where the figure stopped to stare at him before it vanished. He circles around the trees to find any clues, but he finds nothing, while Nanook just sits behind him.

"Like I told you before, you were only imagining things."

"I swear it was right here near these trees where I saw it looking straight at me. I am not making anything up. Let's keep on looking; I know we will find something if we look harder," Amak says, while Nanook rolls his eyes, walking up to him.

"If there was anything here, it would have left footprints, but I don't see any. So, there is no way that there was anyone out here in the middle of the night. Stop being stubborn and just admit it, you are just seeing things!"

Amak still believes otherwise. "There is something out here: I just know it. We are not looking hard enough. These are the wrong trees. Let's go over to those that have bark peeling off. We'll find something there — at least a print or two — just so I can prove to you I'm right."

He hurries over to the trees while Nanook rolls his eyes and sighs as he follows him. They are looking around the trees. Amak calls Nanook to come over when he spots some paw prints covered by dead leaves.

"Nanook, quick — get over here!" Nanook hurries over to him and is surprised when he looks down and sees the paw print. "This must be the paw print that belongs to our 'ghost'."

Nanook crouches down to get a closer look and does not look pleased when he notices something familiar in this print. "Father, look at it."

Amak looks at the imprint and notices it has several broken claws. "It can't be… There's only one wolf on this whole earth with broken claws like that," Amak gasps.

"So, what you are saying is that the ghostly figure you saw last night could be—" Nanook gets interrupted by Amak.

"Yes, it could be Lukka. Who else would it be?"

"What does he want with us?"

"He wants nothing to do with you."

"So, if he wants nothing to do with us, why doesn't he just leave us alone?"

"That's because he is coming after me," Amak declares. "He's calling me out for a challenge. He wants to finish what he started: to challenge me to a fight to claim this land. It was his plan all these years ago and he will not stop until he gets what he wants."

"But that means if you lose, you will get kicked out of the land. He will take over the pack and rule it in your place. I hope you're not thinking of challenging him?" Nanook says.

"It's the only way to get him off this land and leave us alone for good. I have to do it if we are to be safe," Amak says.

"But in order for him to leave us alone, you have to win," Nanook warns his father. "If you lose, you are going to be the one leaving, and he stays. It is too much of a risk to take. I will not let you go on with this."

"I will not lose. Never did; never will. I have faced bigger challenges than him: the cave lion, the hyenas, and the people, and I always came up victorious. He will be no different," Amak says confidently. They walk back to the lair. Nanook, feeling uneasy about his father's decision, looks over at him.

"So, what's your plan?" he asks, concerned.

"I'll stay up and wait for him, in case he comes tonight, and face him.

I knew it would have to come to this, one way or another. If it is a fight he wants, it's a fight he will get, and believe me, I will not go down easily," Amak says.

"And neither will he," Nanook interrupts his father. "He will be the toughest challenge you will have to face, and you are not as young as you used to be, and that worries me"

"I got this. I still got some fight left in these old bones. There is nothing for you to worry about. I will be fine," Amak replies with confidence. They arrive at the lair and before Amak walks over to Sakkara, he looks over at a worried Nanook. "I understand you want to help me. I'm grateful for that, but you have to promise me you will not interfere. This is between me and him only and it does not concern you."

He walks away toward the others while Nanook just looks at him, worried, before he joins his family to eat.

Meanwhile, over by the people's camp, Khi'da is the first to emerge from his tent. He gives a stretch after a long night and walks to the rock the guard was last sitting on while watching over the camp and smiles when he doesn't see him there. He walks over to the guard's tent to check if he is asleep, but is shocked when he finds the tent empty. Worried, he rushes over to the lead hunter's tent and wakes him up.

"Dress and come out here quickly" he says, sounding nervous, which makes the lead hunter concerned. He gets up and puts on his clothing, then rushes over to Khi'da who is standing near the boulder, staring out into the forest.

"What's the matter?"

"The guard hasn't come back yet. That bladder of his must have been full for him to be away this long," Khi'da says, before walking over to take hold of his spear.

"Maybe he is in his tent, asleep already. If that were me and I stayed up all night, that's what I would have done," the hunter volunteers.

Khi'da hands him his spear, shaking his head as he walks past him. "He is not there. I already checked."

"Where are you going? It's early to go out hunting. I haven't eaten yet!" the lead hunter calls out when he sees Khi'da walking into the forest.

"We are not going hunting. We are going to search for that poor man.

I just hope he is all right and nothing has happened to him," he says, concerned. The lead hunter lays his spear on his shoulder and follows him into the forest to help search. They call out, hoping that if he is anywhere nearby, he will answer, but after many attempts they give up when they get no response. They stand side by side as they scan the entire forest.

"It is not like him to just leave without telling us," says Khi'da.

"Maybe he got lost, and he is waiting somewhere until someone finds him," says the lead hunter.

"I sure hope you are right about this, and it's not anything worse," he replies, worried. "This is enough standing around. We have to look around for any signs of where he could be."

The lead hunter agrees, but they do not have to go far for their first clue. It was one that none of them would want to find: they spot a fern that has blood splatter on it and then they see a trail of blood leading away from it. They follow the trail, and it leads them to a large bush and as they get near, they smell the odour of rotting meat, which causes the lead hunter to throw up.

Khi'da moves some leaves away with his spear and panics when he sees the half-eaten remains of the guard. He runs out of there in such a panic that he trips over a rock near him. As he gets up, he spots a wolf print right in front of him, making him angry.

"I knew we could never trust them," he mutters, as he gets up. The lead hunter walks over to him and spots the track and looks over to him, surprised.

"You don't think it was the wolves that did this?" he says, when he sees the look on Khi'da's face as he stares straight at their lair.

"They will pay for this. After I risked my life by helping them fight off those hyenas, this is how they repay me — by killing one of us!" he shouts out with fury.

"Maybe it's a rogue that did this. There's no way it could have been any of those wolves. They have not attacked us since we got here," the hunter says, trying to reassure Khi'da, who looks over at him with an icy stare.

"That's what they want us to think. Get the body and bring it back to camp. We will give our comrade a proper burial after I deal with our neighbours," he spits out.

"What are you going to do to them?" he asks.

"Something I should have done a long time ago," he says, running over to the camp. Once he arrives, he does not even look at the others as he continues to stride toward the wolves' lair. Kho'ta wonders what has gotten into him and runs over to him.

"What's the matter, Father?"

"Your wolves killed our guard last night," his father mutters, but Kho'ta does not want to believe it.

"What proof do you have that it was them?"

"I have seen one of their tracks by the site where I found our guard's half-eaten remains," Khi'da insists. "I am going to wipe them out and rid this land of them if it is the last thing I do." Kho'ta tugs at the sleeve of his shirt, but his father pulls it away. "You will not stop me. I had enough of your foolishness. They will never bond with us. They are animals. We can't ever trust them."

As he is about to step over to the wolves' lair, he hears the lead hunter calling out to him. The hunter approaches Khi'da, and as he catches his breath, he explains what he has discovered. "It was no wolf that killed him, but something much worse. Come with me and I will show you," he urges. Khi'da calms down and lowers his spear, much to Kho'ta's relief, and follows the lead hunter to the forest.

They stand over the body and while plugging their noses, the hunter removes pieces of clothing away from the guard's torso to reveal some huge claw marks spread across the chest, much to Khi'da's dismay.

"There's no way a wolf could cause such a wound this size," says the hunter. "Then as I stepped inside the shrub, I spotted some prints near the body, and I think they might belong to …" he gulps, "…a bear. And a big one from the size of these prints."

Khi'da feels nervous as he scans the forest, to check if the bear is still nearby. "We will take the body and bury it far from the camp so the bear will not find us."

They each grab the body by both arms and drag it away. Later, the entire tribe gathers around the grave with their heads lowered before they walk back to the camp. Kho'ta stays behind with Khi'da.

"If it were not for the hunter showing me what killed our guard," murmurs Khi'da, "I would have done something dumb and broken our bond with the wolves. I am sorry, my son, for letting revenge get to me once again," he says with regret.

"It's all right, Father. I forgive you. Besides, I knew it could not have been them. They would have eaten the whole body, bones and all, and leave nothing behind."

"You sure know more about them than I do," Khi'da admits with pride.

"That's because I did not let old tales get to my head. I got to understand them and learned to respect them, instead. That's why I am never afraid of them," Kho'ta responds, while his father lowers his head and nods as they walk into the camp.

It is now night, and it is foggy. In the wolves' lair, Amak and the others are fast asleep. Amak wakes up when he hears the rustling of leaves coming from the forest behind him. He spots something move past the trees, and believing that it might be Lukka, he walks over to the forest to follow him. He sneaks past the others so he will not wake them up, but Nanook hears him and follows him.

Once inside the forest, Amak looks for the figure but is startled when he hears a noise coming from behind him. He looks back, thinking that it might be Lukka sneaking up on him, but is greatly relieved when he realizes it is Nanook walking out of the fog. Amak walks over to him, not happy that he has followed him.

"I thought I told you not to interfere," he states, but Nanook is not fazed.

"I came to help. We all did."

Amak looks past him, and is surprised when he sees the others walk out of the fog and stand next to Nanook. He just stares at them, unimpressed.

"I told you I can do this on my own. I do not need any of your help!" he cries out.

"But we want to help. We are a family, and we always stick together," Nanook says.

Sakkara walks over to Amak, worried. "You are not young like you used to be. Who knows what tricks he might have?" she says.

"I know Lukka only too well. I know all his tricks and besides, I've got my set of tricks, as well," he retorts.

"He is very experienced now," Sakkara reminds him. "He has lived on his own his whole life. Who knows what else he has planned? This is the toughest challenge you will face, and I worry for you."

Amak looks away. "I can fight my own battles. I do not need any of you to tell me otherwise, and for once, you need to stop worrying," he replies, while Sakkara looks astonished. "I am going now, and I'd better not see any of you behind me. Do I make myself clear?" he demands harshly, before he turns around and runs out into the dark.

The rest of the wolves turn around to head back to the lair, except for Nanook. He runs to catch up with his father while Sakkara calls out to him, concerned.

"Nanook — it is better that you stay."

"And just sit around and do nothing as he suffers out there? I am not going to do that. I am going to help if he likes it or not. You can come, too: the choice is yours. But remember, he has sacrificed his life for all of us. I think it is time we all do the same for him," he states, as he runs after Amak.

Sakkara sits back and watches as he disappears into the fog, while Alornek stands next to her.

"What do you want us to do?" he asks, while she looks over at him.

"I will tell you what we are going to do and that's not stand around here," she says, as she runs out into the fog with the others following close behind.

Deep in the forest, Amak slows down once he has found himself away from the others. He looks back once more to make sure they have not followed him, before he continues to stroll through the misty night. He stops when he spots a figure standing in the middle of a clearing, looking straight at him without a single blink of its eyes. Amak lowers his body and snarls when he believes it could be Lukka.

"What do you what from me? Show yourself, you coward!" he cries out in an intimidating tone, but instead of answering, the figure just walks toward him. Amak feels nervous but still stands his ground fearlessly as the figure approaches him. He calms down when he recognizes the figure is his brother, Tiyani.

"Coward? That is no way to address your brother," Tiyani says, as he circles around Amak with a smirk on his face.

"What are you doing here, brother?" Amak asks, surprised.

"That's funny. That's the same question I am here to ask you."

"What I am doing here is nothing important," Amak says, while Tiyani lets out a giggle.

"So, you just going out for a walk in the forest in the middle of the night," he smiles, while Amak looks away, not saying nothing. "If you will not say what is going on, then I will. You are here to meet Lukka, so you can settle the score with him, am I right, my brother?" he whispers to Amak's ear.

Amak shoves his brother away from him and walks away. "I said this does not concern you" he mutters, but before he can get any further, Tiyani is already there, waiting for him. "Will you knock it off!" he yells.

"I will 'knock it off' if you tell me I am right about you confronting Lukka."

"Yes, you are! There — are you happy now? Now go away and leave me be," he states.

"I think you are going the wrong way. Isn't your lair that way?" Tiyani says.

Amak stops. "I am not going back. You don't understand: I need to do this," but Tiyani does not approve.

"There is no way that I will let you go through with this foolishness," he says, concerned.

"And how will you do that?"

"I am not the one who is going to stop you. I have someone else here with me who will," he says.

"So, show me who else is here and make it quick."

"Look behind you and find out for yourself," Tiyani states.

Amak turns around. A glowing light appears before him and he stares, astonished, when he sees a wolflike figure appear before him. He cannot believe his eyes that he is staring at his own father, lost long ago.

"My son — look at how much you have grown and the proud alpha you have become," he announces with pride.

"Father… Is that you?" Amak murmurs, choking up.

"Yes, it's me, my son, and I am here to tell you that what you are doing is wrong. You are risking your own life if you continue with this."

"Then tell me why I shouldn't, Father, after what that traitor has done to me — and to you!" he cries out, trying to hold back tears.

"I know what he did was wrong, even after we had welcomed him into our pack. But that is the past and you need to forget about it and look forward into your future," Amak's father says.

"I have to do this, Father, whether you like it or not. My future does not matter, but my family's future does," Amak says, while his father looks down at him.

"Why are you so stubborn? Lukka has grown a lot stronger since you ran away from here. He knows this part of the land more than you do. I am sure he will kill you, and your family will not have a future without their alpha."

Amak continues to ignore his warning. "But I must, and you will not stop me. My family could not stop me, and I will not let two ghosts do that, either. Now leave me alone."

He runs away while his father looks on. He looks over at Tiyani with sadness in his eyes, before vanishing back into the sky world. Amak stops by some trees to catch his breath. Tiyani startles him when he appears before him once again.

"How many times do I have to tell you to leave me?" Amak cries out.

"I just came here to tell you I am leaving, since you do not need my help."

As he is about to head back to the sky world and join the others, Amak stops him. "I remember our last encounter before I left the old lair. You sounded like you tried to warn me about something that day and that's what made me realize you knew about Lukka. Why didn't you warn me then?" he asks.

"I thought you would have found out yourself eventually, but it seems you have found out much sooner than expected," Tiyani utters, while Amak looks annoyed.

"Thanks for letting me know and if you had warned me sooner, I would have been ready for him when he showed up."

"I was thinking of warning you, but I thought it would be best I did not," Tiyani says, as he starts to fade away.

"Why not?" asks Amak.

"Because I knew you would not listen… Goodbye," Tiyani says, before disappearing once again.

"Goodbye and good riddance!" Amak shouts out, while looking up at the sky. He then turns swiftly when he hears the snapping of twigs close by. When he notices his family is standing there, he feels some relief. He walks up to them, smiling, and begins rubbing noses with Sakkara. "Let's go home. I have decided not to go on with this any more. Besides, it looks like he is not showing up, like the coward that he is."

Sakkara stares at him with a smile on her face. "I am glad you did," she said.

As they are walking back to the lair, Sakkara notices, the worried look on Amak's face.

"You look troubled," she says. "I am just thinking of the outcome had I not changed my mind about challenging Lukka to a fight," he says, concerned.

"What made you change your mind? When you left us earlier it looked like you had no plans to turn back on the challenge," she says.

"I had very helpful guidance," he says, looking up at the sky, while Sakkara smiles.

"Whoever gave you that guidance, I am glad you listened."

Amak stops when he spots some movement coming from his right.

"What's the matter?" asks Sakkara.

"I thought I just saw something move across those trees."

They both look straight ahead when they spot something move right in front of them. They all stand in the middle of the forest as the mysterious figure continues running around them; appearing and disappearing several times.

"What do you think it could be?" Nanook asks.

"I am not sure, but whatever it is must be fast to be in every direction at once," Amak states.

The figure stops immediately when it spots them all staring at it. Amak stares back and stands his ground, along with the others. The figure walks toward them and as it steps out of the mist Amak snarls.

The figure is Lukka. He stops a few feet from Amak and stares at the pack with a smirk on his face.

"Well, well, what do we have here? And it looks like you have the whole family with you. No surprise," he mocks.

Amak continues to look down at him, while still growling. "What do you want, Lukka?" he says, aloud.

"I just wanted to check up on an old friend and finish what I started," he states, lowering his body and preparing himself for the challenge.

"Well, Amak — what do you say? Let us settle this, once and for all, and the winner will control this land. Of course, we all know who that will be and if you're thinking it will be you, that is where you are wrong, my friend," he snarls.

"You are the one that's wrong," Amak responds. "You see, I have already won and that's because you are outnumbered eight to one. You will not stand a chance with all of us. This challenge will be over before it even starts, so it is best that you turn around and go back to where you came from."

The other wolves stare straight at him, but Lukka is not fazed. "Typical of you, always hiding behind your family and never facing your problems on your own. Again, you are wrong because you see I am not here alone. I've got a pack, as well," he says.

Amak does not believe him. "Oh, really? Then why are they not here?"

"They are here," he retorts. Seven other wolves appear from out of the mist and walk past Amak without looking at him. They stand in front of the family, to keep them from helping him, while Lukka takes on a sinister grin.

"Now it looks like we are both alone," he hisses. "Are you still feeling confident, now that you don't have your family to help you? So how about it? Are you ready to lose everything that your father risked his life for?"

The two wolves both rush at each other. Just as Lukka is about to tackle Amak, the alpha dodges him and bites his back leg, causing Lukka to fall hard on the ground. He gets up once again and attempts to tackle Amak, and this time, he succeeds. The painful cries fill the night sky as Amak tumbles to the ground while the others watch, helplessly. He struggles to get up. Nanook tries to get past one of Lukka's pack members, but she stops him with a glare as she growls.

"Please… you have to let me help him. He could be injured," Nanook pleads, but she refuses to give way as he watches his father on the ground, looking helpless. Lukka notices they are all eager to help and he grins as he steps over Amak and lowers himself down to his ear.

"Look at you, just lying there. You are nothing without your family. They are always there to help you, whenever you need them, and now here you are in trouble again and this time, they cannot do anything. Now, it's time I end you once and for all and take this land for myself."

He crouches down and just as he is about to kill Amak, an arrow zips past him and strikes a tree. He looks up and around, wondering where the arrow came from. More arrows crash down on them, striking two of the wolves and making the others run off. Denali and Alornek chase after them, while Miki, Ila and Nanook rush over to Amak and help him up.

Outnumbered again, Lukka runs away, as well, but stops and looks back at Amak, who stares at him with a grin on his face.

"A lot has changed since our last encounter, Lukka. My pack grew bigger and stronger," he states. Kho'ta and Khi'da and the lead hunter walk out of the forest and ready their arrows. They set aim at Lukka as he stares, shocked to realise they have teamed up with the people. He snarls, staring at Amak once more.

"You may have gotten stronger now but just like all of us, you have a weakness and I will find it. And when I do, I promise you our next encounter will be different, and you had better be ready."

"I will always be ready," Amak says, with the other wolves in his family and the people standing by his side. Lukka runs away into the forest to catch up with his pack, while Amak watches him disappear into the darkness.

As they head back to the lair, Nanook stops when he hears whimpering coming from the forest. He walks toward the noise, and it surprises him when he spots one of Lukka's pack members lying on the ground with an arrow stuck to its thigh. He walks up to it, and as he lowers himself down to pull the arrow out, he realizes that this is the same female wolf that didn't let him help his father, even after he had begged her to let him go.

He gets up and walks away, but feels ashamed when he hears the agonizing cries coming from the wolf. He feels hesitant about going over to help, but he turns around. He pulls out the arrow, and the wolf lets out an agonizing yelp. Nanook picks her up and lays her across his back and carries her back to the lair.

Once he arrives at the lair, the others are shocked when they see Nanook bringing back a member of Lukka's pack. Amak immediately disapproves and stands in Nanook's way.

"Do not even dare think about walking in here with that traitor's supporter!"

Nanook does not agree. "She needs our help. Can't you see she's injured?"

Amak stares at him, astounded. "She does not deserve our help. If that traitor cares so much about her, he will come back. If I were you, I would have just left her there to die."

"But I am not you. I will help her, even without your aid," Nanook says.

Amak will not tolerate it and snarls, "Take her back to where you got her, right now. We welcome no outsiders into this pack."

"What about when you welcomed Lukka into the pack? Was he not an outsider?"

"That was before I knew the traitor he is now, and you know nothing about her," Amak retorts.

"I will once I help her get better, so please, Father — trust me and let me do what needs to be done," Nanook pleads.

Amak lets out a sigh. "Fine, she can stay but once she gets better, she will have to go," he says, ungraciously. Nanook smiles, nodding to show his gratitude, and places the wolf near his den, then begins licking her wound to stop the bleeding.

CHAPTER 18

Three months have passed since Lukka last stepped off the land. The pack is now more at peace with the people. Amak is trusting them, too, since they saved him from Lukka. Over by the den, the she-wolf is still lying by Nanook's den, looking like she has still not recovered. She then raises her head, begins looking around and gets up when she does not find anyone.

Then she shouts out, "Ready or not, I will come find you!" She looks all over the lair. She sticks her head inside every den but cannot find what she is looking for. She catches some movement coming from behind the boulder and sees a wagging tail and sneaks over to the boulder, pretending she has seen nothing.

"Wherever could you be?" she says. She tries not to make a sound but she hears laughing. She crouches down behind the boulder and yells. "This is where you are!" Three pups jump out of hiding and begin cheering, jumping up at her while she laughs as she rolls over on her back. She has recovered after all. She is only playing a game with the pups, having been given the duty of babysitter, while the pack is out hunting.

"You are great at this game. You keep finding us all the time!" one pup says, cheekily.

"This was one of my favourite games when I was your age and besides, nothing can hide from this nose of mine," she laughs.

"Well, we had better look for better hiding places!" another pup giggles, as he gets up and begins looking around for likely spots. She is about to help but stops when she notices the others are back. She watches as everyone walks by her, ignoring her. Nanook sits by her side, and she looks at him, upset.

"I don't understand why they are still not talking to me."

Nanook smiles. "That is because you were fighting against us when we first met, and they are finding it hard to trust you."

"But why do you trust me?"

"Because I am the only one who knows you were just doing what he told you to do," Nanook says, as he walks away, then he stops and turns around to face her. "You never told me your name."

She looks away. "It is better not to tell you my name. I'm not sure I will stay here long enough for you to even remember what it is," she says, walking away. Nanook watches her, then lies down by the den, when he notices Amak staring at him, unimpressed.

Moments later, Amak calls Nanook and the she-wolf to come over to him. They sit down to face Amak and he looks over to Nanook.

"Did you forget your part of the deal when you first brought her over to us?"

Nanook looks at him with regret "No, I haven't, but I do not think it is fair. She was only doing what she was told, and she is not bad like Lukka is, as you can see for yourself."

The she-wolf looks confused. "What deal are you talking about?"

"I said that the moment you got better, you would have to leave right away," Amak reconfirmed.

She looks at Nanook, shocked. "Why did you never tell me this before?"

"I am sorry, but you must leave. I am also doing what I am told. He may be my father, but he is also alpha of this pack, and I must do what he says."

It shocks the she-wolf when she hears Nanook. The same gentle soul she was talking with earlier is acting in a new way toward her, but she obeys, anyway, and without looking at any of them, she immediately runs away into the forest.

Nanook watches, feeling regretful for what he has done. Amak stands by his side.

"That was part of the deal. It had to be done. We can't trust her," the alpha states.

"That is not fair. She has nowhere to go."

"She has Lukka to go back to," shouts Amak and walks over to the boulder to sit by it. Nanook goes to lie down by his den and Sakkara, who was nearby and heard the conversation, walks over to her son.

"You did the right thing. You do not even know her."

"But enough to know that she is not what she seems! I will bring her back, and if I get myself exiled from this pack. So be it," Nanook declares.

Months have passed since the she-wolf went away and Nanook has been going out to the meadow in secret to meet with her. Every morning, the others notice that he has been sleeping much longer than usual and Denali, along with Aurora, worry about him. They decide to find out what he's up to.

Night has come. Nanook is sneaking out of his den and as he is about to run off into the forest, he is surprised when he sees Denali and Aurora are already waiting for him there.

"Where are you going?" says Aurora, while Denali walks up to him with a smile on his face.

"I know where he is going. He is going to look for his girlfriend, isn't that right, Nanook?" he says, making smooching sounds. Aurora feels annoyed and pushes him aside. She stares at Nanook.

"I hope that's not true," she says, concerned, while Nanook looks away without saying anything. He then turns around and runs into the forest. "You know what Father will do if he finds out!" she cries, but he ignores her warning and vanishes into the darkness.

Waiting in the meadow, the she-wolf walks over to Nanook when she sees him. Nanook is glad to see her, but she is not as happy.

"What's the matter?" he asks, when he sees the sad look on her face.

"I don't think this is right. You should not be meeting me out here. You are at risk of getting exiled from your lair."

Nanook looks at her with a smile on his face because he knows they are not doing anything wrong.

"It is a risk I will take." They approach the waterhole and sit by the edge, and as they are looking up at the sky, Nanook asks her, "How did you end up meeting Lukka?"

She looks away. "He has been finding a lot of strays like me, ever since the people arrived and he welcomed us all to join him."

"And how long has this been going on?" Nanook asks, astonished.

"For quite some time; long before you arrived here. Why do you ask?" she says, sounding baffled.

"If he has been forming a pack all this time, that means he was never alone. He was only using it to trick my father into welcoming him back into our pack. What a coward… I am sorry to say this, but is there anything else I need to know?"

"Yes, there is. He also mentioned that when he and your father were young, they were out hunting when they got ambushed by the people. He said your father just ran off to save himself and left him alone to fend for himself."

"None of that is true. It was the other way around. He led the people to us, and he was the one that ran off. They killed his entire family, but he, my uncle and my mother were the only ones that survived."

Nanook turns around toward to the lair as the she-wolf looks at him. "Are you going in such a hurry that you can't even say goodbye?"

"I've just thought of a way that might just make my father think differently about you and welcome you back to the pack," he cries out as he begins to run.

He arrives at the lair but sees everyone is asleep, so he waits out until morning to break the news to them. He lies down by his den and smiles as he closes his eyes to sleep.

The sun rises over the land once again. Nanook is the first to wake up: he stands in the middle of the lair and calls out for everyone to wake up. "Everyone — please get up! I have some important news to announce!" Everyone gets up, and they are shocked to see he is the first to have risen. They all gather around him as he looks around, but he does not see Miki. He notices he is still lying down by his den, and he walks over to him. Miki is startled when he sees Nanook staring down at him, displeased. "I said I have important news to say. Are you hard of hearing?"

Miki gives out an enormous yawn and stretches, before walking over to the others. He sits down and stares at Nanook. "This had better be good."

Nanook looks around once more to make sure that everyone has gathered. He then sighs with guilt before he begins his speech.

"Every night I have been meeting with the she-wolf—"

"You have been meeting with her, even after I ordered you not to?" interrupts an angry Amak. "What are you thinking? She is the enemy. She could be just tricking you—"

"Just like you got tricked by Lukka," Nanook butts in.

Amak is about to walk over to confront him, but Sakkara stops him.

"Enough of this. You are acting just like Lukka, or worse. Just listen to what he has to say."

Amak stares angrily at Nanook, then walks away and lies down, far from them, so he will not have to listen to anything. Nanook looks over at him, disappointed, before he continues.

"Last night, she had told me that Lukka had a pack long before we got here. He was telling us he was alone, just so he could gain Father's trust. It was a plot all along, so he could get close to Father and then attack him when he least expected it. I am sure that he would have exiled us from this land, the second he got rid of Father, so his pack could take over instead and he would get all the credit for himself." Everyone looks shocked by the news. "She has also said that Lukka told them it was Father who had betrayed him and ran away to save himself. But we all know that is not true. He is as much of a liar to them as he was to all of us!"

He notices Amak listening to the news by the den and he walks over to him. He looks down at him with a smile. "If she was bad, like you say she is, she wouldn't have told me any of this."

Amak still does not agree with him. He gets up and stares directly at Nanook, while baring his teeth. "I still do not trust her and from now on, you will never sneak off at night to meet her." Amak walks by him without looking at him. He calls Alornek and Ila over. "Make sure that he does not sneak off any more. If he does, I give you the order to exile him." Amak walks away, leaving Alornek looking shocked.

It is now night and Nanook emerges from his den, and it shocks him when he notices his brothers standing right outside. He attempts to sneak past them, but they hear him and stop him.

"Come on, guys. You got to let me go," he pleads.

"I am sorry, Nanook, but Father told us to make sure you never sneak off again." Nanook sighs and walks over to his den to lie down while his brothers keep an eye on him. "And just so you know, in case you manage to sneak off in the middle of the night, Father also gave us the order to exile you, so I would think twice if I were you," Ila says, sarcastically. Nanook looks annoyed.

Meanwhile, out in the meadow, the she-wolf arrives and when she does not see Nanook she begins to believe that his plan did not work, and she sadly walks away.

It is now late fall, and the sun rises over land. It is quiet out in the meadow. The honking of migrating geese echoes throughout the land as they fly overhead. One goose suddenly falls toward the earth, followed by three more. Kho'ta and Khi'da are standing over the geese as they lie dead on the ground. They pick them up, pull out the arrows, placing them back over their backs, and walk back to the camp with their kill. They arrive and place the geese near the fire pit.

Khi'da places down his bow and arrows and as Kho'ta leaves his arrows near his tent, he looks up, noticing movement coming from the forest. Khi'da notices him staring ahead and walks up to him.

"Do you see something?" he asks, but Kho'ta just shakes his head.

"I thought I did, but I guess it must be nothing." He walks over to the fire and begins to pluck the feathers off the geese. Khi'da sits by him and helps.

Meanwhile, over at the lair, Amak is standing over Nanook as he sleeps. "Wake up, Nanook."

Nanook looks up at his father and gets up. "What is it now? You want to talk to me about how you're going to hold me prisoner in my own den?" he says, sarcastically.

"No, I do not want to talk about that. It is more about her. Come with me to the meadow, where we can talk in private," he says, as he walks toward the forest. Nanook follows him. They are out in the meadow, and Amak sits down by the waterhole, so he walks over to him. He sits by his father as he continues to stare out into the water.

"What do you want to talk about?"

"I want to talk to you about your friend."

"Why is that? You don't even trust her," Nanook replies.

"And that is the reason I brought you out here to talk. You need to be careful when you are around her."

"I understand, Father. You worry for me, but that is not a reason to hold me captive and threaten to get me exiled," Nanook states, sounding irritated

"It was very wrong of me to act that way, but I am only looking out for you."

"What for? There is nothing for you to worry about. I trust her and I know she trusts me," Nanook ripostes.

"You do not even know her."

"But that is not a reason for you to think that she will hurt me. If that was the case, she would have done that much sooner. During the three months she stayed with us, she could have harmed us at any time, but she did not. Besides, the pups love her. If they are okay with her, then tell me, why aren't you?" Nanook states.

"That's because she is with Lukka and that is what concerns me," Amak replies.

"She can change just like you have changed. Before, you hated the people and would stop at nothing to get rid of them. Now you live at peace with them. Don't you understand what I am getting at?"

"Yes, I do, but I still believe I need to keep an eye on her, just in case. Her head is filled with his lies and unless she shows me that she has changed, I will not fully trust her," Amak declares, as he walks away.

It is late in the afternoon. The people are now sitting by the fire eating the goose that Khi'da and Kho'ta brought over earlier in the morning. Kho'ta gets up and lies down in the shade of a tree after he finishes eating. Just as he is about to doze off, he turns when he hears falling branches coming from behind him. He gets up when he spots something move behind the trees. He picks up some rocks and throws them toward the trees, hoping to get something to come out of hiding, and it catches his father's attention. He and the other men sense that something is wrong, collect their spears and stand by his side.

"What is the matter, son?" asks Khi'da.

"I think I just saw something walk behind those trees ahead," Kho'ta says, nervously. Khi'da, with his spear in hand, walks toward the trees and he sees nothing. As he is about to walk back to the camp, he turns around when he hears what sounds like coughing coming from behind him. He crouches down when he sees four figures walking toward him and readies his bow and arrow. When he notices they are people, he lowers down the arrow and breathes a sigh of relief. He waves his arms to get their attention and they rush over to him.

Once they arrive, it shocks him to see their condition. "Who are you and where did you come from?" he asks.

"We are from the far east of here. We got attacked by something not from this earth," one man replies in a shaky voice.

"Attacked by what?" Khi'da asks with concern, but before he can receive a reply from him, the eldest member of the group passes out. Without hesitation, he picks up the old man and leads the others over to the camp and sits them by the fire. He gives each of them some goose and they eat. He and the lead hunter sit across from them and watch them.

"How long ago was it you got attacked?" Khi'da asks another of the men, but all he does is stare at him and say nothing. Another man, next to him, speaks on his behalf.

"It happened five nights ago and was so fast. It just appeared out of nowhere and caught us off guard. We had no chance against it. Fifteen of us escaped but as you can see, only four of us survived," he mutters weakly, while Kho'ta stares astonished.

"What happened to the other survivors?" asks the lead hunter.

"The rest got killed by that creature. It chased after us as we ran through the night and dragged us off, one by one," another, younger man replies.

"What creature?" Khi'da asks, sounding a little worried.

"A bear... but not just any bear. It had only one eye, and it had strength enough to break a man's back, and I believe it was hunting for sport. No bear could do that unless it is otherworldly. Please, you've got to help us," he pleads, trying to hold back tears.

Khi'da calls his son over. "Bring them over to our tent so they can rest. They look like they need it," he says. Kho'ta does as he is asked and leads them over to his tent so they can sleep.

Khi'da gets up and gathers the other men. "I think those men got attacked by the same bear that attacked our sentry that night he disappeared. That bear now has a taste for our flesh, so we have to be more vigilant and keep an eye out in case it comes back. And I am certain that it will," he says.

Meanwhile, over by the lair, Amak and Nanook are eavesdropping on the people when they hear a commotion coming from their side. They are standing by some shrubs near their camp, wondering what is going on.

"Something is not right over there. What do you think it could be?" Nanook asks.

"I do not know, but I know is that it can't be good," says Amak, sounding concerned. "And that means whatever it might be, we will have to prepare to step in. This is not like before, where we would have our own problems and they would have theirs. This is different now: anything that threatens them is also a threat to us and we need to be ready to step in when they need us," he says. Nanook looks over to their camp, worried.

"I have a bad feeling about this…"

"And so do I," Amak echoes, worried.

It is now night. A sentry hears noise coming from the forest. He readies his spear and searches for any signs of whatever might be prowling in the forest. He turns around when he notices a shadow being cast over him. He lets out a scream when a figure suddenly drags him away into the darkness, before anyone can hear him.

Meanwhile, by the fire, Khi'da and the lead hunter are sitting across from each other.

"Did you spot anything yet?" Khi'da asks.

"No, not yet. I have sentries keeping an eye out from every spot of the camp. If there is anything out there, I am sure they'll let us know. And let us not forget about the wolves. We will know something is close by when we hear growling coming from their side," he says, before taking a bite out of a goose leg.

Another sentry notices a broken spear by some shrubs and runs out into the forest. He sees some blood splatter on some rocks and spots bear prints leading out into the woods. He does not hesitate and runs to warn Khi'da and everyone else. He gathers them all by the fire to break the news.

"The bear is here. I saw its tracks leading away from our camp and it has killed another sentry," he cries out, while the others look astonished. They all gather around the site where Khi'da notices tracks and begins to follow them.

"Khi'da, where are you going?" calls out the lead hunter.

"These tracks could lead me to its lair and that is where I will get him."

"I will come with you," says the lead hunter, but Khi'da gestures for him to stay back.

"You should stay here and protect our camp in case it returns," he says, while the lead hunter looks concerned, watching his friend leave. Moments later, Khi'da spots a cave nearby. "That is where that monster might be," he mutters to himself.

As he gets close to the entrance, he notices there are bones scattered everywhere and realises that most of them are human. He spots a rag with some blood on it, and suspects it could belong to the sentry who went missing. He stands by the entrance and gulps before he walks in, but stops instantly when he hears a noise from behind him. He turns around and readies his spear, believing it's the bear, but when he realizes it is the lead hunter, he lowers the spear while breathing a sigh of relief. He walks up to him.

"What are you doing here? I thought I told you to stay back and watch over the others," he says.

"I followed you in case you needed help. There is no way that I was going to stand there and let you confront that bear alone. Besides, they are safe. I told them to hide in their tents. The bear will never suspect they are there, and it will lose interest and leave."

Khi'da does not agree with his decision, and as he is about to order the hunter to go back, he cringes when he hears a growl coming from inside the cave. They both hide behind a boulder as a gigantic bear comes out.

"Look at the size of that bear! It's just how that young man described it. I have seen plenty of bears my whole life, but none this size. It's incredible," Khi'da gasps, amazed. They run to the other side of the boulder when the bear walks by. It stops and begins sniffing around the boulder, rearing up on its back legs to look over it, but sees nothing and continues on its way. The two men sneak out from behind some shrubs near the boulder and hurry in the opposite direction to warn the others at the camp before the bear arrives.

The bear is moving through the forest. As it passes the camp, it catches the smell of cooked meat and walks toward it. When it approaches the settlement, it notices the cooked meat stacked on some rocks and it lumbers over to them. It takes a few bites before raising its head when some sounds come from Kho'ta's tent. Meanwhile, his family panics when they hear the growling coming from the bear just outside. Kho'ta pulls out his dagger, in case the bear peers inside the tent.

Meanwhile, Khi'da and the lead hunter are about to walk into the camp but stop when they hear the bear is already there. Khi'da was about to head over to his tent to warn his family, but the lead hunter stalls him. He points him toward his tent, and it shocks him when he sees the bear already standing over it. He is about to run in and attack the bear, but the lead hunter stops him once again.

"Are you crazy? You can't just walk in there without a plan," he whispers.

"That monster is standing over my tent. My family is in there. I'm not just going to sit around here and watch," Khi'da hisses. "I know you'd do the same if that was your family."

He gets up and readies his spear to throw it at the bear. He releases it but the spear strikes the ground just near the bear, which stands up to scan the area. It spots the two men hiding near the shrubs and lets out a roar before charging at them. The men dodge it in time, just as it runs past them. The bear continues to run ahead and disappears into the darkness of the forest. Khi'da does not hesitate and races to check up on his family. He opens the tent-flap and cries with relief when he sees that his family is safe. He goes in and gives them a hug. The rest of the others come out of their tents and cheer as they gather around their leader. He stands on a log and looks down at all of them.

"Listen everyone: this is no time to cheer. That menace may have left for now, but it doesn't mean it won't come back again. We will need to keep watch and ready ourselves before it arrives," he says. "We have grown much stronger, ever since we allied ourselves with the wolves. The moment we hear the wolves, that should be a clue that danger is near and that will give us enough time to prepare. We must trust them and together we will succeed!" he cries out with confidence. He steps off the log and everyone gathers around him to greet him. Over by the forest, the bear is watching them. It lets out a low growl before it lumbers away once more.

Meanwhile, Nanook is out in the meadow looking for the she-wolf. He lets out a howl, hoping to get a response from her, but hears nothing. He turns around and heads back to the lair, thinking she may never return.

Amak is lying down next to Sakkara when he sees Nanook walk over to his den, looking upset. He gets up and walks over to him.

"What's the matter, my son?"

"I have not seen the she-wolf in a while. I think you may be right about her."

"I am sorry to hear that, but I believe that's the only way you will see for yourself the truth about her. But if she is everything you think of her and if she thinks the same way about you, she will return. You just need to be patient," Amak whispers. He heads back to Sakkara and settles down, while Nanook lies down, staring into the forest.

It is late into the night. Nanook wakes up when he hears sounds coming from the forest. He gets up and looks toward the forest, believing it might be the she-wolf coming back. He moves in closer to get a better look, to make sure it is her, but he sees a bulky figure moving. Amak and the others notice him standing by the forest and run over to him, when they hear him growling. Amak feels uneasy when he stands by his side.

"What did you see?"

"I saw this large figure move across those trees straight ahead. I thought it was the she-wolf at first, but it was too big to be her," Nanook replies softly, while Amak stares toward the forest. Suddenly, they spot an enormous figure staring at them before it bustles in the opposite direction, which makes them growl.

Meanwhile, over in the camp, the people gather near the graves of their fallen tribesmen. Khi'da looks toward the wolves' lair when he hears them growling.

"What's the matter?" asks the lead hunter.

"Listen. The wolves are growling. That means the bear must be close. I think it's time we get ready. Get your spears and come meet me by my tent."

The lead hunter does what he says and calls out to the other men to get their spears. They all gather by Khi'da's tent and wait for him to come out. Khi'da and Kho'ta walk out of the tent and stare at the others, who are already outside.

"Once again, thanks to the wolves, we have realized the danger before it arrives, unlike before," admits Khi'da. "I feel the same bear who attacked us last night has returned for more, and that's what I think is troubling the wolves. That bear has a taste for our flesh now and it's hunting us down, one by one. The Last two night, it killed two of the bravest and finest sentries that I have ever known. These four brave men you see, standing next to me, escaped with their lives when that same bear attacked their entire clan. This is no ordinary bear if it can take down an entire group of people in a single night. We need to get rid of this monster and send it back to where it came from," he states.

"And how will we do that? For all we know, it could be stalking us right now," cries out the elderly man.

"I have a plan that will prove that tonight the hunter will be the one that's going to be hunted," Khi'da responds. "It has messed with the wrong tribe. We have faced many other dangerous predators far worse, and this bear will be no different. I have located the cave where it lives. We will ambush it and get it trapped in its own cave and then take it down. It will not stand a chance!" he shouts out, raising both fists into the air. The others cheer along with him.

Amak hears their cheering and walks over to the others. "Are you guys ready?" he asks, and Nanook and the others nod. "Then let's go over to their side and let them know we are here for them."

They all walk over to the people's side and stare at all of them, while Khi'da smiles when he notices them arriving.

"The wolves have also joined us and that gives me the confidence that we will not fail!" he cries out once more, as the wolves let out a howl followed by the cheering of the people. The howling and the cheering coming from both sides echo through the night.

In the middle of the night, the people and the wolves are approaching the bear's home. The others all feel uneasy when they get their first glimpse of the cave.

"There it is — the bear's cave." whispers Khi'da. "Pay no attention to those," he adds, as he sees his comrades staring at all the bones leading to the entrance. He turns around and looks at the nervous men. "This will not be easy. This is going to be one of the hardest challenges we have ever faced, but I am confident in all of you and that's why I know we will come out of this victorious, and free ourselves of this monster. But we are going to need to have each other's backs if we are to succeed. Together, we will stop this menace once and for all before it takes down any more of us.”

He gathers them all so he can tell them how they are going to bring down the bear. He calls the three youngest of the survivors over to him and hands them each bows and arrows. “I will have you three hide behind those shrubs over to your left, and make sure you have your bows ready, because once that bear runs by, you will jump out and shoot. Make sure you pull them back nice and tight because I assure you that bear’s hide is thick as stone,” he warns them, before sending them off to their post. He looks over to the remaining hunters and grins, looking at the top of the cave. “Now, for the rest of you. Lie in wait just above the entrance and you will strike at the bear with your spears from above just as it rushes out, but you will have to be careful and stay out of reach in case it rears up to knock you down. This will not be easy, but I know we will beat it as long as we work together.”

“What about you? What will you do?” asks the lead hunter, sounding concerned.

“I will go in myself and lead him out.”

“I have a bad feeling about this. That bear is not like any other. It will need a lot more than spears and arrows to bring it down,” says the elderly man.

“And that is where the wolves come in,” Khi’da smiles.

“Are you sure we can trust them?”

“Yes, I am sure and that is because of my son. Although we may have had an unpleasant history with them, I feel we can trust them because my son here does: I feel they can understand each other,” he states, looking down at Kho’ta with a smile. “Go show them what I mean, my son.”

Kho’ta walks over to Nanook and kneels by him. He reaches out his hand so Nanook can lick it. He strokes him behind his ears. Nanook feels his hand trembling as he is stroking his ear and whimpers when he looks up at him.

“I bet you are just as afraid as I am, but we will win; you can bet on it. We will need your help, though, if we are to beat that bear and together, I know we will beat it. That’s why I am going to need you and your family to cooperate if we are going to get out of this alive. I am going to need you and your family to go behind those trees right next to you. I am sure the bear will try to escape and that is when you come out of hiding and stop him from escaping. I will signal to you by whistling three times to let you know when it's heading toward you. Now tell the rest of your family what I just told you," he said.

Nanook turns around and heads over to the others. He sits down and the others all gather around him while he stares at them. "He told me to ask you to hide by those trees behind us. He will signal to us the moment the bear runs in our direction to escape, and that is when we will jump out and trap him," he said.

"What if he tries to break through us?" Alornek asks.

"We will continue to stand strong. We cannot allow that bear to escape or else it will keep on terrorizing us; first it will be them and for sure we will be next. So let us do our part and cooperate with them and we will win this, but we have to work as a team. I guarantee you we will succeed," he says. The others hesitate, but Amak is the first to go and hide behind a tree and the others soon follow, while Nanook smiles. He looks over to Kho'ta, who is already at his post, and he gives him a gesture of gratitude. Nanook hides behind a tree next to Denali and waits there for the signal.

Khi'da is standing by the entrance. Before he walks in, he checks one last time to make sure everyone is in their positions. He looks into the cave and takes a deep breath as he walks inside.

Once inside, he lights up a torch to help see his way through the dark. He is walking deeper inside the cave while trying not to make a sound and that's when notices a crack up ahead and creeps toward it. He peeks inside to look for the bear and pulls back when he spots it sleeping on the other side. He takes a deep breath and mutters a prayer to himself.

"Please guide me through this, great ancestors, and I promise I will show more respect towards you if I make it out of here alive."

He sneaks up behind the sleeping bear and screams at the top of his lungs. The bear immediately wakes and spots Khi'da. It rears up while Khi'da stands there, momentarily frozen in fear, as he looks at its sheer size. He snaps out of it when the bear lets out a roar, and he runs back through the opening just as the bear swipes at him. The bear gets a hold of his sleeve while Khi'da tries to break free before the bear drags him in. He struggles out of his jacket and runs out with the bear close behind him. He rushes out and signals for the men waiting on top of the entrance to ready themselves.

The bear lumbers out, and with no hesitation, the men throw their spears, but they miss because the bear spots them just in time and dodges each one. It is about to go after the men, but stops when it hears Khi'da calling out. The bear charges at him and he runs straight toward the shrubs where the archers are waiting. The moment they notice the bear run by them, they jump out and shoot their arrows, but with little training, none of the arrows hit their target. They just zip past the bear and disappear into the darkness.

Khi'da realizes the plan has failed. The bear is still after him and he does what he can to shake him off, but suddenly he steps on a rock and sprawls to the ground with a sprained ankle. The bear is standing over him and roars at Khi'da before raising his enormous paw to swipe at him.

Kho'ta realizes the danger his father is in and whistles three times to signal the wolves to come out of hiding. Nanook does not hesitate and races out from behind the tree to bite the bear in the hindquarters. The bear lets out a roar in pain and shakes his foot to get Nanook off him. Amak and the others run out and jump on the bear's back and they each bite it on the shoulders. The bear, in desperation, twists and turns to get the other wolves off his back.

Kho'ta sees the wolves are keeping the bear distracted. He jumps down to the ground, pulls out his bow and arrow and shoots. The arrow strikes the bear in the midsection of its back. The beast turns around and runs toward Kho'ta. He shoots another arrow, followed by another, but that does not stop the bear. Khi'da sees the bear charging toward his son, who is standing there, frozen in fear, and screams to get Kho'ta to snap out of it. Khi'da gets up and runs to get to his son before the bear does.

The bear stands and readies himself to swipe at Kho'ta just as Khi'da runs in between them both and pushes his son out of harm's way. In that second, he is struck instead. Kho'ta watches in horror as his father is flung aside by the mighty bear. It walks toward Khi'da and just as it's about to kill him, it stops and turns around, hearing loud barking from Nanook and the others.

The bear loses interest in Khi'da and runs straight toward Nanook, who stands his ground.

Suddenly, appearing out of nowhere, the she-wolf leaps in the bear's way to distract it. She runs to lead the bear away from Nanook and the others. She leads it toward the cave entrance, where the other men are still waiting on top, and they shoot their arrows at the bear the moment it gets close enough. The men by the shrubs also shoot their arrows, but the arrows just feel like bee stings to the bear's thick hide. It raises itself up, and stands on its rear legs, letting out a roar to show them it is still ready for another fight, despite being struck by all the arrows.

Kho'ta pulls out his last arrow and aims at the bear's head while it is still roaring and shoots it directly in the mouth. There is a sudden silence. The bear has stopped roaring and just stares at Kho'ta. Just as it is about to charge at him, it collapses by his feet. The bear lies there, motionless, and everything is quiet. When Kho'ta gets his breath, he pokes at the huge beast in case it is still alive. Suddenly, the bear lets out one final, faltering roar before it dies.

The other men stand around it and cheer while chanting Kho'ta's name. The wolves see that they did their work and walk away, except for Nanook. He notices Khi'da just lying on the ground and whimpers as he walks toward the body. Amak turns and walks up to him. He licks Khi'da to try and wake him up, but he does not. Amak lets out a sad howl and so does Nanook.

Kho'ta hears them howling. He sees his father lying on the ground and rushes toward him. He swiftly turns him over onto his back and attempts to revive him, but fails. He pounds at the ground and screams aloud, his sorrow and anger echoing through the night, heard by the wolves and the other men, as he grieves his father's death.

The lead hunter picks up his friend's spear and walks over to Kho'ta. He pats him on his back and murmurs to him.

"Kho'ta — I am so sorry for your loss. Not only did you lose a father tonight, but I also lost a brother," he says, choking up.

"I wish it was me, instead of him," Kho'ta sobs, his hand wiping away his tears." He slowly gets up and looks at the lead hunter. "Who will lead the tribe now?"

The lead hunter looks down at Khi'da's spear while trying to hold back tears. "There is… There is something he told me before we confronted the bear," he says, sniffing loudly. "He wanted you to be the new leader if anything happened to him. I was uncertain of his decision at first, but tonight you showed me I was wrong."

He hands Kho'ta his father's spear. Kho'ta manages a half-smile while he looks at the spear that his father once held with pride, and he raises it slowly toward the sky. The lead hunter goes down on one knee, and so do the others.

The lead hunter looks up at him with a smile. "From now on you will be known as Kho'ta the Wolf Tamer," he utters with pride.

The next morning, Nanook walks over to the she-wolf and greets her by rubbing noses with her.

"What made you want to come back?" he asks gleefully, while she just smiles.

"I realized I was on the wrong side. This is where I belong, with you guys," she says, and is about to continue, when she stops and turns around, having heard Amak. He walks over and sits in front of her, as she stares at him, nervously. "I just want to say thank you for saving my son last night. I was wrong about you. If it were not for you, I would have lost another son and for that you have my thanks. You are always welcome to stay. The choice is yours."

The others, including Nanook, stand and stare as they wait for her answer. She smiles at all of them before she looks at Amak.

"My answer…" she hesitates. Nanook holds his breath. "…is yes!" she cries out joyfully. Nanook jumps with happiness. The others gather around to welcome her to their lair. She walks over to Nanook and smiles. "You still want to know what my name is? I now think this is the right time to tell you. It is Nuka."

She reaches in and licks Nanook before bounding away. Nanook smiles and runs over to her, and they rub noses while the others look on.

"They are perfect for each other" smiles Sakkara.

"He reminds me of us, when we first met," Amak replies.

Nanook and Nuka walk over to them just as the pups rush over to her and beg her to play with them. With no hesitation, she agrees.

Meanwhile, over by the people's camp, Kho'ta is standing on the stump, and he is wearing ceremonial attire. Everyone gathers around him and they place wreaths around his neck. His mother looks at him as she smiles. She gives him a hug as she tries to hold back tears.

"Your father would have been proud to see you now," she says, tearfully, while Kho'ta smiles a little. She turns around when she hears the lead hunter coming. He looks at Kho'ta and places both his hands on his shoulders as he stares at him.

"This was once your father long ago. I still remember the look on his face. He looked like he was about to pass out, but don't worry if you do because your father did pass out when it was his turn," he says, trying not to sound choked up, but Kho'ta can see it in his eyes and reaches out to him to give him a hug.

The lead hunter cries and holds Kho'ta in a tight embrace. He then releases him, reaches behind his back, and bows down as he extends his arms to show him his father's spear. Kho'ta the Wolf Tamer takes it and raises it up in the air, as everyone cheers for him.

Meanwhile, by the lair, Nanook hears the cheering coming from the people's side and smiles at the others.

"It is time," he says. He is about to walk over to their side, but Nuka calls out to him with concern.

"Where are you going? Don't you know the people are over on that side?"

Nanook just smiles. "You don't need to worry about these people. We are safe with them."

He walks over to their side and the others follow him. Nuka hesitates at first, but soon follows them to join the ceremony. Kho'ta had felt nervous when he couldn't see the wolves, but he immediately gains confidence when he sees them walking out of the shrubs, led by Nanook. The rest of the tribe looks behind them and notices the wolves arriving. They clear the way so they can pass. The wolves look up at them as they pass by, and then stand by Kho'ta as he looks at them all with confidence.

"For a long time, wolves and people have been fighting one another for this land. This land belonged to the wolves, and we drove them away and felt no remorse. We thought Nuna would never see peace again as this hatred continued…" he looks over to Khi'da's grave and his voice falters. "My… My father thought as wolves as soulless demons, but I viewed them as living beings, just like we are. He thought we had nothing in common with one another, but I always thought that we did — and this is the will to survive. We killed them when they took our food, but they had every right to take it because it was theirs. We were the ones taking the food from them with no remorse. I thought this hatred would never end, but one day I met one of them when he got caught in our traps. I wanted to kill him, but I decided not to because I am not like that. I freed him instead, and that is when our alliance began.

We both learned the truth about ourselves as our bond grew, and that's when we thought it would be great that we were to unite and stop this fighting. It was a lot of work, but here we are today, united as one. So, I am proud to say that a violent era ends and a new one begins with us in peace. Along with that, Nuna is at peace and it is up to us to keep it that way," Kho'ta declares.

His words are met with silence, but then he hears clapping coming from his mother and the others all joining in mass applause. Kho'ta begins to smile. He looks down at Nanook, then kneels before him, buries his head in his fur and hugs him. He reaches out his hand and all the wolves take turns licking it. The rest of the tribe do the same and the wolves lick them, as well. They all walk over to Khi'da's grave and kneel before it. Kho'ta pulls out his spear and lays it over the grave, trying hard to hold back his tears.

He gets up, looks at the others and he howls, followed by the wolves. The entire tribe joins in and they all fill the land with the echoes of their howling.

Deep in the forest, hiding behind some trees, Tiyani smiles as he watches the ceremony, before heading back to the sky world. Meanwhile, over at Amak's old lair, Lukka is looking for anything that will bring Amak to his knees. He is about to leave when he hears a faint cry coming from the den, underneath the log. He looks inside and sneers when he sees a young pup looking up at him.

"I have found your weakness, Amak," he mutters. He picks up the pup and walks back to his pack.

Two years later, the sun rises over the land; the dawn of a new day. A herd of wild boar wallow by the pool, oblivious to the people hiding in the forest near them. They humans are behind the trees and have camouflaged themselves in mud to cover their scent, so the pigs will not know they are there. A man steps out into the open. It is Kho'ta, now much older, and the leader of the tribe. He signals to the others to follow him. They all crawl along their stomachs as they creep toward the boars, keeping as low as they can to blend in with the grass. Every time the boars look up, they stay still, only to move again once they go back to grazing.

When they are close enough to the herd, Kho'ta looks back at the others and grins as he counts to three, when they all stand up and charge at the pigs, who scatter the moment they see them. The largest of the boars stops and faces the men and then charges toward them. Kho'ta grabs a rock and throws it at the pig, but it does not stop it. It charges past them and knocks down some men as it rushes to get away to the forest.

Kho'ta lets out a whistle and Nanook and the rest of the pack jump out of the shrubs and have the boar surrounded. They distract the pig while Kho'ta gets the bow ready. He takes a deep breath and shoots. The pig has its back turned as it tries to ward them off, and the arrow strikes it just at the base of the neck. It drops instantly to the ground. They all gather around the pig and shout with joy as it lies there, lifeless.

The people tie it up to the spear and carry it back to the camp. Later at night, they gather by the fire and eat their fill. The wolves have also joined them in their feast, instead of being in their lair. The echoes from their laughing fills the night sky as they eat; humans and wolves at peace.

The following winter, Nanook is in his lair getting ready to go hunting in the meadow with Kho'ta. He does not notice a figure staring at him from the forest. He growls when he sees Kho'ta approach Nanook and continues to stare at them as they walk out into the meadow. The figure growls once more, before turning around and heading back to his pack over at the other side of the meadow.

THE END?